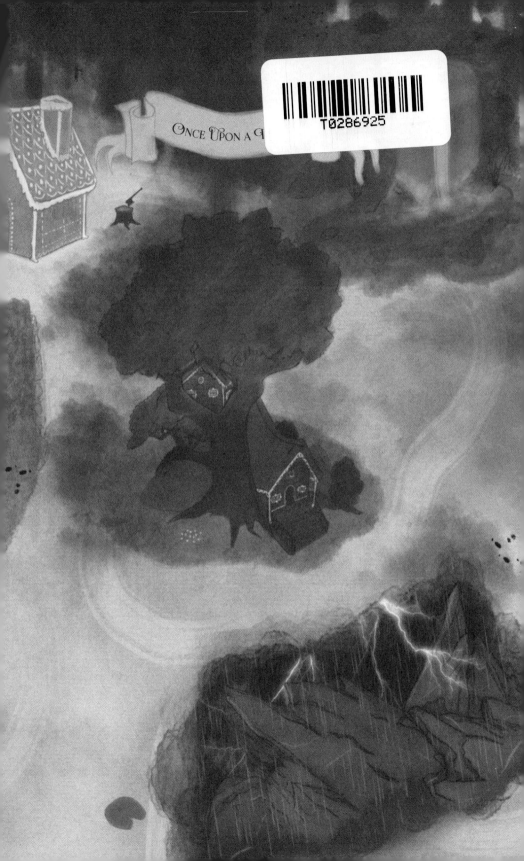

For those who wander through these pages, listen well to the tales of ages... for deep within one's heart will find, their past and present, intertwined.

UNTIL THE LAST PAGE

CHANTAL GADOURY

INIMITABLE
BOOKS
UNFORGETTABLE STORIES

Published by Inimitable Books, LLC
www.inimitablebooksllc.com

UNTIL THE LAST PAGE. Copyright © 2024 by Chantal Gadoury.
Map copyright © 2024 by Finn Honeycutt.
All rights reserved. Printed in the United States of America.

Library of Congress Cataloguing-in-Publication Data is available.

No part of this book may be reproduced in any form or by any electronic or mechanical means, including information storage and retrieval systems, without written permission from the author, except for the use of brief quotations in a book review.

First edition, 2024
Cover design by Keylin Rivers

ISBN 978-1-958607-30-5 (hardcover)
10 9 8 7 6 7 6 5 4 3 2 1

For all the dreams you carried in your heart, the love you never stopped believing in, and all the frogs you rescued from the yard.

To mom, for all the instances of "darting" you helped me delete.

And to Taran, who will always be the prince of my heart.

Someday you will be old enough to start reading fairy tales again.

-C.S. Lewis

PROLOGUE

The twinkling of the candlelight against the glimmering crystal chandeliers made everything in the large, open ballroom sparkle with magic. The ambiance of the room, the women in their elegant ball gowns, and the men in their finery—it was amazing. An evening set for a magnificent celebration. The dancers moved in time with the music, waltzing under the crystals in nearly perfect circles as they flowed across the marble floor.

I stood in the middle of it all, dressed in my own beautiful gown. While many ladies were wearing different shades of blue and burgundy, I wore a shade of pale gold with a sheer overlay, which sparkled from the hand-stitched stars throughout the fabric. The sleeves reached to my elbows, and the gown's back plunged to my waistline in an open vee. Small laces lay at the bottom of the bodice, ensuring the dress fit perfectly against my body.

A solid gold band encircled my head, accenting the soft, dark curls that fell over my shoulders.

I could feel the gaze of the onlookers. I knew they were wondering who I was. But at that moment, my identity didn't need to matter to them. I only knew I was meant to stand out—to be seen by all those around me—by *him*.

Music filled the room. There was something about this experience that felt so oddly familiar. I'd been here before—somehow. I had seen these faces before, heard their laughter and conversations.

He appeared out of the crowd, bowing to a woman dressed in the softest blue, a diadem of rubies adorning her head. Straightening, he turned his gaze to me and flashed a warm, welcoming smile.

My heart fluttered in recognition.

He walked toward me.

I knew what was coming next.

I knew this story, didn't I?

He would ask me to dance, and we would, and then a clock would chime at midnight. Those initial chimes would be a warning, a notice that only a few precious seconds with him remained. And then? It would make one final chime to call me away, back to my world, away from the dancers, the ballroom, and the magic.

Away from *him*.

I choked on the sadness that came with the thought.

His gloved hand reached for me as his green eyes met mine.

"Jo…" he whispered my name. "You finally came."

His arm circled around my waist as he pulled me closer into his embrace. He smelled like the earth, like the fresh scent from a morning bike ride through the park, so warm and comforting.

"I wasn't sure you were going to come."

I leaned in closer. Would it reassure him to hold me tight?

We spun around the room, as he carefully navigated each turn. It could have gone on for hours, but then I heard the first chime from a distant clock.

I froze. Hadn't I just arrived?

My partner eased away gently, and I held his gaze.

His eyes searched mine. An unspoken hurt passed between us as the next chime tolled.

We both knew what came next.

"Jo…" The man leaned in and murmured against my ear, "I'll wait for you."

I closed my eyes against his soft promise and felt the imprint of his lips against my cheek.

Dread settled in my chest, knowing the weight of the farewell the kiss carried.

In seconds, I would be alone again.

Alone. Just as I had been before.

Before *him*.

Before the kiss.

ONE

"Find your gas pedal, you slowpoke!"

Jolting awake, I turned toward Mom and saw one hand holding the steering wheel while the other pressed on the horn. I bit my lip to keep from smiling.

She hit the gas and lifted her hand at the car we were passing.

If it wasn't *me* the passing driver glared at, I might have laughed at my mom's unique brand of road rage that never improved with age. But I was, so I sank further into my seat, wishing I could disappear into the leather.

Noticing me, Mom said, "I'm sorry, Jo. I didn't mean to wake you." She gestured to the surrounding cars with her right hand. "All the *stupid* drivers are out today."

"It's okay," I mumbled, doing my best to clear the raspiness from my voice.

"I'm glad you agreed to come along with me to the estate sale," she said, adjusting her sunglasses on the bridge of her nose before lowering the volume of the radio with the knob. "It's too nice of a day to be stuck in the house," she continued, flashing a smile at me.

It was a nice morning. Sunshine beamed into the front of the car, filling the space with a comforting warmth. Already seventy-five degrees, with the promise of sunshine and June temperatures that would most likely lure us to the family pool later that afternoon. But while Mom was right about the beautiful weather, I'd only agreed to come with her because the alternative was watching more *Fix-My-Car* episodes with Dad. I didn't want to endure another day of *that*.

I *could* have stayed in my bed all day again, but being alone just made everything so much harder to process. I would get lost in my thoughts, and time would disappear in the blink of an eye. Determined to not let this day pass by me, I'd begrudgingly pulled myself out from the covers and dressed in a pair of jean shorts and a simple, white knotted top.

"Sure," I murmured, keeping my gaze on the passing scenery. The green mountainside, covered in summer growth, was in full bloom. A large, blue lake surrounded by upscale homes and wineries lay at the bottom.

With only a few dozen houses, a post office, a fire station, and an antique store, Oaks Corner was too small to be considered a town. More like a set for a romance movie. Everyone knew everyone here, and nothing ever changed. Everything was just like I'd left it two years ago. This place was beautiful, but there wasn't any space to grow. It was now strange to think how my life had led back here after I'd promised I'd never return once I'd set off for college.

"Betsy told me there was a wonderful little writing desk she wanted me to see," Mom explained. "Do you think it will work?"

She had assigned Dad a new renovation project—a home office. As a medical transcriptionist, she spent most of her weekdays at the kitchen table, with her laptop on one side, and her paperwork spread all over on the other side. To create less of a hassle for Mom, we all agreed to take our dinner plates to the living room to eat, usually watching the news while we did.

A pang of guilt spread through me. If I hadn't returned home, my room would have already been transformed. But I'd come back with no job, a car full of belongings, and nothing more than a thousand dollars in my bank account. It was a far cry from where I'd imagined I'd be at twenty-five.

Biting my bottom lip, I did my best to swallow the lump forming in my throat. The last thing I wanted to do was cry again. I'd spent too many days crying over too many things.

"Sounds great," I replied softly, giving a small nod for emphasis.

"Maybe we should stop and get some coffee first," Mom suggested, reaching over to grasp my hand, her palm warm but firm as she squeezed my fingers, trying to get my attention.

But I was too afraid to look up. The tears were too close to spilling as it was, and meeting her pitying gaze would be game over.

"Jo," she murmured softly when I didn't look at her. "It's going to be alright. But I know it doesn't feel that way right now, honey."

"*Mom*," I groaned before pressing my lips together. Her words made me want to go back to sleep. Back to that strange and beautiful dream, where the unknown and charming prince waited for me. I tried to pull my hand away from hers, but she held on tighter.

"Jo, I'm serious," she continued. "You've been walking around the house like a ghost. Believe me, I know what heartache feels like—I know you're having a hard time, and that's okay. It *will* be okay."

"I don't want to talk about it," I managed.

"Eventually, you're going to have to."

When I had first arrived back at my parents' house with only a brief understanding that *something* had happened, they'd welcomed me with open arms. Mom had even helped me cancel the wedding venue and DJ without asking any prying questions.

I was too embarrassed to admit to her what had actually happened. But I didn't even know how to *start* the conversation—how to talk about the end of my two-year engagement.

To be honest, I was still processing the entire situation. At night, I analyzed and relived the moment I'd discovered him with his best friend. Both of them, completely naked, and my heart—*broken*. I couldn't erase the memory of their faces as they stared back at me in shock as I stood in the bedroom's doorway.

Within three days, I'd gathered my stuff and left the city—left Nico standing in the entryway, staring at me with a strange and cold expression of regret.

I still wasn't sure if he was sorrier he'd cheated on me or for hiding the truth about his sexuality from me for three years. But I didn't want to think about it anymore.

"Whatever happened, I'm sure you could go—"

"I'm not going back," I interrupted, turning my watery eyes up to her. I swallowed again, hoping the forming tears would stay put.

She stared at me for a moment, unspoken questions lingering in her eyes, before turning her attention back to the road. Mom had always liked Nico ever since the first Thanksgiving I'd brought him home. I credited the apple pie he'd brought. Little did she know, it had been store bought.

Dad had been the harder sell, watching Nico with a heavy eye from across the table. It was *Dad* who had asked the intimidating, hard questions—or, tried to, at least.

Nico had won them over with his charm, his laughter. He'd *been* perfect—emphasis on the past tense.

"I think this is it," Mom said, bringing the car to a stop. She pointed toward a painted red-lettered *Estate Sale* sign sitting in front of a small, off-white ranch home. Its lawn was in dire need of cutting, and the building was showing early signs of neglect.

There were already people gathering outside, surveying objects on the tables in the driveway. It was a garage sale—but on steroids. Furniture lined the edges of the black asphalt. A sofa, a cushioned rocking chair, a nightstand, tall standing lamps, and, oddly enough, a stove.

"I think so, too," I added, then unclasped my seat belt.

Mom pulled the keys from the ignition and grabbed her wallet with a smile. "Let's see what we can find!"

Taking a sip of my already melting iced coffee, I followed her. Even in my jean shorts, the morning summer heat was already becoming uncomfortable. I could feel it through the asphalt under my sneakers. Shutting the car door, I looked around the neighborhood. It was as though everyone had taken a slice of their cookie-cutter American Dream pie here and made the most of it.

Everyone's yards had perfectly shaped bushes, freshly planted beds of flowers. A pristine sidewalk connected the driveways. The houses were situated too close next to each other, barely giving any privacy to neighbors. At least they all had billowing white curtains in their windows.

I was grateful for how my parents' neighborhood was simply imperfect. I liked that the houses on our street weren't the same color and there was ample space between them.

"Jo! Come look!" Mom called, pulling me from my thoughts.

I stepped toward the estate sale, searching the crowd for her.

"Jo!" she called again, her hand in the air. She laughed as she lifted two colorful margarita glasses from a side table in the garage.

I crossed the driveway to where she stood amongst a few gray-haired shoppers.

She lifted her finds higher with a smile. "How about some drinks tonight?" She didn't specify the occasion, but perhaps the fun discovery was enough for her.

"Is there one more for Dad? Can't leave him out."

She grinned. "Sounds like a good idea. We can make some strawberry daiquiris tonight with dinner." She peeked at the yellow stickers on the items before turning to another table.

I spotted two other matching ones close by and lifted them from the collection of kitchen plates and a strange assortment of vases. How did one come to own so many things?

Mom reached the end of the table and turned her attention toward the house's entrance, where more people eyed the other furniture.

"I'm going to go inside to see if anyone can show me where the writing desk is. Why don't you go look around while you wait for me? I promise I'll be quick."

I nodded, and she went off.

Curious about the other trinkets, I turned my attention to the tables beside me. One table displayed a strange assortment of decor—four painted wooden apples in a brown bowl, faux goldenrods in one tall, white vase, and two unlit apple-scented candles. The next displayed a wax pumpkin with tiny sculpted mice scurrying on the stem.

A nearby overflowing bin contained nothing but footwear. Men's dress shoes, sneakers, a pair of black flats, silver glitter high heels, and some pink high-top sneakers. There was also a pair of wooden shoes, just like the ones tourists returned with from Holland, sitting on top.

I wandered to another table, finding an assortment of vintage cards with green frogs wearing crowns. Soft pink hearts surrounded the two-dimensional amphibians. Lifting one, I read the message.

To my love, Katherine.
May you always remember how much I truly love you, dearest.
—ML

I felt a little foolish for the twinge of jealousy that filled me. It was even sillier that seeing this made me want to text Nico and ask him the million questions I hadn't been brave enough to ask before I left. Quickly putting it down, I turned away, hoping to find something else to focus on for a distraction from my aching heart.

From the corner of my eye, I noticed stacks of books on a long table. There weren't many shoppers there, and I felt strangely drawn to the tomes. It was like they were one side of a magnet, and I was the other. After lowering the two margarita glasses onto the first empty spot near me, I started browsing the eclectic array of titles.

Sense and Nonsense in Psychology. Witchcraft, Magic, and Alchemy. Interaction of Matter and Energy.

I recognized none of them, so I moved on to the next group, which appeared to be primarily children's books. There were dozens of them all stacked on top of each other. The cover of the forefront book had a familiar character, posing happily next to three words—*The Magic Book.*

"What type of book are you looking for?" a gentle voice asked beside me.

Startled, I dropped it back onto the table and lifted my gaze to the woman. I hadn't heard her approach.

She chuckled and reached for the tome. "I'm so sorry. I didn't mean to startle you."

"It's okay," I managed, doing my best to collect myself quickly, examining her closer now that my heart wasn't racing.

The woman had striking white-blonde hair and a collection of wrinkles around the corner of her eyes. But, her smile was warm and kind. Everything about her radiated friendliness.

"Are you looking for anything in particular?" she asked again.

I gestured to the collection of strange books. "I was just looking."

"Oh, I thought you might be one of his students..."

"Students?"

"My uncle was a professor at the community college. He taught Psychology and Literature for almost thirty years."

"Oh," I replied before gesturing to the title in her hands. "Pardon my curiosity, but why did he have so many children's books?"

Her smile met her eyes as she hugged the book against her chest.

"One of his greatest joys was reading to the children at Oak Corner's Hospital. He'd perform magic tricks and read to them for hours." She paused, a small glimmer of sadness filling her eyes before she looked away.

I searched for the right thing to say, but nothing came to mind. "I'm so sorry for your loss," I finally replied. "I've never lost someone, but..." I allowed my words to drift to silence. Anything I would say beyond that would sound silly.

"Thank you," she said, placing *The Magic Book* back on the table. "He was truly a wonderful man. But, mystical and rather special."

"Mystical?" I asked curiously.

"Oh yes. These books bring back so many wonderful memories of when I was a young child. He would read from a giant book of fairytales whenever I came for a visit. And when he read those stories, they felt so *real*. He just had a way of bringing them to life."

By the way she described the memory, I nearly believed he had *literally* done so.

"I grew up loving books," I offered, nervously tucking my hair behind my ear. "So much that I went to school for Literature. I always find myself drawn to books, no matter where I am."

She smiled at me encouragingly.

"I have more friends in books rather than in real life," I finished.

"I can very much relate, young lady," the woman agreed. "Books can truly be an escape if we allow them to be."

She seemed nice enough, and what her uncle did—the kind of person he appeared to have been—sounded almost magical. But when she studied me, I felt strangely uncomfortable.

I tried to smile at her and gestured toward the house. "Well, I better go find my mom. But it was nice to meet you." I gave her a polite parting smile and turned away, wringing my hands.

"Hold on a sec!"

I turned to see her lifting a finger, as though she were waiting for a thought. She turned toward the table again, her hands working quickly as they sorted through a couple of books I hadn't noticed before.

"I know it's around here somewhere," she murmured as she moved on toward another stack.

The ones here were aged and yellowed, their titles slowly disappearing from their spines.

I could barely read the name of one.

Psychology: The Cognitive Mind and Curiosities of Literature.

Still didn't ring a bell. I apparently only recognized children's literature in this man's vast collection.

"I knew it was here!" The woman finally pulled out an aged book of deep tan leather. Her fingers carefully slid over the front before offering it to me.

It was old, well-worn, and yet majestic. The fading gold leaf details glistened in the sunlight overhead.

The glimmering lines looked like a magical swirl from a magic wand had been captured in time. I stared at it for a moment, then looked up at her.

"What is it?" I asked as she pushed the book closer to me.

"Fairytales." She caressed the worn cover again. "I don't know anything better to comfort an aching heart than a book of hope," the woman said as she studied me again.

Goosebumps traveled down the length of my spine as she stared at me, as though she could feel everything that I was feeling—everything that I'd spent an entire month hiding from my parents.

"But it was your uncle's book," I replied. "Surely you don't want to give it away to a stranger?"

"There's something in knowing that a piece of your loved one will live on through the joy of another person," she began. "I know it would have delighted him to know his book was going to someone who will cherish it."

Just by looking at the book's exquisite cover, I knew I couldn't afford its monetary value.

She continued to hold it out to me, her arms steady despite its heavy appearance. Her curious eyes scrutinized me. "It's my gift to you," she said with an encouraging nod.

A gift? For *me*? I stared at her before lowering my gaze to the book again. "Are you sure?"

The woman laughed with a nod and she reached for my hand with her free one. "Yes. I'm *quite* sure. Please, this is my gift to you."

"But you don't even know me," I replied, shaking my head. "I didn't do anything to deserve a gift."

The woman only smiled as she placed the book in my hands. "You were kind to a stranger. Does that not warrant a gift if the stranger says so?"

She removed the yellow price sticker from the cover. "I'll talk to the cashier," she explained with a grin. "Just promise me you'll take the time to read the stories. They can be quite wondrous."

A man cleared his throat from behind me.

I turned and saw him looking at the woman.

"Ms. Lynn, can you please come assist us inside?"

"I'm on my way, Thatch," she replied. "Enjoy the book," she said to me, winking, before trailing after him back into the house.

I watched her disappear inside, stunned at the sentimental gift she'd just given me. As I ran a hand over the cover, I softly promised, "I will."

TWO

Mom emerged from the house about ten minutes later with a wide smile on her face and the two margarita glasses. She lifted a small, white receipt, presumably successful in buying the desk Betsy had told her about.

I placed the small, golden apple I had been admiring back onto the display table, then lifted the matching drinkware, balancing them in my arms with the gifted book.

Drawing closer, she gestured to the old tome.

"Did you find something for yourself?"

"I guess," I replied with a shrug. "A member of the family here gave it to me."

"*Gave* it to you?"

I nodded. "The lady said she was the niece of the guy who lived here. We talked a little about the books he had, and that I went to school for literature."

Mom raised a brow before glancing back at the cover. "Are you sure it's free?"

"She said she'd take care of it with the cashier."

Mom hesitated then nodded again. "Well, I got the desk!" she said, showing the receipt to me once again.

"That's great," I replied.

"I asked about picking it up later this evening. We'll have your dad bring the truck. I underestimated just how big it is."

I nodded in understanding as we both headed back toward the SUV. As we slipped back into our seats, Mom's gaze shifted back to the book in my lap.

"So, what kind of book did she give you?"

I brushed my fingers over the golden detailing. "It's apparently a collection of fairytales."

"Well…that's *nice*," Mom slowly responded, no doubt weighing her words as she turned the keys in the ignition.

By her tone, I could tell she wasn't impressed.

"It looks a bit old," she added, not taking her eyes off the road.

"It does," I replied. "I'm interested to see if there are any stories that I'm not familiar with."

My fingers drift over the intricate swirls on the leather cover before opening it to reveal a long table of contents.

There were quite a few titles that I recognized. *The Frog King or Iron Heinrich, Hansel and Gretel, Little Snow-White, Aschenputtel,* and *Rumpelstilskin.* But there were several others I was not familiar with. *The Goose-Girl at the Well, King Grisly-Beard, The Twelve Huntsmen,* and *Allerleirauh…*

Under each title, there was a small illustration highlighting an infamous scene. Rapunzel, at the window of her tower, gazing down at the prince just below. Snow-White with the poisonous apple as a dark, shrouded elderly woman looked onward with a snarling smile. Just under the beginning title, a frog wore an intricate crown as he sat upon a lily pad.

Flipping back to the first page of the book, I examined the scribbling in the top right-hand corner that caught my eye on the way to the list of stories.

> *For those who wander through these pages,*
> *listen well to the tales of ages…*
> *for deep within one's heart will find*
> *their past and present, intertwined.*

Why were the words inside a book of fairytales?

Were they intended for a specific reader?

The woman had said the book had belonged to her uncle, and that he'd read to her often as a child. Perhaps he'd meant to give the book to someone else but had passed away before that happened? My gaze drifted to the name written just below.

Professor Merle Lynn

I let out a soft laugh. His parents certainly must have had a sense of humor.

"So," I say, looking up from the page, "get this. The guy who owned this book...his name was Merle Lynn."

"Merle?"

"Merle Lynn. Get it? Like *Merlin*." I lifted the book to prove to her that I wasn't making it up.

Mom quickly glanced at it and said, "That's...*interesting*," before returning her attention forward.

"I can only imagine how much he was teased growing up," I replied before closing the book. I shook my head again, smiling. Out of the corner of my eye, I caught Mom sending me a smile of her own.

I imagined she was relieved to see me happy, even if only for a moment—even if it was over something as simple as a strange name.

Dad was sitting in his recliner when we emerged from the garage. I walked right into the dining room and laid my new book on the table.

"Honey," Mom called, placing her purse and keys on the kitchen counter.

"Hmm?" Dad asked, his gaze focused on the television in front of him.

Mom called again, "Honey?"

"Yes, dear?" he replied, looking over his shoulder at us. His gaze drifted from Mom to me, eyes sparkling with curiosity.

"We have to go back to get a desk I bought."

"Ah, so you were successful, then?"

"It was a really good deal," she responded, moving toward where he was sitting.

"Your definition and *my* definition of a 'good deal' don't always mean the same thing."

Mom sighed and gripped his upper arm gently, pressing a small massage into his muscle. "If it reassures you, I didn't break the bank," she teased.

"So, you'd rather break my back instead?" He chuckled at his own joke.

They smiled at each other for a long moment before Mom rolled her eyes.

"I'll *help* you," she promised with a smile.

His grin only grew wider. "So, what else did you girls get yourselves into?" Dad asked, turning to me. "You were away almost all day."

He was right. After we'd gone to the estate sale, Mom wanted to venture to Target to pick up decor items for her writing desk. She always had a good time shopping there. She'd go in prepared with a short list, and always emerge with at least a dozen impulsive purchases.

"We did some shopping," I said before Mom could reply.

"I expected that," Dad teased.

"But not enough to break your back," I chimed in, parroting him.

He chuckled at my response and pretended to wipe his forehead with relief.

"When do we need to go back to get the desk?" he asked, rising from his recliner, glancing at Mom as she eased back into the kitchen.

"Once I finish making dinner," she said, gesturing to the fridge.

"What *is* for dinner?" Dad asked with a small, uncertain chuckle. "Did you get something weird at Target again?"

He still hadn't forgotten the *one* time Mom had claimed to have grabbed a chicken bake from the freezer section in Target. It turned out to not be chicken at all! To this day, I was still unsure what exactly she'd tried to feed us.

I rolled my eyes. "Mom said it was taco night."

Dad stared at me for a moment, almost as though he were searching to see if that was code for something else.

"Are these…*homemade* tacos? Or are we going out and bringing them back?"

"Well, there's an idea," Mom tossed over her shoulder as she eyed the fridge's contents. "Which would you prefer?"

Knowing him, any reason to avoid her homemade ones was good enough for him to choose fast food instead. The last time Mom had attempted them, she had melted and burnt the meat and cheese together. Apparently, that one had taken the cake.

"Why don't we all just pick up something to eat on the way back from picking up the desk?" Dad suggested. "Fast and easy. And no one has to worry about being on dish duty."

"You mean *you* don't have to worry about being on dish duty," Mom corrected with a laugh.

"Anything to avoid you adding more to your 'honey-do-list'," he replied with a smirk.

The term had come from her regularly asking him to do things — even if she had never actually said the words, "Honey, do this for me?"

I couldn't stop myself from smiling as they bantered back and forth. While Dad subtly teased Mom about her lack of cooking skills, and she retorted with all the things she wanted to add to his growing list of tasks, he still gazed at her with the sort of love I envied.

Maybe it would be better to stay home instead of going with them. It would give them an opportunity to just be themselves again. *Without* me.

"I was honestly thinking about staying here while you both picked up the desk," I confessed, easing into one of the dining room chairs. The fairytale book sat in front of me. "But by all means, please go out and get something to eat."

Mom narrowed her eyes as she crossed her arms. "You don't want to tag along?"

"I wouldn't be much help, anyway. You and Dad will be just fine picking up the desk, and then you both can go out and enjoy a nice meal together."

"Aren't you hungry, Jo?" Dad asked, raising a brow.

"Not really," I lied. "I think I might just shower and settle in with my new book."

They stared at each other before turning back to me. I could see the worry in their eyes. The sort I'd been careful to avoid ever since I'd returned from the city.

"Are you sure you don't want to come? We could go to your favorite place."

"Don't tempt me with a good time," I said, flashing a smile. "But seriously, I'll be fine! You two should go out and enjoy yourselves. I'll be here when you guys get back."

Dad's forehead wrinkled as he skeptically watched me for a moment more before glancing over at Mom.

"Really," I continued as I gestured toward the old book in front of me. "I'm looking forward to paging through this. I got it at the estate sale today."

"Oh, so you got yourself something, too?" Dad asked, watching me curiously as he awaited my answer.

"I did!" I replied. "A new book." Well, new to *me*.

"If you're sure…" Mom said, lifting her purse and truck keys.

"I'm sure," I reassured her. "Don't worry about me. I can take care of myself."

I might not have proved that point since I'd been home, but maybe it was time I showed I could move on. Not only for their sake, but for mine, too.

"We'll call when we're almost home again. That way you can come out and help us move the desk inside," Mom added as she walked toward the door that led into the garage.

"No problem," I replied with a nod.

Dad looked back at me and winked in my direction, then followed Mom out the door.

A moment later, the truck rumbled out of the driveway and down the street.

Then I was all alone.

I swallowed my instant regret about not going with my parents. As much as I might have sometimes craved time to myself, it was startling to suddenly experience it—to have to cope with the silence of an empty house. In the silence, I knew I couldn't escape the constant nagging of my own thoughts.

Nico cheated on you. He didn't love you. You weren't enough. You'll never be enough. There is something *wrong* with you.

With Mom's remote working schedule, and Dad being retired, someone was always in the house, filling up the space and silence. In those first few weeks of being home, no matter how much I struggled, no matter how bad I might have been feeling about my situation, there was always someone around.

But not now.

But I'd wanted this.

Releasing a sigh, I turned my attention back to the book in front of me. In the glow of the dining room light, the gold vines and flowers on the book's cover were even richer than before.

The handwritten verse on the first page once again echoed in my mind. *For those who wander through these pages…*

A sudden, unexpected vibration from my pocket startled me. I fished my phone out and woke it up to see who'd texted.

My stomach twisted when the name *Nico* stared back at me.

I placed my phone face down on the table and stared at it. Did I even want to read it?

Why was he texting me? Why *now?* What could he possibly have to say? Maybe the landlady had reached out to him about removing my name from the lease.

Taking a deep breath, I carefully turned the phone back over. As I touched the screen, Nico's message appeared.

Hey Jo. We should really try to talk about what happened.

My fingers trembled as I typed out my response.

There's nothing to talk about.

I was going to keep it short and to the point. I could almost hear my mother telling me, "Don't bring emotions into this." Biting my bottom lip, I waited for his reply.

Can I call you?

Was he kidding? He wanted to call me? No way. With a groan, I quickly texted my reply.

Now is not a good time.

When will be a good time, then?

As I studied my screen, I felt warmth spread across my cheeks. I wasn't sure if I should feel infuriated or devastated. It had taken him nearly a month to ask me to talk things out with him.

Can't you just leave me alone?

I still want a friendship with you, Jo. You mean so much to me.

As I wiped away a tear, I shook my head at his response.

You're not entitled to a friendship with me just because you want one.

You forfeited that when you cheated on me with Bryce instead of just being honest.

You didn't understand what I was going through.

You never gave me the chance to understand.

You kept everything a secret from me, Nico.

Can I please call? I want the chance to explain.

You had your chance before I left.

Even as I packed my bags and left, he hadn't bothered to explain himself. Didn't tell me anything more than he didn't want to be together anymore. As if *that* hadn't been perfectly clear when I discovered him with Bryce.

Please, Jo? Won't you please talk with me?

I couldn't deny that I wanted to hear his voice. That I missed the friend I'd had in him. But I knew nothing good would come from having a conversation with him. At least, not so soon after everything. The questions I wanted to ask would only hurt me even more.

Instead of responding, I held the button on the side of my phone, turning it off. It was easier to remove myself—remove any sort of temptation. Another tear slipped over my cheek as I shoved it into my pocket. This entire experience was one of the hardest things I'd ever been through.

Pushing Nico away was heartbreaking.

I turned back to the book in front of me. Holding the collection of fairytales against my chest, I rose from the chair and walked to my room. For now, the best distraction was to read my book, curled up in bed.

I remembered many childhood evenings spent listening to Mom read to me in my room. She read stories about magical worlds and daring adventures with memorable characters.

Those memories belonged to a little girl who had truly believed that one day her life would be like a fairytale. A little girl who believed in a charming prince, who would appear almost magically, to save the day. And maybe even, to save her too.

But there was no such thing as magic, and there was no prince charming coming to save me. Real life did not resemble fairytales.

I could feel my own tears stirring to life. Why had anyone ever allowed me to *believe* in fairytales? I brushed the back of my hand over my eyes, wiping away the tears that rolled more freely down my cheeks. I promised myself this would be the last time I'd ever shed a tear for him again.

Depressed by my thoughts, I didn't bother changing and peeled back the blankets, quickly slipping under them.

Through my blurred vision, the golden vines, and flowers on the cover of the old book gleamed.

After adjusting myself into a comfortable position, I propped it up in my lap and tried to keep my thoughts away from my silent phone.

Carefully, I opened the book, revealing worn, yellow pages. The scent alone was comforting enough, and I eased further back into my pillow, looking through the first few blank sheets. Black ivy vines adorned the edges.

It was older than I had originally thought. Wondering just how old the book was, I turned back to the copyright page. I was disappointed to find that the page was torn, taking the date with it. But behind it was the handwritten verse I'd seen earlier.

What did it mean? Who had it been written for?

I trailed a finger over the handwriting, silently studying it before whispering the words out loud.

"For those who wander through these pages," I began, "listen well to the tales of ages…"

I paused, noticing a flicker from the light above me. Furrowing my brow, I wondered if the light bulb was going bad. Maybe there was a storm off in the distance? I listened for a moment, waiting to hear the distant rumble of thunder, but heard nothing. Releasing a breath, I turned my focus back to the book in my lap.

"For deep within one's heart will find," I continued. "Their past and present, intertwined."

The lights above flickered once more before a searing streak of blinding light from *the book* flooded my room. It seemed *alive*, somehow pulling me face-first into the book. It felt almost like a vortex, sucking me inside.

I shut my eyes to avoid being blinded and opened my mouth to scream, but nothing emerged.

In a single, sweeping moment, the entire room was gone and there was nothing but darkness.

THREE

A groan startled me awake, but I couldn't distinguish if it was mine or someone else's. My body felt heavy as I laid flat on the ground. My fingers moved from my side to my temple. What had happened? Had I hit my head? I didn't remember falling out of bed. It would be just my luck if I'd given myself a concussion from being startled by an exploding light bulb.

At least I knew my name and age. That had to mean something, right?

I slowly sat up, trying not to worsen the aching pain throbbing in my temples. I couldn't open my eyes against the sheer pain, and they watered as I tried to pry them open.

Giving up, I pressed my fingers gently against the inner corner of my eyes and tried to recall my last memory before blacking out. Nico had texted me, upsetting me so much I had ended up in my bed with my new book…

The *book* had sucked me in. The whole scenario felt so wildly unrealistic, I felt stupid just thinking about it. There was no plausible way for it to happen.

The pain in my temples grew more intense than before. Trying to keep myself calm by pressing a hand to my forehead again, I heard another groan echo. This time, it was much clearer than before. Whoever it was, they were suffering.

I struggled to open my eyes again, wanting to see who it was. Was it Mom? Dad? Were they home already? I pressed my fingers to my tear ducts, wiping away the gathering wetness.

"Mom?" I called as loudly as I could through my pain. "Dad?"

But the only response I received was the soft chirping of what sounded like…*birds*? Despite the stinging, I forced my eyes open—and did *not* see my bedroom.

Woodland scenery surrounded me. The sun was bright in the sky above, illuminating the vivid, green leaves on the nearby trees. It was almost as if I'd stepped into a piece of art, or maybe a movie. This had to be one of the most vivid dreams I'd ever had. I could even smell a sweet scent of jasmine carried on a soft breeze.

My surroundings were beautiful. The sky was a pleasant shade of blue, the grass was soft and lush, and the air was warm. It was nearly too perfect.

I suppose it could be worse—like being in a desert without water or at the bottom of a cliff. I just didn't know how I was going to get home when I didn't even know where I was.

"M-Mom?" I called out again. It was the only thing I could think to do. None of this was familiar to me. There was no explanation for how I'd arrived…*here*.

The groan sounded again, and I quickly rose to my feet. They felt wobbly, making it a struggle to stay upright. With my new perspective, I spotted a small pond close by. Its reflection glittered under the sun's glow.

"Hello?" I called out, slowly spinning to find the source.

Another moan followed, clearly coming from the water.

Getting closer, I spotted a strange green lump in the grass near the pond. Tilting my head, I narrowed my eyes, trying to figure out what exactly I was looking at. I realized the lump was actually a frog, lying on its back. Its eyes were wide open and black, and its mouth emitted a groan every time it opened. The rapid rising and falling of its chest looked like it was gasping for air.

"Oh, God. What do I do?" I asked aloud, contemplating if I should pick him up. Was I brave enough to put my fingers on his scaly, slimy skin?

Taking a deep breath, I slowly knelt beside it. I didn't know the first thing about helping an amphibian with a breathing problem. Hesitantly, I poked a finger at its belly, wondering how it would respond—but the creature didn't move.

Did it need water, or was that a fish thing? Maybe that's why it was so close to the pond? Gritting my teeth, I resisted the urge to grimace as I picked up the frog in my palm.

His body was limp and oddly light—not that I knew how much frogs normally weighed to begin with. His heart pounded wildly against my fingertips.

I wrinkled my nose at how clammy and bumpy he was, and quickly but carefully eased him into the cool water.

"Come on, little guy," I murmured, releasing my hold.

But he immediately started sinking. He was too fast to grab and promptly disappeared from sight, into the depths of the pond.

"No!" I exclaimed, before releasing a heavy sigh.

Easing back, I pressed my wet hand against my forehead, completely frustrated with myself. What was I going to do? I was in a place I didn't recognize—everything that I knew was gone...and I'd apparently just *killed* a frog. Accidentally, but still.

As I stared up at the clear sky, the tears I'd done so well at repressing since Nico's messages threatened to fall. Helplessness I didn't know how to combat, swarmed me. Swallowing it down didn't work as well as it usually did, but I knew I had to focus on the problem at hand.

I reached for my phone, only to find that it wasn't there. My heart sank into my stomach when I realized I was without any source of contact. I had no phone, no internet, no watch, and no money.

My stomach twisted with a new fear. What if I was trapped here?

A loud splash startled me from my thoughts, causing me to turn back to the pond again.

The frog now clung to a long piece of grass, sputtering and coughing as it struggled to pull itself from the water.

"You...nearly...drowned...me..." it croaked, speaking in an un-expectedly gentle and masculine voice. There was a touch of a foreign accent there as well, but I couldn't pinpoint the country.

And then a delayed shock shot through me. I blinked. Had the frog just *spoken* to me?

Maybe I had hit my head harder than I thought. Because what other explanation was there?

"Excuse me?" I asked, shaking my head. If this was a delusion, maybe playing along would help end it.

"You...nearly...*drowned*...me..." it repeated, turning his head up to look at me as he pulled himself safely onto the ground.

The frog was actually speaking...to *me*.

I wasn't sure how much time had passed since its mouth had opened and actual words had uttered from it.

The frog finally settled and caught its breath, then perched forward among the tall grass.

I cringed when it flicked its long pick tongue over its eye.

I brushed my fingertip over my forehead, wiping at the sweat that had formed there. "Did you just speak?" If I could understand it, surely it also could understand me. To myself, I added, "There's no way you could have. I'm hearing things. Or is this a dream?"

All of this being a dream seemed like the most reasonable explanation for all this. I didn't remember falling off my bed, which meant I couldn't have hit my head. Maybe it was a result of too much stress. I had been through a lot in the past few weeks—a broken engagement, moving back in with my parents with no job, and crying myself to sleep over countless evenings...This dream *had* to be the result of my inability to handle everything.

And I was a heavy sleeper—pinching myself might not work. I still tried, squeezing my skin between my forefinger and thumb, hoping it would jolt me awake. But I remained in place, surrounded by a forest with a *talking frog*.

One who appeared to be watching me more closely with a twinge of amusement. As if it could actually *show* emotions on its face.

"This is just a dream," I muttered through gritted teeth as I tugged at my skin harder and squeezed my eyes shut. Only to find, yet again, that the pain was real, but did nothing to wake me.

"This is not a dream. You are, after all, standing before me," the frog—I guess I could call it a *he*—replied in his gentle tenor.

I gave up on the pinching, releasing my skin, and stared at him.

"I would like to know *who* you are, and whence you arrived. Are you from the Southern Lands?"

I wrinkled my nose, doing nothing to hide my look of confusion. Whence I arrived? Who spoke like that? "What?"

"Surely, you must be from the Southern Lands. Just look at your attire," the frog continued, waving a small, webbed hand at me.

I slid my gaze down to my white knitted top and jean shorts before meeting his gaze again. "These are my clothes." Was that really the best I could come up with?

"As I can see. Such attire *must* come from the Southern Lands," it replied before adding, "where the peasants get their clothes from the rag bin."

Now, this animal was just being offensive.

"You're a *frog*," I retorted, as though that should have been enough to refute his insult.

"For now," he responded. "And you are the girl who nearly *drowned* me."

"I thought the water would *help* you," I snapped.

"As I said, I nearly *drowned* thanks to you." The frog scowled and crossed its arms against its chest. It was weird he not only talked like a human, but acted like one, too.

"Well, I'm sorry," I quipped, rolling my eyes. I couldn't believe I was having this conversation, with a *frog*, nonetheless.

This was going on record as one of the most bizarre dreams I'd ever had in my life. As a child, I'd always dreamed of possessing the ability to speak with animals like nearly every fairytale princess could. But I had never imagined *this*—a creature of such a small, slimy stature, rudely criticizing my clothes.

"Perhaps we could start with introductions," the frog continued, rising to his feet.

My jaw dropped, unable to hide my astonishment at his ability to stand on two legs.

"Uhh…"

"Is that your way of agreeing?" he asked. "Or is that your name?"

"Neither. And I'm not giving you my name," I replied, shaking my head.

"And why not?"

I looked down at him, still incredulous I was having this conversation. "It doesn't really matter, does it?"

The frog frowned. "Have you forgotten it?"

"No, I haven't *forgotten* it," I snapped, shaking my head.

"Then perhaps you are running from someone…" he remarked. "Are you a thief? Is there a bounty on your head?"

"No!" I exclaimed. "I'm not any of those things." I squeezed my eyes shut. *This wasn't real.* "This is only a dream," I said, my heart throbbing in my chest.

"This is *not* a dream," the frog responded. "Has pinching yourself at least twice not already proven that?"

When I didn't respond, a small smile formed on his wide lips. It was completely unnatural to see a frog *smile*.

"Dream or not, I need to get home," I finally responded, my eyes opening and darting around, hoping to find something familiar.

"May I assume you will also refuse to share with me just where *home* is for you?"

I sighed down at the ground, feeling entirely overwhelmed. "You would be correct," I said, steadying the tremor in my voice.

When he didn't argue against my caginess, I looked up to find him regarding me with curiosity.

"Perhaps I can help you," he said, shrugging carefully. "If you agree to help *me*."

This dream was getting ridiculous. A frog was trying to *negotiate* with me.

"How on earth do you expect me to help you?" I scoffed. "You're a *frog*."

"A frog *prince*, to be precise," it replied, still standing on its feet.

My eyes widened with surprise. "Wait, did you just say *prince*?"

"Do you struggle to hear properly as well as dress yourself?" he asked, tilting his head curiously. "'Tis no wonder you struggle so."

I glared and bit down on my lip to prevent myself from arguing.

"Indeed, it is what I said. But I was not always this way," he explained. "I am both a frog and a prince."

The book of fairytales— *The Frog King* had been among the titles I recognized. And now I was speaking to a self-proclaimed frog *prince*. Were they the same story?

"So, back to introductions. After all, it is only polite," he tried again, sounding mildly impatient.

I huffed, then gave into his request. "Jo. My name is Jo."

"Seems like a rather strange name for a woman."

"You know, for a prince, you certainly lack manners," I retorted.

"I did not know peasants required a mannered response."

Had he just called me a peasant? "If I'm just a measly *peasant* to you, then I guess you can find more qualified help somewhere else." I looked around us, finding the woods to be completely void of any other being. Just as I presumed.

"My manservant Henry left nearly a fortnight ago, searching for a cure for this curse. But I fear I must take matters into my own hands, as the imbecile has not returned."

Good for Henry. Maybe he was no *imbecile*. Maybe he'd just had enough of the pompous frog, too.

"Such a large matter for such *small* hands," I sneered, raising a brow. "Prince or not, you're just a frog."

"Hardly," the frog responded with disdain laced in his voice. "I am Prince Aneurin James Arthur Quinn—"

"One name is enough," I interrupted. "A person only ever needs *one* name."

"A *prince* needs many," he said with a frown.

How a frog *could* frown was beyond me, but the way his lips slanted revealed he was displeased with my commentary.

"What name do you want me to call you then?"

"*Prince* Aneurin."

His name sounded right out of an epic fantasy novel, not a fairy-tale for kids. It felt even weirder to call a frog by so many names.

"Alright," I replied. "Now that we have that settled, are you going to tell me how you can help me?"

The amphibian stared at me for a moment before his lips curled into a smile once again.

"Ah, yes, of course," he began. "In order for me to help you, you would have to agree to help me break my spell."

"Break your spell?" I repeated, doing my best to avoid gazing at his lips. I was *not* going to kiss him. Maybe there was a small part of me that was curious about what he might've looked like before the magic transformation…if all of this were actually true. But not enough to follow through with pressing my lips against his slimy… There was *no way*.

"Is it not obvious?" he asked, gesturing to himself. "I was not always as I appear now."

"I presumed as much," I murmured as I chewed my bottom lip.

"'Tis not every day one speaks to a frog," he said, almost desperate now. "Especially not someone from the Southern Lands."

"You can say that again," I agreed, ignoring his commentary about my supposed place of origin. I wasn't going to fight him on it. Maybe it was better that he didn't know where I came from.

"If you help break my spell, I will help you find your way home."

"How do I know that you'll be able to?" I countered.

The frog shrugged. "I am a prince. How hard could it be to help you find your way south?" he asked, flicking his gaze over me again.

"So, how do we break your spell?"

"I must find a maiden who will love me, share her plate, allow me to sleep upon her pillow, and be kissed with true love in her heart."

That's what he thought. I was familiar with how this story ended. The princess did the first begrudgingly, took the frog to her room even more begrudgingly, and, disgusted at the idea of sharing her bed with him, threw him across the room. *That* was how he became a true prince again—a near-death experience. Not a kiss of true love. Then the princess, having a change of heart upon seeing his human form, agreed to marry him.

To be married only for his looks? Even for a fairytale, it felt like the *Frog King* got the short end of the stick.

"Do you know where this *maiden* is?" I asked. If he had an idea, then this would be easy, and I'd be going home in no time.

The frog crossed its green arms against its chest while it stared at me again. "Did you not hear me? I need to *find* her."

Narrowing my eyes, I gazed at him closely. "Do you even have a maiden in mind?"

The frog glared at me. "Of course, I do."

I raised a brow. He was lying. Because if he did, wouldn't he have already been on the pursuit?

"So, you're asking me to help you find your princess?"

"For a person with ears, you do not seem to use them as you should," he remarked.

Okay, this little green frog was aggravating with his little jabs.

"If you're going to be rude, I won't help you," I retorted.

"And *I* don't have to help you find your way home," he replied, pressing his hands against his slimy, green hips.

We stared at each other for a long minute.

"*Fine.* I don't need your help!" I tossed my hands up in frustration. "I'll get there…eventually."

"As you say. But do you realize that you are in the King's Forest? Guards lurk about. Eventually, one will find you and drag you before the king, who will take one look at you and most likely accuse you of witchcraft."

I snorted. "Witchcraft?" *Me?*

"Just look at you," the frog said, gesturing to my attire again. "Do you often frolic in your undergarments?"

"What? *No!*" I replied, quickly crossing my arms over my chest, and glared at him. "These aren't undergarments. What would you know? You're just a—"

"You are brave to take such a tone with me. Lest I remind you, *peasant*. I am a royal *prince*."

What he was, was a total *asshole*.

I wasn't a peasant, and he wasn't a prince. He was a *frog*! And if he couldn't call me by my name, he could forget me using *any* of his.

"Be lucky I don't like to eat frogs," I muttered under my breath.

His long, pink tongue slipped between his lips and licked over his eye before he sat back on his legs.

Grimacing, I wrinkled my nose. There was no way I was going to get used to that. He was *disgusting*.

"What did you do to get yourself turned into a frog, anyway?" I asked. "Let me guess. It was a witch. Did you turn her away from your castle on a stormy night? Did you deceive her with your obvious charms?"

Maybe I had too many fairytales confused with each other, but they did seem to have a lot of similarities.

The frog's eyes narrowed. "Of course not. My appearance was the consequence of a quarrel between a dangerous, magical man and my parents," he replied, enunciating his words as if he was afraid I was actually deaf.

"Your *parents* are why you were turned into a frog?"

I could tell he was getting frustrated with me by the agitated way he was twitching, but I didn't care.

"It doesn't matter *how* I became a frog, does it?"

"I just thought the details could be important. If I were this infamous woman destined to kiss you, I'd want to know why you were under a spell."

When he didn't respond, I felt bold enough to continue.

"But I guess at the end of the day, all that matters really, is that you're nothing more than a weird, little talking *frog*."

He lifted his hand, pointing a long, green finger at me in a snap. "Help me find the princess, *peasant*, and I promise I will find you a way home."

The promise made my stomach clench. All I wanted was to be back in my bed before Mom and Dad returned with the desk. What would they do if they came back to an empty house? I could only imagine the scene they'd find in my room—me missing. Both of them would be so worried.

"So, will you help me or not?" the frog asked again, drawing me from my thoughts.

"It seems I don't have a choice," I murmured.

FOUR

This was crazy.

I was wandering in the woods. With a frog who was trying to keep up with me because I had refused to pick him up when he'd insisted on riding my shoulder. As a prince, his servants must have listened to every command, but *I* wasn't from his world. And I wasn't one of his servants, no matter how many times he called me a peasant.

"Can you…walk a…little…*slower?*" he called from behind, wheezing as he hopped after me.

"If I walk any slower, it'll take all day to get anywhere."

"You…do not…even know…where…you're going…"

That was true.

"Look, I just want to find your princess, and get home."

"As you have…*said*," he replied breathlessly.

"I have to get home before my parents flip out when they see I'm missing."

"Flip?"

I released a breath. "Before they get too worried. Dad will probably come looking for me, or…"

"I find it quite hard to believe that you are not the sort that already causes her father quite a measure of distress."

"At least mine cares about me," I muttered. "Maybe yours should have worried about you more. Maybe then you wouldn't have become a frog."

"Touché!" The frog called, jumping faster than before from one patch of grass to the next, until he reached the edge of my shoe. "But you know not the troubles my parents faced, nor the guilt they felt after my curse."

I rolled my eyes. There was no point in arguing with him.

"*Please*," it wheezed, "let me rest on your shoulder."

"If you tell me where we're going, I'll contemplate it."

The frog stared at me. Then its pink tongue slicked over its eyes again. "Well, I *would* tell you if I knew where we were headed."

"Didn't you say that you had a servant with you? Henry, was it?"

"Yes, he left a fortnight ago."

"Sure, whatever that means," I said with a sarcastic nod.

"Two weeks," the frog replied with a breathless groan.

"So, you've been hanging out by the pond for two weeks?"

"Well...no," the amphibian said before stopping on the road.

"No?" I asked, turning to look at him. "What have you been doing for two weeks, then?"

It was strange to ask a frog what he'd done to occupy his time. Wouldn't most frogs just be eating flies or something? But something in my gut told me he was keeping quite a bit of his post-transformation story to himself.

"Well, there were two children who had found me in the wooded area where I had last seen Henry before he departed. They were incredibly distraught."

"Two children?" I asked. "Where are they now?"

"Well, I can't be sure..." the frog said, his gaze drifting toward the line of the forest. "I was placed into the pocket of the young girl for a time. A horrendous place to be, I might add."

"Oh, I'm sure there are worse places you could have been stuck in," I retorted and knelt down before him. "Do you remember anything about the children?"

The frog kept his gaze away from mine as his tongue flicked over his eyes again.

There would never be a time when I would not find that completely disgusting.

"Well, the boy was taller than his sister. He was leaving bread-crumbs behind them, which, at the time, I inquired about. It appeared to be such a waste of good bread. The boy said it was so they could find their way back home. The little girl, however, was weeping beside him."

I felt the blood drain from my face once I realized who he was talking about. Hansel and Gretel weren't going home anytime soon. They first had to outwit a child-eating witch. If they hadn't already been devoured.

I rose to my feet again and studied the pristine scenery. There was no sign of the horrors I now knew lingered just out of sight.

"You seem distraught now, too," the frog responded.

"I am," I said with a sigh. "We have to save those kids."

"Save the children?" he asked.

"Yes!"

"But what indicates they require our assistance?"

How was I going to explain that this entire place was just a story? I couldn't even say I knew their names without having met them.

"Call it a woman's intuition. Look, I'll pick you up, but you have to show me where you last saw the two. We have to find them."

"The little girl did seem rather upset." The frog crossed his arms against his chest. "As did the boy, now that I think about it."

"Do you know where they were going?"

"Before I fell out of the little girl's pocket, I heard the boy promise her that he would take them home."

That meant this was just the beginning of their story.

"How long ago was this?" I was almost too afraid to ask. It must be too late to prevent them from going to the witch's house, but I hoped it wasn't too late to stop the rest of the story.

"Perhaps nearly a week ago now. I imagine they have arrived home since I saw them last." The frog tilted his chin curiously and studied me. "But you seem to have a differing opinion. Do you know these children?"

"I don't know them personally. But I know *of* them."

"I fear for their connection to you and your…*Southern* origins."

"Can you stop with your insults already? You're not helping anyone—including yourself—each time you make a jab at me. You either want my help or you don't—Southern origins be damned."

The frog flicked his tongue over his eye again, then uncrossed his arms with a sigh. "Fine. My apologies, *miss*."

"Just call me *Jo*, okay?" I corrected before redirecting my gaze back toward the denser parts of the woods. "I can't believe I'm about to do this," I muttered to myself before lowering my hand to him. "We'll be faster if I carry you."

"As I have been saying all along," he remarked as he took a nimble step onto my palm.

I cringed at the feel of his foot on my skin. He was soft and smooth, and yet strangely gummy.

"I would like to remind you," he continued, "that you are in the presence of *royalty*, and I should be addressed in the manner my title commands."

"Please," I huffed under my breath. As if *titles* were the most pressing issue in the situation. I placed him on my covered shoulder. I waited until he grabbed onto my shirt before moving forward.

"I am inquiring why you think the children are in danger."

Pressing my lips together, I tried to answer in terms that he might understand. After all, this was a fantastical world, and I was sure they had their own lore to explain away their reality.

"Don't you know the stories about the woods, Your Highness?" I asked. It was vague enough.

"Obviously not," the frog replied.

"Witches live in the woods." I picked up my pace, doing my best to keep my balance against the rocks and tree roots.

"Well, they certainly have no place in the villages," he replied, almost dismissively, as though—*of course*—there would be no witches wherever he once ruled over.

"But there are several types of witches—"

"I know," he replied quickly.

I couldn't tell if he was lying this time.

"Well, *Your Highness*," I emphasized on purpose. "In these woods, there is a story of a witch who lures little children to her home, which is made of all the sweets a child could imagine. She keeps them with her until she decides to...*eat* them."

From the corner of my eye, I saw his quick, startled look at me. My words were finally beginning to sink into that small, little pea-sized brain of his. *Yes*, I thought, as if he could hear me telepathically. *She is going to eat them. You let the children disappear while you worried about a missing princess and a kiss you were never promised.*

"So, you believe that they—"

"It's not a matter of believing," I said, tripping over a smooth rock before catching myself with a thick, long branch of a tree jolting from the trunk. I felt him adjust on my shoulder, his small hand getting twisted in my hair.

"You know this...*how?*" he asked.

I stopped and eyed him. Was that really what he was focusing on? "Are you deaf? Didn't you just hear me tell you?"

"You told me of a tale of a witch in the woods. I know of several stories about goblins, wizards, and dwarves. Who is to say that the children could not be with one of those creatures instead?" he retorted before his voice hitched in mock fear. "You claim you are not a witch, yes?"

"You did say I'd be accused of witchcraft for my outfit," I retorted. "But I'm obviously not."

"Is it *truly* so obvious? You know so much for a peasant. A peasant *woman*, at that."

"Is this the real reason why Henry left you behind?" I asked suddenly, becoming more and more irritable by his jabbing banter.

I was over this slimy, eye-licking frog who claimed to be a prince with way too many names. It wasn't like I asked to be here—I hadn't even willed myself to even believe in the possibility of traveling through books. *Whatever* this was, I didn't want any part of it.

"My manservant is searching for—"

"I know," I interrupted. "A *princess*."

The frog continued to stare at me before flicking his tongue over his eye once more.

"I hope you end up with a real gem," I added, before turning my attention back to the rocky path ahead.

"I am a *prize* to be had, peasant."

"Oh, I'm sure," I remarked, doing nothing to hide the sarcasm from my tone. This appeared to annoy him all the more—which I didn't mind at all. "You know, I do have a name. I would appreciate you calling me by it."

"Are you sure? Such a ghastly sound to it. *Jo*."

"What's so *ghastly* about it?" I asked, mocking his accent as I did. And had we not already had this stupid conversation near the pond—*before* we ventured into these woods?

"'Tis so plain. What does it even mean?"

It was hard not to feel slightly insulted by his bluntness about my name. But I supposed a man—or *frog*—that had so many of his own entitled him to his own opinion.

"It's short for Josephine. My mother named me after her favorite character in a book."

I paused, realizing yet again how strange this all was to me. I was speaking *to* a fictional character.

"But the name means to grow," I continued. "There have been several famous women in history with the name Josephine."

"I prefer it, in truth," he remarked. "There is a ring of dignity to it. So much more than what is left to find in *Jo*."

"I don't care what you think about this. We can talk about names for days with the list you have just on your own. But it's a conversation that we're going to have to hold off on until we find and save those kids."

"*You* are the one walking," the frog said, slipping his fingers back into the fabric of my shirt. He tugged it gently, motioning for me to move forward.

I decided to ignore the indirect insult of being treated like a horse and stepped around a jutting tree limb.

This was going to be a long journey.

I could only hope it would be worth it.

FIVE

How far away was this witch's cottage? I didn't know how far I'd been walking, or for how long, but my feet were killing me. Was I even going in the right direction?

The sun was starting to go down, and the forest was becoming thicker, darker, and creepier. I wasn't thrilled at the idea of spending the night alone, with the protection of just an amphibian...especially in what I knew to be a forest housing a child-eating witch.

The frog had been everything but helpful in trying to get any sort of directional detail. He couldn't tell the difference between one path and another.

"Do you suppose we're close?" the creature in question asked with a yawn. "I am rather tired and would like to have my supper."

I paused and met his gaze. "And just *what* are you planning to eat?"

"While I do not delight in the diet of a frog, I have come to accept that I am one..." he explained, once again flicking his eye with his elongated tongue.

"Of course! How could I forget?" I slapped my arm and pretended to hold a small bug in between my thumb and forefinger. "I think there's *bug* on the menu."

The frog stared at me, unamused.

"I wish I knew where we were," I confessed, changing the subject quickly. "I'm starting to feel like this has become a fool's errand."

"Saving children is no fool's errand—"

"But not knowing *where* the children are is making it one," I retorted. "It's not like there's a clear pathway leading us to exactly where they are."

"Are you sure?" The frog stood up on my shoulder, eyeing the forest. For the first time, he'd taken an interest in our surroundings. Just the mere action annoyed the crap out of me.

For hours, it was *me* who'd had to decide where to go while the prince on my shoulder treated me like his chauffeur. But as I eyed the supposedly transformed prince, I *did* smell a hint of waffle cones in the distance. Was it just my imagination because of how hungry I was?

"Do you smell that, Jo?" he asked, turning ever so slightly. "Something warm and delicious. Like baked bread."

"I can *guarantee* you there's no bread baking anywhere nearby."

"I cannot deny what I smell," the frog countered, pointing a long, webbed finger toward a lone path just behind us.

I wondered just how far his little frog nose took him.

"There's a glow just beyond the hill there," he said.

Out of spite, I ignored the direction he indicated. "So *now* you care," I mumbled. "You're probably seeing things." As I'd walked by the path, I hadn't seen anything to give me any indication it could be where the children were—or a witch.

"You're not even *looking*, Josephine," the frog complained. "It's behind you." Then he pressed a hand against my cheek, forcing me to turn.

His cold, slimy skin against mine sent a jolt through me, and I did everything to resist the urge to wipe away the residue. I turned further away, hoping he wouldn't touch me again, and focused on where he pointed.

Just as he mentioned, beyond the hill from where we stood, was a hint of a light. *Something* was there, and the scent of waffle cones seemed to come from there, too. Deep down, I *knew* what it was.

"What do you think it is?" the frog asked. "Perhaps we should venture closer to get a better look?"

"How did you even see that?" I asked, turning my attention back to him.

"As a frog, I do have quite a gift of sight," he explained.

I wish I'd paid more attention back in school about biology. Maybe that would have been more helpful in navigating the how and why of this interaction.

My attention drifted back to the strange glow off in the distance. The forest was growing colder in the fading sunlight. I shivered—not dressed to be wandering all night in a forest. But the mere thought of getting any closer—to what I *knew* was a dangerous situation—kept my feet planted where they were, a streak of nerves and terror filling me.

Where had all of my bravery gone?

If it were still daytime...maybe I would have be okay. But if the light really was from the witch's house, what would we find there? Would it be just the way the story said? Did she truly live in a house made of chocolates and sweets, with standing cookies that resemble children? Would we find the gruesome evidence of bones and discarded clothing belonging to those who had not been so lucky as to escape?

My stomach turned at the possibility.

"I'm not so sure about going..." I whispered in response.

The frog's slimy hand touched my cheek again, making me flinch.

"Did you not tell me it was up to *us* to save the little girl and boy? We cannot falter now."

"*You* could just go, you know," I replied quickly. "You're the noble here, after all. And you'd have the easiest time going unseen by the witch."

His amphibian features twist with his own nerves, as though his royal title suddenly no longer mattered. Maybe he was starting to realize it didn't.

"Do you have a plan?" I asked, crossing my arms against my chest. "We have to have one if we're going to keep going."

"You are the one who knows more about these children and the witch," the frog countered. "Should it not be *you* who has a plan?"

He was right. I knew that Hansel and Gretel were lured into the witch's grasp thanks to their empty bellies and would narrowly escape danger. Did it matter if we came to their rescue? Their story was destined to end how it was written—right?

But something told me not to rely on that certainty.

"The plan is…" I trailed off. How could we help them and make sure we all got out safely?

"Could we not simply approach the cottage and wait for the children to come out?" the frog asked.

"I don't think it's going to be that easy," I countered, shaking my head. "Even if one emerges, they won't be together."

"Then what do you suggest?"

"We'll have to come up with it as we go," I replied. Before he could object, I added, "I don't have a plan and I don't hear you croaking out any suggestions, either."

"I suggested we approach the house and wait—"

"And I told you that wasn't going to work. It's better for us to keep moving before the sun completely disappears."

I didn't leave any room for negotiations, or any time for me to second guess myself. I had to force myself forward, or I wouldn't be able to help the children at all, leaving us to wonder what happened to them. A mystery that would certainly haunt me.

As I ventured forward down the hidden path, the scent of the waffle cones wafted through the air, drawing me in. I could feel my mouth water from hunger. It was now all I could think of.

"If I'm not mistaken, I can smell Ms. Alden's sponge cake…" the frog murmured, gripping onto my blouse more tightly.

I'd have to ask who she was later, but I couldn't let myself get distracted right now.

"It smells like a fairground to me," I replied, resisting the urge to lick my lips. "Waffle cones and funnel cake."

The frog looked at me, clueless.

Maybe they didn't have waffle cones and funnel cake in his kingdom. But if we were smelling different things—things we obviously craved—this had to be a trick.

I slowed my pace and I willed myself to remember what we were doing there. We were saving children. Hansel and Gretel.

"Is this how she does it?" I asked softly, pressing a hand to my stomach. "She makes you crave your favorite sweets?" The fairytale I knew had never mentioned this, but what else could explain it?

"Is that what it's doing to you?" the frog asked, sliding his tongue over his eye.

The act alone should have caused me to lose my appetite, but I could still smell the fresh sweet scent of the baked goods lingering in the air.

"It's almost all I can focus on," I replied and closed my eyes.

"Aye. If I didn't know any better, I'd expect to see Missus Alden waiting for us just over the hill with her sponge cake."

"Was she a woman in your bakery?" Did castles even *have* designated bakeries?

"The best," the frog answered.

I peered at the small figure on my shoulder. I realized I didn't know much of his story. He'd said a quarrel between a dangerous, magical man and his parents caused his transformation, but nothing more. I knew his fairytale began as the princess lost her golden ball in a pond. And the prince was already under the spell by then. But what happened to his kingdom when he turned into a frog? Had *everyone* turned into amphibians, too? What happened to his parents? Were they looking for him?

"What happened to her?"

"I suppose Missus Alden is still there, baking away as usual. I imagine the entire kingdom is still...just as I left it."

There were so many questions I wanted to ask him, but I'd have to save them for later. For now, I had to keep my focus on the children who needed our help.

Night had started enveloping the forest by now, casting strange shadows through the trees, making it appear as though little children were watching from afar. I braved a look over my shoulder and I could almost make out their faces and small, glowing eyes, watching us. A chill ran down my spine.

"I suggest we keep going," my companion murmured softly. "The children must be waiting. I imagine if the witch has cast a spell, it will only become harder to resist the more you fight against it." For once, his logic was sound.

Biting my bottom lip, I nodded and took a step forward on the path. I pushed myself to walk faster, fighting the urge to run away.

Once I climbed over the small, wooded hill, I spotted the cottage made of sweets. I could feel the looming danger that I was charging toward. What we were about to face was something no fairytale book had—or could—prepare me for.

"I can't believe this is actually real."

"What?" the frog asked, tilting his head. "The house?"

"How often do you actually see a house made out of…what is that? Gingerbread?"

"A closer look could confirm that."

"Let's not." I shook my head. "I'm not *that* curious."

His stomach rumbled. "Are you not?" the frog asked, staring at me before flicking his tongue over his eye. Was this his way of admitting that he was?

While I might have been curious—which I didn't want to admit—I was more eager to just get to the kids and get out of there. It would be even better if we could avoid how the rest of the story was supposed to play out.

"Okay, maybe a little," I admitted. "I just don't want the witch to see *me*." Seeing a frog probably wouldn't raise an alarm, but me?

With my modern clothes? It was a sure way to let her know something was wrong.

"One could stay away from the windows," the frog suggested.

"*Genius* idea," I replied with a frustrated sigh.

"You could look inside them. Perhaps you could get a better idea of what exactly is taking place inside."

"Can you just…" I wanted to tell him to shut it. But I didn't feel like getting lectured if I didn't say it in his polite, *royal* terms. Instead, I bit my lip and focused back on the house.

It was held up by wooden beams jutting out from the sides and walls, which were made of thick, golden gingerbread. Between each side was an oozing cream resembling marshmallow fluff. The roof was similarly constructed, but had square cookies for shingles instead of gingerbread.

"I didn't think it was possible," I murmured, shaking my head. "But I guess…"

I checked around us again before taking a step toward the confectionary building. As we got closer, small flaws—missing pieces—became visible. Little holes in the walls, gaps in cream where small hands had swiped through to the underlying brown layer of gingerbread. They must be where previous victims gorged themselves.

A shiver ran down the length of my spine.

"I can see why the children would come to a house like this," the frog said, breaking the silence between us.

"Yeah," I whispered, curiously pressing a finger to the sugary "cement." Just as I suspected. It *was* marshmallow fluff. And when I lifted some to my tongue, it was just as sweet as in my world.

The frog lifted a webbed hand and pressed a finger into it, mimicking my movements. But he was unable to pull his hand away.

Wrinkling my nose, I quickly, but carefully, pulled until he escaped the sweet trap.

"Just keep your hands to yourself," I replied, throwing him a dark glare.

Before the frog could point out my hypocrisy, a deep, cruel laugh came from inside the cottage. A sound that belonged to the fifty-year-old creep in a clown suit that smoked a pack of cigarettes a day that sometimes starred in my nightmares.

I lifted myself up onto my toes and peered through the closest window. Through the frosted candy panes, I could barely make out two shadows. A larger figure—the witch—waddled across the room while the smaller figure—a girl—trembled in place. I could almost *feel* the sadness emitting from her.

"Poor Gretel," I whispered, shaking my head. "We have to save her." *Somehow.*

"Lead the way," the frog replied, pointing his marshmallow-covered hand toward the other side of the cottage.

"We have to have a plan first," I hissed.

"Ah, yes," he replied in between licking some of the cream between his webbed fingers. "We have made it thus far without one, but *now* you require a plan."

"Any good leader would agree, *Your Highness*," I shot back. "You don't just march right into danger."

"Of course not. One merely knocks on the door and says, 'Good evening, Miss Witch. We're here to rescue the children. Please allow us entry.'"

Was he serious? "Who *says* that?" I whispered.

The frog shrugged and continued cleaning his hand.

"I should stick you back in the marshmallow fluff," I threatened. "Maybe she likes to eat frog legs, too."

"You are certainly proving what I imagined you to be with your Southern manners."

"You know, where I come from...people in the South are *known* for their manners."

The frog scoffed before shaking his head.

"I don't have time to argue with you." I turned to peer into the window again.

Only the girl remained, moving back and forth in the room.

"Gretel!" The witch's voice echoed through the gingerbread walls. "Go get some firewood!"

I ducked and held my breath, hoping that we hadn't been spotted. When no one appeared in the window, I nudged my frog companion and motioned to the side of the cottage.

"I think I have an idea," I whispered.

Six

I've never had the knack for planning. Even when I knew I had to leave Nico, I hadn't made a checklist to follow. I'd needed to get out, so I *left*. It wasn't until I'd found myself back home, eating popcorn on the sofa with Dad that I realized I still didn't know what to do going forward.

But when the witch sent Gretel out to get firewood, I knew this would be our only chance to see her. To let her know that I—*we*—were there to help her.

"Stay quiet," I warned the frog. I crept along the edge of the cottage, still smelling the sweet scent of the gingerbread wall. It was so *strange* to see the building standing before me.

The gingerbread stopped just as brick and stone began and curved toward the back of the home. In the middle of the stonework was a lone, little wooden door with two wooden steps that descended to the ground. My eyes followed the small stone path that led to a half-stacked pile of firewood. Just beyond, was a dilapidated well, with a rotting bucket tied to a frayed rope. It was a far cry from the sweet-looking home from the front. The rotting scene seemed to encompass what horrors lingered just within.

I recalled from history books that historical homes often separated their kitchens from their living quarters. This house didn't look modern, so I hoped it was the same.

"Trust me," he said, "I have *no* intention of saying anything."

"Good." I replied. The last thing I needed was to worry about him, too.

The little wooden door swung open with a startling force.

I ducked behind wall just in time, but my heart pounded in my ears. Taking a deep breath, I tried to calm myself.

Sobbing filled in the air.

Gretel.

"It's the girl!" The frog said as I rose carefully to my feet.

I peeked out from my hiding spot and watched the frail little girl descend the two steps. She couldn't be any older than five or six at most. She was so small to be given such a difficult task.

The collar and sleeves of her white blouse were adorned with flower embroidery. Dirt was smudged against her skin, and her brown dress had traces of what looked like flour. She was in desperate need of a change of clothes. Her long braids that hung over her shoulders were starting to become unraveled. Her brunette curls were matted together in some places. Her face was flushed red as tears rolled down her cheeks.

he stumbled toward the pile of firewood, and my heart went out to her. This was no place for children.

"She looks dreadful," the frog whispered to me. "A far cry from when we first were acquainted."

"What do you expect?" I retorted. "She's been a slave to a child-eating witch."

"I do not wish to admit that I did not believe your tale…" the frog hedged, "But this was not what I was expecting."

In all honesty, I had to agree. The dazzling illustrations I'd seen in multiple iterations of the story, the scenes of the witch's cottage were magical and light-hearted. But *this* was pure horror, and it being night only made it worse.

Gretel started to picking up the logs. Her grunts blended into her sobs. She looked up and over her shoulder toward the house.

Did she think the witch would do something to her brother without her present? Did she worry that she'd return with the firewood only to face their end?

Taking a breath, I stepped out from behind the wall.

"Gretel?" I whispered, trying not to startle her.

She froze, then quickly turned around in her little black shoes. Her eyes were wide with alarm before they shifted into curiosity.

"Are you Gretel?" I asked again, kneeling slowly.

Her gaze flickered from me to the frog perched on my shoulder. She must have recognized him, because instantly, her lips cracked a small, guarded smile. But then fear enveloped her once more.

"Mister Frog," she said quietly before jerking her gaze back to the witch's house. She was trembling when she refocused her blue eyes back onto me.

"I know you don't know me," I managed, following her gaze to where I knew the witch was waiting. "My name is Jo."

She tilted her chin curiously, watching me.

I licked my bottom lip then glanced toward my companion. "Mister Frog and I are here to help you."

"Y-You're here to help me?" Gretel shifted the two logs in her arms. "And Hansel?" she added after a pause.

"Yes." I nodded, offering a comforting smile. "We're here to help you and your brother."

Her eyes began to well up with tears before she shook her head. "But he's…in a cage. Inside. The witch said she'd eat him."

Her hands trembled as the tears erupted from her again. Her grip on the two logs loosened, and they fell to the ground with a loud thump. She pressed her hands against her face just as a small cry emerged from her tiny body.

"Look," I began, starting to feel a little nervous from the amount of noise coming from her. It would only be a matter of time until the witch would hear and come looking. "No one is going to eat you or your brother."

"But she said…" she continued, brushing the back of her forearm against her eyes before meeting my gaze again. "I want to go home. I'm so afraid."

"It's alright to feel that way," I replied softly, trying to give her my bravest smile. "We all get a little afraid sometimes."

She sniffled, turning her curious gaze back to the frog. I had almost forgotten he was there, for how quiet he had become.

"Even Mister Frog gets scared," I continued. "Isn't that right?"

"Frightened? Me?"

"*Yes*," I replied, glaring at him.

His green gaze met mine before his long tongue flickered over his eye.

I bit the inside of my bottom lip, ready to push him back into the marshmallow fluff like I'd threatened earlier. Maybe that would give him the scare he deserved.

"Of course," he said kindly, turning his attention back to Gretel. "Strangers can be terrifying."

I moved closer, keeping myself low so the witch couldn't see me through the window. "We're here now, and we're going to help you."

"Gretel!" the witch's voice echoed from inside. "The firewood!"

The girl tearfully drew her gaze back toward the wooden door. "I don't want to—" she stuttered through her shaking breath as she lifted the logs back into her arms.

I reached for her arm. As I brushed my thumb over her elbow, I could feel just how cold and frail she was. As rage flared inside of me, I bit back my own urge to cry and gazed at her tenderly.

She would not withstand another day or so of the witch's cruelty.

"Mister Frog and I are here to save you and Hansel." I hoped my reassurance would help to calm her.

But she simply continued staring at the well-lit door. I understood her fear. Of being caught. Of not being able to leave. Of the witch and what she might do. I couldn't even begin to imagine what awaited her inside.

"There, there child…" the frog murmured.

Gretel redirected her tearful gaze toward the frog, a faint glimmer of hope sparked in her small, blue eyes.

I turned my attention back to him. *He* was the only one who could go inside undetected by the witch.

"I think Mister Frog should go in with you," I said, smiling at the carefully. "He's going to help me get inside."

"No, I'm not!" The frog interjected, his voice rising with concern.

"Would you like Mister Frog to go in with you, Gretel?" I asked, ignoring him.

"*Gretel!* What is taking you so long! Get in here with that fire-wood!" The witch's voice echoed through the walls of the ginger-bread house. It nearly felt as though it rattled the forest floor itself.

Gretel turned to look at me, tears began to flood her eyes again, though this time I could tell she was trying to swallow them. I just wanted to take her—and her brother—far away from here, to safety. It mattered more than my bone-chilling fear.

"She said it's time to cook Hansel. I am to bring her kindling."

It was almost as though she were trying to explain away her tears, and what had caused her to be so upset. But I knew why. I knew it was crucial for my makeshift plan go as well as it could. There was so much on the line.

"Jo, you cannot mean to send me—" the frog began, but before he could finish his thought, I pulled him from my shoulder.

"You have to do this," I explained, looking at him directly. "You're going to go in with Gretel. You're going to prop the door for me, and give me the chance to sneak inside, undetected. It's that simple."

"I have a strange feeling nothing is ever *that* simple with you."

"I'd say the same about you," I sighed.

"But I cannot—"

I glared at him and lowered my voice while Gretel lifted a small stick, adding it to the two logs in her arms.

"This little girl is *afraid*, Your Highness. I imagine you might know, after your transformation, what it is to be afraid. Her and her brother's lives are hanging in the balance. You said you wanted to help. So, *help*."

"You did not tell me that sending me in with the child was a part of your plan."

"To be honest, I don't *have* a plan," I admitted. "But if you can help me get inside, then I'll do the rest."

"How do I know you won't get us all killed?"

"The only one who is going to die is the witch…"

The frog continued studying me.

"You have to trust me," I continued. "To be fair, I don't exactly trust you either. But that little girl needs you. Didn't you see her face when she saw you?"

"If I hear you call me 'Mister Frog' one more time…"

"You're going to have to deal with it until this is over."

He flicked his tongue over his eye before oddly raising what should have been his brow. If he had one.

"I'm taking your silence as a yes," I sighed.

"What choice do I have? You have already made it for me."

"I'm glad you're so *willing* to go along with this," I snarked at him. "I'm going to give you a stick, and just as Gretel goes through the door, I need you to drop it to prop it open."

He continued to stare at me. I wasn't sure by the way he looked at me if he necessarily was following my idea.

"That way I can sneak in," I explained.

"And you think this is going to work? A mere *twig* is going to allow you entry?"

"You know what? You're right. I could just barge in and hope for the best," I snapped. "Why didn't I think of that before?"

"If it were so simple, wouldn't the children have tried it themselves?" he asked.

I looked over my shoulder, watching as Gretel tried to gather her courage before marching toward the house's door again.

"They are *children*, and they're terrified," I said softly. "I'm not sure if this will work, but it's worth a shot. Either way, we have to get them away from the witch." And *I* had to get the witch into the oven.

The frog released a heavy sigh, pressing his webbed fingers against his face. I'd never seen a frog react so human-like—it was weird to say the least.

"Be the prince I know you are," I tried to encourage. "Think of this as practice for protecting a damsel in distress. But *this* one is five-years-old, needs a bath and wants to avoid becoming a meat pie along with her brother."

"Must you be so grotesque? It is entirely unbecoming."

"And you're rude and gross, *Your Majesty*, so we're even," I said back. Before he could say anything more, I shoved a small stick from the ground into his webbed fingers.

I rose to my feet and approached Gretel, then dropped his slimy body into her pocket.

"Mister Frog knows what to do," I said with a smile. "Now, go inside with that firewood. I'll be right behind you."

SEVEN

"I'm not doing this for you, peasant," the frog muttered before Gretel walked back into the house. At least, I'm pretty sure that's what he said. It was hard to tell while I followed a few paces back, praying he'd swallow whatever pride he held within that tiny, slimy body of his, and did what I asked.

Gretel pulled on the latch and shoved the wooden door open. A pool of light emerged from inside.

Now that I could see, I easily spotted the tiny, green amphibian pop up from Gretel's pocket and drop the stick. The door slowly began to close but stopped short from locking.

I crept toward the door, gathering my courage. I couldn't remember ever being this afraid in my life. And not just for myself—for Gretel, her brother, and even that stupid frog.

This was *so* much worse than I arrived back at my parents' house after everything. I had been so afraid of what to tell them, not wanting to see the disappointment in their faces. It had taken me nearly ten minutes just to get out of the car, and control how fast my heart had been beating.

My parents were always accepting and forgiving of any mistakes. Like when my mom had surprisingly been unfazed when I'd accidentally washed a red shirt with a load of whites, and everything had come out a soft shade of pink.

She'd simply said, "Everyone learns."

There'd also been a time when I'd brought home a less-than-satisfactory grade on my report card. I'd been told just to try harder…to do better next time.

But when I'd come home after Nico, there'd been something bigger that had scared me—facing the disappointment in *myself*. I'd failed being a successful adult. I still needed my parents, when, by society's standards, I was supposed to have my life together.

But I couldn't afford to break down today. My mom wasn't waiting for me behind this door. Hansel and Gretel were relying on me.

I might have bitten off more than I could chew, but it was too late to turn back now. "You got this," I whispered to myself as I extended a hand toward the door handle.

Find the oven, I told myself. *Just as the story tells and push the witch into the oven*. I wasn't thrilled at the idea of having to murder someone—but at least my victim was a child-eating witch. But that made it no less gruesome.

"Bring me your brother," the witch snarled from behind the door. Her voice was gruff and slightly deep. There was a hint of annoyance—probably at her not already eating her latest victim.

Gretel whimpered.

How were she and Hansel supposed to live after this experience? How were they ever going to be able to trust anyone again—let alone their parents? If I could recall the story correctly, it was due to their stepmother's jealousy that they were in this predicament to begin with. I could only imagine the nightmares they might suffer in the future.

But did it matter? As soon as the story came to an end, so did the existence of Hansel and Gretel. Right? But did that still apply now that I'd been thrust into their world?

"If you don't *stop* your blubbering—"

I heard the echoes of a slap, and my hand moved on its own accord. I pushed the door open with no thought but to find and protect Gretel from that god-awful woman. Thankfully, my entrance was silent as I entered a large, wide kitchen.

There was a large fireplace in the wall beside me, ablaze with the two logs Gretel had brought in from the pile in the yard. Perched over the flames was a large, black cauldron—exactly the kind one would imagine a witch having.

Along the adjoining stone wall, was a long counter made of dark, stained wood. Pots, pans, and herbs were strung along the upper wall, and led to a larger, round brick oven with an iron door in the front. The door was tall enough that an entire person could almost step inside without any trouble. I pushed aside what that meant.

Next to the long, wooden counter lingered the witch. She was broad and large, reminding me almost of a villainous headmistress. Her cheekbones were wide and high, and her nose was long and pointed, and even had a little wart on the tip.

Just as she turned to look over her shoulder in my direction, I heard Gretel say, "No Mister Frog! Stay in my pocket!"

He jumped out of nowhere, landing on the witch's upper skirt.

The witch jumped back in surprise, releasing a screech of alarm.

I moved to the side of the island, ducking out of sight.

"A frog!" the witch cried out.

I wasn't sure if it was from fear, or if she was thrilled by the sight of him. If she enjoyed eating children, I could only imagine that frog's legs were on her list of delicacies.

"Oh, catch him, girl!" The witch commanded, as I heard a frying pan banging against the counter. *Thump!* Again. *Thump!* Again.

"Get him! Get him!" she repeated as she released a deep, throaty laugh. By the sound of her guttural laughter, my unspoken question was answered. If she caught the frog prince, she'd eat him, too.

I peeked around the island and saw Gretel chasing the frog.

Behind her, the witch towered, holding a glistening cleaver.

I felt my heart sink into my stomach at the sight.

"Mister Frog! Mister Frog! Come back here!" Gretel shouted. She lurched forward each time he landed on the floor, on the shelves, on the counter—I'd seen cartoons play out in similar circumstances.

And then I realized he was shouting my name.

"Jo!" he called. "*Jo!*"

If only he'd remained in Gretel's pocket. Then, perhaps, this wouldn't have escalated to the witch chasing him and Gretel around the kitchen. I wasn't sure exactly how I was supposed to intervene, only that I had to.

The frog hopped onto a tile on the floor, and Gretel's hands wrapped around his little body, finally catching him.

Immediately, the witch snatched the frog from her hands and lift him high up into the air. "Just the thing I've been craving," she said with a snicker. "Frog's legs with a side of frog's heart!"

"Please let him go!" Gretel cried out as she reached on her tiptoes for the frog.

The witch snarled in response before turning back to the counter where she'd been working. Her long fingers reached for a lone glass jar as she gazed back at the frog with a smile. "What a treat I'll have," she continued. "A roast with a side of a frog fry."

"I command you to release me!" he yelped from the witch's fist.

Completely unfazed, the witch didn't blink at his ability to speak. Instead, she started pushing him into the glass jar. But he resisted, holding onto the sides.

"Jo!" the frog called out again. His voice cracked. "Jo, *please—*"

Maybe it was the way he pleaded for me—the helplessness resonating in his voice. Or maybe it was the combination of watching Gretel's fearful expression as the witch attempted once more to force him into the glass jar. Regardless, I slammed my fist against the nearby counter, announcing my presence, and glared in her direction. I just hoped whatever bravery I'd been able to muster wouldn't dissipate now that I needed it more than ever.

The witch shifted her gaze toward me, her piercing blue eyes on mine. A peculiar, gaping smile formed at the corner of her mouth, revealing teeth of a yellow-green hue, some visibly absent. It was only then that I observed the thinness of her hair, its off-white and gray tones standing out. She was *old*, more than I expected. It was almost as if time itself was decaying her.

"A new face has joined us, I see."

"Let go of my friend," I ordered, gesturing toward the panicking frog. His green eyes met mine before I glanced at Gretel. "And you're going to let the children go, too."

"Oh no, dearie…You wouldn't deprive a poor, old woman like me from her meal, now, would you?"

"Children aren't meals," I retorted. "And I can already tell you that frog is more trouble than he's worth."

"No trouble, dearie," she said with a laugh. "It only takes a single cut through the belly." She lifted the frog, tracing his white stomach with her pointy fingernail.

The very idea of her dissecting him made me grimace. Going through that in high school biology class had been more than sufficient for me. "How dare you!" the frog shouted as he wriggled his legs. "I *order* you to put me down!"

The witch considered him, as if she had just registered that he was speaking. "This one seems to be enchanted," she said thoughtfully. "That'll only make him all the juicier." Her smile widened before she lowered the frog toward the opening of the glass jar.

"I came for the children," I interrupted. "Hansel and Gretel."

"You can have the girl. She's no use to me," the witch remarked. "Look at how frail and thin she is. I shall keep the frog and the boy." Without waiting for my reply, she thrust my animal companion vigorously into the glass jar and slammed a nearby saucer on top, blocking any easy escape.

His webbed fingers pressed against the side as he gazed in my direction. Like I would know precisely how to free him.

I shifted, unsure of how I would manage to rescue everyone, myself included. Though I had the advantage of being nearer to the door, I was the farthest from those I needed to protect. "I'm not here to negotiate," I forced out. "I want all three."

The witch must have seen my hesitancy, because she smiled again—exposing her crooked teeth between her tight, thin lips.

"Well, you can't have all three." She lifted the glass jar for me to see. "Frogs happen to be my favorite delicacy, and it's been quite a long time since I've seen such a large, round one."

Offended, the frog glared at the witch before shifting his gaze back to me. He *would* be the type to take offense to the opinion of a cannibal witch.

"You're going to let them go. *All* of them," I reiterated, struggling not only to find my voice but also any trace of the bravery I had just moments ago. I needed to stay strong and steadfast. I had to see this through. I already knew how this was meant to end, but it felt like an incredible weight rested on my shoulders to ensure the witch met her fate in the oven…and that Gretel and Hansel went home.

"You are rather bold for a mere girl…" The witch scoffed, raising an amused brow. "There is nothing to stop me from eating you, too."

"Not if I kill you first." The words slipped out of my mouth before I had a chance to think. Despite all the mysterious criminal documentaries I might have watched in the past, I never had imagined myself to be in the sort of predicament where I was contemplating someone else's demise. But this didn't count, right? The witch wasn't even real. *None* of this was real.

The witch began to cackle—the sort that echoed in my ears and traveled down the length of my spine with chills. It told me I hadn't been the first to threaten her life. But I would be the last.

I surveyed the table before me, strewn with the ingredients the witch had assembled to prepare Hansel for cooking. Bags for sugar and flour were open and positioned in the center, accompanied by wooden spoons and sizable mixing bowls. At the far end, a long carving knife stood ominously.

I wouldn't be fast enough to snatch the blade from the witch, but I could create enough of a diversion to get within reach. Without a second to spare, I took a step toward the table, grabbing a handful of the flour from the open sack and threw it toward the witch's face.

She released a strange yelp before taking a step back, wiping the white powder from her eyes.

Without waiting for her to regain her balance, I hurled another handful at her face, inching my way closer with each throw.

She twisted and turned, attempting to dodge my attacks. Gradually, she edged away from me, accidentally dropping the jar with the frog, causing it to shatter on the floor.

Despite the distraction, I remained focused on her, unwilling to divert my attention.

Gretel dashed out of the way, watching me with wide eyes.

I frantically grabbed the nearest sack beside me, eager to continue with the progress I was making. If I could get her close to the oven, then this would be all over in just a few minutes. The newest one I'd grabbed had small specks of white, which could only be one of two things—sugar or salt. Either would be even worse than mere flour. I tossed another handful, and another when the witch's yelp turned into a sharp, piercing scream.

"You horrid, *foolish* child!" she screamed, rubbing her eyes. "I shall carve you alive!"

Disregarding her warning, I countered with another handful of what I had discerned to be salt.

As we finally rounded the corner of the table, she stood in front of the looming, large oven. I had no time to lose.

"Gretel!" I shouted, gesturing toward the iron door.

The little girl didn't hesitate, understanding my meaning. She struggled, holding onto a rag as she tugged open the door.

Inside, I could see large, yellow flames awaiting their next victim.

"I'm sorry I have to do this," I muttered under my breath, as I tossed one more handful of salt into the witch's face before dropping the sack onto the floor. With another step, I pushed her, using all my strength to move her toward the roaring oven.

She reached for me blindly, trying to grasp any part of me she could find.

Determined, I pushed her once more, driven by desperation to push her into the oven before she could drag me in, too.

Her body slammed back against the hissing bricks, tearing a sharp scream from her. She opened her eyes, exposing just how bloodshot they'd become. And lurking just beneath the surface, I could see the sheer rage she had for me.

"You won't get rid of me so easily," she hissed, grabbing me.

A wave of pain swept over me as her fingernails pierced through my shirt and into my flesh.

Her bloodshot eyes were wide with fury as she snarled at me. "I'll grind your bones, girl!"

"You've killed countless innocent children!"

"They're *beasts*," she growled quickly. "Ones no one wanted. No one came to claim them. The lowly, hungered beasts were left for dead. I did them mere favors."

I struggled as her nails dug into me more deeply.

"And if you kill me," she continued. "You're no better."

Gasping, I tried to ignore the intense sting of her nails as they pierced my skin. She was trying to force me to release her.

"We'll be the heroes," I bit out, pushing her as hard as I could, into the roaring opening of the oven.

The witch's lips twisted into a manic grin as she clutched at the edges, halting my progress.

"You think you're so clever, but in less than an hour, I will be picking your meat from my teeth."

If she had it her way, I knew all of us would be dead. But I wasn't going to let her win. That's not how this story was supposed to end.

"The kitchen is closed," I sneered and shoved again.

In a sudden flurry of movement, two small bodies appeared between us. With remarkable speed, their tiny hands pressed against the witch's waist, propelling her backward with unexpected force.

A startled cry escaped the witch's lips, reverberating in the air, as my focus shifted swiftly to the children.

There stood Gretel and her brother, their determined gazes fixed on the oven where they had boldly confronted the witch.

"The door!" I shouted and reached for the handle. The heat seared my skin, but adrenaline let me fight through it. I couldn't let the witch escape.

Gretel was quick to move beside me, pushing the rag she'd used into my hand.

I wrapped it around my palm and, with a forceful slam, locked the iron door locked into place. Once it was closed, I did my best to drown out the piercing scream of the witch just beyond. Soon, she dwindled into nothing more than a looming shadow swallowed by the fiery glow.

EIGHT

"Is she gone?" the frog croaked, its voice barely louder than a whisper, as he emerged from the other side of the kitchen, where the witch had dropped the jar on the floor.

Relief washed over me as I saw he was alright, despite the fall and the shattered glass. Releasing an exhausted sigh, I slowly sunk to the floor.

Beside me, Gretel and Hansel embraced each other tightly and wiped away each other's tears.

Despite his time having been locked away, Hansel appeared rosy-cheeked and warm. But they both were very much in need of a bath.

"You were so brave, Gretel!" Hansel said to his sister with a smile. He brushed his long, blonde bangs from his eyes and hugged her again. "We can go home to Papa, now."

Gretel spoke into her brother's shoulder. "But what if Papa forgot about us?"

"Of course he didn't," Hansel replied, easing her away just enough for him to peer at her. "Just wait until I tell him about all the things you did to protect me from the witch. Surely, Papa will be so proud."

I lifted a hand, pressing it against Gretel's back gently. She turned to look at me, her eyes were clouded with unshed tears. The lingering fear in her eyes prompted me to offer my most reassuring smile. I could see the fear still lurking there, so I gave my gentlest smile. "Your papa will be so proud of you both," I reassured her.

Hansel nodded his chin in my direction in acknowledgment. "Thank you for helping us, miss," he said. "For helping Gretel."

"Thank you for coming to *my* rescue," I admitted, shaking my head. "I don't know what I would've done if you both hadn't been there to push her with me."

"I freed Hansel from the cage while she wasn't looking," Gretel admitted, looking back and forth between the two of us, as though she were afraid she'd done something wrong.

I released an exhausted breath and smiled again. "You did the right thing. You helped to save yourself, your brother, and me."

"And me..." the frog said as he hopped closer to the three of us. "I must thank you both for your tremendous bravery."

Narrowing my eyes, I glared in his direction as he approached.

"If only you had done as I *told* you," I blurted, raising a brow. "I would have had more control over the situation."

"I was merely trying to help," the frog insisted. "As *you* directed."

"I didn't tell you to jump out of her pocket," I corrected.

He shifted onto his hind legs. "I do not do well in them."

"*You* put yourself in that situation," I retorted. "And it made everything more dangerous for everyone."

"I trusted that you had a plan."

That frustrated me even more. He'd *assumed* I would save the day. That *I* would solve his mistake. I swallowed back the words I wanted to say. "And what if I had failed?" I asked, shaking my head. "What if she had succeeded in boiling you for lunch today?"

The frog merely stared at me as he crossed his arms against his chest with a shrug. "But you did not."

"But what if I *had*?" I snapped back.

"'Tis a good thing neither occurred. You did not fail, and I did not become someone's lunch," he remarked before turning his gaze back to the children.

A thick silence, and the disturbing smell of...roast meat...drifted from the oven between the four of us. My stomach turned.

"We need to go," I said, rising to my feet.

Gretel peered between the frog and me. "Before we go, there is some things I would like to take," she interjected meekly. "With the witch gone, she will not need such things, right?"

"What things?" I asked with a small, curious smile. "Show me."

Gretel hesitantly grabbed my hand and took a small candle from a nearby table. She led me down the cramped, dimly lit hallway, into an adjoining room as the faint flicker of flame cast eerie shadows on the walls and uneven wooden floors. In the far corner, bathed in the faint glow of the hearth, stood the iron cage that had once imprisoned Hansel.

The mere sight of it sent a shiver down my spine.

The little girl guided us to the center of the room and placed the candle down beside her black shoe. She released my hand and knelt down and, with determined fingers, tugged on a crooked floorboard, attempting to pry it up. The wood creaked in protest as she unveiled the hidden secrets beneath the floor.

"One night, when the witch thought I was asleep, she pulled this out," Gretel explained. She lowered her arm beneath the board and pulled a small burlap sack from the shadowy spot. Then she opened it and poured small stones into her hand.

"Jewels?" I asked, kneeling beside her and tilting my head to examine the prize.

"Did you say jewels?" the frog's voice sounded from behind me.

I spun around to see Hansel standing in the doorway, holding the amphibian carefully in his hands.

Gretel emptied her palm back into the bag and opened it further. In the dim candlelight, I could see inside there was a solid gold bracelet and two rings, a few rubies and yellow diamonds as large as my thumbnail, several gold coins, and a few round pieces of what appeared to be sapphires and emeralds.

"These are beautiful," I said. "And I'm sure they will help your family when you go back home."

Gretel flashed me a relieving smile and pulled the treasure against her little body.

Hansel took a step closer, clearing his throat. He released the frog, who came to sit beside me. "I think we should give them a token of our gratitude, Gretel. Without the pretty lady and her frog..." But he didn't finish his sentence.

"Oh, no. I don't—" I began before the frog cut in.

"A coin or two would be much appreciated," he said hastily.

"It's enough to know that you both are safe," I interjected.

Hansel ignored me and tilted his head.

Gretel rose to her feet, looking a little disheartened as she brought the sack to her brother.

With a tender smile, he took the bag from her and opened it. He reached in, grabbed something in his fist, and turned his eyes to me with a cute smile. It was the first time I took in his boyish charm. He had to be at least eleven or twelve. Old enough to be considered a man in his world—responsible to tend to his family if needed.

In *my* world, boys his age were too busy riding bikes and playing video games to be bothered with real responsibility.

"I owe you so much," Hansel said softly. "And you...and you protected my sister." He extended his hand out to me, revealing a ruby, a sapphire, one of the golden rings, a larger yellow diamond, and four coins. "Is this enough?" he asked, looking from the offered treasure to me.

I peered at the items before glancing back at him and then to the frog. I didn't know exactly how to respond. It seemed more than enough to me. But given my companion didn't complain, he appeared to be more than appeased.

"Uh, yes..." I lifted my hand and watched as Hansel carefully dropped the jewels into my palm.

He then tied the sack's top and slipped it into his front pocket before turning toward his sister. Extending his hand to her with a smile, he revealed a charming dimple on his cheek. "Let's go home."

"You're leaving?" My tone was unnecessarily harsh. I couldn't stand the idea of letting them go back out into the woods again. At least, not without knowing they'd be safe.

The frog cleared his throat, but I ignored him.

"*We're* going to need to find a place to stay for the night," I explained, tucking the jewels into the pocket of my shorts then rose to my feet. "We can try to find your home when it's daylight again."

"But I know the way home," Hansel insisted. "It isn't far."

"Isn't that how you found yourselves in this predicament to begin with?" I challenged, crossing my arms against my chest. "Let's just focus on finding a safe place to stay for the night."

"Only if you're sure," he said, looking reluctant but relieved at the notion of having our company a bit longer.

Gretel was smiling ear to ear.

"I'm in agreement." The frog tugged on my shoelace. "Could I reside on your shoulder again?"

Resisting the urge to roll my eyes, I picked him up and did just that. At least he'd *asked* this time.

Hansel looked at his sister, who anxiously nodded in turn. They were understandably eager to leave. She lifted the candle from the floor, protecting the small flame with her free hand.

We left the room, walking back through the hallway and out through the door of the kitchen. I glanced back at the oven once to make sure the iron door was still in place. The last thing I wanted was to find that she somehow managed to escape. But there was nothing. But a peculiar scent of sweetness and meat still hung in the air, wafting from the chimney stack on the opposite side of the house. I hoped that once we all had put enough distance between us and the cottage, we coulde'd leave behind any reminders of the ordeal we'd all just endured.

We opened the door, but stopped at the dark night that met us.

"Wait," Hansel said, and reached for the lantern hanging by the door and turned to his sister. "May I borrow your candle?"

Gretel nodded and passed it to him.

Taking it into his hand, Hansel used it to light the lantern's wick. "Good thinking," I said.

Together, we rounded the side of the edible cottage. I examined the gingerbread's intricate siding before breaking off pieces to save for later. At least I'd have something for all of us to nibble on.

"Good idea," the frog whispered into my ear. I nodded silently, stuffing a few pieces into my free jean shorts pocket.

The forest was different in complete darkness. I couldn't see where I was going, and couldn't trust anything around me. Earlier, I remembered seeing the shadows of the children, but now…there were only tall trees, their large trunks, and the long branches covered in voluminous leaves.

"Come on," Hansel called over his shoulder to me.

"Where to?" I was well aware none of us had a clue as to how to escape the forest—none of us knew where home *was*. And none of us had a plan of where to sleep.

"Papa always said to walk east and eventually you'll run into a body of water…"

"And is that where home is, Hansel?" I asked, doing my best to catch up to him and his sister. "East?"

"It'll at least give me a better idea of where home is," he replied.

Gretel turned to her brother.

I could hear her softly tell him that her feet were hurting. He encouraged her to keep going.

We continued walking quietly for a while, threading our way through the intricate twists and turns of the forest.

Turning to the frog on my shoulder, I found him alert—his eyes attentively scanning the surroundings behind me.

Eventually, Gretel stopped, lifting a finger in the direction of a distant light in the trees.

We all froze, watching in silence as the glow flickered back and forth, almost as if it were dancing.

"What do you think it is?" she whispered. "Is it another witch?"

I felt the frog shift on my shoulder. "It better not be," I replied. But I could hear a voice off in the distance. And by the way Hansel stood attentively, he heard it, too.

I couldn't make out the words, but I could tell it was a man. A man that was desperately shouting. "What is he saying?" I asked.

The boy lifted a hand, shaking his head. "I...don't know."

The frog cleared his throat before saying, "He's calling for you. *Hansel...Gretel...*" He said their names in a different tone, obviously mimicking what he heard.

Then the voice got louder. *Closer.*

Before I had a chance to react, Hansel bolted through the woods, leaving his sister behind with me.

"Papa!" he screamed. "We're here! *Papa!*"

Gretel looked at me once, then took off running after her brother. She, too, began to cry for her father.

I ran after them, wanting to ensure they were safe. The distant light came closer and closer until I could make out the larger figure, wrapping his arms first around Hansel, and then little Gretel. The man held them tightly against him, kissing their foreheads.

Tears of relief flooded my eyes. It was fate that we were all in the forest together. After everything they'd just gone through...they'd found their father.

"My children!" he cried. "My children!"

I stopped myself a few feet away and caught the man's eye.

He raised his chin and, in the dim light of his lamp, I could see his cheeks were damp and he was smiling.

"My children..." he repeated, looking back down, as if he were afraid they'd disappear again if he didn't have eyes on them.

"Tugs at the heartstrings, does it not?" The frog asked softly. "To see a father so joyful in being reunited with his children?"

I wanted to say that I hoped he'd learned from this experience, but at that moment, that felt cruel. Instead, I nodded in agreement.

"If only mine had shown such devotion," he murmured softly.

I stared at the frog, recalling the short tale he'd shared with me. My heart tightened in sympathy.

After a prolonged moment, the father rose to his feet and extended a hand in my direction. I could sense his confusion as he observed my attire. Unlike my meeting with the frog prince, this man chose to not say anything.

"Is it you I should give my thanks to for saving my children?"

"Only briefly," I admitted. "I'm sure they'll explain everything to you tell you their story with time and some understanding."

"I've been searching for weeks after their stepmother..." He trailed off and peered back down at their faces. "She died unexpectedly and I-I'm so very sorry for what transpired."

He muttered the words almost as if he believed a simple apology would fix everything.

Just like Nico.

If only apologies were enough to patch deep wounds.

This man had abandoned his children and only regretted the decision because his *wife* had died?

"I think you owe them much more than just an apology," I replied. "After you find out what they've endured, I hope you never choose to leave your children again."

He stared at me long and hard, struggling to respond.

But I didn't care. As long as Hansel and Gretel were safe and sound, how they healed was up to them.

"You're right," the father replied and tugged his children close to him again. "And I hope," he said to them, "with time, you both can learn to forgive your poor papa."

Gretel clung to his side, wrapping her fingers around him. "I want to go home, Papa," she confessed

"And home we shall go, my dearest Greta. We're only a day's walk away." Their father lifted her into his arms and tucked her against his chest.

"Goodbye, Mister Frog," she called from her father's arms.

Hansel watched his family for a moment more before grabbing his father's lamp from the ground. "I'll lead the way," he offered.

His father flashed him a proud smile and nodded.

"Be a good lad and take us home."

The boy started off.

Before the man turned on his boot to follow, he bowed his head toward me. "Thank you for tending to my children. I may not know as much as you do but...I can see they've endured much. And I hope—I'm grateful to have my children returned to me."

I swallowed, not confident in what to say. Eventually, I whispered, "I'm just glad they found you."

Realizing his father wasn't following, Hansel turned back and offered the lamp from the witch's cottage to me.

I took it, grateful for the light it would provide. I stood there with the frog on my shoulder, watching as they disappeared into the darkness.

And then, there was only us.

The story was over.

"And where shall *we* stay?" the frog asked.

I sighed again. "I think your options are a cave if we're lucky...or a hollow tree. I hear they're popular in enchanted forests."

I had only mentioned a hollow tree as a joke, but after walking another twenty minutes or so, the frog gestured ahead at a large tree loomed in the distance. "Well, there's your hollow tree."

Fortunately, the space was large enough for me to crawl in and sit comfortably. While it was far from a five-star hotel, it did offer some shelter and warmth under the cover of night.

After everything, exhaustion finally hit me. Before I fell asleep, I imagined how I'd wake up in my bed, realizing everything I had experienced was all a dream.

Because there was no plausible way for me to have traveled inside a book of fairytales. Much less to have met a talking, walking frog—who claimed to be a prince under a spell—and to have saved two small children from a cannibalistic witch who could have easily killed me, too.

NINE

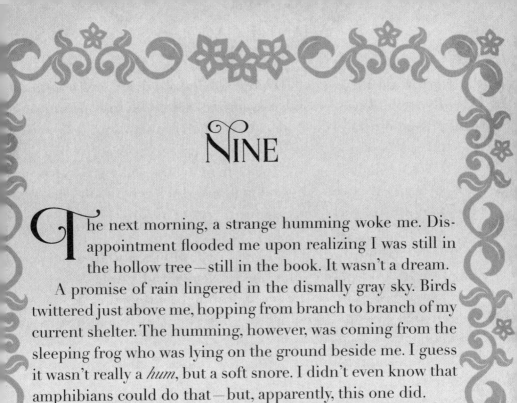

The next morning, a strange humming woke me. Disappointment flooded me upon realizing I was still in the hollow tree—still in the book. It wasn't a dream.

A promise of rain lingered in the dismally gray sky. Birds twittered just above me, hopping from branch to branch of my current shelter. The humming, however, was coming from the sleeping frog who was lying on the ground beside me. I guess it wasn't really a *hum*, but a soft snore. I didn't even know that amphibians could do that—but, apparently, this one did.

In just my shorts and shirt, a chill started creeping into my bones. The forest felt significantly colder compared to last night. There was *some* warmth to be found inside the tree, but not enough to not wish for a jacket or some full-length jeans.

It didn't help that I was also starving. Thankful for my past self stealing some of the witch's house's gingerbread, I pulled a few of pieces from my pocket and carefully bit into the hard cookie. I didn't need ants coming after any crumbs.

It wasn't anything fantastic. Nothing to lose your life over. If anything, it just tasted stale.

"Are you going to share?" the frog asked, suddenly breaking the silence.

I hadn't realized the soft humming had come to a stop.

"There's not much left," I murmured.

"So? Should you not share with your betters?"

I stared at him in disbelief. "Did you really just say that?"

"I *am* a prince."

Narrowing my eyes, I lowered the cookie from my mouth. "I know you think you're above everyone, or maybe just me, but...so what? You being a prince doesn't mean anything."

"Of course it does."

"Does it?" I challenged. "You're lying on the same ground as me. You're currently two inches tall and are stuck relying on people to pick you up and carry you around."

"My legs tire easily."

I wrinkled my nose. "I have seen real princes, and they don't act like you. It's no wonder you've been turned into a frog."

"I *am* a 'real prince,'" he scoffed, straightening himself.

"If your parents were anything like you...this must be a lesson for you all."

"I am nothing like my parents," he retorted, shifting on his feet. I must have struck a nerve.

"Is that a blessing or a curse? I haven't had the pleasure of finding out yet. But I can say, most definitely, that you're insufferable."

"All because I asked you to share some of the cookie you stole from the witch's house?"

"It's not like you can eat it, anyway. Your royal highness doesn't have teeth." I still tossed the cookie in his direction. Just to shut him up.

I rose to my feet and stepped out of the hollowed tree. Our current surroundings didn't look any different from where I'd first met him. I was almost certain there was nothing but trees for miles.

I was never going to find my way home.

Instead of allowing myself to slip into a spiral, I started exploring. What else could I do? If I could walk off irritation, maybe I could do the same with fear and hunger.

I trampled through the maze of trees and thickets, pausing to enjoy the slight breeze the late morning had brought. Remaining motionless, I focused on the rustle of leaves, attempting to calm my annoyance with the prince.

In the stillness, I heard water flowing in the distance. Hansel had instructed us to head east, promising that we would eventually encounter some. And I could very much use a wash. The frog surely wouldn't want to pass up the opportunity of dipping his toes in. Turning on my heel, I moved toward where I'd left him.

"Your Highness!" I called out as I quickly approached. "Frog?" I wasn't sure which name I cringed over more.

"I do have a name…" the frog replied, hopping out to stare at me as I came to a stop in front of the hollow tree.

"You're right, you did inform me of quite a few."

"If we're going to be traveling together, I think it best for you to address me by my name," he said, staring at me, unamused.

"And not, 'Your Highness?'" I really needed to stop talking before I said anything more stupid. Here he was, trying to be civil with me, and here I was…being a brat. "What would you like me to call you, then?"

"By my name. *Aneurin*," he said, crossing his arms over his chest.

"No title? When did you decide this?"

"Just now," he replied curtly. "Now, what is it you were calling me about, Josephine?"

"Jo," I corrected. "If we're laying down rules about names, my name is *Jo*."

He flicked his tongue into the air and stared at me. "Jo," he repeated after a moment.

"I came back to tell you that I heard water nearby. If we can find it, we can wash up. After everything, that might be nice, right?"

The frog—or rather—*Aneurin* seemed to contemplate what I'd just shared with him before slowly nodding. "A wash would be nice, yes," he agreed. "Just as long as you have no plans to drown me."

"We're supposed to be working together," I replied. "I need you. Just as much as you need me." I approached him and extended my hand downward. "Would you like me to carry you?"

"Are you asking out of pity?"

I *had* struck a nerve with him earlier. Instantly, I felt bad for how I'd treated him. How we both had treated each other. Maybe we'd just started out on the wrong foot.

"No," I replied, shaking my head quickly and letting my hand drop. "Of course not."

"I can most certainly hop beside you."

"Yes," I agreed. "But if I carried you, we'd stick together easier. You could save your strength for whatever else we come across."

"Another witch?"

"Who knows?" I replied honestly.

"And so, where does that leave you and I now?"

"I guess that's a good question," I replied. "And I have a feeling we'll find out soon enough." I extended my hand again, giving him a smile that was more believable than before.

He flicked his tongue over his eye instead.

"Fine, if you don't want me to—" I straightened, lifting my hands. At least I had tried.

"No, no. Jo—" he called out, hopping quickly toward me. "You may lift me." Aneurin sat at my feet, proudly turning his head to the side. As though he wanted me to witness him giving into me.

I contemplated squeezing him a little when I picked him up, but I imagined my doing that would only hinder any hopes of us getting along. Instead, I simply placed him on my shoulder.

If there was one fact I'd come to accept about him—he was bizarre. I wondered what he'd been like as a human. He must have been arrogantly handsome. It seemed all the men who were beautiful from my time, and knew it, used their attractiveness as a way to explain away bad behavior.

The river water was far from refreshing. It was cold—bitterly so. The kind that reminded me of all the frigid showers I'd endured at Camp Whitmeyer. But at least there it was the only way to endure the grueling heat in the middle of the forest.

I've never been the type that enjoyed summer—not with the humidity. Not unless I was at Oak Corners Lake. Everything was right when Mom got treats out and Dad set up the Slip 'N Slide. There was no better way to spend a hot day away than with the garden hose and some frozen popsicles.

If it were warmer, the water might have been a saving grace, but it wasn't for me, nor the frog—Aneurin. Addressing him differently was going to take some getting used to. Aneurin. Not "frog." He had a name. Was a person. An actual prince.

Not that I cared.

It's no different from a pet having a name.

"I beg your pardon?" I heard him croak beside me.

My cheeks heated. Had I really said that out loud? Damn it.

"I didn't say anything," I quickly replied, glancing away as I dipped my hands into the river again.

"I am not a *pet.*"

"I never said you were," I remarked, wiping a few strands of my wet hair away from my face.

He scrutinized me, likely noticing my embarrassment and realizing the extent of my dishonesty. However, he chose not to dwell on it, merely shifting his gaze away from me to the flowing river.

"Do you think Henry is looking for you by now?" I asked after a moment. I hadn't forgotten that his servant was still out there, searching for help.

"My servant is doing as I requested of him to do. He is searching for the cure of my curse."

"A princess to kiss you."

"Indeed."

I glanced back at the water. "Well, we won't find one here."

"Which is why I must insist we leave. As soon as you are through in your bathing."

"I'm done." I flicked my fingers free of any remaining droplets. "Where would you wish to go, Your—I mean, Aneurin?"

He flicked his gaze back to me, his shoulders sagging and his eyes worried. "Are you saying you know not where to go?"

"Aren't you the one who is supposed to be helping me get home?"

"Only *after* I am freed from my curse."

"My point is that I don't know my way around here. I don't have a single clue where we are, other than in the middle of the forest. A forest, mind you, that once was the home to a child-eating witch."

"No need to mention that heinous wench," the frog—Aneurin—retorted, his voice laced with disdain, before lifting his webbed finger across the water. "Is that not a boat, Jo?"

A boat? I squinted in the direction he indicated, struggling to discern anything amidst the rippling currents. Aneurin's eyesight was beyond good, not to mention his ears—as he'd proved with Hansel and Gretel's father. If he claimed to see a boat, then it was most likely there.

It was hard to see against the dark hue of the river, the thickets of bushes and branches, and the gray sky above. But I looked where he was pointing and saw a wooden boat. It was tied against a large, flat rock just down the bank from where we stood. It was an extremely lucky find.

"How did you see that?" I asked, unable to hide how impressed I was.

He flicked his tongue into the air, quickly pulling in a passing bug before glancing back at me. "My frog instincts."

I stared at him, completely unsure of how to answer. An honest reaction would be to laugh at the absurdity of it all.

"Right…" I lowered my hand to him. "Should we see if we can get to it?"

"And what will your plan be? Ask the captain for a ride?"

I turned in a circle, checking to see if the owner was anywhere in sight. "I can be the captain. It would be a lot faster to travel by water, don't you think?"

"You know how to steer such a vessel?"

I shrugged as I nodded. I paddled a canoe a few times during summer camp. It couldn't be that different.

"Actually," I said, surprising myself with my own confidence, "Yes. Don't all the peasants of your kingdom know how to steer such a vessel?" I asked back with a smirk.

Aneurin didn't respond. Instead, he silently hopped into my hand. That was a first. He remained mute while I navigated through the tangled roots of trees, all the way to our destination. As we drew nearer, I spotted a single oar resting across the lone seat. Almost as though it had been waiting for me. In the far corner of the small fishing boat, a small sack was perched on the floor.

Stomach rumbling, I hoped the sack contained some forgotten meal. Despite my companion's ability to snatch bugs from the air, I knew he wouldn't pass up the chance for human food.

He'd made that apparent with the reference to the cookie earlier.

"I don't swim," he said, breaking my thoughts as he crawled up the side of my arm. It was still freaky—how small and slimy he was against my bare skin.

"I don't understand that." I replied, narrowing my eyes curiously. "You're a frog."

"But I'm a prince," he corrected.

"Princes don't learn how to swim?" I bit my lip in amusement. "Isn't this the setting where men learn how to do everything, and know how to do everything, and keep women at home?"

The frog shifted his small legs on my shoulder blade. "I know no such nonsense," Aneurin replied. "Women tend to do just as much as the men do in my kingdom. They work in the fields, they raise their children—"

"Do women learn to read?" I asked, challenging all the things I'd assumed to be true. "Can they *teach* children to read?"

"I'm sure some do," he whispered, unsure. "Can you?"

"Of course I can," I explained. "This is a…" Book. And then I stopped, realizing that I was about to say too much. I couldn't just give away that this world wasn't real, could I? Would it ruin the time-space continuum like countless time-travel films? Could I actually *ruin* the entire fairytale world?

"I was lucky enough to receive an education," I corrected quickly before glancing back at the boat. "And, I won't let you drown."

"Are you confident in your abilities to steer us?" he pressed.

"It won't be that hard," I said, taking a step toward the vessel. "I've done it before."

"Do you understand that this is a serious matter, Jo? If I were to drown—"

"Your little feet won't even get wet," I groaned, glaring at him. "I swear, I won't let you drown. If you do, then I will, too, okay?"

Aneurin stared at me as though I had offended him and his feet.

It was all I could do to stifle my laughter by his expression. "You can trust me, okay?" I tried again with a smile. "We have to start trusting each other."

"I trust you," he replied.

"I'm glad," I remarked. "After all, I did save you from becoming...what did she call it? 'Delectable frog legs?'"

"Let's not speak of that wench ever again."

"Good thing she wasn't a princess, huh?"

"God's teeth," he muttered as I clamored into the boat.

It was wobbly, to say the least, and it took me a moment to find my footing. To keep him safe, I moved the prince from my shoulder into the bottom part of the boat. I was nearly certain that he was turning a darker hue of green than his usual complexion.

"Are you sure this is a sound decision, Jo?" he asked me, his tone reminiscent of a nervous child about to meet a mall Santa Claus.

With the oar in hand, I turned to him, determination coursing through me. "I don't think the owner will miss their boat."

After unraveling the rope from the stone with my free hand, I pulled it inside the boat and felt the current pull us forward. I slid the oar into the water and started rowing, quickly finding a steady rhythm. Back and forth. A rhythm I remembered from years ago.

"I think this beats trampling through the woods for a few hours. And it might be safer this way. Most rivers lead to villages." That had to be true in fairy tales too, right? "We should find one soon enough where we can rest."

The frog clung to the inside of the boat with fear in his large eyes. He turned toward me. "I appreciate your civility with me since this morning," he suddenly confessed from my feet.

I looked down at him. "Civility?"

"Naturally. Perhaps you have even become fond of me?"

I wrinkled my nose as I jerked my gaze back up at the river. That was a stretch. "I don't know if I'd say that."

"Would you not? Surely your actions since this morning's incident have been caused by your change of heart?"

Where was this coming from?

"Just because I'm being civil with you, doesn't mean that I like you," I replied, pushing the oar against the current of the river. At the answering silence, I looked down at Aneurin, only to find him glaring up at me.

"Then I care not of your opinion of me," he retorted.

I rolled my eyes. "That's very clear. You're the type that feeds off validation. Your ego can't handle somebody not liking you."

His tiny mouth fell open. "That is not true!"

"Yes, it is. And it's jarring to you when your god-awful attitude pushes people away."

"I do not surround myself with such lowly—"

"Oh, don't start with this again. I thought we'd moved past the whole 'peasant' thing," I said, rolling my eyes again. "If I'm so lowly, then why are you so adamant in my staying? Why did you bother to come with me?"

"Did you not agree to assist me with my mission?"

"Why are we even arguing?" I chuckled bitterly into the wind. "This is just ridiculous! I'm fighting with a *frog*!"

"A frog *prince*, Josephine!" he shouted as he rose to his feet.

But the speed of the boat immediately jolted him backwards, forcing him to sit.

"*Don't* call me Josephine!" I argued back.

Our spat left me breathless, but we continued to glare at one another in silence. For a frog, he sure was stubborn.

"Fine," he seethed. "I confess I prefer your company to the alternative of being alone. I do not appear to have any other options," he continued as he adjusted himself against the side of the boat.

"So, desperation lowers your standards?" I retorted, pushing the oar angrily. "I should have left you in the woods. Or maybe you would have preferred the witch we pushed into the oven?"

"Do be serious," he replied. "Of *course*, I prefer your company to that old hag. And besides, she is dead."

"As if that helps your case."

"Does it not?" he asked, peering at me.

"Can you just stop talking?"

He had more to say. It was evident in the way he parted his lips as if to speak, yet something held him back. Instead, he flicked his tongue over his eye.

I shook my head. "You're disgusting."

"And you lack propriety," he shot back. So much for being quiet.

"How so?" I asked. If he was going to insult me, he might as well explain himself.

"Did you not wish for me to remain silent?" Without waiting for my answer, he added, "And so, I shall." He turned on his heel without another word, crawling up the side of the boat to gaze out over the water.

It was all I could do to resist the urge to push him into the water with my oar. But that wouldn't get me home. But, goodness, it was so tempting!

Raising my eyes to scan the expanse of water before us, I came to a stark realization — I had no clue where our journey was leading.

There was no sign of civilization in sight. Where was Gretel and Hansel's home? Had they made it back safely with their papa?

My thoughts drifted to the two children, and just how brave they'd truly been in that horrible experience. If something like that had happened in Oaks Corner, it would have been plastered all over the news...

"Gretel was sweet, wasn't she?" I asked, breaking the silence as I recalled her little face. She'd place herself in real danger to save her brother. And he'd looked at his sister with such love in his eyes.

I was surprised by Aneurin's soft response.

"Yes. She was." After a brief moment, he continued, "And her brother was quite a brave lad. A little slow to come to the rescue, but brave nonetheless."

I held back my snarky remark in defense of Hansel and decided to continue the conversation politely. Maybe that's what I needed to do. Stay positive — at least until I found him his princess.

"They were in quite the predicament," I replied.

"I'm rather curious to know just how you knew what would oc-cur," he remarked. "I did not have time to ask at the moment, but how *did* you know?"

I bit my bottom lip, pressing the oar into the water again. "I told you...the stories."

He was quiet, considering his words. "I think you know more than you are telling me."

"It was a lucky guess," I snapped. "That's all."

"*Too* lucky," he replied, before jolting back against the side of the boat again.

I looked down at the water. It water was moving too fast. The cur-rent had changed. Lifting my gaze, I could see the stream opening to a wider, deeper area ahead. And just beyond, a line of...nothing.

Then roar of the falling water echoed in my ears.

A drop.

"Oh, no..." I tried to turn the boat sideways with the oar.

But the current was far too strong.

"What are you doing?" the frog shouted.

"Do you see that?" I replied, lifting my oar and gesturing to the line of water. It wasn't helping, so what was the point in continuing to struggle?

His silence was all the response I needed.

"The water is too strong," I continued, panicking. This couldn't be the way things ended for me. In a boat, with a talking frog.

"I told you I can't swim!" he exclaimed.

The boat continued to move.

The oar felt useless as I tried to brace us against any jutting rocks. But I couldn't get a grip on them long enough to hold us still.

"We could jump out now!" the frog exclaimed.

I shook my head at him. "It's too late. We'll go over either way. The current..."

The boat approached the edge and, before I could say anything more, the front tipped down dangerously.

I saw the frog peer over his shoulder at me, his large eyes even wider with fear.

We went over the edge, sending my heart down into my stomach.

I screamed.

TEN

The blinding burst of light was familiar. I *knew* that light. Did it mean I was going home? Had this *all* been a dream after all? Was I going to find myself back in my bed like Dorothy?

The light slowly enveloped me, sliding over and through me, inch by inch, until I became a part of it too. I searched for a way out, tried to see through the strange shadowy shapes forming before me.

Squinting, I could barely make out what appeared to be a woman—gazing into a gleaming glass mirror. Her features were soft, and her eyes doe-like and black. Her skin was pale and smooth, and her lips were perfectly shaped. In my world, she would have been envied by everyone.

But when I looked into the glass and saw her horrifying reflection, a scream erupted from somewhere deep within me.

I could hear the woman's voice echo in my ears, ringing out the rhyme I knew so well.

"Mirror, mirror, on the wall…"

Another burst of light expelled from the mirror, sending the searing beams towards me like darts. I squeezed my eyes shut, hoping…praying that I'd wake up.

As swiftly as the flash of light ensnared me, it released me, carrying away the image of the woman and her mirror.

I continued to plummet, until the sensation of water enveloped me entirely. The impact was immediate, the chill flooding over me as the current dragged me down.

But Aneurin. Aneurin needed my help in escaping his curse.

I opened my eyes, glancing up towards the glittering sunlight, just above the surface.

Air. I needed air.

My lungs stung from the effort of holding my breath, and I propelled myself toward the sunlight, just inches above. Breaking through the water's surface, I gasped, inhaling as much air as possible before descending one more.

I can't swim…

Aneurin's confession rang in my ears, and I turned my attention to the cloudy water surrounding me. I needed to find him—he needed me. But where was he?

I pushed my hands blindly through the water, hoping I would knock into his little body by accident. But there was nothing. I pushed to the surface, gasping as I squinted against the sun's rays.

This sky was certainly not the same one we'd just seen in the forest. It was a beautiful shade of blue, and the clouds were a pearly white. I scanned the scene, realizing that I—*we*—were in a small pond, with a bank on either side only a few feet away. No waterfall or dizzying cliff in sight. And, of course, there was another thick forest surrounding the pond. Still, I instinctively knew this one was different from the last.

But I didn't have time to focus on the details of where we were now. I needed to find Aneurin. Could he have been left behind? Was I the only one who could be transported by the strange light?

"Aneurin!" I called, moving my hands through the water. A gentle breeze blew across the surface of the pond, sending shivers down my body. I wasn't dressed for any part of this excursion—walks in the forest, falling into ponds, searching for magical frogs…

A moan echoed nearby. One that I instantly recognized.

I spun in place, searching across the surface of the pond again. My eyes roamed the tops of lily pads until I came across the small of his body.

He was clinging to the side of one, hanging on tightly with his small hands.

Relief flooded me as I realized Aneurin had come to this new place with me.

"Aneurin!" I managed, swimming forward.

"Over here," he groaned, his eyes desperately searching for me.

I pushed myself towards him, swimming as quickly as I could.

"*Jo!*" he croaked. "Jo, I can't swim!"

It was so strange that a woodland creature—one that was primarily found in water, couldn't swim. Even if he was originally a human. Why hadn't his frog instincts affected his ability to swim when it had heightened his sight and hearing?

As I neared him, I extended my hand, helping to shift him fully onto the lily pad.

He collapsed, exhaling a profound sigh. "I was certain 'twas the end of me," he managed. "And then I landed here in this pond."

I studied him and his exhausted form before asking, "Did you see the woman in the mirror?"

"The woman?" Aneurin asked, shifting his large green eyes in my direction. "What woman?"

"Maybe she wasn't real," I murmured. And maybe that was what I needed to remember. No matter how real this all might feel right now, none of it actually was. It was only a matter of time that I'd wake up with my parents circling around me with deep concern in their eyes. I could already hear Mom insisting that I go speak to a therapist about my ex-fiancé.

"Jo?" the small, accented voice called out to me, drawing me back from my thoughts. "Jo? You don't think we died, did we?"

It was all I could do to not roll my eyes at him. But I guess if there was ever a moment to cut him some slack, this was it. After all, we *had* just tumbled off the side of a waterfall.

"Do *you* think we died?" I asked, doing what I could to hide my amusement. I was relieved just knowing that he was alright.

"God's teeth, I hope not," he replied. "For, if heaven awaits me, I should hope I will not remain a frog."

His remark stirred an unusual curiosity within me. It felt out of place given the current circumstances, but I couldn't help but wonder again about his appearance as a human. I imagined a man sitting in the reeds, drenched like myself.

Not just a man, but a *prince*.

Did he have brunette hair? Blond? I knew, at least, that his eyes were green—an almost emerald hue.

Would he resemble those men gracing the covers of romance novels, with meticulously styled hair, wearing 1 billowing white shirts and sporting dimples in each cheek? Would he look like one of the amazingly dashingly handsome actors, starring in historical pieces left and right? Or maybe he'd appear more relatable and down-to-earth, like the boy next door?

I quickly dismissed the thoughts. What did his appearance matter to me anyway? My focus needed to be on finding his princess and somehow persuade her to summon the courage to kiss him—as a frog—so I could return home. How much time had passed since my unexpected descent into the book? What if Mom and Dad had already come back from picking up the desk? My mind was racing with so many thoughts that I was taken aback when Aneurin cleared his throat, staring up at me once more.

"It all seems a little strange," he began. "One moment we were cresting the edge, and the next there was a brilliant light, and suddenly...we were here. Wherever *here* is..."

The bright light had enveloped us, just as it had when I'd said those handwritten words in the book. At first, it had sucked me into the forest, to where I found Aneurin. But, this time, I'd seen a queen and her magic mirror. The light had sucked the Aneurin and me into a new place, or more specifically...into a new story. Right?

"Kind of like magic, huh?" I asked aloud, glancing back at our surroundings. It was hard to see through the bushes what might be just beyond. If this was the story of Snow-White, as I suspected, shouldn't there be some sort of cottage?

Another gentle breeze swept through, causing me to shiver once more in my water-soaked clothes. The only plan I could devise was trying to find the dwarfs' cottage as soon as possible. We needed to dry off and understand where—and *when*—we were in the story.

I turned to look back at my companion again and motioned towards the shore. "We can't stay here."

"Obviously not," he remarked, shaking his head.

"We'll try to find a place to stay…"

"I'd prefer it not to be a place that resembles sweets, or one that houses a child-eating witch," Aneurin retorted.

"I don't think we'll have to worry about that," I replied, peering at him and then back to the shore. "Right now, we have to figure out how to get you to the other side."

"You could carry me," he said, motioning towards my hand.

"You could also just learn how to swim," I mumbled under my breath. However, when I looked back at him, his large, green eyes were fixed on me. I detected a glint of fear as his gaze shifted back towards the shore. "You know I won't let you drown, right?"

"You did try to before…"

"That was purely an accident," I corrected.

His small face bobbed up and down as he adjusted himself on the lily pad. "Forgive me, Jo. I was merely jesting…"

The whole exchange between the two of us was odd now. We'd done this dance with each other, making little jabs since our first meeting. But they felt different now. I suppose after everything we'd been through in the past few hours, there would be a sort of bond that would develop, right? Trauma bonding, or something? I knew we weren't friends, but we were. In a weird way.

"It's alright." I gestured to the lily pad. "Maybe I could just pull that to the other side as I swim…If you hold on, it should keep you from going under."

He stared down at his floating refuge, flicking the sides with his long, webbed fingers before nodding again. "I trust you."

I trust you.

I didn't know how his words made me feel, but I didn't want to disappoint him. Smiling, I gently plucked his refuge from the water.

He released a small gasp when I struggled to snap the stem, but I kept my hand carefully balanced underneath to ensure his safety. As soon as I felt it break, I started swimming, pulling it along.

The water felt colder now. Probably thanks to my prolonged exposure, the biting breeze, and my inadequate attire. I wasn't sure if I'd be successful in getting a change of clothes at the dwarfs' cottage, but it was worth hoping for.

When I reached the opposite bank, I placed the lily pad on the ground first.

Aneurin released a heavy sigh of relief and immediately hopped onto a patch of grass.

Inhaling deeply, I prepared myself for the cooler air then I hoisted myself out of the water. Goosebumps prickled my bare legs as I scanned our surroundings once more. And I couldn't help but smell a strange odor coming from me, the unfortunate result of an unexpected swim in a pond.

"Where do you think we are?" Aneurin asked.

I squinted at the tree line. There had to be some sort of indication we were close to where the story would take place. "W-We should go l-look for shelter," I stuttered between my chattering teeth.

Aneurin was silent as he surveyed the glade as well, before settling in one direction. "I see smoke through the thicket. Just there." He lifted a webbed finger towards a small opening in the foliage. It looked like nothing more than a shadow from where I stood.

But the longer I studied it, the clearer I saw small billows of smoke rising between the tree branches. That *had* to be the cottage — had to be the home of the seven little men.

Even if it wasn't, we were about to find out.

ELEVEN

"I believe we have passed this tree twice already," Aneurin croaked by my ear.

I paused in place and released a heavy sigh. I hadn't walked far. Not enough to be remotely lost. But it was taking forever to get closer. "I'm going toward the smoke," I said, glaring at him as I pointed in the direction of where we'd seen it.

It didn't help that I kept trying to recall the story of Snow-White and all the versions I'd heard growing up. There were seven men, right? Or dwarfs? Was it even *okay* to call them that? Should I call them "little people" instead? I didn't want to offend anyone.

I glanced back at the frog, wondering if I should warn him against doing just that. The last thing I needed was for him to jeopardize our safety because of an ill-considered remark.

"Can you just do me one favor?" I asked, tucking a strand of hair behind my ear.

Aneurin seemed to hesitate, shifting his little feet on my shoulder before clearing his throat. "What is this favor?"

"Promise to be on your best behavior to the next set of individuals we meet?"

"Are you implying that I did not acting accordingly before? The woman wanted to eat me."

I grimaced. "I'm not implying anything. I'm just asking you to be polite to whoever we come across next."

"I will act as I do with any stranger. I shall introduce myself and establish an understanding of our ranks and stations."

I groaned. "We're in the middle of the woods, *Your Highness*," I retorted. "No one but you has a rank or station here."

"As long as that is understood, we should not have any issues."

"You're incorrigible," I sighed, moving ahead once again through trees and brushes, keeping my eyes set on the stream of smoke. I tried to ignore how wet and cold I felt, but my shoes were squeaking against the soil with each step I took. At least, I could take comfort in knowing that there was no imminent danger this time. I wasn't leading us towards the clutches of a child-eating witch.

Curiosity sparked within me as I wondered what awaited us in this unfamiliar reality. It would most likely diverge from the beloved animated film of my childhood. Certainly, that vision would not be found within the original pages of a Grimm fairytale. Still, relief filled me at the sight that met me when I finally emerged from the dense foliage.

While still quaint and warm, the home before me was, in the truest sense, a *tree* house. Three robust plants, reminiscent of the towering sequoias back in California, stood just beyond the edge of the forest where we'd just come. Their branches intertwined seamlessly, almost as if they were a single entity. Wrapped around the middle trunk was a circular staircase, leading up to a porch. The entrance, adorned with neatly carved windows and a curved door, exuded charm. It was easy to see the structure was at least two or three stories high. Built entirely into the three trees. It was certainly large enough to house seven grown—albeit *little*—men.

Aneurin sucked in a shocked breath, which landed right next to my ear thanks to his place on my shoulder. "Is that a home…in a *tree?*"

"It is," I replied, nodding. "A tree house, to be exact."

"Why would *anyone* wish to build a home in a tree?"

I wrinkled my brow, looking at him curiously. "Why not?"

"If one does not have an aversion to heights…" he went on. "Are you?"

He crossed his little arms against his chest and glared at me.

"It's alright to admit that you are," I said with a smirk. "I'm not a huge fan of them, either. But this is our only option."

"Tis better than the home of the witch, I suppose," Aneurin said cheekily, releasing a soft sigh.

I nodded silently, brushing aside the unsettling thought that another witch would soon visit this place. Maybe it was why we were here—to thwart her attempts to harm Snow-White! And maybe, just *maybe*, Aneurin was the prince destined for Snow-White.

Turning back to the tree house, I saw a figure move on the upper porch. I squinted to see better.

That had to be her. She appeared youthful and stunningly beautiful, and not at all dressed for outdoor living. Her radiant presence made it understandable why the queen had been consumed by envy. Any woman in my world would have felt the same way.

A woman, dressed in a maroon gown, adorned with a ribbon of gold around a low neckline, adjusted a long rug over the porch railing. he fabric of the gown seemed to be tied up in places around her hips and waist, preventing her from tripping. Her attire didn't match the chores she was attending to. Her graceful hands moved to a stray piece of her ebony hair, tucking it back into a crevasse of the braid that encircled her head.

"You there! Maiden!" The frog called out, startling me.

I felt my heart race with panic as he rose to his feet, waving his small hands in her direction. From this distance, he would be nearly impossible for her to see from the porch. She'd only see...*me.*

"Aneurin!" I whispered sharply, feeling my cheeks flush with embarrassment. There was something about meeting a real princess that completely took me off guard. She, a *royal* figure who had always existed merely as a character in a story, was now as tangible and human as I was.

The woman turned in place, moving her gaze over the railing and down to where I stood with Aneurin on my shoulder. Her eyebrow rose with a slight confusion before her lips broke into a wide smile. "Hello there!" Even her voice was soft and sweet as she called out to us. She lifted her hand to her eyes, blocking the sun as she peered down. "Can I help you?"

As the princess peered at me from above, I was struck with the familiar discomfort I used to feel at the countless parties I'd attend with Nico—all those social gatherings I longed to escape. I would grapple with a strange sense of alienation when he went off with his friends, and a strong inadequacy among the women who seemed effortlessly beautiful in ways I felt I could never emulate. They exuded a confidence that I knew I lacked, were slimmer, better dressed, and always had flawless makeup. I had blamed my appearance for why Nico would pay more attention to Bryce than me.

Everything made sense now. But those wounds on my confidence remained deeply ingrained.

Nevertheless, I was okay with being completely ordinary. In the grand scheme of things, I realized that was not a flaw, but rather proof of my authenticity. At least, that's what I told myself.

Aneurin nudged me with his hands, pushing against my shoulder when I didn't respond.

"She is addressing you!"

"*You're* the one who called out to her," I hissed between my teeth before slowly lifting a hand into the air.

"Hello!" I called back hesitantly, doing my best to keep my awkwardness in check. "My friend and I...are a little far from home." That was the truth. Right? "We accidentally fell into the pond..." My words drifted into silence.

The woman approached the railing, making her face a little clearer to see. Now her brows reflected alarm and concern. "Oh, dear!" she exclaimed. "Are you alright?"

"Yes," I continued. "Just a little wet."

A soft laugh rang from her, and she waved her hand, motioning towards the cottage. "Well, then, please come up! I'd be delighted to assist!" she responded eagerly, making her way towards the staircase. With a warm smile, she descended swiftly.

She was too friendly. Her kindness would ultimately be her downfall in her story. However temporary it might be. But maybe with us—me—here, I could help her navigate the infamous meeting I knew would occur. And maybe, with her assistance, Aneurin could be on his merry little way to his own happily ever after. Even if he didn't deserve it.

"Introduce me," Aneurin murmured in my ear.

"You can introduce yourself," I snapped back softly.

"Not to a *lady*!"

"We're in the woods. No one cares about formality."

But before the frog could slide in a quip, the princess appeared in front of us, her smile warm and bright.

As she approached, I couldn't help but wonder if children at amusement parks experienced a similar sensation when their beloved characters approached them. It felt both strange and surreal to have Snow-White standing this close to me.

Snow-White's eyes were a rich shade of green, and her lips were full and red. It was just as the original story described. She was beautiful, even more than her mother probably had ever imagined for a child who would be, "as white as snow, red as blood, and as black as…" I couldn't remember the exact text, but knew the story had qualified which features would be assigned to each color. But even then, the description wasn't completely accurate.

"Oh, indeed…" Snow-White remarked, her eyes sweeping over me. "It's clear you have journeyed quite a great distance."

My cheeks burned hotter as I peered down at my attire. My shorts and shirt were grimy, even more so thanks to the pond we'd fallen into. And I knew the stench wasn't helping anything. When I lifted my gaze to hers again, I found her smiling even wider than before.

"I was taught it is polite to exchange names at the beginning of a friendship." She held out a hand. "My name is Snow-White."

I stared at her hand for only a moment before I pressed my own into hers. "Josephine." It seemed better than *Jo* in this situation.

"What a lovely name!" she exclaimed, then shifted her attention to the small frog perched on my shoulder. Arching her brow inquisitively, she wrinkled her nose with a smile.

"What a sweet creature. Is this your traveling companion? Does it have a name?"

Before I could respond, I felt him rise on his nimble legs.

Snow's eyes grew wide with surprise as he bowed—formally.

"I am Prince Aneurin James Arthur Quinn Bartholomew Jensen Alexander—"

"She gets it. You have lots of names," I cut in.

But he ignored me and kept going. "Crown Prince and heir to the Luria Kingdom…"

"Does anyone really need as many names or titles as you have?" I muttered quietly.

But it appeared he caught my remark. "All members of *royalty* do," he jabbed. "Not that you would understand."

I could almost hear the underlying hiss of "peasant" in his tone.

Before I could protest further, Snow-White began to giggle, observing the exchange between us with amusement. "My nursemaid, Matilde, used to regale me with the most marvelous tales of enchanted frogs."

"I am a *prince*," he corrected her sharply, turning to her again.

"*And* a frog," I added.

Snow's smile persisted as she shifted her gaze between us.

She was so young. It was obvious in the way her eyes glistened with awe and amazement as she watched the two of us. She couldn't have been more than eighteen or nineteen years old.

"Oh, the men will be so delighted to meet you both."

"The *men*?" Aneurin asked, sitting back down on my shoulder.

"Oh yes," Snow replied. "There are seven men, in fact, who reside here."

"You're *alone* with seven men?" the frog asked again, his surprise not at all subtle.

"What's wrong with that?" I interjected, shaking my head.

The frog glared. "No woman should reside with—"

"I'm going to stop you right there," I said, tapping his head with my finger.

He squeezed his eyes shut, probably bracing for a harder blow.

Redirecting my focus to Snow, I offered her a warm smile. "We'd be happy to meet your friends."

"If you're willing to come inside," she continued, keeping her gaze only to me. "I can obtain a fresh change of clothes for you. I've been trying my hand at sewing, though I must admit I'm not as nearly as talented as Stitches."

"Stitches?" I asked.

"He darns the warmest of socks and has been working on a simple working gown for me. As my attire…" she brushed her hand over the fabric of her dress. The maroon and gold fabric seemed rather heavy and elaborate. It wasn't exactly practical attire for living in the middle of the woods. "In a setting like this, my gown feels out of place," she lamented.

I tried to piece together what I knew of her tale, of the trials she must have already faced. She would have escaped the huntsman after being lured to the woods to be killed after his conscience had prevailed over the queen's order, and he urged her to flee and seek refuge in the depths of the woods.

As I looked down at my own outfit, I replied with an earnest nod. "I can very much understand."

Snow-White glanced at me curiously, her gaze lingering on my attire—no longer pristine white shorts and lace shirt. Yet, she remained silent, refraining from questioning about my unusual clothing choices.

"I insist you come with me," Snow said, gesturing toward the staircase with a sweep of her hand, motioning for me to follow.

With her turned away, I glanced at Aneurin. "Remember our agreement," I whispered.

"I have been *nothing* but polite and dignified."

"Just...don't ruin this for us." I stared at him, hoping he knew just how serious I was about all this. We hadn't just gone through all that trouble for him to ruin a chance of safety, however brief it might be.

"*Me?* Ruin things?"

When I didn't answer, he sighed deeply and nodded. "Fine."

Snow-White spoke, her voice catching me off guard. "Josephine, may I ask where you and your friend are venturing from?"

I looked up and saw her disappear around the first curve of the tree trunk.

How could I provide a plausible explanation that would make sense to her? Should I just say a neighboring village?

Aneurin answered, "We have been lost and wandering in strange woodlands. We do not know precisely where we have come from. But I do know it has been long and tedious."

I knew I'd need to thank him later for that. It only proved that two minds were better than just one.

The princess slowly nodded as she tapped her hand on the bark. "It's difficult to be far from home, isn't it?" she asked. "To not feel... disconnected and a bit lost?"

"Are you far from your home as well?" Aneurin asked.

Snow-White responded with a melancholic smile before nodding. "It's for the best, I'm afraid," she murmured softly, gesturing towards the steps ahead. "Come, let's get you both settled before the men return from their day's work."

TWELVE

As we reached the top of the porch, I hadn't expected my legs to feel like gelatin. It was evident just how out of shape I was, considering the house wasn't situated that high up.

Snow was already waiting by the door, showing no signs of heavy breathing unlike myself. I assumed she had grown accustomed to the climb through practice, making it second nature to her now. She seemed to read either my mind or face, because she smiled as I leaned against the panel of the house.

"My legs have only just begun to not ache from the steps," she admitted. "And I've been here for at least a fortnight."

Had the queen already come? I couldn't recall exactly what the queen had brought, but I knew enough that her *first* encounter hadn't been with the poisoned apple.

Snow-White swung open the wooden door, revealing the entrance to the grand home. It far surpassed the simple image of a tree house I had envisioned in my mind.

"Come along," she said with a smile, turning into the space.

I couldn't pinpoint why I felt so hesitant to follow. I didn't fully know Snow-White, but I did, in a way.

She wasn't a stranger to me, unlike we were to her. Yet, despite her own circumstances, she was open and welcoming.

With countless questions swirling in my mind, I found myself stuck where I stood and at a loss of how to continue.

"Aren't you going to listen to her, Jo?" Aneurin asked, breaking me away from my thoughts.

I nodded, a soft exhale escaping me as I followed after the princess. When I crossed the threshold, I was immediately met with a rich aroma with earthy, woody tones. It was as if the very essence of the forest had woven itself into the fabric of the tree house, enveloping me with open arms.

Planks of wood, stained with a lacquer that made it rich with color, lined the room. And there were wide, long windows that made the space feel large and well-lit with sunlight.

I found myself standing in a simple, yet inviting kitchen.

There was a long table, carved from a long shaft of a tree trunk, surrounded by an eclectic assortment of wooden chairs, each one bearing its own unique shape and size. It was as though the craftsman behind them had been experimenting, their imperfections only added to their charm. I couldn't help but imagine that each one symbolized the personalities of the seven men who inhabited this space. After all, they were named after their traits, right?

On the table, each place setting had its own plate and bowl, awaiting whatever contents Snow-White was cooking for them.

Even more dazzling was the craftsmanship of the fireplace in the far corner of the room. Crafted directly from the trunk, its intricate carvings and sturdy structure added to the enchanting atmosphere. It felt like I was standing in the middle of a fairytale cottage.

Snow-White moved towards a set of simple wooden steps and waved her hand at me. "Over here, Josephine!" she called, smiling.

I hurried towards Snow, my steps quickening as I took in the unique features of the home. As we ascended to the next floor, I discovered rooms adorned with expansive glass windows and thick drapes, offering glimpses of the surrounding forest just beyond them. These rooms were interconnected to walkways and other smaller structures that moved throughout the tree.

Our host paused at a door located at the top of the final set of stairs. "This," she exclaimed with a smile, "is undeniably one of the most beautiful rooms. It has a view that cannot be matched."

The curiosity on my face must have been so noticeable that Snow opened the door almost immediately.

In the far corner of the room was yet another fireplace, encircled by small white stones.

Against one wall, a built-in structure enclosed what seemed to be a bed, providing a level of privacy I hadn't ever seen before.

A perfectly fitted window adorned the opposite side of the bed, offering a breathtaking view, just as Snow-White had promised.

Though it was simple, it exuded a quiet beauty and an inviting coziness I sorely needed after my adventure so far.

I was taken aback a bit by her warmth and hospitality. To offer us a place to stay without hesitation went beyond my expectations. I never thought staying in the cottage would be so easy...but here I was.

"Will this do for you and His Highness?" Snow asked, glancing at me and the frog on my shoulder.

When Aneurin didn't say a thing, I checked my shoulder to see if he was still there. He seemed to be curiously taking in the surroundings of the room.

"This is more than enough," I admitted with a nod. "Thank you."

Snow-White crossed to a small trunk in the corner. Opening the lid, she pulled out a few pieces of fabric and then turned back to me. . "You'll have to excuse the poor needlework," she said sheepishly. "It's not my best work. But I hope they'll do for the time being."

I took a good look at the clothes in her hands as she crossed the room. In her hands, she held a long piece of green clothing, and a simple white blouse.

Was this her room? Was she giving us her place to stay?

"Snow…" I began softly, shaking my head. "I don't want to take your room."

"Oh no, no. You're not," she replied with a smile. "I've only just helped Stitches to clean up the space a day or so ago. I'm glad we took the time to do so."

"Are you sure it's alright us...for *me* to stay here?" I asked softly. "I don't want to cause any trouble for you or anyone else. I can assure you that if Aneurin and I—"

"*I* certainly will not bring any trouble," he interjected.

I paused and cleared my throat. It wasn't entirely true. He had at the witch's house. But if he wanted to feign his innocence and pretend he had nothing to do with it, then so be it.

"Please," Snow-White began, pressing the clothes into my hands. "If I can offer assistance to someone in need..." She paused, pondering her next words carefully. "There is far too much cruelty and pain in this world. And I feel it is my destiny to bring joy to others around me. Even if they cannot bestow the same upon me."

Her words saddened me. I knew how cruel the queen ultimately was to her...I bit my lip and nodded. "We appreciate your kindness, don't we, Your Highness?" I asked, glancing back at him once again.

The frog nodded slightly, as his tongue flicked over his eye.

"Oh, he is darling," Snow-White said with a laugh. "What a prince you must have been, indeed."

"You know," I began, cheekily. "He is looking for his princess..."

As soon as I said the words, Snow's smile disappeared. Her cheeks turned pale. She studied me, as if trying to discern the true intentions behind my words. The atmosphere in the room shifted suddenly, and I couldn't shake the feeling of unease that settled over us.

"Snow?" I asked, searching her face. "I'm sorry. I was only—"

"A princess," she said quickly, feigning a smile as she took a step back from me. "What a silly idea, surely. Me?"

How could I have been so stupid?

She hadn't introduced herself as a princess. Of course, she'd want to keep her true identity hidden. I was no more than a stranger. For all she knew, I could have been someone from...wherever she was from. I'd said too much without thinking, which was normal for me, but so badly timed in this situation.

Desperate to recover from my mistake, I grabbed her hand gently, dropping the clothes to the floor. I needed to save the moment—to keep Snow's trust.

"Right?" I asked with a small laugh. "What an idea. It's his horrible luck that he's stuck with us ordinary women."

Snow continued to watch me as I attempted to offer her a reassuring nod.

"Perhaps with your help, I could find him a princess sooner! If you happen to know of any, that is."

Oh, I was only digging this hole deeper. I needed to learn to keep my mouth shut. In the meantime, I had to explain this away. "We'll have to be on the lookout for a princess to kiss him."

Her hazel eyes fell onto Aneurin, and her lips quivered into a small, tender smile. "Of course," she replied softly.

I could tell by her tone she was unsure what to think of me and my now-talking-frog-prince. *Great.*

Snow pulled her hands free of mine and retrieved the clothing I had dropped. She placed them back into my arms and offered the both of us a faint smile before making her way toward the door. "You'll want to wash up before you change. I'll bring up a bucket of water for you."

"Thank you," I said. "That would be lovely, actually."

She nodded in acknowledgement and left.

As soon as the door shut behind her, I released a heavy sigh. How was I going to earn her trust now? "Well, shit."

"Is that how folk from your village speak?" Aneurin asked, shifting on my shoulder.

"Didn't you just experience the same conversation that I did?" I shot back, moving towards the open doors of the box bed.

"Apparently not," he retorted. "Do you plan to repeat whatever conversation I seemingly missed?"

Without a second thought, I picked him up from my shoulder and held him in my hands.

He squirmed momentarily before finding his balance between my thumb and fingers. "This is undignified," he croaked.

"Just try not to pee on me, okay? I know frogs tend to do that when they're scared."

"Ladies do not speak of…such *things*."

I wrinkled my nose and shook my head. "Wait. Does referencing your bladder upset you, too?"

"I am beginning to doubt whether you are truly from the southern lands," he remarked.

"I've been telling you that all along," I chuckled. "Anyway…"

"The conversation…" Aneurin stated, his little webbed fingers held onto my thumbs tightly as he peered at me. For being a little frog, he was kinda cute. Especially the way he looked at me with those big, green eyes.

I sat down on the side of the bed.

"This is another story I'm familiar with," I began. "And it involves a princess who has to remain hidden from her evil stepmother. The stepmother is actually the queen of the land, and desperately wants to be the most beautiful woman in all the kingdom."

"How absurd," he said, tilting his head. "It is preposterous to think that only one woman can be the *most* beautiful."

I smiled a bit more, nodding. "I think that's the most reasonable thing I've heard you say all day."

"'Tis true," he continued. "Beauty is subjective. One could find even *you* virtuous and beautiful, though I beg to differ."

"You were doing great…" I mumbled, lowering him to the bed.

The frog hopped a few paces away from me before giving me a small smile. He tilted his head slightly, watching me. "With a bit of distance, I might also come to find you somewhat beautiful, Jo. In your own way."

Should feel insulted or flattered? I definitely felt a little of the former. And for a frog to be telling me that I was beautiful? Weird. "I'd say thanks but…I'm not sure if I should," I replied.

Aneurin nestled into the blanket of the bed with an indifferent shrug. "It matters not to me whether my words bring you pleasure or not. My point is that your beauty should only concern you. If someone can find beauty in you as well, then all the better. But the opinions of others should hold no weight."

"But the opinion of others matters to *you* a lot," I remarked, lifting the two pieces of clothing that Snow had given to me curiously. I wasn't sure exactly how to wear them but from the length of the white garment and the heaviness of the green dress, I assumed one was to be worn over the other.

"Well, in some particular cases, opinions do matter," Aneurin continued. "But those concerns come from the responsibilities of the crown."

"How so?" I asked, glancing at him again.

"Should I not expect, if not *require*, the good opinion of my people?" he asked. "If I do not have that, then they possess no respect for the crown. The crown and I are one."

I'd heard that before in some Tudor drama Nico and I had watched together. The memory felt as though it belonged to a different time and place altogether now. I could even remember the way Nico casually shoved a handful of popcorn into his mouth as one of the queens made her way to her own execution.

"It is my responsibility to take care of the people," Aneurin said, drawing me just as quickly out of the memory. "To keep their best interest in mind as I make decisions for the good of the kingdom."

"But you've never ruled…" I replied softly. "Right? Didn't you tell me that your family—"

"When I return to my kingdom…with my bride," he said, with a hint of annoyance in his tone. "I shall finally take my rightful seat to rule."

"Ah," I nodded, raising a brow. "I see." Of course. The answers were always found in the future.

When he returns. When *I* return.

For some reason, we seemed to think that whatever we were capable of—it would be found in time, but not *now*. And it felt slightly disappointing. How much longer was I going to have to wait to live my life? To be happy?

"I'm glad you do," he finished. Lifting a webbed hand, he gestured towards the gown in my hand. "'Tis a simple kirtle," he explained. "But I do see the potential in her craftsmanship."

"A kirtle, huh?" I repeated the term as I examined the dress. "I like it. It has character."

"I have seen better fashions—"

"Beggars can't be choosers," I said with a smile. "Besides, I'm lucky if I can sew a button straight."

"Clearly, you were very useful in your village," he snorted.

"At least I'm not fragile like you," I said with a smirk.

Just then, there was a knock on the door. It opened again, and Snow-White entered with the bucket she'd promised.

"It's a little cold," she explained, setting it down on the floor. "But I brought soap and a rag. It should suffice for the both of you."

Before either of us could respond, she swiftly turned on her heel and shut the door behind her.

I could feel Aneurin's stare piercing into me.

Meeting his gaze, I asked, "What?"

"I must share bath water with you?" he questioned, scandalized.

I glared at him. "You could always go back to the pond if this is beneath you, *Your Highness.*"

THIRTEEN

The blouse proved relatively easy to manage once I adjusted it. It was a little too big for me, but that was okay. After doing my best to fold the white fabric in place, I rolled the sleeves to my elbows, and left the lone button around my neck open. The green kirtle that went over it fit snugly against my body. It ultimately helped to keep everything in place. While the skirt didn't flow quite as elegantly as I'd imagined in fairytales, the fact that it had pockets made it a win-win in my book.

As I tried to brush my fingers through my wet, tangled hair, I turned to where Aneurin remained on the bed. In the sea of blankets, his little green form was hard to miss. I studied him as I braided my hair, letting the lone strand rest on my shoulder.

When was I going to wake from this dream? That's what this had to be, right?

It seemed impossible any of this was actually happening.

Maybe all the crying, all the avoiding I'd done since leaving Nico, was starting to catch up with me. I'd been tired for so long. And maybe…*maybe* this was my way of processing everything that had happened to me.

That would be easier to believe because nothing about this world felt real to me. To be in a shared space with a frog who claimed to be a prince. To have the real Snow-White only a few floors below me. *Real.* What did that even mean? She was still just a part of a story. One I was now fully immersed in.

"Have you finished yet?" Aneurin asked as he turned his head just slightly.

"I have," I replied and shifted my hands to my sides. "What do you think?"

I was surprised to still find the jewels that Hansel and Gretel had given to us still in my original clothes before hanging them up to dry on the back of a chair. I pushed them into the pocket of my new dress, just to keep them safe. Just in case. Now, I just needed to figure out how I could wash my shorts and top so they could stop reeking of sweat and pond muck. And my shoes needed to dry out.

Aneurin hopped on top of the blanket. He studied me for a long moment before tilting his head slightly. "'Tis strange to see you finally attired in what is expected..." he admitted. "Despite the poor craftsmanship, that gown strangely suits you."

"I'm never really sure what to think of your comments," I sighed, shaking my head. "You didn't like my clothes before, and now..."

"It suits you," he said again with a nod. "From afar, I might also come to find you somewhat beautiful, Jo. In your own way." There was that stupid comment again.

"Should we venture downstairs to see if we can find Snow-White?" I managed, trying to shift the conversation.

"And what will you do when you find her?"

"I imagine asking her if we can stay would be important, don't you think?"

"And do you think she will deny the request?"

"No, but in the end, it's ultimately up to the seven men to make that decision."

"Ah, yes. The seven men we have still yet to meet."

"You better be on your best behavior when you meet them."

"You make it sound as though I am some brute, lacking even the most basic behaviors of decorum."

"You do *lick* your eye a lot," I pointed out, half-teasing as I was unable to suppress my smirk.

"Only to irritate you," he countered, his retort accompanied by a mischievous flick of his tongue over his eye. "If it means so much to you, I will do my best to be as regal and polite—"

"Just be polite," I interrupted. "I think sometimes your definition of 'regal' gets you in trouble." I extended my hand to him then and tilted my head towards the door. "Shall we go find Snow?"

"Yes, fine, fine." With a resigned sigh, Aneurin hopped into my hand, his small form resting on my palm.

I carefully placed him on my shoulder before opening the bedroom door and starting down the stairs. I was pretty sure I heard him murmur something about it being humiliating to be carried around, but I just ignored him. Watching him attempt to navigate all those stairs on his own would be quite a spectacle, I thought with a silent smirk.

Barefooted, I moved from room to room and floor to floor. As I did, I took in the details of the home.

The railing of the stairway was all crafted from tree branches, interwoven to look as though they were emerging from the floor and walls. The steps had small little paintings of flowers, and vines, as though someone had been bored and used them as a project one rainy day.

Most of the rooms contained bunk beds, each equipped with wooden ladders, and never more than two. Toward the lower level of the treehouse, there were two rooms furnished with single boxed beds, resembling the one Aneurin and I were occupying.

One room appeared cluttered, filled with books and papers strewn about, while a desk was covered in odds and ends. Its walls were lined with dark wood paneling, and a faint scent of cigars lingered in the air.

The other, on the far end, was spacious and clean. A bouquet of wild purple flowers sat in a vase near the bed, adding a touch of vibrancy to the serene space. The windows were open, allowing a refreshing breeze of cool air to gently billow through the curtains.

Not a single item seemed out of place, leading me to surmise that this was where Snow White was staying.

As I paused on the last step, I thought I heard Snow singing softly to herself. Glancing at Aneurin on my shoulder, we both stared at each other as we listened to her soft song.

'Tis when my love will come to thee,
And I will wait upon thy knee,
For those who find my lover, dear,
Please tell him I am waiting near,
And deep within our hearts will find,
Our past and present, intertwined.

I recognized the last part of her song as part of the rhyme inside of the book from the estate sale. The same one I was now *inside*.

I wasn't sure how much my expression had revealed my astonishment, but evidently, it was enough to prompt Aneurin to glance at me curiously.

"Are you alright?" he asked gently.

I slowly nodded a realization forming in my mind. Everything in these stories were interconnected...somehow. And I had a feeling the only way I was going to manage to get out of the book was to solve the connection.

I finally stepped onto the floor as Snow-White began to sing the words again, her melodious voice filling the air. Nestling myself against the wall, I peered into the kitchen, watching and listening intently. I wanted to hear the song again, just to ensure I had caught her words accurately. The words from the pages echoed in my mind as I tried to piece together a deeper meaning. Was there a hint—a clue—of what I needed to find? To discover?

"Jo?" Aneurin asked softly, watching me curiously.

"Do you know that song?" I asked.

For those who find my lover, dear,
Please tell him I am waiting near...

Her voice sounded even more beautiful than any animated princess I'd heard. To top it off, she was nimble. Even her movements of placing vegetables in the large, black cauldron were as graceful as a ballerina. How was she *real?*

"I cannot say I am well versed in common folks' songs," he admitted after listening to the refrain, shaking his head.

"Right," I replied.

Snow-White likely knew more about common things than Aneurin did. After all, she had worked as a servant in her own castle, a consequence of her stepmother's jealousy.

> For those who wander through these pages,
> listen well to the tales of ages…
> For deep within one's heart will find,
> their past and present, intertwined.

"She is rather beautiful, is she not?" Aneurin whispered, pulling my attention back to the present, to the room where a secret princess was working diligently in the kitchen over the stove.

She was everything I had imagined and more—a vision of perfection in almost every sense of the word. Even as she stirred the cauldron with a large wooden spoon, mopping her black curls from her face. Off in the far window, I could see a bird perched upon the windowpane, seemingly entranced by her voice. Listening.

"She is," I murmured back. It was so easy to see why the queen had become consumed with jealousy. To envy Snow-White was to envy any beautiful woman who possessed grace and a kind heart. I even found myself wishing I could be just like her.

Maybe then I would have been enough for Nico.

And suddenly, I was back in my old apartment, unboxing an order of Chinese food on the kitchen counter. Nico was flashing a smile at me before pressing a soft kiss against my forehead and turning his attention back to his cellphone. It was common for him to get distracted by either a funny video on social media or having one of his work friends text him.

"I'll be right back, Jo," he had promised as he turned on his heel, disappearing into our room.

I had continued to focus on dinner, carefully portioning just enough rice into our two bowls, along with our coveted egg rolls. I wanted everything to be perfect. *I* wanted to be perfect. To embody everything Nico wanted and more. To be the sort of woman that could live up to the role of future wife.

Once everything had been ready, I grabbed his bowl and headed towards the bedroom door, only to find it closed shut.

"Nico?" I had called out, my voice echoing in the silence of the apartment. Stepping closer, I had reached for the doorknob and pushed the door open.

Inside, I had found him lying on the bed, the top of his pants wide open as he exposed himself to his phone's camera. It felt surreal to stand there, holding the two bowls of Chinese food, while he took pictures of himself so blatantly. But for *who?* It certainly wasn't for me...

Yet, I had remained silent, unable to voice the questions swirling in my mind. What could I have said? So, I just stared, standing there like a fool.

Then our eyes had met, and for a moment, there was a blank silence between us. I had stumbled upon him in a vulnerable state, one that he couldn't easily explain away. Maybe he wanted to offer an explanation, but I was unable to confront the truth, unable to bear the weight of whatever revelation lay behind his actions.

I wanted to be enough and for things to work. If I could just swallow my pride and pretend moments like those didn't exist... maybe then, everything would be fine.

I needed to stop thinking like that. I needed to stop trying to condemn myself in ways that were entirely unrealistic. The truth of the matter was that Nico hadn't been enough for me.

I'd lied to myself over and over, trying to have him fill a space within me he could never successfully occupy.

"Perhaps she could be the one to break my spell," Aneurin said, jolting me from the bitter memory. "If she is truly...a princess."

"And what if she isn't?" I asked, my tone a little harsher than I'd expected. "Are you telling me that her title is the deal breaker?"

"How many times do I have to go over this with you, Jo?" he scowled. "I am a prince, whether you've come to accept this as fact or not. And with such rank, I am expected, nay, *required* to wed a princess. The title has nothing to do with breaking the spell. But it has everything to do with the longevity of my future nuptials. I could not imagine myself returning to my family with…a peasant for a wife."

I didn't know why his bluntness stung the way it had, but it did. Maybe it was his tone, or the sharpness of the way he used the word. But my stomach twisted with an anger I hadn't felt since Nico. "But what if you really loved her?" I asked, glaring at him as he shifted on my shoulder.

He peered up at me for a long moment before shrugging indifferently. "I would do as my title requires. Even if I loved such a woman, I could never consider nor consent to a marriage that would not benefit my country."

"Then I pity the woman who ends up with you," I mumbled under my breath, shaking my head.

"Pity?" he asked, his eyes wide. "Why do you pity her?"

"Because you won't love her."

"Marriage is not always about love, Jo."

I knew that. I'd witnessed enough reality television shows to realize how people could exploit others for their own gain. It could be about name, job, or wealth. Exclusive commitment didn't guarantee genuine love, either. And, apparently, it wouldn't for Aneurin and his potential princess bride.

I bit my lip, turning my gaze away from his. There was no way that I was going to admit he was right. He could *know* he was right, and that would have to be enough.

"And you?" he asked, inching closer to me on my shoulder. "You have not mentioned a suitor of any sort."

"Because I don't have one," I retorted, sharply.

"And why not? Can I not find a reason to pity you in return?"

He could have found plenty of reasons, but I didn't want his pity. Nor did I want my parents' sympathy. I had seen it in their eyes the moment Mom had opened the door that day. Nico had not only cheated on me, but lied—broke my heart. And I'd run away. To be honest, I'd given up on myself.

"I'm not going to talk about this with you," I said.

"You might be a little...lacking..." Aneurin continued, his lips curled into a tight, knowing smirk. "But with the right match, I am sure you could find a reasonable balance."

"Let's work on finding your own match first," I replied.

"You carry the expectation to fall in love first, do you not?" he continued. "And you have been gravely disappointed."

I wrinkled my nose at his observation. Of course, I'd be that obvious. "In my world, dating isn't exactly a walk in the park."

"Dating?"

"I don't know what you call it here. Courting?" I tried, searching for some word that he'd understand. "You go out to eat a meal, talk, and if it goes well...I don't know, hold hands, kiss..."

"And there are no such suitors who wish to court you?"

"Are you really asking me that?" I asked, raising my brow.

"I am surprised. Surely there is a lad who finds something to admire about you."

His sharp dig felt a little more painful than I wanted.

"*Aneurin*," I sighed, shaking my head. "I'd appreciate it if you didn't press this anymore. I didn't mean to offend you. I may pity the woman you marry, and I may even pity *you* more. But even if you are a bit pompous, you deserve a happy life. After all, aren't you supposed to live happily ever after?"

"Happily ever after?" Aneurin repeated. "What does that mean?"

I chuckled cynically, shaking my head. Wasn't that the million-dollar question of the century?

"I don't know," I replied. "I guess I'm hoping to find out."

But if happily ever after didn't exist in *fairytales*, where else would they?

"Oh! It's you!" Snow-White said suddenly, peeking from around the wall of the kitchen.

I hadn't noticed she'd approached until she was right in front of us.

"I thought I heard talking, but thought it might be too early for the men to return."

"We were just admiring your cooking skills," I replied, forcing a smile. "I'm horrible in a kitchen." At least that part was the truth.

She turned back to the small pile of uncut vegetables waiting for her on the wooden table. But not before I saw her cheeks flush.

"Oh, it's nothing," she said with a small giggle. "I've had many hands teach me their secrets." She smiled at us. "You both must be famished," she continued. "I have soup on the fire for supper. But I just made a fresh batch of bread."

"I have always been in favor of fresh bread," Aneurin replied.

Snow smiled at him as he remained on my shoulder. "I can even provide one of my freshest jams. Herb and I—"

"Herb?" I asked, tilting my head curiously. "Who is Herb?"

"Oh, Herb is one of the men who live here. He's the gardener."

Herb. With a name like that, of course, it made sense that he would be the gardener.

"Who are the others?" I asked with an eager curiosity. So far, none of the names I had heard seemed familiar. Herb. Stitches.

Snow-White moved slowly back into the kitchen, waving for me to follow. She walked to the table, where a perfectly shaped loaf of bread awaited her attention. The smell of it was divine.

"Well," she said, pulling a long cutting knife from a drawer by her waist. "There is Arch. He's the eldest of the group and I would argue the leader as well." She began to cut into the bread. "He's also the kindest."

"Arch?" I asked.

"He is the one who designed and built this house."

Architect. Of course. When I nodded, Snow continued.

"There's Hunter and Trapper. They're brothers. And then there's Axe. And there's Topper, who is Herb's brother."

"Topper? That's quite a name," I replied, wrinkling my nose. What did *that* stand for?

"He is a fantastic cook," she said with a broad smile. "He's taught me quite a few things since I've arrived."

"So, Hunter and Trapper are brothers," I repeated. "And Herb—"

"Herb and Topper."

"That seems almost too convenient," I replied.

"And then there's Bones," Snow-White said. "But Bones is with the men today."

"Bones?"

"He's their dog. He's rather old, but very good."

A *dog*?

Snow must have noticed the way I nervously looked at Aneurin, for she laughed again. "Don't worry. Bones might sniff your friend. But nothing more. His Highness should be just fine."

She brought two slices of bread to me, one a little larger than the other. Both were covered in a soft red strawberry jam.

Aneurin hopped down from my shoulder and began to quickly nibble on his portion. It was a relief to know he was finally eating some real food, not just the various bugs I'd seen him snatch with his long tongue.

"This is delicious, miss," Aneurin said between mouthfuls. "Almost as good as a sponge cake from my home."

Snow sent a quizzical look in my direction, and I could only respond with a smile. I remembered his mention of a servant in his palace when we were at the witch's house—Missus Alden.

"I'm glad you're enjoying it, Your Highness," she said with a laugh. "It brings me joy to hear that."

The frog flashed her a smile before he took another small nibble of the bread and jam. He wasn't being rude or condescending—a significant improvement from my own interactions with him.

Maybe it had something to do with the fact that he knew she was a princess. Maybe he was hoping she'd be the one to break his spell.

I watched them briefly before turning my gaze to the piece of bread in front of me.

"Are you always this warm and welcoming to random strangers?" I asked, after taking a bite of my own piece of bread. The flavor was unlike anything I'd ever had in my life.

It was warm and fresh and so very different from the store-bought bread I was used to. The strawberries were also warm and fresh, and so very sweet.

"Of course," Snow replied with a nod. "For I know how little kindness there is out there in the world. If I can be a beacon for others. To give something as small as a shared smile—"

"Yeah, but...you have to be careful," I interjected, shaking my head. "People will take advantage of your kindness."

Snow studied the bread in front of her, then turned her hazel gaze to mine. "I know," she whispered in kind. "I know all too well that my kindness does not always provide the results I wish to see."

I knew what she was speaking about, even if *she* didn't know that. I knew *who* she was speaking about.

She turned her gaze back to the bread and lathered her own slice with the soft red jam. "But I am grateful," she continued softly. "The seven men have opened their home to me and, in turn, have promised protection..." Her words slowly drifted to silence as her gaze flickered back to mine. Her expression was frozen, as though she'd realized she'd said too much.

This was my opportunity.

"Protection?" I inquired, tilting my head curiously.

Snow-White licked her bottom lip as she stared at me, before slowly nodding. She seemed hesitant to say anything further. But before either she or I could continue, I heard footsteps outside, ascending what I assumed were the spiral stairs outside.

"Oh! That must be them!" she said, turning her gaze to the door, her mood suddenly shifting again.

"Them?" The frog asked, glancing at me.

I sighed and lowered my bread back onto the plate in front of me. "Remember what I said," I mumbled under my breath as I looked at him. "Your *best* behavior."

FOURTEEN

I stood by the door with bated breath, waiting for the men to appear. Honestly, I was half expecting to see the familiar little men from the animated film filter through the door, singing their snappy working song. But I knew this experience was far from any sort of *happy* coincidence.

Aneurin took one more bite of his bread before rising onto his feet on the table, and stood tall, awaiting the strangers.

I prayed with everything in my being that they would at least let us stay, and that Snow would endorse the idea. I was sure, after being in a house full of men, a woman would be a welcomed companion. And if I could earn her trust, I would let her know she was safe with me.

Maybe *that* was the reason we were here. To help her avoid her encounters, rather than simply enduring all that she originally had.

And maybe Aneurin could be her prince in the end.

I didn't know just how jumbled these stories could get, but…it could work, couldn't it?

Finally, the footsteps crested the landing, and the tread of them followed in the same direction. A moment later, the front door opened, revealing four men.

They were slightly shorter than both Snow-White and I, but not at all as small as I expected. They weren't at all "dwarfs" in any sense of the word.

"Welcome home!" Snow-White exclaimed with a radiant smile, lifting her hand in greeting.

The four men turned their attention away from their conversation to her, their faces lighting up. It was apparent, even in the short time together, they had grown to care and appreciate her.

The first two entered the house, lowering their bows and arrows, along with a line of rabbits that hung from one of the men's backs.

"I brought home meat for the stew," one said, flashing a smile in Snow's direction.

I observed each of them closely, taking in their distinct features.

The man with the dead animals had golden-reddish hair and wore a dark forest green tunic. His eyes were dark, and his nose and chin were chiseled nearly perfectly.

The other man had crystal blue eyes, with dark brown, curly hair. His brows were thick as he raised one, glancing to the man beside him. His tunic was a dark mud color, probably best in hiding the grime of the day.

"*You?*" he scoffed. "How about *we?*"

The golden-haired man shook his head. "You merely set your traps and waited. T'was *me* who used the arrows today."

"You both did well," Snow-White said with a laugh as she approached the men. Her attention seemed to shift to the two others behind them, taking an offered basket from the one. "What did you bring back today, Herb?"

"Blueberries," the man replied with a smile full of pride. He nervously brushed his soft red hair from his eyes and slid his fingers down the short length of his beard.

It was the first time I'd seen a fully grown man be so nervous around a woman before.

The other man beside him rolled his eyes and lowered a sack of potatoes to the table. "While he was in the forest, I was in the gardens, pulling these."

"Oh, these are perfect!" Snow-White said with a nod.

"I'll tend the gardens tomorrow, Topper," the hearty man named Herb said, wrinkling his brow and staring at the one who just spoke.

"Who is that?" the man who had carried in the rabbits asked, gesturing in my direction. Was he Trapper?

Suddenly, all four of the men were staring at me, and I sucked in a breath.

Snow-White slowly turned in place and smiled back at me. "This is my new friend," she explained when I didn't speak. "And she's come with a royal companion."

"A royal companion?" Trapper asked, his blue eyes scrutinizing me closely, as though I were secretly an enemy. To them, I could be. After all, I was a stranger in their home.

"Why yes," Snow continued with a soft giggle as she pointed to the frog, standing quietly on the table, his half-eaten slice of bread still waiting beside him.

The men stared at him for only a moment before returning their attention back to me.

"And what's your name?" The man with the sack of potatoes asked me. Was he Herb? Or wait, Topper?

"M-Me?" My voice suddenly broke from nerves. I just needed to calm down. Nothing bad was going to happen. At least, nothing remotely as bad as we'd experienced at the hands of the child-eating witch with Hansel and Gretel.

"Who else?" Trapper—I think—replied sharply. I could tell by the way his blue eyes bore into mine, he was a man of little patience.

"My name is Josephine," I quickly said, nodding. "Though, you can call me Jo if you like. And this," I gestured towards my companion on the table. "This is Aneurin."

The frog lifted his hand to his lips and cleared his throat. "Actually," he began. "I am Prince Aneurin James Arthur Quinn—"

"He has a lot of names," I laughed, interrupting him as I nervously picked him up. He wriggled in my hand as I gently set him on my shoulder. I wasn't entirely sure why I felt compelled to keep him close, but I supposed it was just in case I decided to make a dash for the door.

The four men turned their gazes to each other before glancing back at Aneurin.

"Well, that's new," the one with the reddish beard murmured. "In all the hours I've spent outside, I've never once met a talking frog before."

"A talking frog *prince* at that," the blue-eyed man scoffed.

"You are all clearly uncultured," Aneurin mumbled.

I coughed to cover up the insult.

But no one responded. Either they hadn't heard him or chose to ignore him.

"We'll certainly have enough to feed everyone tonight!" Snow-White exclaimed, thankfully shifting the conversation back to food.

"And is she to stay?" Trapper asked, pointing directly at me.

"We should wait to see what Arch has to say," Hunter said with a nod. "After all, Snow-White did say she was her friend."

"But you came here with no one," Trapper said, turning his anger towards Snow. "You *told* us you had no one. You ran away from that witch and we—"

"*Trapper,*" a voice said suddenly from behind him.

My eyes shifted to a man standing in the doorway. He carried himself with a sense of authority the others didn't.

"That is not how we speak to our friends," he stated firmly, his voice carrying a note of reprimand.

The four men stepped aside to make way for him, allowing me to take in his appearance. Like the way his hair flowed over his shoulders in loose waves. His beard and mustache reminded me of a tamed version of the men in those wilderness shows on TV. His eyes, a warm shade of brown reminiscent of rich chocolate, held a depth that hinted at wisdom and experience. His broad shoulders and narrow waist gave him a sturdy yet agile build, further accentuating his commanding presence. For a moment, our eyes met, and I found myself momentarily captivated by the intensity of his gaze before he redirected his attention to Snow-White and Trapper.

Trapper slid a hand through his hair before taking a step back. "We have a new guest, Arch," he explained, his voice tinged with a hint of apprehension.

"I see," Arch said with a nod, glancing back at me again.

My cheeks warmed under his scrutiny.

He raised a brow at Trapper. "And you thought to welcome our guest with hostility?"

"She could be one of them," Trapper retorted, grabbing the lapel of his jacket. "How can we trust that she's not a spy for the queen?"

Snow stood motionless in front of the sack of potatoes. She lowered her hand onto the table, looking to Arch with an expression I couldn't quite place.

I knew this had been a fear of hers all along, ever since I'd mentioned finding a princess for Aneurin. I knew she had harbored doubts about me. How could I convince them that I wasn't a spy?

"But I'm not," I said abruptly, shaking my head, breaking the tense silence that had settled over the room.

All eyes turned to me, their gaze piercing.

Turning to face Snow-White directly, I continued, "I'm not a spy. I'm not from any kingdom…I'm…"

"Anyone could say the same thing," Trapper interjected, his voice skeptical. "We can't trust you."

"If you can't trust me, the last thing you'll want to do is throw me out then," I retorted, narrowing my eyes at him. "If you really think I'm from some queen's palace, would you be so quick for me to send me back to her and risk me informing her about all of you?"

"She's clever at least," Arch said as a small smirk tugged at his mouth. He strolled casually to the table, plucking a blueberry from the basket that Herb and Topper had brought in from the garden. "Appears you've done well today," he continued before popping one into his mouth.

"Is that all you have to say?" Trapper asked, his gaze volleying between me and Arch. "She's *clever?*"

"What more do you wish for me to do, brother?" Arch asked. "Snow herself has vouched for Jo as a friend. Why should we question that?"

"But—"

"And just as Jo has said herself. The last thing we want to do is release a person we do not trust back out into the wild, for if she is lying, would she not bring the queen here to find Snow-White?"

Snow's face paled, and she nervously bit her bottom lip, revealing the unspoken truth she had kept hidden. Her fear of being discovered was palpable.

"We know nothing of such a queen," the frog responded, crossing his arms as he rose to his feet. "And I am offended, sirs, that you would think so lowly of us. Of *me*."

Arch raised an eyebrow in curiosity. "A talking frog?"

"A *prince*," Aneurin retorted. "Jo here is my friend. We have not come here to *harm* the princess. In truth, I am in search of one."

The man that went by Hunter finally shut the door and settled into a seat by the table. "This shall be worth hearing," he mumbled under his breath, shooting a wink at Herb and Topper.

The two of them smirked in response before casually leaning against the table.

I realized that the five of them were now watching us—Aneurin and me.

"In search of a princess?" Hunter asked with a chuckle. "Are ye short of pretty lassies, frog?"

I could tell Aneurin was annoyed by the way he flicked his tongue over his eye—a gimmick reserved for expressing irritation, typically directed at me. Normally it would be followed by his favorite insult, "peasant." But this time, he remained still on my shoulder.

"Well go on," Hunter encouraged. "You have us all listenin'. You're here for our Snow, are yeh?"

"I am in search of a princess who can break my spell," Aneurin said through gritted teeth.

"Ahh, so you've been cursed."

"I wouldn't say *cursed*," I interjected, shaking my head.

"And are you the one who did the cursing?" Hunter asked amused, crossing his arms against his chest. "Are yeh a witch?"

I wrinkled my nose with annoyance and sighed. "No," I said firmly. "I'm not a witch. And I didn't do anything."

"But yet, here you are with an enchanted frog," Trapper interjected, his glare emphasizing his disbelief in my story.

"I found the lady by chance," Aneurin explained, thankfully keeping out the part where I almost accidentally drowned him. "For she claims to be under a spell, just as I am."

"Two curses?" Hunter laughed. "And what is your curse, lassie? Can't you find a man to wed?"

I rolled my eyes at Trapper and Hunter, before releasing another irritated sigh. I couldn't help but feel a surge of frustration at their dismissive attitudes. "You know, actually…" I began, my voice tinged with defiance. The words spilled out before I could stop them, the truth slipping past my lips without a second through. "I once was engaged to be married."

As the confession hung in the air, I felt a wave of vulnerability wash over me. Revealing such personal details to virtual strangers was unsettling. It was a part of my past that I didn't like to bring up, buried beneath layers of pain and regret.

Even Aneurin's surprised expression didn't escape my notice, his eyes widening in astonishment.

"But that has nothing to do with why I'm here," I added quickly, as if to deflect any further questions. But even as I spoke those words, I couldn't help but wonder if I was being entirely honest with myself. Wasn't everything that had happened to me recently because Nico had cheated on me? Was it fair for me to place all the blame on him? Hadn't I ignored all the signs he'd given me?

Arch cleared his throat. "So your frog friend is a prince, seeking a maiden to break a spell. And you are…under a spell as well?"

"I'm looking for a way home," I confirmed.

"You are lost?" he asked, popping another berry into his mouth.

"Yes, you could say that."

"And to break your spell?" Snow-White asked, glancing at the frog. "What would a princess do to help you, Prince Aneurin?"

It was the first time someone addressed him with his title, and I could see the pride swell in his eyes, a small smile forming on his lips. It obviously went straight to his head.

"I require a maiden to share a plate of food with me, to allow me to share her pillow, and to bestow a kiss of true love upon my lips."

She seemed appeased by the answer, for she nodded in return.

"A kiss of true love," The gruff man named Herb glanced between his brothers with a small smile. "I've been told kisses are quite powerful things, indeed."

"Clearly you've been sniffing among the flowers far too much," Trapper snorted.

"I do hope you will find your princess, Prince Aneurin," Snow-White replied, offering a small, sad smile.

The hope that I'd seen in his eyes vanished quickly. Slowly, he lowered himself back into a sitting position on my shoulder.

It was an outright rejection if I'd ever heard one, and I felt a twinge of pity for him. We'd already come so far, and that was just with me. I had no clue what he and Henry, his manservant, had been through before my arrival.

"I thank you," he said with a polite nod.

The tension in the room dissipated, leaving the five men exchanging uncertain looks, unsure of how to navigate the aftermath of Snow-White's gentle dismissal.

"Well, there is nothing more we can do about this situation," Arch said finally, breaking the silence. "Josephine and her frog will stay the night with us." He lifted his hand towards Trapper before he could respond. "And she will be a *welcomed* guest, will she not?"

Trapper glared at Arch before releasing a huff. He nodded.

Herb and Topper exchanged an uncertain look before turning their attention back to Snow.

"Have you seen Stitches, Snow?" Topper asked, brushing his auburn bangs from his eyes.

While he and his brother shared their reddish locks, Topper remained clean shaven. Despite being the younger of the two, he had a certain firmness about him that contrasted with Herb's looks.

Herb had a more robust physique, looking as though he belonged on one of those historical Vikings shows. Yet, as he gazed at the blueberries in the small basket on the table, it was clear that he possessed a kind and gentle demeanor.

"He said he was going to tend to the laundry today," she replied. "He should be back from the river soon."

"And Axe just finished with a few trees out in the forest," Arch interjected. "We should tend to supper soon."

"I've just begun," Snow said, turning to the cauldron over the fireplace. "I have soup started."

"We thank yeh," Hunter said with a nod. "God knows I was tired of eating Topp's rabbit stew."

Topper seemed slightly offended, for he pushed his hand against Hunter's shoulder. "No one ever said that *you* couldn't cook for us."

"I hunt," Hunter replied. "That is my job in this house."

"Perhaps yeh should stop bringing home rabbits then, hm?" Topper retorted. "There are other animals in the forest. Or is that all yeh can catch?"

The banter between them seemed natural, probably a regular occurrence. Despite the apparent irritation in Hunter's gaze towards Topper, there was an underlying mutual respect between them. They all seemed to have an ease about them that was familial. And even with Snow…as if she had always been a part of their group.

"Help me set the table?" Snow-White asked Herb, passing a stack of plates and bowls to the man before glancing at the door. "Since Stitches hasn't returned yet."

"He'll be angry with me for having taken his job," Herb explained, shaking his head as he lifted his hands.

"I'll help," I offered, reaching for the plates.

She turned her hazel gaze to me. "Thank you, Jo. Topper, perhaps you could make those delicious potato hotcakes tonight?"

"Hotcakes," Trapper cooed with a smile. "I do love hotcakes."

Aneurin turned to me as I moved towards the table with the plates. I took care to ignore the stares of the men who remained in the nearby seats.

"Hotcakes?" he asked ever so softly to me.

I raised a curious brow. "You've never had pancakes before?"

"'Tis a common dish, is it not?" he asked.

I shrugged. "I guess it is. I never thought about it."

"It seems there is much I have yet to experience..." he mumbled.

"Just think of all the stories you'll be able to share with Henry when you see him again."

"I'll have *too* many," he replied.

"Won't we both?"

When Stitches finally came through the door of the house with his pile of clean sheets and shirts stacked in his arms, his deep blue eyes forlornly found me and Aneurin and the table already set with plates and bowls. He stood there, a picture of conflicted emotions, his mop of golden curls framing his face. Strands of hair brushed against his shoulders, adding to the disheveled but charming look. His nose, though long, seemed perfectly proportioned, and his lips were pressed into a thin line, betraying his inner turmoil.

Herb had been right about his reaction.

I think it only took him thirty more seconds to realize I was wearing the gown he and Snow had worked on together, and I could see the faint blush creeping up on his cheeks as the realization dawned on him.

"W-Who are you?" he asked, almost accusingly, as his hand gestured toward the table. "W-What have you done?"

"Oh, let it be," Topper said quickly from the stove, where he and Snow-White were making hotcakes. "We weren't sure when you'd return from your task."

"I *always* set the table," he retorted, pushing a hand to his hips.

"Tis only since Snow has been here," Topper replied, winking at him. "You never helped in the kitchen *before.*"

"That's not true!" Stitches exclaimed, his cheeks burning with an even darker shade of pink. He looked in Snow-White's direction, waiting for her reaction.

But her focus remained on cooking.

Stitches relaxed. "You haven't answered my question," he said, returning his attention back to me.

"You missed it," Hunter called from a seat in the other room. Herb, Trapper and himself had all moved into the room adjacent to the kitchen, tending to a fire in the small fireplace there, while Arch remained at the table. "The frog is apparently a cursed prince, and Jo...is lost," Hunter finished.

"They're my friends," Snow-White remarked, turning on her heel as looking at the men. It was the first time I'd seen her show a hint of annoyance. Her hazel eyes held Stitches' gaze and gestured to me. "There is no danger here."

"So, they're your friends?" Stitches continued to look at me curiously. "Then have you escaped from the queen's palace, too?"

"You're such a halfwit," Trapper retorted from the room.

Stitches remained silent then, moving to the table to look at my handiwork. He adjusted a plate or two with his fingers carefully, before glaring at me.

"And did Snow give you that dress?"

"I fell into a pond," I gestured toward the door, almost as an explanation of the reason why I was wearing it in the first place. His eyes scanned the green fabric as he took a step back.

"There are a few folds that should be worked out," he murmured to himself. "But overall, it does show your improvement."

It took me a moment to realize he wasn't talking to me at all, but rather, about the dress.

He looked over his shoulder at Snow-White.

"I understand why you suggested a more appropriate behavior," Aneurin murmured into my ear softly as I eased myself back into a corner of the room.

I felt so awkward, in not knowing any of the men, and feeling a twinge of unwelcome.

"I didn't want you to offend anyone," I said. "You never know…"

"I have the first plate of hotcakes ready," Topper called out to everyone. "And the soup is ready."

Trapper, Hunter and Herb suddenly appeared at the table, joining Arch, their eyes gleaming with anticipation as they glanced at the dish of hotcakes.

"Where is Axe?" Arch asked. "And Bones?"

"Should be here soon," Herb replied with a nod.

Arch looked at me with a curious brow. "Aren't you hungry?"

"I wasn't sure I was allowed to sit," I replied curtly, shooting a glare in Trapper's direction.

The man met my gaze and returned it with a glare of his own.

Arch clicked his tongue with a soft chuckle.

"Come, come. Sit and eat. If you've been traveling as you said you have, I imagine you and your companion must be hungry."

"We are," Aneurin quipped. "And I thank you for your hospitality, sir."

Leave it to him to chime in with his charm and politeness. At least it would give us a chance to fill our stomachs with real food, rather than the leftover gingerbread from the witch's house.

Snow-White took to placing large bowls of the soup around the table so everyone could help themselves. The smell was divine. Whatever it was, my mouth watered at just the scent.

Arch motioned to an empty chair beside his own. "Please, take a seat."

I hesitated, hoping I wasn't taking someone else's spot. Of course, Trapper was seated beside me.

"No one is sitting there," Arch reassured me, as if he could read my mind.

Sitting down, I smoothed the skirt of my dress underneath me.

Arch reached for a plate of potato hotcakes and offered it to me.

As the sleeve of his shirt exposed his wrist, I noticed a small dull circle was scarred into his skin, with what looked like a *B* inside it.

"Help yourself to as many as you'd like," he offered, drawing my gaze back to his face. "Topper is one to always make more."

At all the gatherings I attended with Nico, even when I felt like an outsider, nothing compared to this moment. Despite Arch's efforts to make me feel welcome, I couldn't shake the feeling of being watched by Trapper and Hunter. I wanted to confront the former about his attitude towards me. Hadn't we already established that I wasn't working for the queen?

Taking a hotcake with the two-pronged fork, I placed it on my own plate with a nod of gratitude. "Would you like one?" I asked, looking at my biggest objector.

"I can manage myself," he retorted.

"Of course," I replied with a nod and took the plate from Arch before pushing it in his direction.

"I'd like to learn more of where you're from, Jo," Arch continued as he lifted a ladle from one of the soup bowls, pouring a heap of what looked to be cooked vegetables into his own bowl.

"Me?" I asked, keeping my gaze locked on the hot soup.

Arch chuckled as he took the ladle and poured some soup into my bowl. My stomach growled almost in response. How long had it truly been since I'd last eaten anything?

"Jo," the frog whispered into my ear. "Would you please share your soup with me?"

Right. *Aneurin.* He needed to eat, too. I nodded with a defeated sigh. The thought of sharing with him wasn't exactly appetizing. Imagining his slimy tongue touching my spoon made my stomach churn. In an instant, the soup lost its appeal, the craving dissolving into disgust.

The frog hopped from my shoulder and landed onto the table. In what seemed a mere split second, his webbed fingers were in the bowl, pulling out chunks of the carrots and onions.

"Yes, you," Arch said, raising a brow as he watched us.

The table suddenly erupted with activity, as most of the men sat around it, tearing into their hotcakes with their fingers. Snow, on the other hand, sat at the end, gracefully sipping on the soup.

I could sense Trapper's stare on me, an unsettling feeling creeping up on me. Another heavy sigh escaped my lips.

"Are you not hungry?" Arch asked, his eyes shifting between me and my bowl of soup, where Aneurin was contentedly nibbling on another piece of carrot. His little round cheeks were puffed up as he continued to chew.

"Oh Jo," Aneurin said between bites. "This…is…delicious!"

I tore a bit of the hotcake from my plate and slipped the piece into my mouth. At least the flavor was so much better than what I was expecting.

"I'm from a place called Oaks Corner," I finally said to Arch as I swallowed the first bite. "It's a small town near quite a few lakes. It's quiet and it's home."

"Oaks Corner," Arch repeated. "I've never heard of it."

"You wouldn't," I said, pushing another piece of hotcake into my mouth. "It's…really far away from here."

"As you and your frog friend have mentioned," Arch agreed, his tone carrying a note of understanding. "And do you have a family? Will they be looking for you?"

The mere thought of them stirred a whirlwind of emotions within me. How much time had passed since I had been sucked into the pages of the book? What was going to happen when they found me gone? Would they frantically search for me, assuming I had actually returned to the city, or would they suspect something more sinister? Perhaps they would even reach out to Nico, adding another layer of complexity to an already tangled web of emotions.

I could almost envision Mom's worried expression, her frantic phone calls, and her sleepless nights. And Dad...

The memory of that first morning back home flooded my mind. Dad, sitting on the sofa, a solitary figure in the early morning, indulging in his favorite breakfast ritual of sunny-side-up eggs and toast, while the television played in the background.

"Come sit here, honey," he'd said to me, patting the spot on the sofa beside him.

Like the zombie I was, I had plopped down staring blankly at the television and thought about everything that had happened. The image of finding Nico in bed, his expression a mixture of guilt and defiance, was etched into my memory like a scar that refused to fade. I felt the sting of not only his betrayal, but of my own. I'd betrayed myself.

Then I'd felt Dad's arms around me, hugging me. I could smell the faint hint of oil and his cologne on the collar of his plaid jacket. He didn't say anything. I guess in a way, he didn't need to. Instead, he just hugged me. As the television show returned from commercials, Dad kept his arm wrapped around my shoulder, keeping me close to him.

I couldn't even imagine what he was feeling right now.

The sound of Aneurin's lip-smacking interrupted my thoughts, pulling me back into the present. I shot a questioning glance at Aneurin, but he didn't meet my gaze. It was clear that he didn't have a care in the world. He was being fed, had a roof over his head, and an assured pillow awaiting his royal head.

"I imagine they will be, yes," I replied to Arch's question, my voice tinged with resignation.

"And you, Your Highness?" Arch asked, turning his attention to the little green soup-fiend. "What of you and your family?"

Aneurin swallowed a piece of cooked cauliflower and shrugged. "My parents reign in the Kingdom of Luria."

"If I'm being honest, I have not heard of it," Arch replied with a raised brow.

"No? It is a beautiful place," Aneurin said thoughtfully. "A land with vast mountains, lush gardens, prosperous villages…"

"You must miss your home," Arch commented.

"Yes," Aneurin replied. "I do. But I shall not return until my spell is broken."

"What led to the casting of such a spell, Your Highness?"

I bit my lip, listening intently to the conversation between Arch and Aneurin. Looking around the table, I saw everyone's eyes were on them as well. And I hadn't even noticed the new face that had joined the table until now.

Axe, who appeared to be one of the older in the group. He bore a long, deep scar over the right side of his face and across his eye. His hair was nearly salt and pepper, and his beard around his chin was thick and long.

The only member of the family I hadn't seen or met was Bones.

"My spell," Aneurin said with a sigh, drawing my attention back to him. "It is a story I have not, in truth, told aloud to a soul. Not even Jo knows the entirety of it."

I remained still and silent in my seat, not wanting to interrupt.

He took a deep breath. "But I suppose, if there's a time for me to share my story…it should be now."

FIFTEEN

During our first interaction, he'd vaguely mentioned his parents' altercation with a mystical figure, leading to his transformation. However, I always had suspected there was more to the story. What had been the *real* reason for him being turned into a frog?

Aneurin straightened on his hind legs, assuming a posture that hinted at his human nature and the regal lessons he must have had growing up. It seemed improbable that an ordinary frog could maintain such a dignified bearing.

"My parents had a love story that I was sure would be told throughout the ages," Aneurin began, waving a hand in the air. "My father, once cursed himself to live a life in darkness and despair, was saved by mother…a woman who, at that time, held very little rank. My father wished to have her hand in marriage, and so struck a deal with a mysterious magical man."

I couldn't say that it sounded like it was a love story worth noting. It wasn't a tale like Romeo and Juliet with a love worth dying for, or Beauty and the Beast, with a love that could break any curse. Although it did sound like perhaps their relationship started out like the latter.

"Bargains with old men never end well," Hunter scoffed, shaking his head.

"Indeed," Aneurin replied. "The man wished for lands and riches, in exchange for arranging the frowned-upon marriage."

"After my father married my mother, the man came to claim his reward, but my father sent him away each time. For years."

"So, your father was unwilling to uphold his end of the bargain…" Hunter interjected again.

Aneurin released a heavy sigh and nodded. "Yes. It is as you say."

I felt a twinge of pity and sadness for him. With all the privilege that came with being a royal, I guess I'd forgotten how complicated it could be, too.

"On my twenty-fifth birthday, the man appeared again. But this time, he did not allow the guards to lead him away. Instead, he breached the throne room and threatened to take my life in front of my parents. When they pleaded with him to spare my life…he cursed me instead. With a touch of his finger, I transformed." Aneurin slid his webbed fingers over his green skin and sighed.

I felt for him then. To be punished for his father's misdeeds? What had happened to him was so unfair. More so than anything I'd personally experienced in my own life. I wanted to find a way to break his spell all the more.

"He knew the worst way to hurt my father was to rid him of his heir. I was at the prime age of seeking a wife and settling down. I had already become aware of my duties, and the expectations of what was to come when I became king. In an instant, all of that was gone. And then he disappeared immediately."

He released a shuddering breath before whispering, "I began this search to find either him or a princess who could release me from this spell."

"It seems you've been unjustly punished," Arch replied.

"At times, I tell myself that exactly. My manservant, Henry, often reminds me as well. On the days in which I truly hate my existence."

"Where is yeh manservant, then?" Herb asked, shoving a piece of his hot cake into his mouth.

I'd nearly forgotten we'd had an audience.

"He left me to find help," Aneurin said with a sigh, turning to look at the rest of the table. "He went in search of finding a lady who might sympathize with my predicament."

"Is that how yeh found this lassie?" Herb asked, gesturing to me.

My cheeks began to burn as I felt everyone's gaze drift to me.

Aneurin lifted his webbed hands and shook his head. "Henry would have never brought such a lady to me," he replied, in a tone revealing he found such a possibility absurd.

I lowered my gaze to my plate, where my half-eaten potato hot cake was growing cold. His response stung a bit, even though I recognized that neither of us had begun our interactions on the best terms. Back then, I'd been far from sympathetic to his situation.

Perhaps I didn't fit the conventional image of a princess, lacking the instinct to gracefully wave my hand or execute the perfect bow. I didn't know all the titles and ranks in the aristocracy, but I had managed to watch enough historical mini-series and documentaries to navigate my way if needed. Maybe I didn't have all the required etiquette that a princess should know. But if a secret princess could successfully learn from her queenly grandmother, I was sure I could too. Not that I wanted that opportunity.

"No?" Hunter asked, easing back in his chair. "If Jo isn't the sort of lass yeh'd want for yourself, who would you want?"

"'Tis not a matter of who," Aneurin replied. "I require a *princess*."

"A princess," Hunter scoffed, shaking his head. "Why would anyone want a prin—"

"Yes, *Hunter*," Snow-White interjected, her laughter cutting through his scoff. "Why would they?"

I bit my lip, biting back a laugh as Hunter's face went white. Talk about putting your foot in your mouth.

"Well, I didn't mean you," he corrected. "You're not really a—"

"A princess?" she asked, amused. "But I am."

"Not really, when yeh think of it, Snow," Hunter continued. He was most definitely trying to backpedal on this one.

I wasn't sure if Snow would allow it.

"I'd dream of a woman like you," he explained, gesturing towards her. "One that cooks and cleans and is as beautiful as a flower…"

"There's a reason why you're still unwed," Trapper chuckled.

"Oh?" Hunter asked, raising a brow. "And who would yeh wish for, *brother*? Would you not want a woman like Snow?"

Trapper's gaze lingered on Snow for a moment before he quickly averted his eyes, crossing his arms and clenching his jaw.

Stitches shifted in his chair before shrugging. "There's no shame in admitting I would be honored to have such a woman as a wife."

"We already know that," Trapper retorted, his sigh carrying a hint of frustration. His eyes flickered briefly towards Snow before he masked his emotions behind a neutral expression.

Stitches' face flushed a shade of red reminiscent of a rope of licorice before he returned his focus to his plate.

I broke the remainder of my hotcake into smaller pieces and lifted one up to my mouth. I hoped chewing would distract me enough to keep from saying something stupid.

Arch watched me as he eased back into his chair. "I must say, this has been quite an exciting few days. First in finding Snow to now welcoming a new friend, and her talking frog prince."

"Is this what I've missed?" The man that I presumed to be Axe asked from across the table, gesturing to me and Aneurin with his fork. "I was wondering what was going on here."

Arch nodded and leaned his elbows on the table. "We missed you earlier, Axe," Arch replied. "This is Josephine, and her friend..." he trailed off, casting a glance at the frog.

Before he could proceed with a lengthy introduction, I interjected, "Aneurin. His name is Aneurin."

He didn't object to my brief explanation and nodded at Axe.

"I suppose it would only be polite for us to introduce ourselves as well," Arch continued. "With all of us here, it's much easier."

He rose from his chair and pressed his hand against his chest.

"I am Arch. I'm the eldest of the group."

"He's our respected leader," Trapper interrupted.

"I gathered," I replied. "And I know that you're Trapper."

"Aye, I am," he quipped, in the friendliest tone he'd spoken to me with yet. "And I have my brother, Hunter." Brushing his dark curls from his eyes, he gestured toward the one who had come into the house with the rabbits.

Hunter lifted his hand with a smile.

The two would be the easiest to remember, in just by their response to me and Aneurin both, earlier.

"Then we have Herb," Arch said, gesturing to the bearded man with kind and gentle eyes. He smiled in return, nodding his head. "And his brother, Topper."

"The chef," I added, observing Topper taking a sip from his cup.

"We also have Axe here, whom you just met." Arch pointed to the man with the long scar across his face. "And Stitches."

Stitches offered me a firm but uncertain smile, a clear indication of his wariness towards me—a sentiment that seemed justified. After all, I was a stranger to them all, someone who hadn't yet earned their trust.

"And you know Snow-White," Arch finished, gesturing to the princess seated across the table.

She dipped her head with a warm, wide smile.

"I'm curious," I began, looking from one side of the table, back to Arch. "How did you all come here? Or...why are you here?"

"*Why* are we here?" Hunter asked, the strain of sarcasm laced in his words.

"Yeah," I said. "Why are seven men living in a tree house?"

Maybe it wasn't the best description, but I didn't know what else to call this place. It wasn't at all the cottage I'd seen in the movies. And by the looks they shared among one another, they didn't seem to know how to handle my question.

"It's a long story." Arch lifted his cup from the place setting and took a sip. He swallowed, then continued, "But I suppose we could share a bit of the tale if you'd like to truly hear it."

"Oh, I would!" Snow-White said with an eager nod.

Trapper clutched at the fork in his hand, his knuckles growing white as he peered at his brother.

What was the big secret they were keeping?

Aneurin redirected his attention to the cooling bowl of soup, already starting to nibble on another carrot before glancing back at me. The expression on his face suggested that perhaps I had posed a question I shouldn't have. But at least Arch's willingness to share proved it wouldn't make us run around another kitchen, narrowly escaping with our lives.

He lowered himself back into his seat before clearing his throat. "We came here to live a better life than the ones we'd known before." When neither Snow nor I replied, he continued, "I think it's safe to say that we all experienced…ridicule for our appearance."

I surveyed the table once more, searching for clues to what he meant. They were a far cry from the original description of the seven men, who had been classically described as dwarfs. *These* men weren't little, disfigured, or hunchbacked. Even if they *were*, it wouldn't matter. They were human, just like me. "How you—? I don't understand."

"We all bear scars in some form," Arch replied. "Ones that have been branded on us at birth." He carefully rolled up his sleeve, exposing the circle I'd seen earlier.

"And what does the B stand for?" I asked softly, sitting back in my chair.

It was Aneurin who spoke up, lowering the vegetable back into the soup. "Bastard."

"Aye," Hunter said from across the table. "Bastards. We're all illegitimate, unwanted bastards."

Snow appeared to cringe in her seat as she glanced across the table at her friends.

I noticed Stitches gazing at her silently, his lips parting as though he wanted to speak. He averted his gaze, his expression tinged with shame. Something I didn't think he knew how to express.

"It was Axe and I who grew up with each other, who experienced much of our village's prejudice together," Arch explained. "One day, we devised a plan to escape our troubled homes and ended up here," he murmured, his voice carrying a reverence for their sanctuary. "That's where we stumbled upon Hunter and Trapper. They looked like they'd been living there for years."

Trapper snorted, his tone laced with a hint of amusement. "Hunter just refused to bathe. Always stubborn, that one."

"What was the point?" the man in question interjected, his self-deprecation evident in his voice.

I couldn't help but smile, the image of a younger Hunter and Trapper, covered in grass stains and mischief, painting itself vividly in my mind. Two boys who had managed to survive on their own in a world that had let them down.

"And then Herb and Topper…"

"Topper saved us all from starvation." Hunter laughed. "I don't think I could have mustered enough strength to eat one more bowl of Arch's mushroom mush."

"I was the last," Stitches said softly, lifting his spoon from the table. "I grew up in my grandfather's house until I was ten and seven. He was a tailor in the village, tending to rips and tears, creating gowns and jackets alike. It became my dream to have a shop of my own. But when he died, it seemed like the entire village abandoned the shop. They wouldn't even acknowledge me when I walked past."

I raised my brow with curiosity. "Did they treat you like that when he was still alive?"

"Of course," he nodded solemnly. "They would only do business with my grandfather. Only pay him. If not for this *stupid* brand…"

My gaze flickered back to his wrist, where I saw the same emblem that matched Arch's. It was horrific. How would anyone do such a thing to someone else? Especially *children*.

Stitches slid his gaze back to Arch, who, in turn, responded with a small, sad smile.

"It was a happy day to have you join us, lad," Arch said.

"So, you just...came out here?" I asked, my curiosity piqued by their shared journey to the forest.

Stitches leaned back in his chair and nodded. "I often heard tales of the cottage in the forest. Villagers spoke of it as the place where the bastards gathered. There might have been a time or two that I'd heard of Arch...he was well-known after all."

Arch clicked his tongue with a chuckle as he shook his head. "Hardly, Stitch."

"At least the villagers treated you kindly," Stitches remarked.

"Only because they were unaware of my true identity," Arch replied with a wink. "Ignorance worked in my favor more than once."

"So, you all built this place," I asked. "This...house in the tree."

"I wouldn't say it's huge," Arch responded. "But it serves as our home. There's ample space for all of us to live comfortably. And it appears it has space for guests too."

Snow-White's cheeks flushed a delicate shade of pink as she pressed her lips together. "Your kindness means so much to me," she admitted. "I didn't know what to do."

"You won't have to worry," Stitches reassured her, gently taking her hand in his. As he caressed her knuckles with his thumb, it was clear to me that he harbored feelings for her, a fact he unwittingly advertised in front of everyone.

Feeling awkward for witnessing the moment of intimacy, I averted my gaze, not wanting to intrude on their moment.

Snow offered Stitches a tentative smile before delicately withdrawing her hand, letting it rest in her lap. "I'm sure you want to understand the men's hesitancy in having you here," she continued, her gaze fixed on me. "It's only fair to explain my situation to you."

I attempted to hide my surprise, though the warmth spreading across my cheeks betrayed my effort. I wanted to tell her that I already knew the situation—understood why Trapper and Arch and the rest of them were so protective of her.

"You see," she whispered, sliding her gaze in Arch's direction before sighing. "My father was the king of this land. He was great and good and wise, but he believed he couldn't raise me alone. I suppose having an heir was also of great importance, for I was a girl…and my father's only child. So, when I was about six or so, a few years after my mother's death, he remarried. My father brought a great woman from a faraway land. A woman renowned for her beauty and wisdom. When she first arrived, I felt…" Snow shuddered in her seat. "I was terrified of her. There was something unsettling about her demeanor, the way she regarded and spoke to me…I knew immediately she harbored no affection for me. I confided in Papa, and he reassured me it would improve with time." Snow looked down at her hands, her face was growing warm and pink. Her chin trembled, revealing she was about to cry. "But time ran short. One winter, my Papa caught a chill…and he died quite suddenly."

"I'm so sorry," I replied.

She shifted in her seat. "It was a grief I'd never known before. With my being so young when my mother died, I didn't truly understand the loss of her. But with Papa…I knew him. I loved him. And he left me with her."

Her. The queen.

"The day after his death, I was forcibly removed from my chambers and placed in the servants' quarters," Snow continued, her voice quivering with the weight of her memories. "I cried myself to sleep that night, overwhelmed by the sudden loss of my status, and the cruelty of my stepmother's actions. By the next morning, I was expected to wait upon her every whim, to perform any task she demanded. I was no longer addressed as a princess…"

"No one deserves such treatment," Trapper snarled beside me, his fists clenched in anger.

"One day," Snow whispered. "Papa's best hunter came to me and told me he required my help. He'd caught a buck out in the field and wanted my assistance."

I furrowed my brow That was how he'd lured her out?

"I did think it strange," Snow admitted, her voice growing somber, "to be asked to help with such a task. But I'd always been eager to lend a hand, no matter the request. So, I followed him out into the meadow just beyond the walls. It was then that I discovered I was not there to assist the hunter with his kill, but to be killed *by* him. He raised his dagger over my chest…"

As Snow lifted her gaze, meeting mine, I could see tears building in her eyes. I could see the years of grief she'd kept to herself.

And I could see myself there, all the tears *I* still hadn't processed over Nico.

"As I began to cry, the hunter took pity on me. He told me to flee into the forest and never return. Never claim to be who I truly am. To live…" She sucked in a breath as she shook her head. "If the queen ever discovered that he disobeyed her orders, that man would face dire consequences. He would die in my place."

I silently absorbed the gravity of her words. But when no one spoke, I asked, "Do you think she knows?"

"It is my hope that she doesn't," Snow replied, her tone tinged with uncertainty. "But I've come to accept that I must live in seclusion. I imagine if she discovers that I was allowed to run away…she will do whatever it takes to kill me. I am, after all, my father's heir. Girl or not."

"*You* are the next in line," I agreed.

"So it is in her best interest that I vanish without a trace."

I leaned back in my chair, suppressing the deep sigh that lingered in my throat. Compared to the cannibal witch we'd left behind, I couldn't even begin to fathom how Aneurin and I were going to help Snow. How were we—me and an enchanted frog—supposed to come up against an even more powerful witch, when we'd barely been able to escape with our lives after encountering the first one?

As I looked at her, and then slowly to all the faces of the men around us, I realized I couldn't do this on my own. But wasn't that the point? We were all here, for one reason or another, seeking help. The men were avoiding a world that had rejected them. Snow was hiding away from a stepmother who was both cruel and dangerous. Aneurin needed to find a princess to kiss him.

And then there was me. I needed to find a way to forgive myself from the past, and find a way home.

Snow was a step towards that.

"I'll help you," I said softly with a determined nod. "I don't know what that means, or what it entails, but…I'll help you."

"But you are helping *me*," Aneurin said, turning on his foot to look at me.

I shot him a quelling look. I was fully capable of helping more than one person at a time. "*We'll* help you," I corrected, volunteering the frog's help just for being selfish. "While Aneurin and I stay here, we'll keep an eye out for the queen. If the men need to go anywhere, I'll stay here with you."

"What could *you* do?" Trapper asked, raising a brow.

"What is that supposed to mean?" I asked, turning in my seat. "I used to live in a cit—" I paused, biting my bottom lip. None of them even knew what a city *was*.

"I used to live in a big village, all by myself…and I managed."

"You didn't have a queen with a vengeance after you…"

"Maybe not," I replied curtly. "But I know how to defend myself. There's nothing you can do that I can't."

Trapper snorted and eased back in his chair, smirking with challenge. "Is that so?"

Sixteen

As it turned out, there was *one* thing Trapper could do that I most definitely could not.

I was taken aback by how swiftly he rose from his chair and strode across the room, vanishing around the corner. When he reappeared, my eyes widened at the unexpected sight of an accordion in his hands. In response to my surprise, Trapper approached me with a smile.

It caught me off guard, too. It was a rare occurrence, especially directed at me. In the short time I had known him, he was always scowling in my direction.

"You've gotta be kidding me," I mumbled under my breath.

Stitches and Herb rose from their own chairs, disappearing into the next room.

"Now, now…" Arch said with a chuckle as he watched the two turn the corner. "You started it now, Trapper."

Trapper clicked his tongue. "Technically, *she* did."

Stitches returned to the table with a long flute-looking instrument that I didn't recognize, while Herb returned with a larger version of a ukulele. Of *course*, they could play instruments. Why wouldn't they?

Herb and Stitches situated themselves back at the table and looked towards Trapper, who started a melody. They joined in gradually, echoing back their own versions of the song.

Their performance seemed to captivate not only me and Aneurin, but also Snow-White. It was clear she hadn't experienced their musical talents before.

Her smile broadened as Stitches leaned in her direction, his fingers dancing gracefully along the wooden instrument.

Even Aneurin was entertained to watch the musical group from his bowl of soup.

As the song closed out, Trapper turned to me with a raised eyebrow, silently challenging me to contest what we had just witnessed.

I lifted my hands with a laugh. "Defending myself and being musically gifted are two *very* different things," I explained.

"I heard a challenge," Trapper retorted, a hint of mischief in his eyes. "And I accepted it."

I laughed. "Yeah, you did. There's no denying that."

"That was delightful," Snow-White exclaimed, her smile widening even further. "I had no idea how talented all of you were."

"Well, not *all* of us," Topper said, gesturing to the rest of the men who had listened quietly.

Axe was leaning back in his chair, his arms crossed over his chest, while Topper and Hunter finished the food on their plates.

"I used to play in my youth," Aneurin said, gesturing to Herb's ukulele. "But with fingers like these..." He lifted his small, little hands with an expression of disdain.

"You'll be yourself once more, my friend," Arch said. "Don't lose hope yet."

"Of course. What is one without hope?" Aneurin replied before looking up to me.

It was the first time I'd seen a weary glimmer in his eyes. We'd both been through so much just within the past few hours. The witch, the children, the waterfall, and now this tree house with the men and Snow-White.

"You both appear exhausted," Arch said, breaking the silence.

I lifted my gaze from Aneurin and nodded slowly, mustering a polite smile for our host. "I think we are. It's been quite a long day."

"I understand Snow-White has already shown you to the room above." He gestured to the staircase. "Please, my friends, go rest."

I felt hesitant at first to just get up and leave the table without helping. Not after everything they'd already done for us. But when Arch gestured again towards the staircase and Snow-White gave a nod of approval in my direction, I opened my hand to Aneurin and placed him back onto my shoulder before rising from my own chair.

"Thank you," I managed as I stood up.

"Be sure to take a candle on your way up," Arch said.

Right, there were no electric lights.

When Aneurin didn't express his own thanks, I obnoxiously moved my shoulder and gave him a sideways glance.

"Yes, yes," Aneurin quickly chimed in as he grasped onto the fabric of my dress. "Thank you for the meal and hospitality."

Once I rounded the corner and grabbed a candle as Arch instructed, Aneurin mumbled, "Next time, don't almost drop me."

Rolling my eyes, I started up the stairs. "Remember your manners next time."

Out of the corner of my eye, I saw their dog, Bones, lying beside the hearth of the fireplace, sleeping soundlessly.

Aneurin sighed. "I'm too exhausted to argue with you."

"Then don't," I replied, holding the candle out in front of me. We both were silent as I maneuvered through each room, and each level of the tree house, until we arrived back at the door where Snow-White had led us earlier.

It was relieving to find that candles were already in the tall holders, sitting on shelves scattered about the room. As I lit them, the room gradually brightened against the backdrop of the setting sun outside the window.

"I'm exhausted," I whispered, gently taking Aneurin off my shoulder before placing him on one of the pillows on the bed.

"As am I am," Aneurin agreed.

As I moved back to where I'd left my clothes to dry, I was struck anew with discomfort. Despite the shared experiences we'd endured, the lack of privacy in our room left me uncertain. After all,

I found myself sharing quarters with a frog—an enchanted one at that. But what could I say? Whether I liked it or not, my pillow was going to be shared with him too.

Breaking the silence, Aneurin cleared his throat. "You never mentioned you had once been betrothed," he said suddenly from the pillow, breaking the silence.

I bit the inside of my cheek, exhaling slowly. "It's not something you needed to know," I replied, making my way back to the bed.

"Perhaps not," Aneurin conceded.

Sitting on the edge of the bed, I slid my hands over my knees.

"Will you not tell me what occurred between you and your betrothed?" Aneurin asked, once again breaking the brief silence. Startled by his question, I turned to look over at him.

"What's there to tell?" I asked with a shrug. "I was once engaged to a guy, and now I'm not. End of story."

"End of story…" He echoed my words, as if searching for some hidden meaning behind them. His green gaze sharpened on me. "But…is it ever truly the end? Our hearts still beat the same, and our thoughts continue on."

His question made me pause. My heart felt like someone had squeezed it, and I shifted uncomfortably.

"What are you trying to get at?" I asked, narrowing my gaze.

"Is that not why we crossed paths in the forest?" he pressed on. "Were you not running away from your…situation?"

But I *hadn't* been running away. Not this time, at least. To be honest, I hadn't even walked away from home. But…I had run away from Nico and all the things I couldn't emotionally handle. When Nico tried to reach out to me to talk, I wasn't ready. I wasn't sure I'd ever be *ready* to hear his explanation or his excuses.

Maybe that didn't matter any more.

After all, I'd been pulled into this strange story, where I was sitting on a bed in an unknown forest. Talking to a frog prince.

"I guess I was," I admitted. "And I have been for quite a while."

"You've never told me where you're really from…" the frog continued. "Oaks Corner?"

"It's a place, far away," I replied vaguely.

"As you said at dinner." Aneurin acknowledged. "I have never heard of such a place."

"There are probably a lot of places you're unfamiliar with," I replied with a nonchalant shrug. I didn't want to get into the reality of my world with him just yet. I knew Aneurin enough now to know he wouldn't believe me.

"You must be tired," he said softly, his green eyes studying me intently. Did he want to get out of this conversation? Or maybe he'd finally noticed just how drained I was.

It wasn't just the exhaustion from dealing with the seven men—including one who kind of hated me—the pond, or the cannibalistic witch. It was *everything*. Even before my breakup, I had been tiptoeing around Nico, constantly on edge with knowing something wasn't right, but I couldn't quite put my finger on it. I had worn myself out trying to be the woman I thought Nico wanted, only to discover that I had lost sight of myself in the process.

"I think I'm mostly tired from escaping being turned into dinner." I confessed the half-truth with a small smirk. "Not to mention having fallen over a waterfall."

"What I meant—" Aneurin started.

"I know what you meant," I interjected quickly.

Aneurin looked down. "I know we argue quite a bit."

"Too much, honestly," I said.

He sucked in a breath and shook his head before lifting it again. "You can trust me though." His small green eyes locked onto mine, and I found myself nodding in response.

"I-I know," I stammered.

"We are friends, after all, Jo," he affirmed.

Friends. The frog prince considered me a friend. The thought made me smile.

"We are, aren't we?"

"Like it or not, we are as I have decided," Aneurin agreed. He patted the pillow with his small, webbed hand. "Now, come lie down and rest."

"Isn't this breaking a rule or something? Isn't this what you're supposed to be doing with a princess?"

"Are you a princess?" Aneurin asked with a wicked smirk.

I rolled my eyes and shook my head. "Clearly not."

"Then worry not," he replied.

I didn't need any more permission than that. Kicking off my shoes, I leaned back into the semi-soft mattress. It was not the kind you'd find in a five-star hotel, but it would at least be a place to rest. And while I didn't have pajamas to change into, I was glad the dress Snow had given me was still comfortable enough to rest in. I was grateful to have something that was clean, and would keep me warm. As I eased under a layer of a few soft blankets, I turned my gaze back to the frog, lying mere inches away from my face.

"You know," I began with a soft yawn. "I would help break your spell if I could."

"Oh?" Aneurin asked, amused.

"I've shared my food with you, several times—in fact. And I'm now sharing my pillow. All that is left is the kissing part."

"'Tis to be a kiss of true love," he corrected.

"Right," I replied sleepily. "True love."

I wasn't sure if I believed in such a thing. At least, not anymore.

"I'm just saying, if I could…if it meant you'd be free to be a man again, and return to your old life…I think I'd help you."

Aneurin silently lowered his head to the pillow. "I appreciate that," he whispered, his gaze feeling as though it delved into the depths of my soul. "Truly."

It was quiet then. The stillness of the room lingered and grew into this great, awkward silence again. Maybe I'd said something I shouldn't have. I shut my eyes, hoping sleep would overtake us.

CHANTAL GADOURY

Suddenly, I heard him murmur, "If I may be so bold as to suggest that I think Stitches has a fondness for Snow."

I all but snorted. "I definitely think he has a crush on her."

"A crush?"

"It just means that he likes her." I said, nodding against the pillow. "I think it's obvious. Stitches didn't exactly keep it a secret."

"But she could never be with someone like him," he replied.

"And why is that? Because of his past?"

"She is a princess," he said. "She is the heir to her father's kingdom. There are certain expectations."

In the tale I'd been familiar with since childhood, Snow was ultimately saved by a kiss from a prince who had tirelessly sought her out. As long as the story unfolded as it should, Snow's fate would align with those expectations.

My heart couldn't help but ache a little for Stitches.

I rose onto my elbow, wrinkling my nose. "Yeah, but...from who?" I asked, shaking my head. "Think about it. Her stepmother, the queen of the kingdom, wants her dead. Her father is gone. If the queen were to die, and if Snow-White ruled, she would have the freedom to select her own companion."

"*That* is where you're wrong," Aneurin said, sitting up. "It only makes the pressure of the decision that much harder. It is not about your own wants and desires."

"But it *should* be. If a man can make decisions based on wants and desires, then she should, too!"

"Perhaps in Oaks Corner," he interrupted, his gaze steady on me. "You'd be quite the match, for any man, Jo. But..."

I shook my head, pressing my lips together. "You've completely discredited what you're about to say with just the word 'but.'"

"Marriage is not about love for people like her and I. Marriage for royalty like us is transactional."

"For people like you, maybe," I corrected. "For men. For princes and kings who choose to abide by the rules. She can choose what

156

life she wishes to have. You and your rules shouldn't apply to her, or to Stitches, for that matter. I don't even think those rules should apply to *you*. Look at what your father did for you."

"Look at what my father did *to* me, Jo," he retorted, pressing a webbed hand against his soft, white chest. "I was a man. A man with hopes and dreams...and now, I am nothing more than an amphibian being carted around in some girl's pocket."

I sucked in a breath as I shook my head.

"You certainly have a knack for aggravating people," I retorted sharply, rolling my eyes. I laid my head back down on the pillow, trying to contain my frustration. "You're exhausting. It's going to be a wonder if you find yourself a princess at all."

"I could say the same about you," Aneurin replied. "It is no wonder you are alone."

That stung worse than I think he had intended. I felt a deep-seated rage fill my chest as I lifted myself up on my elbow again. My eyes stung as I glared at him. "That's right," I shot back. "I *chose* to be alone. I don't need someone to make me whole, unlike you."

"I only need my spell to be broken," he retorted. "Nothing more."

"That's not what you keep saying. You need true love. But whatever that means to you is beyond me."

Aneurin puffed up as he continued to stare at me.

"I've never meant anyone as stuck up as you," I added.

"And I," the frog scoffed, "have never met anyone so stubborn."

"At least I'm not as narrow-minded as you."

This was becoming ridiculous.

"I think like a prince," he countered. "That is something a peasant like you would never understand."

"You're back to calling me that?" I asked, glaring. "I'd rather be a peasant than be completely heartless like you. You look down on anyone who isn't like you—regal or whatever. All those men downstairs are far more courageous than I imagine you actually were when you were a human."

The frog narrowed his eyes on me. "I have a heart."

"Then you choose to not use it."

"I choose not to have it *control* me. Am I not allowed to make a logical match for myself? Do not women do the same?"

"In your world, women don't seem to have much of a choice."

"Are you discrediting my own inability to have a choice?"

"I'm not discrediting anything," I replied. "I just don't see anyone here dictating who releases you from your spell, other than you. From what you said, your spell doesn't come with the condition of the woman being some royal person. *You're* the one making it that way. And I'm telling you, if you stick to that, you're going to be a frog for the rest of your life."

"You told me you would help me to find a princess."

Blood rushed to my cheeks. He was also being selfish. Maybe it was time for me to be as well. "Yes. But if you find someone else—"

"There is not. There is only one person. That person—"

"Don't." I pressed my forefinger and thumb against the bridge of my nose as I released a hiss. "You know...I've learned a thing or two in the past year about love, expectations, and conditions. You may think you have everything figured out. You may even think that there's just this *one* person for you. But...it isn't always like that. Things don't always work out the way you think. And people aren't always the way you expect them to be."

I'd been wrong about Nico. And maybe he'd been wrong about me, too. We weren't what each other needed, even if I hadn't understood that until he no longer wanted me anymore.

"Obviously," Aneurin replied. "I think 'tis a fair thing to say that neither of us are what we expected."

"The person that ultimately breaks your spell could be a lowly servant to some horribly stuck-up princess."

"Stuck-up princess..." he echoed with a soft scoff.

"While you might deserve someone like that, I don't want that for you."

"Should I be thankful for your well wishes, *Josephine*?" he asked, his tone sharp.

"Yes," I said curtly. "You should."

We stared at each other for a moment.

Then the corner of his lips curled into a smile. "If I agree to these terms, will you be the one to explain everything to my father?"

"He'll probably be more relieved to see his son return unharmed than worry about the social status of who broke your spell," I explained. "He's not going to care about it if you found…true love. All I'm saying is that you should be more open in who you think might save you."

Aneurin stared at me for a long moment. He knew I was right.

I even knew I was right.

Releasing a huff, Aneurin finally nodded. "I shall keep my eyes open," he said finally. "But…it is still my desire to find a princess."

I released an irritated sigh. I was done talking about this. I just needed to focus on getting back home, back to Mom and Dad.

"Whatever." I lowered myself back into the pillow and pulled the coverlet over my shoulder.

"If I had a choice," Aneurin continued after a moment. "I would hope she'd be like you."

SEVENTEEN

I squeezed my eyes shut, pretending to sleep, hoping that eventually I'd be able to just block out his voice, and the weight of his words. What had he meant by them?

If I had a choice, I would hope she'd be like you.

Why did it bother me so much? All we ever did with one another was argue. If we were in my world, I'm sure my college friends would tease us for bickering like a married couple.

I would hope she'd be like you.

His comment echoed on a loop in my mind while I struggled to decipher its meaning for what felt like hours. And it was the first time he'd ever used a contraction in his speech. But did it really matter what he'd said?

It didn't matter to me what she turned out to be like—this mysterious future bride of Aneurin. Just as long as his spell was broken…and he was happy.

Lying stiffly on the lumpy mattress, I became acutely aware of the jewels I'd forgotten to remove from the pocket of my dress before bed.

I could see his sleeping form in the dimming candlelight. He had curled himself into the pillow with his large eyes closed. In the dark, he looked like a blob of green and bumps.

I shifted my position, trying to be careful to not disturb him, but probably wasn't doing a very good job. If I kept this up, he'd probably complain in the morning about not getting his beauty sleep. Then that would turn into some sort of bickering argument until someone intervened.

But I found myself imagining—wondering—what he looked like underneath his amphibian disguise. Who *truly* slept beside me?

Was he tall and broad-shouldered? Did he have long eyelashes that would brush against his cheeks when his eyes were closed? What color was his hair? I wanted to know what Aneurin truly looked like so badly. Maybe one day, I'd ask him.

But why did I care?

It's not like he'd ever turn his attention to me. I wasn't a princess. With a heavy sigh, I turned over again, pulling the blanket over my head. This entire situation was crazy. Never in my wildest dreams would I have ever imagined myself here…sleeping beside a frog prince in the home of Snow-White's seven…*men*.

A good night's sleep would help clear my mind. In the morning, maybe everything would start to make sense—the reasons behind how I ended up here and why.

"Just promise me you'll take the time to read the stories," the woman at the estate sale had said. "They can be quite wondrous."

Wondrous my ass. It would be a *wonder* if I ever found my way back home.

I shifted again, and thought I heard Aneurin hiss, "Keep still."

Holding my breath, I willed myself to do exactly that. Eventually, my body gave into its own exhaustion and all of my thoughts finally quieted enough for me to drift into the familiar realm of dreams, succumbing to the same one I'd experienced in the car ride before I got the magical book.

A dashing man stood in the center of an expansive but empty ballroom. Adorned in a tunic of resplendent gold and crowned with a coronet of the same radiant hue, he extended his hand towards me with an inviting smile playing upon his lips.

I recognized those emerald eyes.

"Dance with me?" His voice, rich with warmth, carried the question across the empty expanse of the room.

I took his hand without a thought.

"Josephine," he murmured.

His voice stirred something deep within me. It was as though he had uttered my name countless times before. It didn't make sense.

But while I knew his eyes, the face of this man belonged to a complete stranger.

"I'll wait for you," he said.

I jolted upright in bed, peering around the sunlit room. Unlike Alice and Dorothy, who found themselves awakening from their adventures surrounded by loved ones, I remained trapped in between the pages of a fairytale book. And I was still stuck with a frog who believed himself to be a prince. A prince who needed help in breaking his spell.

I peer over my shoulder.

Aneurin sat quietly, awake and watching me from the pillow.

"Good morning," I murmured groggily, breaking the silence. "How'd you sleep?"

"You talk in your sleep, you know," he replied, resting his chin on a webbed hand.

My cheeks warmed with embarrassment. "What do you mean? N-no I don't..." I said, a little horrified.

"You do," he insisted.

"What did I say?" I asked, raising a brow.

He smiled. "Lots of odd, random words. It would be quite amusing if one was not trying to sleep."

"I'm sorry," I said, biting my lip.

Nico had brought it up a few times, but it was usually only on nights when I was utterly drained. After everything we had been through, it was safe to say that exhaustion had taken its toll and qualified last night for one of sleep-talking.

"'Tis no matter," Aneurin said with a sigh. "But I would like to break the fast this morning soon."

"Breakfast?" I asked. "Is that what you mean?"

Aneurin mumbled under his breath something about me being a peasant again, but I just pretended to not hear him.

Just to avoid another argument. It was too early.

When he didn't give me a clear response, I sighed and pushed myself to the edge of the bed. "I suppose we can see if Snow-White and the rest of the men are awake," I began. "I'm sure they'll have food ready."

After I pushed myself up from the mattress, my fingers instinctively traced over the fabric of my green dress, attempting to smooth out the creases. The rumpled appearance of the garment gave away I had slept in it. I slid my hand into my pocket, happy to discover the jewels from Hansel and Gretel remained. Maybe Arch would have some insight into their significance.

I slipped my shoes back on, feeling the lingering chill from yesterday's pond plunge. They were still damp, but I didn't have much choice. It was this, or going barefoot again. But while the house was clean, I still felt more comfortable with something on my feet.

"Are you ready?" I asked, glancing over my shoulder back at Aneurin, who remained sitting on the pillow. He shrugged and crossed his arms against his chest silently.

Rolling my eyes, I moved to his side of the bed and picked him up carefully into my hands. No matter how many times I held him, I still couldn't get over how small he was. How delicate he felt between my fingers. I could always feel the pounding of his heart, and the way his body jolted in an unexpected fear.

"I'm not going to drop you," I reassured him as I placed him on my shoulder.

"All you'd have to do is squeeze me," he replied. "That would be the end of me."

"But what fun would that be?" I teased, trying to pry a smile from him. "I wouldn't tell people that so freely. It might be too much of a temptation."

"*Josephine.*"

"I didn't say that *I* was tempted," I argued.

"I would hope not," he replied.

There was a certain gravity to his response, a trust building between us that I couldn't ignore. I was responsible for him, just as much as he was responsible for me. In whatever way that worked for a frog.

I didn't say anything more as I began the descent back down the stairs and through the various rooms. As I reached the last step, I could hear Snow-White's humming coming from the kitchen again. This time, I didn't linger to listen. Instead, I moved with a purpose into the space, determined to get the both of us some breakfast.

"Good morning, Snow!" I said as I strolled into the room.

She stood behind the counter in the kitchen, a dusting of white flour adorning her cheeks. Pausing from her baking, she greeted us with a warm smile. "Oh, good morning! Did you both sleep well?"

Before Aneurin could comment on my sleep-talking, I replied, "Yes! We did. Thank you."

"I'm so glad to hear it." She motioned to the counter in front of her. "I'm making an elderberry pie for dessert tonight."

It wasn't one I'd ever tried before, but based on the mess of items around the counter, it looked promising. I was almost always willing to try something at least once.

Snow lifted a bowl of berries and pushed it my way. "I know it's not much, but if you're willing to wait just a few more minutes, I'd be happy to fry up some eggs and toast some bread for you both. I just want to finish the pie first." She hesitated, eyeing Aneurin. "Do frogs eat eggs and toast?"

"I would love a plate," he said with a nod.

Taking a berry from the bowl, I popped one into my mouth and smiled at the sweetness. "I think that sounds fantastic."

"A hearty breakfast sounds wonderful," Aneurin agreed.

At least, for once, there was something we both could agree on—food.

I pulled a chair from the table, bringing it to the counter, where I could watch Snow-White as she finished her work on the elderberry pie. I admired how graceful her hands were with the dough as she kneaded it.

"Where did you learn how to bake?" I asked, lifting my gaze from the half-formed pie.

She brushed a strand of her hair from her nose with a puff of air. "I had to learn much in the castle, and quickly," she admitted after a moment. "But, thankfully, everyone was patient with me. I was required to tend to a great many things, many of which were tasks done by multiple servants. But my stepmother took great pleasure in seeing me struggle. There were many nights in which she would demand a meal made by my hands, and my hands only—knowing I'd been newly appointed to the kitchen. It was unmistakable she wished for me to fail—to humiliate me."

"And did you?" Aneurin asked as he settled more firmly against my shoulder blade.

I winced a little at the odd sensation and carefully moved him to the table. I ignored the side eye he shot my way before he returned his attention back to Snow.

"Oh, of course I did. Everything I made was never good enough. But with practice, I perfected several dishes. So much so, the cook would secretly have me come assist on nights when he needed the most help. The queen was never the wiser."

I sighed. "I'm so sorry about what happened to you. And how she treated you."

Snow wrinkled her nose as she pressed against the dough with her hands. "You need not be sorry for me, Jo. My journey has led me here." She lifted her hazel gaze to meet my eyes and smiled. "I truly believe my father led me to this house. He knew of my trials...he heard my prayers. I would not be here without his help."

It seemed, no matter how tough things had been, she miraculously was still able to find the silver lining to her situation. With her strong belief in her father rescuing her—even if it was from the other side—she was exactly what I'd expected in a fairytale princess.

But a part of me also felt a twinge of anger towards the father who had remarried such a cruel woman. Why were all stepmothers in fairytales awful—or, like this case, straight up evil? As I started to rattle off a few titles in my head, I heard Aneurin ask, "Where are the men this morning?"

"They already left," Snow replied. "Hunter and Trapper like to set out on the trails in the forest by dawn, but they took Axe with them. Herb and Topper went to the gardens, and I believe Arch and Stitches are conducting lessons today by the pond."

"Lessons?"

Snow opened a nearby drawer near the counter, pulling free a long, rolling pin. Nodding, she said, "Stitches apparently has only learned a few words to get by. While his arithmetic is good, for his sewing needs, his reading and writing are a bit lacking. So, Arch agreed to teach him."

"That's really..." I trailed off. It was sad to think that someone hadn't been given the chance to learn how to do some of the most basic things in life.

How many people still suffered from the same lack of education in my own world? Even my dad hated to read because he struggled with turning his letters around. I swallowed, trying to make my response less blunt than what was in my mind. "That's nice of Arch."

"It is," Snow agreed thoughtfully.

"Is that common...for someone to not..."

"Most peasants do not require such knowledge," Aneurin interjected. "And with being an illegitimate..."

Snow dropped the rolling pin on the counter, startling my attention away from Aneurin. "I would ask, Your Highness, if you would avoid using such a term here." Her tone was stern. Her eyes met his, as she slowly shook her head. Her hardened expression a shiver run down my spine.

He seemed flustered, as he shifted his weight between his legs before nodding slowly. "Of course." He didn't add anything more before turning his attention to the bowl of berries.

Snow was quiet then as she continued to focus on rolling out the top layer of dough against the counter.

When she slid the piece over the bottom of the dish, I broke the awkward silence. "It's a little weird how quiet this place gets without the men."

"It does, at first," she agreed as she began to pinch the edges of the pie together. Snow lifted her gaze to the kitchen door. "They all go about their tasks and come back throughout the day."

"I'm sure they've been grateful to have you here, then."

Snow-White smiled but shrugged. "I suppose they are," she explained. "I feel bad they feel the need to check up on me during the day, as though I'm some child."

"They care," Aneurin said with a nod. "And rightfully so."

"They do," she agreed, flashing him a small smile. "I suppose if providing a few meals throughout the day grants me a place to stay, a warm bed to sleep in, and good friends to share it with..." She lifted her finished pie for us to see. "It is well worth it."

"Indeed!" Aneurin agreed.

"Now, how about those eggs, hmm?" she asked and moved quickly about the kitchen.

Snow-White had left her mess on the counter, and I figured cleaning was the least I could do in helping her. Before rising from my chair, I popped a final berry into my mouth. I gathered the porcelain bowl she'd mixed her dough in, and a few of the leftover ingredients. Then I realized I had to find my way around the kitchen.

She smiled at me, pointing to a few of the places where things belonged whenever I paused in confusion.

To be honest, I was mostly lost. This certainly was not a modern set up. There were no garbage bags and no dishwasher. There wasn't even plumbing. At least, not how I was used to.

I did admire the contraption that she explained to me as their "sink." Arch had designed a system that brought up small increments of water to the kitchen through hollowed tree branches and buckets. But only enough to clean a few dishes at a time.

While she fried the eggs in a large iron skillet, I toasted bread over the fire, sitting by the hearth beside her. My childhood was littered with disastrous, burnt marshmallows from Fourth of July parties. But I was proud of myself when I lifted the perfectly golden-brown bread for Snow to see.

She smiled wide in approval.

As we pulled the eggs and toast from the hearth, I decided there was no way I was going to share an ounce of this with Aneurin. No matter how much he might beg me.

Snow-White gave me a plate then loaded a small bowl for him.

Aneurin also seemed delighted at the fact that he wouldn't have to share with me.

I sat back down in the chair by the counter and ate quietly beside the frog. I watched him from the corner of my eye as he carefully and delicately nibbled on the bread and eggs.

When I had nearly finished my plate, Aneurin took a step back from his bowl and focused on the princess, who had already begun a new mixture of dough for a new pie. "I do wish to inquire about your kingdom," Aneurin said as he sat back down on the counter. "If you are willing to discuss such matters with me."

Snow-White lifted her arm against her forehead, brushing a wisp of a flyaway hair from her face before returning her attention to him. "Of course," she replied.

"If the queen dies, what will you do?" he asked, tilting his head as though he were unsure of how to ask his question. "Will you return to your home? Will you go back to claim your crown?"

She pressed her lips together and studied the dough in her hands. "I suppose, if it's safe to do so," Snow-White replied after a pause. "If the people wish for me to be their ruler."

"But you are your father's daughter."

"I am," she replied quickly. "And I know he would want what's best for me."

"If such a thing were to come to pass, what would happen to your relations with these men?"

"*Aneurin!*" I hissed, dropping my fork onto my plate.

"I'm not quite sure I understand," Snow-White said, starting to knead the dough in the bowl again. "What do you mean?"

"It is very clear that the gentleman who sews rather well has taken a liking to you," Aneurin gestured towards the door. "From his display last night, it seems his intention is to court you, if he could."

"Aneurin!" I tried again, this time poking his side. "Knock it off." I wanted to scoop up the frog and flee the room. How could he think asking questions like this was okay?

Snow-White raised an eyebrow as she glanced at Aneurin. "Are you suggesting there could be a future between Stitches and me?"

"I'm simply trying to ask how could such a thing work?" Aneurin clarified. "You are meant to be a future ruler. In theory, we have been ordained by God for our thrones."

"What do you mean? He is a man, is he not?" Snow-White asked.

"He is, but—" Aneurin began.

She cut him off. "It is our hearts that choose whom we love, is it not?"

"Perhaps."

"There is no 'perhaps,' Prince Aneurin," Snow said firmly, shaking her head. "If my heart and his heart speak to each other, it is our decision about what our future will look like. A title is merely a title. Of course, at times, it most certainly can be of great importance…" She shook her head. "But a loveless marriage…I saw what it did to my father. I've suffered the consequences of his decision. I will never force myself into the hands of a noble, purely because of his station. We are all deserving of love."

"That's what I said," I mumbled.

Aneurin glanced at the princess, then turned back to me. "You told me to keep my eyes open."

"Jo speaks the truth," Snow-White interjected. "I know that as an heir to your kingdom, as a man with the expectations of a king-ship, it may not be the same. The pressures of each of our roles can differ. But I can promise you that life is not always about the posi-tions we are born into. It is who we *choose* to be. It is the role we take on by ourselves, for ourselves…and at times for others."

Aneurin peered at her, a glint of a smile growing on his lips. "I have never heard wiser words before."

"I hope that the woman who breaks your spell is everything you've ever hoped for," she said sincerely. "And perfect by no other measure as determined by someone else."

He cast his eyes downward, fixating on his webbed fingers, as if contemplating the notion of having something exclusively his own for the first time.

There was a vulnerability in his gaze, a sense of longing that struck a chord within me. My heart panged in sympathy for him. I observed him, unsure of how to offer comfort in such an unusual circumstance. Was it possible to hug a frog?

Maybe the lack of affection and love was another aspect to this. Maybe his parents hadn't done a good job in showing him what love could be….*should* be. And maybe there was some truth to his own words.

I didn't understand everything about his world—didn't under-stand the politics of a royal family. But I knew what it was to love someone. And I knew what it was to feel not good enough.

"I know that Stitches has feelings for me," Snow-White admit-ted after a prolonged moment of silence. She lifted the dough from the bowl and placed the mixture on the counter. Her fingers began to slowly knead it again. "When I was a servant, I was too occu-pied with work to ever imagine anyone taking a liking to me. I was ashamed. I was a princess suddenly reduced to a scullery maid."

Her words hit me harder than expected. Even though I'd heard her story thousands of times growing up, I hadn't thought about what it would have been like to endure such a change.

"When I found my way here to this cottage, I was neither princess nor maid. I was just...*me*. It was also the first time I had ever held the gaze of a man who did not look at me as a prize or a possession, but an equal." She looked away, a small tear rolling down her cheek. "If I ever had to give up my right to my father's throne, for just a single moment of the pleasure I've felt with him—with all of them,—I would do so without a second thought."

Aneurin's emerald eyes were glazing over with tears.

I didn't know frogs could cry, but maybe he could.

"You are brave," he finally replied, his voice full of emotion. "You possess the heart of a king."

Snow-White flashed a small, sad smile. "I have known my own moments of cowardice. And I would not consider choosing to love being brave."

"I think it counts," I countered. "Loving someone takes bravery."

Her smile grew as she lifted her gaze to meet mine. "Loving and choosing to love can be two very different things."

I laughed. "Agreed."

Just then, several loud knocks echoed throughout the house.

"I wonder who that could be," Snow whispered, peering at me.

I turned in my seat, gazing at the front of the tree house, towards the small living space. "We're the only ones home, right?" I asked.

She nodded.

There was a pause before another series of loud knocks came from the front room.

This couldn't be happening so soon, could it? I shakily stood up, staring at the door. Was I going to find an old hag selling apples outside? My heart sank into my stomach at the thought. We'd just defeated one witch yesterday. Were we really going to have to face another one so soon?

EIGHTEEN

Snow, Aneurin, and I sat in the kitchen, listening to the incessant knocking. The visitor wasn't going away.

I released a breath. "I guess I'll...go see who that is," I offered.

Aneurin's small, webbed fingers gently grasped my wrist, drawing my attention to his earnest gaze. His emerald eyes studied mine, as if he were trying to discern my thoughts.

"Josephine, allow me to accompany you," he said—commanded. His tone more insistent than I'd ever heard it.

I wasn't going to deny him this request. Not when I was scared shitless. If there was one villain who had always scared the living daylights out of me as a child, it had been the queen from Snow-White. There was something about the way she could seamlessly change her appearance from a beautiful, young woman to a creepy, old hag. I'd never quite understood how Snow-White ever fell for that disguise.

However, this Snow-White seemed to have a better understanding of the world. A firmer grasp of the reality she was living in. More so than the two-dimensional version I'd read about in my childhood.

Picking up Aneurin gently, I placed him on my shoulder.

"Do you suppose it's the queen?" he whispered into my ear. He was smarter than I gave him credit for.

But I didn't want to jump to that conclusion. Not yet.

Snow-White was the first to move, her fingers grazing over the tops of the chairs as she walked towards the door.

My stomach started to twist with knots as I watched Snow-White. Aneurin and I had only just arrived in this story, and I actually liked it here. Was this really the infamous moment so soon?

Another knock. This most definitely was *not* one of the men.

"I'm coming!" Snow called as she reached for the doorknob.

My heart raced in my chest as I hurried past her, catching her by surprise. With a quick movement, I reached the wooden barrier and placed my hand on it, halting her in her tracks.

"You should hide," I whispered. "Let me."

Aneurin's webbed fingers were holding tightly on the shoulder of my dress.

Snow observed me with a raised brow, her expression curious yet silent. But she took a step back. Perhaps this wouldn't be as difficult as I had anticipated.

I felt her gaze following me as I reached for the handle, the moment stretching out as if time itself had slowed. With a tug, the door creaked open, revealing a glimpse of the day just beyond.

The sun was shimmering against the dew of the grass just below, and there, on the entrance of the porch, stood a tall, slim woman.

Her hair was brown and curly. It hung past her shoulders. Her eyes were dark, almost a strange shade of gray, while her lips were a lipstick shade of red. Around her shoulders, hung silky shreds of fabric of all sizes—all of them colorful and adorned with different threading, contrasting against her brown and gray clothing.

As she met my gaze, her lips curled into a warm smile. "Well, hello there..." the woman said with a half curtsy. "Are you the lady of the house?"

"There is no lady of the house," I replied. "I can't say I'm all that interested in what you're selling, either."

"No lady?" The woman said with an amused laugh. "Are *you* not a lady?"

"Nope. I'm a...peasant." I doubted my response would work, but it was worth a try.

I heard Aneurin choke on my shoulder, but he quickly recovered, releasing the most frog-like croak I'd ever heard from him.

The woman stared at me, apparently unsure of what to make of my response. "Well…of course," the woman finally said. "Still, I would only implore you to give me just a moment of your time."

"I think I've already given you that." There was something off about this woman. While she wasn't the hag I was expecting, I wondered if this was the queen in disguise.

I started to shut the door, but the woman was quick to grab the handle, shaking her head.

"You need not be startled—"

"But I am," I admitted. "You'd have to be lost in the forest in order to find this place, and you don't look lost."

"Lost?" She tilted her head. "My goodness. All the village raves about this glorious cottage in the woods. All the men who come gather here…"

I shook my head, pushing the door again, but her hand stopped me from completely shutting it.

"Please," she attempted again. "These items may be of use to you and the others. I have scarves, shawls, and sashes. I hoped in a cottage occupied by men, that perhaps one or two would have taken a wife…or employed a maid…"

She didn't finish her thought. Instead, her gaze moved up and down the length of me. I certainly wasn't what she was expecting. It was apparent she didn't know how to handle me.

"You're not selling anything else?" I asked.

The woman raised an eyebrow before glancing over my shoulder. "Not today, my dear."

I narrowed my gaze, watching her for a moment.

She refocused on me and smiled again. "Are you truly all alone?"

Out of the corner of my eye, I saw Snow-White motioned towards herself, just enough to draw my attention away. Her cheeks were growing pink as she remained out of sight.

Arching my brow inquisitively, I attempted to decipher the silent message she conveyed, careful not to reveal anything to the unfamiliar figure in our midst.

"I said, is there someone else at home with you, girl?" The woman's voice grew more insistent, but her attempt to address me "girl" ticked me off.

"How about we start with names?" I replied. "Do you have one?"

"A name?" The woman's scoff was dismissive. "Of course."

Well, that wasn't particularly helpful.

I clicked my tongue before trying again. "My name is Jo. What is yours?"

"They call me Margarette," she replied.

Out of the corner of my eye, I saw Snow begin to emerge from the side. I internally groaned. What was she doing? Didn't she know the risk she was taking? I tried to side-step her—tried to block the sight of her, but it was obvious by the way Margarette's gray eyes widened that she had seen the princess.

The woman might as well be selling apples by the way her lips curled into a smile. "Well, who is this pretty lass?" Margarette asked, her eyes sparkling with interest.

Snow peeked over my shoulder, stepping into full view.

I fought the urge to pull her back behind me.

"Did you mention you were selling shawls?" Snow-White asked.

"Indeed, I did, my dear," Margarette replied in a tooth-rotting sweet tone, pulling a soft pink one from her shoulder. It was lined with several embroidered flowers.

"I have been in need of one for a while now. The nights are starting to cool, and I haven't been able to make one successfully…"

Nodding thoughtfully, the woman pulled another one from her shoulder, this time one of dark blue with dark green embroidered vines. "I think this one might just be your color."

Snow lifted a hand to caress the shawl, her eyes were wide with awe at the beautiful fabric.

I bit the inside of my cheek, silently staring at them. I felt a tug on my shoulder and turned to see Aneurin staring at me.

"Should we not be concerned about this woman?" he whispered into my ear.

"Yes. I don't have a good feeling about this," I mumbled, hoping I wouldn't be overheard.

Margarette pulled one more piece of fabric from around her neck. The red satin was smooth and rich, dotted with small white rose buds that lined from top to bottom. It was much thinner than the other two she'd pulled.

"What about this?" Margarette asked, showing the sash to her. "Such a beautiful woman such as yourself should be wearing things like this."

"You're too kind," Snow-White said, pressing a hand to her blushing cheek.

With a hearty laugh, Margarette lifted her hands with the sash, coming closer to the princess's side. "Hardly, my dear. Would you like to have a try? To see if it truly would suit you?"

"Oh, but I couldn't. I don't have much money, you see, and I could never afford..."

"Nonsense," Margarette replied. "Do not worry so much about such trivial matters."

Since when was money *trivial?* I didn't care if I was stuck in a fairytale. Money was important no matter where you were.

"I'd even be willing to make an exchange," Margarette continued.

Snow-White's face lit up at the idea. "Are you quite sure?"

"Of course, my pet," Margarette cooed. She pulled the long, red satin sash around Snow-White's waist.

I saw the way the woman peered at me as she tied the sash. Her eyes became almost a shade darker, and her lips curled up in an unsettlingly smug manner, as though she were silently saying, "Watch what I'm about to do."

I was almost certain this was the queen. It had to be.

"I don't think that's such a good idea," I blurted in, pressing my hand against Snow's shoulder. I wracked my brain for anything I could say to stop her. "Those are surely last year's fashion—"

She flashed a smile from over her shoulder and shook her head. "Don't worry, Jo. I'll try to not fall in love with it too much. After all, perhaps Stitches could make me something like—"

The woman yanked the sash tightly then, causing Snow to gasp aloud. Her cheeks grew a shade pinker as she pressed a hand against her chest.

"Are you sure it should be this tight? I—" Snow-White started, but was interrupted.

"It is the latest fashion, my dear," Margarette explained with a gentle smile. "They say the thinner the girl, the better the breeding."

"No one says that," I scoffed.

"You'll make the men's mouths water," Margarette laughed. "You'll have countless options." She tugged again, wrapping a strand around Snow's waist again, drawing another ragged breath from the princess.

"That's enough!" I exclaimed, trying to push Margarette away.

"I'm simply showing her how to wear it," she reasoned, yanking on the red satin sash harder. "Beauty does not always come easily." The woman twisted the last portion of the fabric and pulled as hard as she could, her veins poked from underneath her skin.

The princess grimaced, moving a hand to the doorframe to steady herself. "My stepmother used to say that often to me."

"What a wise woman," Margarette replied. "*Snow-White.*"

How had I been so stupid? I'd forgotten about this part of the story. Snow was not just visited once with the poison apple, but a time before with a sash.

The look on my face must've said it all because I heard Aneurin ask from my shoulder, "What?"

I didn't bother to respond. Instead, I acted on instinct, thrusting my hands against Margarette, attempting to push her away from

Snow. My intention was to push her off the porch. I'd already been responsible for one witch's death. Two didn't seem like such a big deal if I was saving yet another person's life.

To my surprise and disappointment, she didn't topple over but merely staggered back a few paces.

"What do you think you're doing?" she demanded, her voice tinged with anger and confusion.

I put my head down and continued to maneuver her down the front of the treehouse.

"Get out of here!" I yelled back, my heart was racing wildly in my chest. "Stay away from us!"

The woman only began to laugh as she clung to the handrail of the porch.

"I don't know who you think I am…or who you think you are…"

"I'm her friend," I countered, digging my fingernails into her hand. "And you're never going to come back here."

"She's deceived you," she continued, reaching for my arms; her fingers sinking into my skin. "She's a devious pretender and—"

"One day, you will pay for what you've done to Snow-White and her father," I hissed through my teeth.

Margarette, or whatever her real name was, smiled broadly. "He was a fool," she countered, her nails piercing my skin. I winced at the pain.

"*You* were the fool, coming here," I ground out.

Then I saw a flick of a pink tongue.

Suddenly Margarette was rubbing her eyes and stumbling back down the stairs.

Aneurin.

"Get back to Snow," he ordered. "We must get her inside."

"Did you just—"

"Now is not the time for questions," Aneurin replied. "Now!"

I turned on my heel and headed straight for the doorway.

Snow was a heap on the floor, the shawls still tight around her.

I placed Aneurin on the floorboards and hoisted her up the best I could. Wrapping her arm around my shoulder, I tried to drag her back inside, watching the door as we moved further into the house. What if Margarette came back? What if she tried to get inside? Not only would she try to kill Snow-White, but she'd most likely come after *us*, too.

"Close the door, Aneurin!" I called, gently laying the princess on the floor of the front room. I wasn't even sure if a frog was capable of doing so, but I wanted to give him the benefit of the doubt.

I turned my attention back to Snow. Her cheeks were flushed, and her breathing was way too slow. My eyes drifted to the sash around her waist. I could see how strained the fabric was, wrapped around her.

"I'm going to call for help," Aneurin called from the porch. "Come shut the door behind me, Josephine!"

"What do you mean?" I asked, glancing at the doorway, only to find it empty.

Aneurin was gone.

Frustration zipped through me. The timing sucked. I couldn't have something happen to him, too. I couldn't lose him.

Was the witch waiting for him at the bottom of the porch? Would she use him for some sort of weird potion? What if she killed him for his disgusting habit of licking his eye?

"Aneurin!" I yelled as I struggled to tug the sash free from Snow-White's waist. Tears flooded my eyes as I turned her onto her side, looking for a way to free her from the stupid piece of fabric.

"I should have known," I murmured, shaking my head. "I *knew*..." A sob lodged in my throat as I struggled against the knotted satin. "I'm so sorry..."

"Get out of the way!"

Trapper's voice startled me from my place beside her. I turned to look over my shoulder to see him barreling towards me, wielding a small pocket knife in his hand. Aneurin was clenched in his other.

Within seconds, his blade sliced through the satin, releasing Snow from suffocation.

Aneurin hopped out of the man's hand and sat beside my leg, watching nervously.

Trapper dropped the knife by his knee and lifted Snow up to sit; his hand gently tapped her cheek. "Get her some water," he commanded, keeping his gaze on her.

I rose to my feet, dashing to the kitchen. I didn't know what to grab. Where was I going to get water?

My gaze locked on a small pitcher by the open window. I grabbed it. Running back through the kitchen, I moved as quickly as I could back to Trapper's side.

His lip curled in annoyance as he looked between the large, wooden pitcher and me. "A cup, Josephine. A *cup* would be helpful."

"But I don't—"

"Never mind," he growled, yanking it from my hands. Splatters of water droplets landed between us.

I sunk back to my knees, watching as he lifted the pitcher to Snow's lips carefully, tilting it just so.

Her eyes were still closed, her lips were only slightly parted.

Please don't be dead.

I felt Aneurin's weight as he hopped into my lap, curling into my open hand. Looking down, I saw his emerald gaze staring back up at me.

A webbed hand patted mine, a silent act of comfort.

"Come on, Snow," Trapper murmured. "Drink the water."

But she remained unresponsive.

Turning his dark gaze to me, he demanded, "What happened?"

I shivered, biting my lip. "A woman came to the door, and she was selling things."

"Christ," he seethed "You both answered the door?"

"Well, *I* did…" I admitted. "It was my intention to send the woman away. But then Snow—"

"You should have never *opened* it!" Trapper argued. "I don't understand why you would, considering you are well aware of Snow's circumstances. That door was not to be opened to anyone but my brothers or myself."

I understood why he was so angry. He cared quite a bit about Snow and her wellbeing. But his words were still frustrating.

"Sir," Aneurin interrupted. "You are not being fair to Jo—"

"And you think this is fair to Snow?" he retorted, gesturing at her with his hand. "Is any of this *fair* to Snow?"

"I didn't just let the woman walk into the house," I countered, biting back my anger. "I tried to make her go away. I fought her off!"

"That explains the strange woman I saw hobbling away," Trapper sighed. "I was coming back after I'd realized I'd forgotten my skinning knife. As soon as I saw her..." He pressed his lips firmly together, before drawing his wide-eyed gaze back to Snow.

As he'd spoken, her hand had slowly found his, her knuckles were nearly white from how hard she was squeezing his hand.

Her eyes slowly opened. "T-Trapper?" she asked.

"Snow..." he breathed.

"W-What happened?" Snow asked, pushing herself up slightly, moving her gaze to me and Aneurin. "What happened to the—"

"What's going on here?" Arch's voice filled the room.

He and Stitches stood side-by-side, watching the three of us—or rather, four—on the floor.

The latter was obviously struggling to contain his emotions.

Arch lifted his hand to Stitches' shoulder and gave him a gentle pat. "Did something happen to Snow?" he asked.

"They had a *visitor*," Trapper snapped. "Snow was nearly killed."

"K-Killed?" Snow asked, her gaze flitting from his to mine.

I could sense the lingering questions in her eyes. I could almost read her thoughts as she studied me. Was it true? Had she almost died? These were questions I was still grappling with myself. All I could manage in response was a slight, terse nod.

"I knew it was your stepmother," I replied softly. "As soon as she said your name."

"My name?" she asked, wrinkling her brow in confusion. "What does that have to do with anything?"

"Neither of us ever told her what it was," I explained as I slid my gaze to Aneurin, still in my lap.

He bobbed his head in agreement.

"There was something about her," I continued. "How she spoke to us. How she looked at you."

"My name," Snow whispered, leaning back against Trapper.

He lifted his hand to cup her cheek gently. "You understand what it would do to us to lose you," he murmured to her.

This was the first time I'd ever seen him be so gentle.

Snow bit her bottom lip as she moved her hand over his. "This is my fault," she said. "I shouldn't have been lured by her kindness."

Trapper closed his eyes and shook his head. He moved his hand away from Snow's face and helped her to sit upright on her own. The piercing glare he sent my way made it obvious that he blamed me. And he was right.

I should have known better. I shouldn't have even opened the door to the strange woman.

"Many are deceived by kindness," Arch reasoned from where he stood. "No one can fault anyone for such a thing."

"So, are we to just stay here day in and day out, to protect the princess?" Trapper asked. "Who will complete all the tasks?"

"I will stay," Stitches replied, taking a step forward. His eyes continued to watch Snow-White on the floor. "My work usually keep me in the home as it is."

"It's clear we cannot leave her alone with the girl—" Trapper continued, gesturing to me.

"That's not fair," I interjected.

"No? You were the only one here with her, and this was the first time anything like this happened."

I moved Aneurin from my lap to the floor and stood up. "I tried to protect her."

"You're more trouble than you or your frog prince are worth."

My anger flared. "If you think for a single moment that I want anything to do with any of this—"

"Go home, then!" Trapper shouted. "Go back to whatever little hovel hole you came from."

"Sir!" Shaken, Aneurin's voice echoed from the floor below, but neither of us paid attention to him.

"Do not speak to her that way," the prince continued.

"I *tried*," I said through gritted teeth.

"And you *failed*," he replied. "If I hadn't come home, Snow would be dead. And it would have been your fault!"

A hand touched my shoulder, pulling me away from Trapper and his angry set of dark blue eyes.

Arch stood beside me, his lips were pressed into a hard line before he said, "*Enough*." Trapper lifted his hand, extending a finger in my direction. But before he could verbally attack me again, Arch added, "I said *enough*. There will be no more fighting about this."

Trapper clicked his tongue before releasing a heavy sigh. "That's *rich* coming from you."

"Go back to Hunter. I'm sure he's waiting for you."

"If anything happens…I will not be one to hear of it," he threatened, turning to look at Snow again.

Stitches knelt down beside her, his arm gently encircled her waist. He stared back at Trapper. "We'll see you and your brother at the evening meal."

The two men glared at one another for a long moment. There was something there—something that felt deeper and heavier than just the occurrence of the witch.

Trapper released a breath and slid his knife back into his belt pocket and turning on his heel

Once he was gone, Aneurin mumbled, "He has a *foul* temper."

NINETEEN

Dinner was quiet. Too quiet.

Not a single person knew what to say as we gathered around the long table. A line of small, yellow candles down the middle illuminating our solemn faces.

While Topper and Herb served a bowl of stew to everyone, I could feel their eyes watching the princess ever so carefully.

Axe had even graced her with a small smile as he strolled to his chair with his steaming serving.

Trapper was the last to join us, and I knew his late arrival had been purposeful. He'd come in quietly with Bones, stopping by the door to remove his dark gray jacket before coming to take his place.

Our eyes met from across the table, just as Snow-White moved to place full bowl in front of him.

"You didn't need to do that," he mumbled, keeping his eyes on the food.

"I did," she replied. "For helping me today."

"I did nothing," Trapper replied curtly. "Now sit."

"Trapper—" she started, but he didn't look up. Instead, he lifted the lone spoon by his hand and dug into the potatoes and carrots.

"There's no need for your hostility," Stitches said as he pulled a hand through his blond curls. He leaned forward from across the table, propping himself up on his elbows.

Trapper shoved a spoonful of beef into his mouth. He obviously wasn't interested in engaging with Stitches.

"You can be as angry as you wish," Stitches continued. "But your anger directed at Snow or Jo does no one any good. We must direct our anger towards the queen. *She* is the real enemy."

"I know who the enemy is," Trapper mumbled between potatoes. "I'm not daft."

"But you're being a fool," Stitches replied. "You've been quick to point your finger at anyone who comes in your way."

Trapper slammed his fist onto the table.

Everyone stared and waited.

Aneurin stayed close to my bowl of stew as he nibbled on a large, round carrot.

"I think we're *all* fools," Trapper replied. "We have truly lost our minds, the whole lot of us. Thinking that we could protect a princess from a witch. And then to allow a stranger into our home," he gestured towards me. "We have sunk *low*, men. And yet, lower we continue to sink." He looked at Stitches then, shaking his head. "Some of us have allowed ourselves to *feel*."

"Is feeling *that* bad for you, brother?" Stitches asked, crossing his arms against his chest. "Is it truly so terrible?"

Trapper's eyes narrowed. "I would stop while you're ahead, Stitches," he warned.

"I would *suggest* that you both stop," Arch said as he took his seat at the head of the table. "Both of you are acting like fools."

They both just stared at one another, their gazes challenged each other to break the silence first, but neither of them faltered. Not even when Snow-White took a seat beside me.

"*Enough* already," Axe replied with a heavy sigh. "Snow is safe and sound. We will all devise a plan to be ready for the queen should she return."

"She *will* return," Trapper retorted, turning to glare at him.

Axe lifted his fork in warning.

It was only then that Trapper slowly lowered his gaze back down to his stew.

The table once again became silent, aside from the soft sounds of eating.

I couldn't help but watch Trapper as he lifted another spoonful of stew to his lips. I saw the way he peered up at Snow-White from underneath his lashes. As though he didn't want anyone to notice.

This wasn't just about the confrontation with the woman. There was something deeper brewing beneath the surface. As his gaze briefly flickered towards Snow once more, it became clear what he had never openly admitted—Trapper loved Snow, too.

"We all know you have no heart anyway," Stitches mumbled, breaking the silence. "You've made that abundantly clear through the years."

"Stitches," Arch warned. "*Enough.*"

Trapper closed his eyes, crossing his arms against his chest, silently seething. He clearly wanted to say a great many things by just the way his brow creased. When he opened his eyes, his blue gaze fell on me.

Maybe I was looking at him too softly—with too much compassion—because Trapper's eyes instantly turned cold and distant.

"You're right," he remarked. "I'm glad I've left no question of where I stand with your absurd sentiments. I care not for anyone, *especially* Snow." He stood up abruptly, pushing his chair back with a harsh scrape against the floor.

"Trapper," Snow-White called, rising to her feet.

He turned to her. "Don't," he commanded.

"But, Trapper, I…" There was a tremble in her voice as her words drifted to silence.

He ignored her and glanced at his brother beside him. "I'll see you in the morning, Hunter." Then Trapper stalked out of the room.

The princess pressed the back of her hand against her lips as her eyes followed Trapper's departure. Glimmering tears rolled down her cheeks, despite how quickly she tried to brush them from sight.

Stitches cleared his throat. "I apologize," he murmured.

"Excuse me," Snow-White gasped as she turned from the table.

We all watched in silence as she fled, her hurried footsteps echoing against the wooden floors as she darted towards the stairs to her room.

Our attention shifted to each other, silently taking in what had just occurred.

Even Stitches appeared surprised by the unfolding events, his cheeks flushed with embarrassment.

"Well, that did not go well," Herb commented, shaking his head.

"*Clearly*, you dimwit," Topper retorted with a huff.

"I should go check on her," I said, pushing my bowl of stew away.

"It should be me," Stitches said with a heavy sigh. He pushed himself up from his chair, keeping his gaze on the table. "I should apologize to her for my part in all that."

"I think you both should give her time," Arch replied.

"Trapper cannot just say he doesn't care—" Stitches started.

"We all know he didn't mean it," Arch sighed. "Even *he* knows there's no truth to his words."

"Then he should apologize! He should take them back!" Stitches said, slamming his fist onto the table just as the man he was condemning had done.

"I'm in agreement," Arch replied. "But not now."

Stitches released a groan before shaking his head. "I'm going to go take a walk," he muttered.

No one stopped him as he grabbed an old, orange jacket hanging on the coat hooks near the door and shoved his arms into its sleeves almost angrily. The cups on the table rattled as he slammed the door, disappearing into the night.

Bones lifted his head from his nap to peer up at the commotion.

A shiver ran down my spine.

"Are you alright?" Aneurin asked gently, releasing one of the soft carrots of the stew and hopped closer to my hand.

I didn't flinch as his webbed hand touched my skin.

There was a strange solace to be found in how he tried to comfort me.

"I am," I replied softly.

One by one, each of the remaining men pushed themselves from their chairs before disappearing up the steps, leaving only Topper, Arch, and I to handle the dishes.

"This is not how I envisioned tonight ending," Arch confessed, pressing his thumb and forefinger against the bridge of his nose.

"I'm sure things will smooth over," Topper replied. "We never fight for long."

"I hope you're right," the first said. "For I feel this to be much different from anything we've experienced before."

Topper leaned back in his chair with a groan before glancing at the table. "I suppose I'll be the one left to do the cleaning tonight."

"If you don't mind." Arch sighed. "To be honest, I would like to speak with Jo. Do you mind tending to cleaning up tonight?"

"Nothing that I'm not already used to," Topper mumbled before yawning and pushing himself up from his chair. The man bowed his head in my direction, then rolled up his sleeves before collecting the plates from the table and disappeared into the kitchen.

"Let's take a walk," Arch said, jerking his chin towards the door.

"And me?" Aneurin asked as he sat atop the table. His eyes narrowed as they drifted between the two of us. "Am *I* permitted to go on this promenade?"

"I would ask that you'd allow me time with Josephine. Alone," Arch said.

"So, I am to just leave Josephine unchaperoned with you?" Aneurin asked, shaking his head. "I will *not* permit such a thing."

"I'll be alright," I said, pressing my finger gently to the top of his head. It was now a gesture of affection rather than annoyance.

The prince looked at me again, as his gaze narrowed slightly. His tongue flicked against his eye.

He wasn't happy, but I didn't understand why.

"I trust you can make it to your room on your own for once," Arch said, gesturing towards the stairwell. "If not, I'm sure Topper would be happy to assist you."

Aneurin was conspicuous with his annoyance as he crossed his arms against the small of his chest. "I can tend to myself, *sir*."

"As I thought," Arch replied with a thin smile. "I won't keep her for long."

Aneurin gave me one last glance before hopping towards the edge of the table, landing on the chair beside me with a quiet thud.

"Shall we go?" Arch asked, getting up from his seat and adjusting his vest as he turned to look at me.

My cheeks warmed under his attention, but I lifted myself from my chair. Peering over my shoulder, I noted Aneurin was already gone. Searching the room, I hoped to see his little body moving towards the staircase, but didn't see him anywhere.

Hopefully he wouldn't get eaten by the dog in my absence.

We descended the house's stairs and walked closer to the pond than I expected to.

Arch sat quietly beside me on a swing I hadn't noticed when I first arrived at the tree house. Secured between two sturdy trees, it was a large, wide swing, adorned with nearly perfect wood carvings. I could not make out exactly what they were, but from the particular swirls I saw in the wood, it clearly had taken quite a lot of time and skill to create.

The forest was mostly quiet, except for the soft hum of the crickets. There was a slight chill and it traveled down the length of my spine. I regretted not grabbing one of the jackets by the door. I hugged myself tightly, hoping to find a semblance of warmth somewhere in the crook of my dress. I'd give anything for a sweatshirt and fleece-lined leggings.

"Cold?" Arch asked as he looked at me.

"Y-Yes," I confessed. There was no hiding my rattling teeth.

Arch moved with a soft chuckle as he carefully removed his jacket and wrapped it around me. He took his time buttoning it, his gaze steady and serious.

"Thank you," I said, grateful for the warmth seeping into me.

"Of course," he replied, easing back into his seat again. He crossed his arms against his chest and released a soft sigh.

"Won't you be cold?" I asked.

"Worry not, Josephine," Arch reassured with a nod. "I've faced much harsher conditions. Besides, we're not far from the house."

I peered over my shoulder, taking in the sight of the candle-lit tree house. The kitchen was still illuminated from a distance, where I knew was Topper working on the mountain of dishes from supper. But most of the other rooms above were dark. I wondered how many of the men had gone off to bed.

If I squinted, I could make out the candle's glow from my room. I guess Aneurin had managed to climb all those steps without me, after all. But I still I felt a pang of guilt as I thought about him struggling up them on his own.

I turned forward again and followed Arch's example by staring up at the moonlit sky.

"It's been quite a day, has it not?" he asked, breaking the silence "A day I suppose we all expected to see at some point."

"Did you expect Trapper and Stitches to argue the way they did? Or was it the appearance of the queen?"

Arch snorted, sliding a hand through his long, tangled hair. "Does it reflect poorly on me if I say both?"

"I didn't expect Trapper and Stitches—"

"That has been a long time coming," Arch replied, resigned. "Trapper has little patience for Stitches. He finds him...weepy, and very much unlike him and his brother."

"There's nothing wrong with being different," I countered.

Arch nodded. "I'm in full agreement. Every man in that house is different. Each of us looks at our manhood differently. Some define it by strength, and some define it by compassion. And some do not wish to define it at all."

"And you?"

Arch pressed his lips firmly and shrugged. "I suppose I am one of the few who only wish to look at life based on principle and morals. Not based on who can bring the most kills home, or who can move a tree from one end of the forest to the other. Those are such trivial ways to determine a man's character."

But what we'd witnessed wasn't just about Trapper's narrow definition of masculinity.

"The first time I saw Trapper look at her, I knew there was a spark in him," Arch continued. "Something in him changed. He doesn't know what to do with that emotion."

"So, he does care for Snow-White?"

"I think he loves her," he replied with a small smile. "I certainly saw the truth on his face today when I came back from the woods. I'm quite certain Stitches did, too."

So had I. And I'd seen the way he avoided and given his place to Stitches—intentionally or not.

Shaking my head, I pressed a finger to my temple. "So, what will happen?" I asked, glancing back at Arch.

He sighed. "I fear I know not, honestly. I suppose the answer lies within themselves. Ultimately, it is for her to decide whom she wants, if she wants either of them."

"I don't think she even knows how Trapper feels."

"I'm sure he doesn't know what he feels, himself. He's spent so much of his life rejected by those around him. And the possibility of having such a thing occur again scares him."

"It *is* scary," I agreed.

"Aye." Arch nodded. "I recall you shared that you've had your own bit of heartache before. You were once betrothed?"

"Yes." I whispered. "And it wasn't that long ago, either."

"Oh?"

I sucked in a breath before continuing, "There's a lot about me I haven't really been forthcoming about."

"Why admit such things now?" Arch asked.

"Am I crazy to say that I feel like I can trust you?"

Arch's lips tilted into a half smile as he shook his head. "I can't say there's much that I find 'crazy,' as you say, Josephine. Perhaps a little outlandish, but aren't we all?"

"I guess," I mumbled.

"However, I am glad to hear you feel this way with me."

I lowered my gaze to my hands, carefully considering what I felt comfortable sharing with him. While I was relieved that Snow-White had recovered from the day's events, I couldn't shake the fear of what was still to come. I knew there was going to be another encounter, and Snow wasn't going to be so lucky.

Should I warn Arch? Should I warn them all? Was I even allowed to? Could I tell them about the poisoned apple?

And if so, who would release Snow-White from its grip? In the fairytale that I knew, it had been a prince who rescued her. One who had heard of her beauty and came to find her in the woods. The piece of apple only dislodged from her throat when he decided to take her home with him, glass coffin and all. Were those events still set to occur? I couldn't imagine any of the men, especially Trapper, allowing a stranger to take her away.

A soft breeze broke through the thicket of trees, sending another chill down my spine.

"I've always known there was more to you than you've shared with the men," he admitted, breaking the silence. "I hope you can be assured, you can say what you wish, Jo. I won't betray your trust."

If there was one thing I was sure of about Arch—he was the most trustworthy of them all.

I bit my bottom lip. "I haven't even told Aneurin the truth," I admitted. "I don't even know *how* to tell him."

"I'm sure you can tell him just as you're telling me. Calmly."

I laughed. "Right, that's always a good place to start." I remarked, taking a deep breath to steady myself.

Arch nodded, encouraging me to continue.

"What if I told you that I'm not really from this world?" I ventured, feeling a rush of uncertainty. . "That I come from a very different place altogether?"

Arch's smile widened, a glint of amusement in his eyes. "I would say these are all things I've already gathered," he replied, his tone teasing. "There is no element of surprise in your confession."

"And if I told you I'm not even supposed to be here?"

"Josephine, if you confessed you came from the skies, I would find no folly in your words. In my many years, I have never quite met a woman like you before."

I could feel the warmth flooding my cheeks, turning them a shade of red that I was certain was impossible to hide. "I don't know if I should be flattered or—"

"If you are saying you're not from this land, or any land surrounding this kingdom, or the next...I would simply then ask, how did you find yourself here?"

"I know this is going to be hard to believe." I couldn't believe I was telling someone my secret.

"Just say it," he urged.

"I'm here because I got sucked into a book—" I blurted before I lost the nerve. "And I have no idea how to get out."

Arch studied me, clicking his tongue before turning his gaze back towards the night sky. "A book you say," he murmured.

"I don't even know *why* I'm here. I was given this book and there was something written inside of it," I explained. I needed to tell Arch everything for it to make sense. "When I started to read it out loud, this bright light filled my room and then, almost by magic, I was in the middle of a forest and found Aneurin. Before I knew it, we were both chasing after a pair of siblings and I pushed the witch into an oven—"

Arch lifted his hand, interrupting my story. "Did you just say you *pushed* a witch into an oven?"

"There really weren't a lot of options," I explained with a shrug. "She was going to eat Aneurin and the children."

Arch fell silent, his gaze returning to the scenery of the forest. Leaning his body back against the swing, he seemed to be contemplating the weight of my confession.

What was he thinking? What was he going to say?

Who would ever believe me if I tried to explain this to someone? If I ever made it back home...

He swallowed hard and let out a heavy sigh. "So, you claim that all of this..." he lifted his hand out, gesturing to the trees beyond. "This is all found within a book..."

"Well, not all of this, exactly," I said, shaking my head. "For instance, Aneurin is a frog prince, and his...story...doesn't have anything to do with the children or Snow-White. Some of the stories have become entangled since I've been here."

"And who is the author of these tales?" Arch asked, pressing his hand against his chest.

"People that are long dead," I replied.

"And you know how these...tales end?"

"Not always..." I admitted. "I don't know *everything*."

Arch shifted in the swing to face me again.

"To be honest," I continued, "I don't know if I'd believe me if I were in your shoes. All of this sounds crazy, even to me."

"It is a lot to take in." He let out a soft snort. "But you have not provided me a reason to doubt you, Josephine."

"It was only yesterday you were all worried I would hurt Snow."

"And yet, you attempted to save her today," he remarked.

"I failed. *Miserably*."

"That was not your fault," he countered.

"But I do blame myself," I whispered. "I knew that something—" I cut myself off and lifted my gaze to meet his.

He raised a brow. "What did you know?"

"I-I knew something was going to happen. But what I expected…was not what occurred." If I had read the whole book before reading the inscription, would I have been better prepared?

"And what was that?"

"I'm not sure I what I'm allowed to tell you. I wasn't given any rules, but I feel like there must be *some*."

Arch studied me, his jaw tight with tension. He wanted to say something, but remained silent. "I can't claim to comprehend what you've been through," he eventually murmured. "But I am familiar with bearing a heavy burden. In knowing something that can bring terrible consequences to a great many people."

"I'll do whatever I can to keep all of you safe."

"And your prince?" Arch asked.

"Aneurin is not *my* prince," I answered quickly, sliding my hands to rest in my lap.

"Josephine," Arch chuckled softly. "Between you and Trapper, I wonder who is more hopeless."

I wrinkled my brow. "What is that supposed to mean?"

"Come now. Surely you won't deny what everyone else sees?"

"What?" I asked, wrinkling my nose. "I don't understand what you're insinuating."

"I think you will, *eventually*. And when you do, I'm sure that will come with its own price to bear."

"Aneurin isn't my prince," I reiterated. "He's looking for a princess to break his spell. Not *me*—"

"We are all determined to have our way in life," Arch interjected. "But I think you know, just as we do, the things that we need are often right in front of us. We must be wise enough, and, at times, brave enough to grasp it."

"Even if you're right, I don't belong here."

He nodded, sliding his hands along his thighs. "If all of this is as you claim, eventually, the story will come to an end."

"I don't know how *this* version ends," I admitted.

"I suppose the important part is that we all live on, beyond whatever ending your storybook provides us."

"But what if…when Aneurin and I leave…" I hesitated. "What if all of this disappears?"

"There was a time before you and Aneurin," he said slowly. "And I'm sure there will be a time after you leave."

"But—"

"Is that not the beauty of life, Josephine?" Arch murmured. "To not always know the outcome of the future? To discover the answers along the way?"

"But that means this isn't real. The men, Snow-White, you—" I started, but Arch lifted his hand, stopping me.

"I can assure you, Jo, even if we only exist in the pages of the book you found, our world, our worries—all of our struggles—everything is very real to *us*."

"I never expected any of this," I confessed softly.

"I'm sure neither Aneurin, nor the rest of us ever expected to meet you either, Josephine. But I am glad we did. I'm relieved to know that we shall keep each other in friendship, no matter where our paths may lead."

I leaned forward in the swing, grappling with what to say. Why did this moment feel like the start of a farewell?

Arch rose to his feet, stretching in place. "It's getting late," he remarked with a sigh. "We should bid each other good night."

"Right," I replied with a nod. "I'll be right in."

He bowed his head and retreated back to the house.

I couldn't shake the feeling that my silence to his previous comment had somehow disappointed him. Maybe what I shared with him might have been too much. And simultaneously not enough.

I lowered my face into my hands. All of this was a horrible mess. I just wanted to go home. How long had I been away by now? My parents had to be worried. What would happen if they called Nico, asking if he'd seen me? Would he tell them everything I'd neglected to say when I'd come home?

Suddenly, a familiar weight landed on my lap, and small hands drew mine from my face.

There, sitting in front of me, was Aneurin. *Aneurin*, who was supposed to be back up in the room.

"H-How did you get out here?" I asked, flicking my gaze between the house and him.

"I have been here this whole time," he answered.

"The whole time?" I echoed. "How?"

"While it might be deemed highly improper, I found a small fold in the skirt of your dress. I was worried you might feel the shift in weight, but…it seems I worried for naught."

"You snuck into my dress?" I asked, staring at him with wide, surprised eyes.

"I held onto a fold of your skirt. While I might be an amphibian, I am still a *gentleman*. I certainly would never find myself inside your dress. Not without your direct permission, that is."

As if I would ever give him *that*. "Let's make one thing clear, then. That will never happen. *Ever.*"

"Duly noted." He rose to his hind legs and set his hands on his waist. "I would like to address some things I heard you speak of with Arch before we return to the cottage."

"What things?" I asked, trying to play it cool. I could guess where this was going, but I had no idea how to talk my way out of this.

"You know exactly what I speak of, Josephine. You are so open with Arch, but will not grant me the same trust."

"You think I don't trust you?" I asked.

"Apparently not enough to tell your most treasured secrets to," Aneurin retorted.

"Nothing I told Arch is a secret," I replied, shaking my head.

"Then why have you not told me of your true origins? Why did you not share—"

"Because you had it in your mind that I was from some southern land," I interjected. "It seemed to be this big thing for you to explain away why I appeared the way I did."

"It was your duty to correct me!"

"Correcting you is now my *duty*?" I asked, suppressing a laugh. "Aneurin, I'm not one of your *subjects*. Your rules don't apply to me. And as far as I'm concerned, they never will."

Aneurin's expression twisted into one of pure annoyance. He flicked his tongue over his eye and folded his arms across his chest, shooting a glance over his shoulder towards the house. He looked as though he were debating on whether he should have a tantrum. But he remained silent and shifted his attention back to me.

I sighed. "You might as well just say what you're thinking."

"As you are aware, you are in my world now," he began. "It matters not to me where you come from. In truth, what is a greater concern to me, even more as you are my traveling partner, is that you value me."

"It's *you* who doesn't value me," I explained. "You've never seen me as an equal. But Arch listens to me. He treats me as an equal," I said, responding to his earlier complaint.

"It is not that I do not listen to you, Josephine," he replied. " It's that I choose not to hear."

"Same thing," I retorted.

Aneurin pressed his lips firmly together then sighed. "You must understand," he murmured, "I was raised to know my place...But it does not mean that I am not willing to learn from you, Jo. If there is one thing that I have learned from the men and Snow, it is that I have lived my life with a narrow view. I am shallow. I know that now. It is clear I cannot live this way forever."

"Are you saying that Snow knocked some sense into you after her talk about marriage?"

"'Knocked some sense into me?'" He tilted his head curiously before shaking his head. "Sometimes your choice of words astounds me…It is not so much changing my mind, as it is my own decision to simply…as you once so graciously said, 'be more open.'"

"Open?" I repeated, staring at him.

"'Tis what you told me." He shifted in my lap. "Now, getting back to the matter at hand…If this world is as you say, and I am a mere character…you must know how this all ends."

"It's not that simple." Hadn't he heard me just tell Arch I didn't know *everything*?

"You've known all along how to help me!"

"That's not true," I tried again, shaking my head. "None of this is how I remember it."

"Then tell me what you *do* know. You—"

"Arch!" a piercing cry broke through the darkness, startling us. Barely a moment passed before the voice called out again, this time echoing farther through the trees. "Arch!"

I turned back to the house, trying to see what was happening. Why was someone calling for Arch? Wouldn't he already be back by now?

Something was wrong.

A shadow crossed the porch.

Was it Herb? Topper?

"What is it?" Aneurin asked softly, tugging on the sleeve of my arm, drawing my gaze back to him.

"I don't know," I whispered. "But I think we should go back to find out."

Picking him up without allowing him the chance to respond or argue, I placed him on my shoulder and rose to my feet.

I heard the voice call out a third time. This time, it was crystal clear who it was.

"*Arch!*" Trapper called out, his tone desperate. "Snow is gone!"

TWENTY

M y heart sank into my stomach. *Gone?*

Aneurin spoke up from my shoulder. "Did I just hear them say Snow is gone?"

I gave a brief nod and picked up the fabric of my skirt before I ran toward the commotion as fast as I could. Thank goodness I decided to wear my wet sneakers today.

The men didn't know about the poison apple—how far the queen went to get rid of Snow-White…but I did.

"Trapper? Arch?" I called out as I approached the house. My heart raced as I scanned the railing above for their silhouettes. Topper, Hunter, and Herb peered over the wooden railing, their faces etched with a concern I hadn't seen before.

The latter paced the floor with arms tightly crossed, his gaze fixed on the darkness just beyond.

I shifted my gaze to the bottom of the staircase of the treehouse, where Trapper and Arch stood together. The former pointed towards the line of trees, but Arch shook his head. Whatever they were saying, they were not agreeing.

"Arch?" I walked toward them. "Where is Stitches?"

He'd gone for a walk, and that had been just before Arch and I had left the cottage. Hadn't he come back yet? Maybe she and Stitches were on a walk together? But I knew in my gut that wasn't what was happening. How much time did we have to find Snow before the queen did?

"Have you seen her?" Trapper asked, his dark, blue gaze meeting mine.

"No," I answered quickly, shaking my head. "I was out for a walk with Arch and then…"

Trapper didn't listen long enough to hear my full response. Impatiently, he turned his gaze back towards the woods, his eyes reflecting a hint of desperation as he peered into the darkened trees. "We can't just stand here," he snapped at Arch after a long pause.

"We need to divide the forest up between all of us," Arch explained evenly, trying to keep Trapper calm. "We need a plan before we start aimlessly searching the woods."

"What about Stitches?" I asked.

"I don't really care about him right now," Trapper snarled. Just as he went to take a step forward, Arch laid a hand on his shoulder.

"We all must work together," he said. "She couldn't have gone far…There's no need to panic."

"We have *every* reason to panic," Trapper retorted. "The queen is out there, watching…waiting. If she could deceive Jo and Snow—"

A snapping stick behind us caught his attention, interrupting his tirade.

The three of us pivoted and saw Stitches' concerned expression. He was panting. Had he been running?

"I heard shouting," he gasped, bending over and bracing his hands on his thighs.

"Snow is missing," Arch explained slowly. "It seems she's left us."

No matter how much he might have wanted to cushion the blow of Snow-White's actions, there was no way to prevent the fear or hurt both other men were probably feeling.

"She *what?*" Stitches asked carefully, as he slowly took a step forward, his gaze locked on Trapper.

"We're all going to go try to find—"

"*You,*" Stitches seethed. "This is your fault. You just had to be so unfair to her at supper."

"Shut up already!" Trapper snapped. "All of us are tired of listening to you pine over your unrequited love for her."

Stitches let out a laugh. "Is that what this is all about? Because you're jealous?"

"Jealous?" Trapper snorted. "Me? *Jealous?*"

"Perhaps if you'd clean your ears out more often, I wouldn't have to repeat myself so much," Stitches retorted.

"You're lucky I haven't skinned you alive by now," Trapper growled, taking a step towards him.

His fisted knuckles were turning white, and I was honestly worried they'd end up fighting each other. Which was the last thing any of us needed.

Arch lifted his hands. "Do not allow something as mediocre as jealousy affect our family."

"I won't give her up to you," Stitches replied, ignoring Arch.

""We don't have the time for this!" I yelled. "We have to find Snow before something bad happens."

Arch raised an eyebrow at me, silently asking what I knew.

Aneurin piped up, reminding us of his presence on my shoulder. "I think it best we listen to Josephine. The two of you can discuss who will woo Snow-White later."

"There is no *wooing* Snow," Trapper retorted. "And there never shall be. She's a princess. Neither of us has anything to offer her."

"Say you," Stitches said. "But I'd like to think otherwise."

"Whatever it is you think, Stitches," Trapper continued. "It is up to Snow what she chooses to do. It is her heart, and she must stay true to it."

It was probably one of the most reasonable things I'd ever heard come out of the man's mouth.

Stitches hesitated, as if he had more to say, but ultimately kept silent. He redirected his focus to Arch, folding his arms against his chest. "Are we going to look for her, then?"

"Yes," Arch said with a nod. "Let us divide the forest amongst ourselves. One of us can stay here at the house in case she returns on her own."

I glanced over my shoulder again, towards the forest. How were we going to see? It wasn't like flashlights existed in this world. And a candle's glow could only illuminate so much.

"I can take the northern side of the lake," Stitches replied, gesturing off into the distance.

"And I'll take the cliffs," Trapper offered. "I know them better than anyone else here. Even Hunter avoids the cliffs."

"I would go with—" Arch began, but Trapper shook his head. "You might as well focus on the southern end."

"I'll go with you, Trapper," I volunteered, locking eyes with him once more.

His deep blue gaze swept over me, just as he had upon our first meeting. He scrutinized me for a prolonged moment, causing heat to rise to my cheeks. "If you fall," he murmured. "There is nothing I can do to rescue either you or your frog prince."

"I beg your pardon—" Aneurin interjected. "Did you just say if we *fall?*"

"I think we're covered," I mumbled, jerking my chin in his direction. "We've fallen off far worse things."

"A waterfall is not what I'd consider the worse out of the two scenarios, Josephine," Aneurin protested.

He had a fair point. But we didn't have time to argue about this.

"We'll be fine," I replied. Then, turning to Trapper, I added, "No one will be falling off anything."

"You better hope so," Aneurin hissed, low enough for only me to hear.

Trapper watched the two of us, then shook his head. "I'll say what I did before. There's nothing that I can or will do—"

"You don't have to go with him," Arch interjected, placing a hand on my shoulder. "You can easily come with me or Stitches, or any of the others."

"I know," I replied. But I didn't take Arch's offer. I couldn't explain the reason why I needed to go with Trapper, but I did.

Trapper removed a small dagger from the top of his boot and he glanced up at me. "Are you coming then?"

"At least leave the prince with me," Arch suggested, glancing at the frog perched on my shoulder.

"I shall follow Josephine," Aneurin declared. "And if it is to cliffs, where there is a chance I might meet my peril, then so be it."

"Don't be so dramatic," I chided, rolling my eyes.

"I'm leaving," Trapper interrupted, turning on his heel. He didn't bother to look back at us to see if we were following and hurried towards the path leading into the darkened woods.

I looked at Arch, uncertain of what to say. On instinct, I wrapped my arms around him in a tight hug. It was a brief one before I pivoted and hurried after Trapper.

"Did you just *embrace* that man?"

"Aneurin," I replied, not doing anything to keep the annoyance out of my tone. "Not now, okay?"

I needed to focus on the dark path ahead and Trapper. I could barely make out his shadow just a few paces ahead of me. He definitely had an unfair advantage in having longer legs than me and knowing the land. I'd always had two left feet when hiking in the woods, let alone running...

Aneurin's webbed fingers clutched the fabric of the shoulder tighter. His body swayed as he struggled to maintain balance.

When I stumbled on a rock jutting out from the ground, I saw him fall onto the ground.

"Aneurin!" I called out, dropping to my knees beside him. "Are you alright?"

He blinked up at me, a bit dazed. "I think so," he replied, pressing his hand against his head.

Up ahead, I saw Trapper turn around some brush, disappearing into the night.

"Come on," I replied, breathlessly, offering my hands to the frog. "We have to keep going."

Aneurin groaned but didn't fight me as I picked him up carefully and placed him into my safety of my dress pocket.

"What on earth are you—"

"Just for now," I explained as I pushed myself back up to my feet. "You'll be safer there."

When he didn't argue, I ran with as much energy as I could muster. I regretted not being dressed in my own normal clothes. Running in a full-length dress was not easy. Least of all on a path I could barely see.

It wound deeper into the woods, nothing was familiar to me.

Off in the distance, thunder rumbled in the sky. There was a storm coming. Great.

"Snow!" Trapper yelled, his voice echoing all around us. "Snow! Where are you?"

"Snow!" I repeated. "*Snow!* Come back!"

Why had she run away in the first place? Why did she feel leaving the house was the only option? Was it because of what had happened with the queen? Because she thought she was putting everyone in danger?

A pang of guilt shot through me. I should have done better. I should have pushed her out of the doorway. I should have...But what did thinking like that solve?

No matter what, the evil woman was going to return.

Maybe Snow knew she would stop at nothing to destroy her.

"Snow!" I gasped, doing my best to swallow back the sob that formed in my throat. It seemed, no matter what I did in this story, the princess would ultimately suffer the queen's wrath. Perhaps it was never my role to disrupt the course of events. Perhaps, I was merely present to facilitate them.

But I hated to be a part of what would hurt so many.

Maybe that was the lesson that I was meant to learn here. We all played roles in each other's lives, whether we liked it or not. For a reason—however brief—to help their story continue on.

Suddenly, I slammed into Trapper's back.

He'd stopped dead center on the path. He was frozen in place, while his hand desperately searched the darkness behind him; I presumed to reach for me.

"Trapper," I hissed, annoyed as I rubbed the back of my neck. I peered down at my pocket, finding Aneurin peeking out.

"Jo," he whispered, "look…"

My heart was racing in my chest as I took a step around him, squinting my eyes to see through the pitch night. But it was hard to make out anything, let alone what he was gesturing towards up ahead. But I kept looking until I recognized two forms standing close to each other.

One was unmistakably the queen, disguised as the old hag. I could almost imagine how she'd taken advantage of Snow's kindness, stopping her in the woods and pretending to be lost.

I wondered if the princess was aware of the true identity of the person beside her. When I started to step forward, Trapper grasped my arm, holding me in place.

"We have to go to her," I murmured, lifting my hand towards the two figures. "It's the queen! We must stop this before it's too late."

"You leave the queen to me, Jo. Get Snow home."

"*We're* getting her home."

"No, I'm not going to let that witch take another breath," he seethed, shaking his head. "*Promise* me you'll get her home."

"We have to move," I replied, avoiding making any sort of promise I wasn't sure I could keep.

He nodded once, then took off, his knife still in his hand. "Snow!" His voice echoed throughout the forest just as another rumble of thunder boomed through the air.

Hopefully, the others could hear him and know to come to us.

The two figures ahead froze. Snow's attention shifted in our direction as Trapper ran closer. But the sight of him didn't stop her from lifting the ruby red apple in her hand to her mouth.

I could almost hear the words uttered from the old hag, standing beside her. I knew those words by just memory alone.

"Make your wish and then…take a bite."

I ran after Trapper. I should have warned him of what was to come, but I'd run out of time.

He pushed forward harder, narrowing the gap between them. His powerful legs pushed him down the path, far beyond my reach, propelled by a strength I couldn't match.

"*Snow!*" Trapper's voice was desperate and pleading.

With her gaze fixed on him, and Snow hesitated in bringing the apple to her mouth.

Despite the distance, I could see her tear-streaked face, a clear indication of her inner struggle.

"*Princess!*" Aneurin's plea rang out from my pocket. "Stop!"

I fought against the fatigue creeping into my limbs, pushing myself to move faster. I wanted to catch my breath, but I needed to save Snow-White. I couldn't fail her now.

"Trapper!" the princess shouted. "I'm sorry for everything!"

"*Snow,*" Trapper shouted again, his voice heavy with emotion.

Her ruby lips pressing into a thin line before lifting the apple once more to her mouth, taking a bite.

Time seemed to slow as the poisoned fruit fell to the ground from Snow's hand.

I watched in horror as the princess reached for her throat, gasping for breath, her eyes wide with panic.

The hag beside her cackled, clapping her hands in triumph. "At last!" she shouted. "Now, I'll finally be the fairest!"

This was the woman who I'd seen as we'd fallen over the waterfall. The one who had sent shivers down my spine.

In the next breath, the old hag turned into the forest, disappearing down a narrow path covered in ferns.

Trapper finally reached Snow, throwing himself onto his knees and quickly gathered her in his arms. "*Snow…*" he murmured.

Glancing over my shoulder, I waited to see if anyone else was coming our way. But there was nothing, and no one.

All I could think about was the disguised queen, dashing through the woods…getting away with her terrible deed.

Trapper's voice cracked with emotion as he pulled Snow against his chest. Tears streamed down his face, mingling with the dirt and sweat. "Don't leave me," he choked out between sobs, his words barely audible amidst his anguish. "I'm sorry I was such a fool…" His voice trailed off, consumed by grief and regret.

"Is she…dead?" Aneurin asked softly, peering up at me from my dress pocket.

I bit my bottom lip, debating on whether I could share everything I knew. Even if I *should*, I didn't have time. Not if I wanted to catch the queen.

"We have to get her," I replied to Aneurin. "That witch has to pay for what she did to Snow."

"*Another* one?" he groaned. "I never wish to see a witch again in my life."

"Hopefully this'll be the last one for the both of us," I concurred. Stepping closer to Trapper, I placed a hand on his shoulder.

He turned his chin abruptly, his tear-filled eyes meeting mine.

"Take Snow," I urged, echoing his earlier sentiments. "Get her home with the others. Aneurin and I are going after the queen."

"But you can't do it all on your own," he countered.

"No one else is here, Trapper," I replied. "I'm not letting that witch get away with what she's done."

The apple still lay by Snow's foot, abandoned and ominous.

Kneeling down, I picked it up, noting the small but significant bite mark where a piece of the fruit was missing.

"A poisoned apple," Aneurin gasped, his voice filled with disbelief. "And I thought such things were figments of children's stories."

"Same," I agreed before passing it to Trapper. "Burn it when you can. So that no one else can suffer from it."

He sniffled, staring at the fruit before hesitantly taking it into his hand. "Are you really going to go after her?"

"We are," I said.

Shifting Snow in his arms, Trapper offered the small hand knife in my direction. "Just in case you need it," he explained. "Aim for the heart if you can."

It felt strange taking it. I had never imagined myself ever being in a situation like this—even aside from the fairytale book and the witches and the talking frogs...

I'd already pushed one witch into an oven, but that was to save others. This was *revenge*. I took the knife and gave him a curt, quick nod before turning on my heel.

"Jo?" Trapper's voice cut through the rumble of thunder.

I paused, turning to glance back at him.

"Thank you." His words hung in the air, leaving gratitude and uncertainty between us. What exactly he was thanking me for, I couldn't be sure.

"Trapper," I began, catching his gaze before he turned away. "She isn't dead."

He gave a short, curt nod. "I know."

"A prince is going to come looking for her," I continued, unsure if I was breaking a rule in sharing too much information. I didn't care. "And when he comes to take her away, it'll dislodge the piece of apple. That's how she wakes up."

He furrowed his brow, a look of confusion crossing his face. But I raised my hand in a silent gesture. "I want you to know...you don't have to wait for some *prince* to save her. You can, Trapper."

But I had no idea what other advice I could give him about dislodging a piece of apple. I doubted he even knew anything about the Heimlich maneuver. But he'd have to figure it out for himself.

"Don't give up on her now," I finished. Without waiting for his response, I turned on my heel and took off running.

My legs screamed in pain with every stride.

"Jo!" Aneurin called from my pocket. "Look!"

A crack of lightning lit the sky, illuminating the looming mountain ahead of us. I flinched as rain droplets fell from above. In mere moments, my dress was plastered to me.

With a second flash of light, I saw the witch hobbling along a narrow path.

It was just my luck—of course she'd go to the cliffs.

But I was determined. The wind picked up, sending a shiver of cold down my spine as I began to climb the dangerous mountainside. This was going to end badly—at least for one of us. Me or the witch. Hopefully, Aneurin would save himself if I didn't make it.

"You alright?" I asked my companion, without glancing at him.

"I experienced a far bumpier carriage ride in my childhood," he replied airily.

His response at least made me smirk.

I pushed my body to climb faster against the pelting rain and steady wind. I was freezing, wishing more than anything to find myself back in front of a warm fire with everyone safe in the tree house. Or, even better, a hot shower and a delivery pizza. If I ever got back to my own world. Assuming I survived tonight at all.

"*Josephine!*" Aneurin's call rang out.

I glance down at him, noting the urgency in his wide eyes.

Following his gaze, I spotted the old hag just ahead of us. Somehow, I'd managed to almost catch up with her.

"*You!*" I shouted, the anger in my chest building as I approached. The rain intensified, causing me to brush my hair from my face. I stumbled on a rock, slipping onto my knees. A cry of pain escaped me before I forced myself back up.

"Careful, Jo! *Careful!*" Aneurin said.

"I'm *trying*!" I exclaimed, releasing a sigh as I turned my gaze back to the witch ahead.

The queen glanced over her shoulder, laughing at the sight of me. "You don't know when to give up, do you?" she scoffed.

Another crack of lightning seared through the sky.

I flinched. It was too close.

"You're going to pay for what you did to Snow-White!" I shouted back, turning my focus back on the queen.

"Only if you can catch me!" she taunted.

That was a challenge if I'd ever heard one, and I wasn't going to let myself fail again when it came to this evil woman.

Another rumble of thunder echoed through the forest the same time I thought I heard someone calling my name from down below. But I didn't look down—I couldn't get distracted. Gripping a wet rock the best that I could with my hands, I pulled myself up onto the side of another boulder.

The queen was only a few strides ahead, her black cloak fluttering tantalizingly close to my fingertips, just out of my reach.

I didn't know if it was possible for rain to come down harder than it already was, but it felt like it was leaving welts on my skin.

"Josephine!" I heard Aneurin calling.

"Just stay where you are!" I called back to him. Everything was happening in a blur. The rain was sending shrills of pain through my body. I was soaked through. The last thing I needed was Aneurin to hurt himself by falling out of my pocket. I'd never forgive myself.

The rocks underneath my hands and feet were slippery as I watched the witch ahead. It seemed with every step I took, she was getting further and further away from me.

She reached the ledge of a rock and pulled herself over, landing on its solid surface. A second later, she peeked over the edge with a dark, cruel smile. The same one I'd seen earlier at the tree house. "It would be such a shame to see you fall, pet," she cooed from above. "But oh, what a sight to see…" With a laugh, she disappeared.

I huffed out a breath then tried to swallow my fear. This was an unfair fight. As I reached to pull myself up to another rock, she returned with an armful of rocks.

"No!" I shouted as she started throwing them.

The few that reached me pounded my shoulders as I tried to protect my head the best I could.

Her cackle filled my ears as she slipped out of view once more.

"Are you alright?" Aneurin's concerned voice reached me.

"I-I think so," I replied.

"It's not too late to turn back…" he suggested.

"It is." I wiped my bangs from my eyes again as I leaned my forehead against the wall of rock. "We can't let her get away."

Aneurin's voice was filled with concern as he spoke up. "I can't let you get hurt."

I looked down at him in the pocket of my skirt. His small face peered up at me, his eyes filled with concern.

"Are you saying that you care about me all of a sudden?"

"It is certainly not 'all of a sudden,' as you put it. Though, would it truly be all that surprising to you?"

"Are you only saying this because your life depends on me surviving this?"

"*Josephine…*" His tone broadcasted his annoyance.

The crunch of the witch's shoes from above drew my attention. This time, she looked down at me, holding a larger rock between her hands. She grunted, struggling to bring it to the edge.

"Press yourself flat against the cliff," Aneurin whispered. "I'll distract her."

"Distract? Aneurin, you—"

Suddenly, he hopped from my pocket and crawled up the rocks. His little webbed fingers gripped each small crevasse as he moved closer to the witch. "For once, just do as I tell you. *Please*, Jo."

"But—"

Before I could continue, I heard the witch call for me from above. "Oh, *Josephine*," she beckoned. "I have something for you."

I dared a peek in her direction.

She was looming over the edge, pushing the larger rock with all her might.

"I already told you," I retorted, holding onto the side of the rocked wall with everything I could muster. "I'm not interested in what you're selling."

"It didn't stop me, did it? And to think it only took a mere apple to trick that stupid princess. And soon, she'll die!"

Another crackle of lightning flashed against the sky.

I lifted my gaze, hoping to see Aneurin. But my heart sank when he was nowhere to be found. Oddly, neither was the witch.

He had told me once to trust him, and I knew I needed to, now more than ever. But it didn't stop me from worrying about him.

I *cared.* The realization struck me as I searched for him through the heavy rain. I didn't know how or when I'd started to care about his well-being, but I also knew I couldn't let something horrible happen to him. I cared if he died, cared if I didn't get any more time with him.

I climbed up the rocks as quickly as I could, ignoring the sting of the rain against my face as I pushed forward.

Once I reached the top, I saw the old woman again, twisted in her misshapen form, grappling with another rock.

I spotted Aneurin hopping towards her, his small body struggling against the wind as he tried to reach her.

His voice called out to her, taunting her from one side of the ledge to the other as he tried to draw her away from her task.

There was another crack of lightning, though, this time it was mere inches away from where she stood.

I pushed myself to my feet, straining against the pain of my weak muscles—exhausted from all the running and climbing.

"You fools!" The witch cackled as her gaze flew from Aneurin to me. "You thought you could defeat me? No one wins but me…"

"Maybe before, But you hadn't met us yet," I countered.

She laughed. "What is a simple peasant girl and her frog going to do?" She bent down, picking up a discarded tree branch at her feet. As she lifted it, she kicked Aneurin with her heel.

He landed on the other side of the rocks. Too far for me to reach him if I was going to fend off the witch's next attack.

"Aneurin!" I screamed, hoping he'd respond. When he didn't, I glared up at the witch, wishing my rage could burn her. I'd never felt this amount of hate for anyone before. But *she* deserved it.

"You will not win," I shouted. "While evil might prevail at times in my world, it never does here! Snow-White and Aneurin will get their happily ever after, and so will—"

And so would *I*. I believed that now. After my unlikely friendships with Arch and the others, and the princess, and my shocking bravery—plan or no plan—with the witch and children...I deserved *my* happily ever after, too. And I'd get it—prince, or no prince.

Before the queen had the chance to react, another flash of lightning filled the sky before landing right in front of me.

I closed my eyes against the brightness of the searing light.

My eyes flew open as the witch's scream filled my ears. The spot where she stood was empty—she was gone. Even the piece of rock she'd been standing on was missing.

"Did that just really happen?" I asked aloud, taking a timid step forward. Looking around, I realized that Aneurin was gone, too.

"A-Aneurin?" I called out, trying to contain my panic. Where *was* he? He hadn't been near the witch when the lightning had hit.

I needed to find him. My eyes scanned the flat rocks, hoping to see his little body lying about somewhere. Maybe the shock of everything had made him pass out.

I moved closer to the ledge, trying not to think about the possibility of him falling after her. He couldn't have, right?

This couldn't be the way things ended for us. This was not the ending either of us deserved.

Then I heard his muffled voice call my name.

"J-Josephine?"

"Aneurin!" I shouted, squinting through the downpour, I spotted him curled against a small slab of rock jutting out from the cliff.

He looked so small. So defenseless.

"I was so afraid something happened to you," I admitted.

Aneurin was lucky to still be alive.

Slowly, he lifted his head. His green gaze held mine steadily, fear broadcasted on his features.

I attempted a reassuring smile, hoping to offer some comfort.

"Josephine," he murmured with relief. "I must confess, I was afraid of the same for myself."

"Stay still," I replied, my teeth chattering from a mixture of cold and adrenaline. "Don't move."

"I don't think I could, even if I wanted to," he managed.

Fighting back the urge to laugh, I tucked myself close to the edge of the deep curve and reached for him. It took everything in me to try not to look too far down. Heights have never been my thing. The pounding of my heart in my chest was echoing in my ears. I wouldn't be surprised if Aneurin could hear it across the way. It seemed no matter how much I tried to stretch myself, I still couldn't reach his small form. He was a lot lower in the curve than I thought.

"Hold on," I replied as I tried to shift my body against the rock.

"Onto what, exactly?" he asked.

"Just stay where you are," I sighed, as I pushed myself forward, lowering myself more into the divot. Reaching out with my hand again, I tried to grab him. But I still came up short. He was just out of reach. I groaned. If I so much as slipped an inch further, I was going to topple over completely.

No matter how much I tried, my gaze kept darting to where the witch had disappeared. She'd been standing there, and in a flash, had disappeared into the abyss. One wrong move, and the same could happen to me.

But I had to save him. I reached out again, straining my arm in his direction.

"Aneurin," I called to him. "Can you try to reach my hand?"

He hesitated then peered over the same edge I was so fearful of. He turned back to me and shook his head, his hands holding himself in place. Maybe he saw my fear in my eyes, or maybe he just recognized his own.

I pulled back so I wasn't hanging over the chasm. There had to be another way to do this.

"You can go back and get one of the oth—"

"I'm not *leaving* you," I interrupted.

"It's okay to leave me behind if it's to get help."

I shook my head. "I'm *not* leaving you, Aneurin."

"I'm not worth dying for," I heard him mutter. "I'm nothing more than a frog."

His words struck me wrong. Maybe in the beginning, that had been true. An annoying one, at best. But now...*now*, he was Aneurin. A prince locked in a spell. A man who had feelings and had tried to be brave. He'd sat in my hand and defended me, small as he was, when Trapper had scolded me. He cared about my secrets...

And somehow, strangely, I'd come to care for him, too.

"You're not just a frog, Aneurin," I replied. "Not to me."

He sniffled.

"Aneurin," I said sternly. "I'm not leaving you. Not ever..." The words fluttered from my lips before I had the chance to hold them back. But there they were, out in the open. And I had no intention of taking them back.

He fell silent, taking them in. Maybe he believed me.

"Now, let's try this one more time," I suggested, pushing myself out over the ledge again, bracing my weight against the bottom of the curve with one hand, while I tried to reach him with the other.

He shifted closer towards me and reached his hand out.

To no avail.

"Come on," I encouraged. "We can do this."

"I suppose I could try to hop," he mused. "I am a frog, after all."

"Hop?" The thought had never struck me. "You can *hop?*"

"I think so. But consider how embarrassing it might be for a grown man—a prince—to hop his way around," he muttered.

"Don't worry about that right now."

"You have to catch me," he warned.

As if there was another option.

Before I could respond, he adjusted his footing and jumped.

I wanted to close my eyes, afraid to see what would happen. But I couldn't—I had to catch him.

As soon as I had him in my grasp, I pulled him close to me, tucking him against my chest. "Thank god," I gasped.

"Perhaps I should have tried that first," he murmured, his eyes wide with relief.

"I'm just glad you're okay…"

Maybe I shouldn't have spoken so soon. Because when I tried to hoist myself back onto the flat of the rock, I no longer had the ease of both hands. My balance shifted and then I was sliding backward, or rather, *down*.

I heard our twin screams in my ears as we plummeted into the darkness of the forest below. Down to where I knew the queen's body lay mangled.

But before we landed, I saw a familiar burst of white, bright light.

TWENTY-ONE

I'd seen this light before. I knew what it meant. Aneurin and I were moving into a different world—a completely different story. I didn't understand the logistics of what exactly was occurring, but it was the second time we'd fallen from one place and landed somewhere new. All I could do was hold onto him, his small, frog heart beating hard against my thumb and forefinger.

Smooth, delicate strings of gold wrapped around us, pulling us through the searing light. Watching as it curled around us, weaving between my legs and arms, I became more afraid than before—where were we going? I closed my eyes, praying to whoever could hear me, to allow us to live. To just get us to land safely…somewhere.

As the light continued to envelop us in its warmth, the storm disappeared—or maybe just could no longer touch us. Now that I was no longer being pelted by rain, I realized just how cold and wet I was.

This fall felt different. Gravity pulled us harder, down into a narrower, darker area. Aneurin grabbed onto my fingers holding him and screamed in fear as we continued to sail through the sky, only stopping when our fall was cushioned by a heap of small but itchy sticks.

Our screams echoed off the stone walls that now surrounded us. I had no idea where we were, but looked down to peer at Aneurin first. He was panting on my chest—I must have let him go once we landed, but I didn't remember doing it.

I closed my eyes and tilted my head back while I caught my breath. Our fall miraculously hadn't given me any whiplash, but I still hadn't recovered from it *or* the fight on the cliff. Blindly, I slid my hand deeper into the pile under us, trying to figure out what exactly it was we'd ended up in. It was dry and brittle under my hands, but didn't feel like clumps. Was it...*straw?*

I hadn't seen a barn anywhere near the tree house. Which meant everything we'd known for the past two days was gone. The seven men and Snow-White...While we'd only stayed a day or so in their home, it felt strange to suddenly be without them. What would happen to them all with Aneurin and I gone?

Even if Arch was right and they continued to exist without us, I wouldn't ever see him again. Even though I'd hoped it wouldn't, the impromptu hug I'd given Arch had turned out to actually be my farewell. There was no way for us to return that I knew of. And I had no way to know if Trapper had heeded my warning and saved Snow with the information I provided him.

I laid still, grappling with the range of my emotions. Tears stung my eyes. Behind my eyelids, I imagined Trapper carried her back to the house and had been met with the support of his chosen family. Hopefully, Trapper had swallowed his pride and admitted his feelings...not only to the others, but most importantly, to himself.

None of this was real. It couldn't be. But everything was becoming more so every moment. My emotions were tied to this world, to the people.

To *Aneurin.*

I had to continue to help him find his princess, to help him receive his kiss of true love, and break his spell.

"Aneurin," I whispered cradling his body so he didn't slide when I pushed myself up to sitting.

He grunted in response.

Opening my eyes, I peered up at the vaulted ceiling above us. It was made of pure stone, curving smoothly with outlined edges.

Sliding my attention from him to the rest of our surroundings, illuminated by a sliver of sunlight through a lone window across from us, I realized our pile of straw wasn't the only one in the room.

Dawn must be breaking, which meant it was a new day...

My gaze snagged to the imposing wooden spinning wheel at its center. My mind began to race with the different fairytale options. A spinning wheel could be two famous ones, but the addition of straw meant this could be only one tale.

"Josephine?" Aneurin asked, diverting my attention back to him by turning my chin with a webbed hand. His eyes were wide with confusion. "Josephine? Do you recognize this place?"

I pressed my lips together, uncertain on how to explain our new situation. I'd never liked the story of Rumpelstiltskin. After her father had lied about her being able to spin straw into gold, she was brought to new rooms, each one larger than the next, with the promise of death in the morning if the task was not complete. Amidst her tears, a little man appeared and struck a deal with her. He would spin the straw into gold for treasures...and her firstborn. After all of that, how could the miller's daughter marry a king who had threatened her life not once—but three times—for his own greed?

"Do you know where we are?" Aneurin asked again, drawing me back from my thoughts. Maybe, after venturing into new worlds after falling off waterfalls and cliffs, he now believed me.

"I think I do."But where were we in the timeline of the story? I peered back around the room again. The piles of straw were high. Was this the third room?

I set Aneurin next to me, finally examining my own appearance. The blouse's sleeves were brown and damp, and the green kirtle had stains of mud all along the front. I looked like a hot mess.

"I must be quite the sight," I admitted softly, shaking my head.

"You always have been," Aneurin replied without missing a beat. He turned his attention to the room again, climbing onto my knee. "Do you imagine we're in the stables somewhere?"

"I don't think so," I answered.

"No? Why else would a room be filled with straw?"

Before I could reply, a large wooden door swung open. Voices filtered in, growing louder as their sources entered the space.

"I have had a third room arranged for you."

I grabbed Aneurin from my knee and pulled him against my chest again while I tried to hide the both of us under a layer of straw. The last thing we needed was to get in trouble with a tyrannical king. I'd watched enough about the Tudor dynasty to know the penalty for upsetting royalty. And I was keen to keep my head on my shoulders. Thankfully, Aneurin got the hint to stay quiet and burrowed into my pocket.

Slowly, a tall—one might say lanky—young man came into view. He wore a large, golden crown on his head and a regal ensemble. Long, unkempt black hair fell to his shoulders It looked as if he'd rolled out of bed, put on some clothes, donned the ultimate sign of his power, and called it a day. *This* was the king. This was the douche canoe the poor miller's daughter had to appease.

He lifted a hand toward the straw as a small smirk appeared on his lips. "Do you see, Esmeralda? This is not such a large task to ask for you to complete, is it?" Even this far into the story, his tone was as condescending as ever.

I suppressed the heavy, irritated sigh that wanted to escape. I couldn't give away our attention.

Aneurin shifted in my skirt and I looked down. His eyes asked if we could move, but I shook my head, lifting a finger to my lips.

"But sire," another voice broke the silence. This one belonged to the woman, Esmeralda. "I'm weary from the past few nights' work. Could I not be permitted just one night of—"

"Do you not wish to appease me, my lady?" the king asked. "For if you accomplish this one final task, all the riches of the kingdom will be yours. *I* will be yours. Would you not wish for such a grand reward?" He actually considered *himself* a reward?

"I can see you are rolling your eyes," Aneurin whispered.

"Of course, I am." I answered just as quietly. "Do you hear him?"

"I do have ears, Jo," he quipped.

"I do wish to make you happy, sire," Esmeralda admitted with a nod, her response tinged with uncertainty. It was evident that she harbored doubts about her ability to fulfill the task at hand. And I couldn't blame her. At this point, Rumpelstiltskin had come to assist her, but she knew there was no guarantee he'd return.

"Of course, you do," the king replied, a large smile on his face. He turned to her, sweeping some of his stringy hair over his shoulder. "If by morning, this room is filled with gleaming, glittering gold, I shall make you my queen."

It was a line straight out of a cliche Hallmark channel movie. I bit my lip hard to stop myself from groaning out loud.

Aneurin spoke up. "I'm sure you'd like to shove this man off a cliff right about now."

My lip twitched into a small smile. I guess in the few days that we'd spent together, he'd learned my personality. And he was maybe taking some of them on—he'd used more modern contractions. A mistake? I wasn't going to bring his attention to it in case it was.

"Your Highness, surely you couldn't mean to marry me," Esmeralda replied, shaking her head.

"Of course, I do," he assured her with a firm nod. He lifted her hand from her side and held it in his own. He studied her it, almost clinically, before lifting one to his lips to kiss. "There is no more worthy of a woman in this entire kingdom. For you are worth more than any riches that could ever be given to me."

"But—"

"But if you do not complete this quite small, menial task," he continued sharply, releasing her, "if you do not spin all this straw into gold by morning, dear Esmeralda, you will die."

His words hung in the air like an executioner's ax.

I held my breath until the woman nodded in understanding.

"Seems a little severe," Aneurin whispered. "Can such a thing truly be done? Spinning straw into gold?"

"Not where I come from," I whispered. "And I'm pretty sure it's impossible here, too." With one notable exception, of course.

"I've never heard such a thing," Aneurin continued, shaking his head. "And to give such a task to the woman under a death threat?"

"Yeah." I sighed. Marrying the king in this world wasn't quite the happily ever after my world had portrayed it as.

Aneurin climbed out of my pocket and sat on my chest again. His little feet wobbled as he tried to keep his balance. All the while, he watched me closely. "And you do know how this is to end?"

I pressed my lips together.

"I simply wish to know what the poor girl's fate is," he explained.

"She doesn't die, if that's what you're asking."

"So, she spins the straw into gold?" he asked, shifting his weight on my chest.

"Not exactly. Some—" I replied.

"Remember, Esmeralda," the king's words interrupted me. "You have until dawn to turn all the straw here into gold. If you succeed this third time, I shall wed you before nightfall tomorrow."

She bowed her head in response, lowering herself to the floor in a low curtsy.

Clearly pleased with her actions, the king turned on his heel to leave. A moment later, a loud thud filled the room as the door shut behind him. Metallic clanking followed—was he chaining it, too? Had that been part of the story? I couldn't remember.

"What would be worse, Jo?" Aneurin mused. "Marriage to him or death?"

"I suppose it all depends on your definition," I replied.

"Marriage is a union made for the duration of a life," Aneurin said. "I do not foresee a happy life for either of them."

"So, you think she should just give up and die?"

"Perhaps it would be a braver option."

"I wouldn't choose either. I'd figure out a way to escape."

Aneurin glanced around the room, lifting a small hand. "But, as you see, there is only one way out. Unless you have a plan?"

I didn't. I had no idea how to get out of the room, or the story as a whole. But my gut told me everything depended on the woman. After all, we hadn't left Snow behind until the main event of the poison apple had passed. Maybe that was the key to exiting stories?

I looked at the miller's daughter.

Her shoulders quivered as she pressed one hand to her face and the other to the wooden door. Despite the distance between us, I clearly heard her sobs echoing around us.

"I don't," I admitted softly, shaking my head.

Aneurin rolled his eyes. Clearly, he wasn't too thrilled by my answer. Irritation grew in his green gaze as he swept his attention from me back to the girl.

"This whole situation seems absurd to me," he whispered. "For a king to promise marriage to a woman merely for her spinning skill."

"It's more that he's set himself to marry a woman who will make him rich." Or so he thought.

"I understand that, but it's still absurd."

I couldn't resist the urge to snort, but covered my hand to muffle the sound. "You're one to talk," I whispered, lightly poking his side.

"Me?" Aneurin retorted, shaking his head. "Are you comparing the two of us? The king and I?"

My cheeks burned under his accusatory look. Maybe that was a bit of a reach, but...he *was*, in a way.

"You've insisted that your kiss can only be with a woman who wears a crown. You will only marry a woman for her title."

"Not this again," he sighed.

"Yes, *this* again," I replied, gesturing towards the woman. "It's the same thing as what's happening here."

"Tis not the same."

"It kinda is."

"I will not going to *force* someone's hand."

"Won't you? What's your plan after this random princess gives you a kiss, and poof, you turn into a prince? Aren't you going to get down on one knee and propose?"

"It's not going to be just some random princess."

"Aneurin, you've asked me to help you *find* 'your princess.' She is going to be a stranger to you. And you, to her."

"There is an art to wooing a woman."

"As a frog?" I asked, raising a brow.

He studied me hard for a moment before flicking his tongue to his eye. "It's possible."

I pressed my lips together, trying to suppress my laugh. But I felt the corners of my lips curl, and I saw his do the same. We held each other's gazes while we smiled at one another. It was odd—given the circumstances—but strangely nice.

"By the time I propose, she will no longer be a stranger. And I shall not force her hand into anything she has not already agreed to." He paused to take a breath. "Besides," he continued after a moment, "the kiss I receive from said princess will be one of true love. Which means she and I will have created a bond so profound…"

"Right," I interrupted, not wanting to hash out the details again.

As if differentiating a normal kiss to a kiss of true love would actually make a difference. The latter one was the sort I'd seen in romantic films. The kind I'd once dreamed about myself. And for a short time, I thought I'd found my happily ever after in Nico.

But I'd been wrong.

Aneurin turned around to watch the miller's daughter again.

Staring at him, I wished *I* had a royal title. Wouldn't it resolve everything? Even if I didn't *love* Aneurin, I cared about him deeply.

I internally shook myself. Why was I thinking this way? Aneurin was a frog, and a fictional one at that. This was just a *book* I'd managed to get myself stuck in. Eventually, I was going to get back out.

Hopefully.

"You really believe in this true love thing, don't you?" I asked aloud, watching him as he slowly turned his attention back to me.

"Do you not?" Aneurin inhaled deeply, as though he were bracing himself for yet another argument with me.

But I didn't want to argue. I was tired of fighting with him. Hadn't we just smiled at one another?

"It's not that I don't believe in love," I replied, pausing to collect my thoughts. "I just...I guess I've just had different experiences. Not everyone is so lucky to find love, let alone *true* love."

I turned my attention back to the woman, now sitting in the middle of the room.

"I hope we find that person for you," I continued. "But I don't think we're going to find her in this story."

Esmeralda's pressed her hands against her face as she continued to weep. She had long dark hair that fell to her waist, and she was dressed in a red gown with tight sleeves. A red ribbon was loosely woven into her hair. Based on her disheveled appearance, she hadn't changed her attire in days. She looked *hopeless*.

Just like I had when I first came back home.

Wiping her eyes with the back of her hands, Esmeralda sat up straight and examined her surroundings.

I could see her chin tremble when she turned towards the door. How scared she must feel, knowing she was so close to freedom. Yet, her fate hinged on a magical man—Rumpelstiltskin.

Rumpelstiltskin! Maybe he could be our way out of here. After all, he'd struck deals with the miller's daughter for treasure, and we had treasure from Hansel and Gretel! I'd totally forgotten that I'd kept the jewels in my pocket all this time.

Shifting in the straw, I slid my hand to the small pocket of my dress, hoping against all hope it was still there. After everything—all the running and falling and cliff diving...would they still be there? When my fingertips brushed against the small bag, I closed my eyes and released a breath of air.

"Is something the matter?" Aneurin asked.

"I might be able to get us out of here," I whispered.

He waited, crossing his arms against his chest. "How, pray tell?"

I pulled the jewels from my pocket for him to see. "We might be able to strike a deal."

Aneurin stared at them, and slowly shook his head. "While I admire your plan, I don't think the king will have any interest in these. Even more so if he's expecting a room full of gold."

"No, no," I replied softly. "Not with the king." As if I'd ever give *him* anything. "But with Rumpelstiltskin."

"Rum— *What?*"

"Rumpelstiltskin," I repeated. "He's the one actually spinning the straw into gold."

Aneurin lifted his head, looking around the room. "So, where is this fellow?"

I put the bag back in my pocket. "I think we have to wait."

"We don't have much time," he countered, lifting his hand towards the woman. "'Tis clear that she's aware of that as well."

"He'll come," I replied. I could at least be confident about that. Rumpelstiltskin would come to strike his last deal with her. Little did he know, he'd be striking a deal with me, too.

Somewhere between the soft sounds of the woman crying, and feeling Aneurin's gentle rhythm of his breathing, I had fallen asleep, nestled in the warm straw as we waited for Rumpelstiltskin to appear.

In my dream, I found myself in my own bed, surrounded by the familiar comfort of my room. The harsh light from above nearly blinded me, making me shield my eyes with a hand. I flexed my toes and stretched my arms. It was then that reality dawned on me...I was *home.*

Sitting up abruptly, I noticed the book of fairytales lying open beside me. I stared blankly at it for a moment. I suppose I expected to find the book just as I'd last seen it, with the stories the way I'd found them. Hansel and Gretel reuniting with their father in the woods, Snow-White receiving her kiss from her dashing prince, the Frog Prince finding his princess in the forest. But I found nothing but blank pages.

Just as I was about to close the book with a frustrated sigh, I felt the mattress dip slightly, Holding my breath, I cautiously turned my gaze to the figure lying beside me on the bed.

There lay a *man*—a strikingly handsome one at that.

His chest gently rose and fell with each breath. He was tall and muscular, with broad shoulders that tapered down to a trim waist. Strands of chestnut hair cascaded over his forehead, partially obscuring his features and lending him an air of mystery. Even then, there was something familiar about him.

My fingers twitched with the desire to brush the stray locks from his face. I fought the impulse, but ultimately succumbed to it.

When my fingertips made contact with his soft hair, he stirred, his emerald eyes fluttering open to meet mine.

I gasped. I knew those eyes. *Aneurin's* eyes.

And from the way they softened, I knew he recognized me, too. The corner of his lips curved into a gentle, tender smile.

I never wanted to lose the chance to see that smile on his face. The idea of suddenly being without him, made my chest hurt.

"Jo," he whispered, sliding his hand to the curve of my cheek. There was so much warmth there. "Josephine," he murmured once again, his voice barely audible. "You have to wake up."

"W-Wake up?" I repeated, my voice trembling with confusion.

A sudden knocking sound shattered the moment, pulling me away from his intense emerald gaze. I turned towards my bedroom door, finally aware of the thunderous knocking on the other side.

Opening my eyes, I snapped out of the dream. My heart pounded in my chest until I realized I was still in the heap of straw with Aneurin safely secured on my shoulder.

Had I really dreamed of Aneurin as a human? Could that really have been him?

He struggled to open an eye as he, too, woke from his nap. Aneurin peered at me sleepily before he pressed a hand to his face.

The moment was interrupted by another round of knocking.

"What in God's teeth?" he asked, turning to look at the door.

"I don't know…" I whispered back. "Hold on. I'm going to sit up and look."

Once Aneurin gripped my shirt, I shifted myself up in place and peered over the top of the pile of straw.

Esmeralda now stood next to the large spinning wheel, holding the small stool at her waist as she knocked against the seat of it with her knuckles. "Oh, dearest man!" she called out, glancing all around her. "Please, I beg you to come and help me." There were barely any gaps of silence between the loop of her loud, desperate pleas.

"Is the 'dearest man' she's referring to, the one you mentioned earlier to me?" Aneurin asked, rising to his feet to see for himself.

I nodded.

The woman, Esmeralda, eventually lowered the stool back to the floor and then knelt on the ground. Lifting her hands, she closed her eyes and leaned her head back. It was definitely a dramatic way to pray. But I suppose if my life was on the line over a pretty impossible task, I'd be a little dramatic too.

"P-Please, sir. Please," she begged more desperately.

"Oh, do stop your tears, my dear," a voice of a man replied from across the room. "I told you I'd return."

So, *this* was the voice of the infamous Rumpelstiltskin.

I leaned forward, trying to catch a glimpse of the man.

He was dressed in leathers. His pants were a shade of dark brown, while his tunic was black, topped by a mossy green vest. His nearly golden shoulder-length hair was tied back with a thin, frayed black ribbon.

Esmeralda stood as he approached her.

He was taller than what I had expected, but he still appeared to be a little shorter than the miller's daughter. The crown of his head easily met her shoulder. He paused by the spinning wheel, stroking a thumb against the wheel as a smile appeared on his face.

"The king has summoned yet another room, has he?"

"Yes," she replied, nodding as she bowed her head.

"He must truly be in need of gold. Three nights of imprisoning a poor, defenseless young woman like yourself…" he continued, shaking his head. "Such a shame."

"You will help me, won't you?"

"Of course, of course," he cooed. "For a price."

This was the night that she would promise her firstborn. A promise that she would later regret and fight to take back. And only succeeds by knowing a name. *His* name.

"But I gave you everything I possess," she exclaimed, lowering herself back to her knees. She pressed her hands against the floor at his feet and looked up at him. "If I become queen, I promise…I promise I shall give you all the jewels you could ever request. Lands…whatever you wish."

"'Whatever I wish,'" he repeated back, pressing his finger to his chin thoughtfully.

Deceit gleamed in his gaze, but she didn't see it.

"Y-Yes, w-whatever you wish," she replied.

"If I help you this last night, Esmeralda," he began. "You will become queen." His voice was stern, almost harsh. As though he wanted her to understand what it implied. "You will become his wife. You will vow to *obey* him, with every breath that you breathe in this world. Is this truly what you wish for yourself?"

"What choice do I have?" she asked, her voice shaking. "Am I to await my death at dawn?"

"There's no need for dramatics," the man replied. "No one spoke of such a morbid thing."

"If I had a choice—"

"*Everyone* has a choice," the man interrupted, shaking his head. "Even for those who feel as though they do not. There is always a choice. It is up to you to be brave enough to grasp it."

"I don't understand?"

"Regardless," he said with a shrug. "What shall you give me then if I complete this task for you?"

"Would you not like lands? A castle? A crown?"

"What good would any of those do for me? A poor, humble old man like me."

I held back a snort. There was nothing poor or humble about the man. But he wasn't wrong about the old part.

"*This* is who you wish to strike a deal with?" Aneurin asked. "I recognize him. Do you know what you intend to do?"

I nodded.

"I must warn you against this, Josephine," Aneurin said, shaking his head. "He does not appear to be trustworthy. Might I suggest that we perhaps—"

"How else are we going to find your princess?" I asked, sliding my hand into my pocket. I showed him the jewels again.

Once again, his eyes grew wide. "You plan to bargain with him?"

"It's worth a shot, right?"

"I have a very bad feeling about this," Aneurin replied.

"Noted." Still, I stood up and dropped him into my pocket, ignoring his indignant yelp.

The air seemed to still as all eyes turned to me. Esmeralda's expression shifted from surprise to curiosity. Rumpelstiltskin, however, regarded me with a mixture of intrigue and skepticism.

Ignoring the flutter of nerves in my stomach, I lifted my hand with the jewels, and fixed Rumpelstiltskin with a bold look.

"I have a deal for you," I declared, my voice stronger now, carrying a hint of challenge.

"Oh, do you?" he replied with a jeering smile, eyeing me with interest. "Pray, *pretty lady*, tell me more."

TWENTY-TWO

I could hear Trapper in my head telling me to be smart. I even heard Arch warning me to remain wary of Rumpelstiltskin, no matter how self-assured I was feeling in the moment. If there was one thing I'd learned in my very short life, it was feelings were fleeting. Love, fear—confidence.

With each step, I second-guessed myself more. Was striking a deal with someone like Rumpelstiltskin a good idea? Maybe this wasn't the right decision. Up close, he intimidated me. Maybe it was the curve of his nose and chin. Or it could have been what I remembered about his particular fairytale. He wasn't someone I'd want to come across in a dark alley. And his amber eyes...they were so dark.

But hiding did nothing to help in Aneurin's quest.

When I finally stood in front of the man, I'd already lowered my hand to my side. Still clutching the jewels in my palm, I held still while his gaze roamed from the top of my head down to the tips of my toes.

An amused smile danced along the length of his lips. "I did not know we had guests," he said lightly, diverting his attention back to Esmeralda.

She shifted on her feet. "I thought I was alone."

"Nevertheless," Rumpelstiltskin continued, "here we are."

"Here we are," I echoed, lifting my hand with the jewels again—this time a bit more tentatively than before.

"I have these valuables," I offered, finally opening my palm to reveal the treasure. "They belonged to a witch, who lived deep in a forest, and captured children to eat." I don't know why I felt like I had to explain where I got them, but the sparkle in Rumpel's eye had turned to amusement.

"Sounds like a questionable pastime," he replied. "But who am I to judge?"

"I think if it involves eating children, we *all* have room to judge," I countered.

"Nasty creatures—children," Rumpel retorted. "But they are good for one thing." He turned his attention back to the miller's daughter, who stared at us with wide eyes. "Sweet Esmeralda," he cooed in a sing-song voice, "if you promise me your firstborn child, I will fill this room with all the gold a king could ever wish for."

"You can't!" I exclaimed, shaking my head.

"And why not?" he demanded. "For if I do as she asks, her rewards are bountiful."

"You know as well as I do that's a bunch of bologna."

Rumpelstiltskin raised a brow. "I'm not entirely sure I understand what you're saying."

Selecting the ruby with my free hand, I lifted it to his gaze. "This should be a fair enough trade to take care of the gold in this room."

"A single ruby?" he scoffed. "You think that is a fair trade?"

"And you think a *child* is?"

"Of course." He gestured to Esmeralda. "And I don't hear her disagreeing. Do you object, my dear?"

I glanced at her and felt a pang of pity for her. She must know she didn't have a leg to stand on when negotiating.

Rumpelstiltskin was just another man, in control of a situation that she was not.

"I have four gold coins," I continued. "Add that to the ruby."

"Is this a trap?" he asked, jerking his gaze back to Esmeralda. "Were you hoping to have someone else pay your debt?"

"There is no debt," I retorted, lowering the gem. "This is an act of kindness. You said that magic comes with a price. I'm paying hers."

He scoffed. "No one simply pays for someone else, expecting nothing in return."

I turned my gaze to Esmeralda and gave her a small, sad smile. "Tomorrow, when the king returns, I hope with all of my heart, you find it within yourself to reject his proposal."

"*Reject*—?"

"Yes," I said more sternly. "You don't want to live your life with a man like that. And the life of a child that deserves your love…it should never be the price of your own."

Rumpelstiltskin tilted his chin, watching me with a strange look. "I don't know if I should consider your advice brave or foolish."

"Maybe a bit of both," I admitted. "But you can help her."

"Me?" he asked, flashing a knowing smile. "What could I possibly do to assist her more than what I've already done?"

"You can help her escape."

Rumpelstiltskin chuckled, crossing his arms against his chest. "What makes you think I could do such a thing?"

"You spin straw into gold," I replied. Wasn't that enough?

As Rumpelstiltskin turned his attention back to Esmeralda, I was almost certain it had been. Stroking a person's ego never hurts in situations like this.

He turned back to me and narrowed his eyes.

"Will you take my payment for her?" I asked, holding out the ruby again.

"I have a feeling you'll offer me a bargain far more amusing," he replied. "If you require me to accept verbally, consider this deal for Esmeralda done." He snatched the gem from my grasp before I could say another word about it.

The treasure Hansel and Gretel had found in the witch's floorboards had finally come in handy for something worthwhile.

As he tucked the jewel into a leather pouch on his waist, I wondered if what I'd just done was even allowed. But I also couldn't bear the thought of Esmeralda marrying the king—or die, either.

With a snap of his fingers, the spinning wheel whirled on its own, as though an invisible being was making the mechanism work. The large wheel moved, the peddle underneath rapidly bobbing up and down. Piece by piece, the straw spooled itself through the device and emerged as a perfect string of pure gold, winding onto a large bobbin. Once it became full, a new one appeared and the process began anew.

I could only watch in awe. I knew I'd never see this ever again.

Esmeralda admired the spinning wheel's magic with wide eyes, her smile continuing to grow. Her expression told me just how grateful she was for the exchange I'd made. Her relief was palpable. A kind I'd only known a few times in my life—especially when I'd confessed my feelings to Nico.

I felt a tug in my pocket. Aneurin. He'd been a lot quieter than I thought he would be. I glanced down and saw his little head peeking out.

Rumpelstiltskin tilted his head curiously in my direction, drawing my gaze back to his.

He smiled, flashing me a brown-toothed grin, inching closer and closer to me. "I am still awaiting this bargain you wish to strike."

"My bargain..." I revealed the rest of the treasures in my hand and extended them to him. "I need you to get me out of here." I let him eye the remaining items for a moment before I closed my palm.

His amber eyes met mine. "And where, pray tell, sweet lady, do you wish to go instead?"

"Some of those are *mine*, Jo!" Aneurin called from my pocket, drawing Rumpel's gaze down to my skirt.

The magic man's eyebrows raised, curiosity brightening his expression, as he brushed a finger against his chin. "Well, well, well," he murmured, reaching for me—well—where Aneurin was hiding. "What, or should I ask *who*, do we have here?"

I took a small step back, covering the pocket's opening to protect the transformed prince. "He's my friend."

"Tsk, tsk, sweet. Aren't you going to introduce us?" he chided. Not waiting for my response, he snapped his fingers.

In an instant, Aneurin's slippery skin slid against my hand, displacing it with an unexpected force.

My shock paralyzed me, preventing me from seizing him before the inevitable occurred. It was a lapse in judgment, one that led to his large, emerald eyes locking onto me as he ascended into the air. Panic clouded his gaze, and Aneurin stretched out his arms towards me—asking me to save him.

Shoving the small gems back into my pocket, I reached for him, nearly going onto the tip of my toes to grab him. Relief only settled in me once I curled my hands around his body and pulled him against my chest.

"What are you doing?!" I shouted. "You can't just—"

"That's certainly not just any old toad you have there, sweets."

"How would you know?" I shot back, narrowing my eyes at him.

Aneurin wiggled in my tightening grasp.

I flattened my palm so he could sit comfortably.

"If I'm not mistaken, this is the long-lost Prince Aneurin."

His words stunned not only me, but apparently my amphibian companion, too, based on the jolt that shuddered through him.

Aneurin peered over his shoulder, glancing back at me, mirroring my own confusion.

I redirected my attention to Rumpelstiltskin. How could he know about Aneurin when they were from entirely different stories? Could he have something to do with Aneurin's spell? Was that even possible?

"What did you say?" I asked, shaking my head in case I had heard incorrectly.

Rumpel laughed, setting a hand on his waist. "It is, isn't it?" His fingers came together in another snap.

Could I tie them together and stop him from doing magic? Even if I could, it was too late.

A cloud of shimmering, golden flecks encircled Aneurin, yanking him from my grasp.

I panicked, reaching out for him again, but the magical mist moved too fast. "Wait!" I shouted. "Let him go!"

"I think you'll want to see this, dearie," Rumpelstiltskin replied with a grin. He snapped his fingers for the third time since he'd spotted Aneurin.

A bright, searing flash filled the room.

But not like the ones that had transported me into the book and between stories.

It dimmed, revealing our surroundings just as it had been before. Except for one thing. In the center of a pool of golden thread, was a young man. Bent over with his hands and knees planted on the floor. His back rose and fell with heavy breaths. He continued to stare at the floor, as though he were unsure of his own strength.

Where Aneurin, the frog, had been was now Aneurin, the *man*.

Unable to look away, I circled him, taking in his new appearance.

Rumpelstiltskin stepped out of my way without a word, as if he wanted me to examine the result of his magic.

Aneurin was somehow dressed in a white linen shirt and black pants. At least he wasn't naked—that would have been awkward.

Given how his shoulders continued to heave, I wondered if he was alright. I peered at Rumpel. *Is it safe to approach?* I silently asked with a raised brow.

He gestured toward Aneurin. "You are more than welcome to go see him for yourself."

I needed no more permission and immediately started slowly closing the distance between me and Aneurin. Nerves built in the pit of my stomach with each step.

Long, dark curls hung around his head, just brushing the tips of his broad shoulders. He had a sharp jawbone. His forearm muscles shifted under the fabric, and his nose was long, but perfectly placed. He was beautiful, just as real as he had been a mere moment ago, even though I could no longer hold him safely in the pocket of my dress. He was a real, breathing person.

And I *knew* him. I'd seen his face in my dreams before.

But what if his gaze didn't meet mine the same way? What if his smile didn't reach his eyes? What if everything that I'd experienced before we properly met was simply that—a dream?

Extending a hand, I brushed a few fingers over his shoulder. "Aneurin?" I asked softly. When he didn't respond, I knelt beside him. "*Aneurin*, are you alright?"

He blinked, as though he finally understood that someone was talking to him. He turned toward me, and our eyes locked onto each other's. His dazzling emerald eyes softened.

I felt my earlier anxiety melt away.

This was *him*.

Even though this was my first time seeing Aneurin as a human, this was more than just my dreams made reality.

But Aneurin had transformed from a frog to a man by just the snap of Rumpelstiltskin's fingers. Without a kiss of true love. Was this change permanent?

As if he heard my thoughts, the magical man broke the silence. "Enjoy the moment while you can, Your Highness." Now standing by the spinning wheel, his voice had to travel across the room. Despite the increased distance, his jeering didn't lose any of its effect.

I jerked my gaze back in his direction, noticing another completed bobbin of golden thread floating across the room to stack amongst the others.

"This is fleeting, to be sure," he continued.

Was it a promise? Or a *threat*?

From what I knew of his story, it was probably both.

"Fleeting?" I repeated.

"Of course!" Rumpel chuckled gleefully. "I did him no favors. I merely satisfied my hunch that he was the missing prince."

"Are you saying you know where Aneurin is from?"

Was it even possible that Rumpelstiltskin knew about other stories? What about other worlds?

"Of course, my girl. I know *everything*." He proudly lifted his finger in the air to emphasize his point. "And I know that his royal parents have been searching far and wide for their son."

"But I don't understand. How did Aneurin end up—"

The man cut me off as he eyed Aneurin. "It appears, however, Your *Highness*, that the king and queen have sadly bestowed your throne unto your little brother."

My attention shot to Aneurin, just in time to see frustration spark in his gaze.

Aneurin had a *brother*? He hadn't ever mentioned one, had he?

He eased back onto his knees, lifting himself slightly to stare at the magical man.

"Why, yes," Rumpelstiltskin continued, though it was unclear if he was still addressing the prince or me. "The dashing Prince Charming. One of the most adored sons in the entire realm, and thus far, eagerly sought by the fairest and most beautiful maidens."

Aneurin pressed his lips together, as though he were deciding what to say.

If his brother was *the* Prince Charming, that could only mean that Aneurin belonged in the Cinderella story. Right? But if his *brother* was Charming...

"Your family," the man said, "has finally given up on you after three years and moved on and gave your birthright to the spare."

"But how do you even know all of this?" I countered.

"Weren't you listening? There is very little that I don't know," Rumpelstiltskin reaffirmed.

The dread in my gut intensified. Was there something more to all of this?

I placed my hands on Aneurin's shoulder.

He still hadn't spoken since the news of him being replaced in the line of succession.

"There's something you don't know," Aneurin finally said.

It was my first time hearing his true voice. I watched the movement of his lips, the way his eyes focused on Rumpel. The only word to describe Aneurin was *regal*. He was destined to be a king.

"Oh?" Rumpelstiltskin prodded, the amusement in his tone. "Pray tell, Your Highness."

"If you seek a reward for my return, you'll be disappointed."

Rumpel waved his hand, as if brushing off the warning. "I doubt your brother would wish to see his rival return to the kingdom. He would have to forfeit his crown, the promise of the throne…"

"My brother has never cared for his title, nor the pomp and circumstance that comes with the throne," Aneurin countered..

"Perhaps before, Your Highness. But, as one often finds, when given a taste of the sweet promise of luxuries, it is hard to resist when they're just within reach."

Aneurin clenched his jaw.

There was some truth in the words, but why bait the former frog prince? I had no idea where this was going. My knowledge of fairytales was useless now that the stories were merging.

"However," the magical man hummed, "you still need to lift your curse, with a kiss of *true love*." He pinned Aneurin with a probing stare. "How long do you plan to continue your search?"

"Until I find her," Aneurin retorted sharply through gritted teeth.

I resisted the urge to hold his hands, to bring solace to him in the way he had for me when Trapper had been yelling at me in the tree house. Instead, I slid a hesitant palm over the curve of his back. I felt oddly relieved when he didn't recoil from my touch.

Rumpelstiltskin's lips spread, revealing a gleaming smile. "What if I could promise you I could help you find your true love?"

"Your help is not the sort I wish to indulge in."

"No?" Rumpel asked, pressing a hand against his chest in feigned offense. "And yet, you partnered yourself with…" He gestured to me, unable to definitively finish his sentence.

I hadn't given him my name, just as he hadn't given his to us. Even with things diverging from the traditional story, I knew a name held power.

"I agreed to help the prince find his princess," I explained. "In exchange for returning home safely."

"And yet, no luck?"

"Believe it or not, princesses are hard to find," I snapped.

"Perhaps," Rumpelstiltskin continued, "we could strike a deal, Your Highness. You and I."

"About?" Aneurin asked, turning his gaze back to the man.

The man let out a huff, as if he was put-out that he had to *explain* his offer. "I could take you somewhere filled with eligible royals. Surely, you will find your kiss of true love there." When Aneurin still didn't respond, he crossed his arms against his chest. "Shall I spell it out for you, Prince Aneurin?" he asked, his words more forceful now. "I shall send you where you'll have the chance to break your own spell. And I shall give you twenty-four hours to do it. If you find your kiss by midnight there, you win. Your life, your freedom, and your happiness."

"And if I do not?"

The magical man shrugged. "I like to focus on the positive side of things. But if you do not succeed…then you'll transform back into your frog-self and belong to me."

Aneurin couldn't agree to this. There was no way. We could still do this—him and me.

"I'm sorry," I cut in. "Did you just say he'd *belong* to you?"

"What a duo we would be," Rumpelstiltskin said with a laugh, completely ignoring me. "It's not every day a being like me has a prince under his control."

Aneurin turned, catching my gaze, and squeezed my hand.

A knot tightened in my stomach. "Aneurin," I murmured, shaking my head. "You *can't*…"

"If I ensure your return home, as I promised you originally—"

I cut him off. "We can still find your princess. We were only getting started."

He lifted my hand, his touch gentle against my skin, and pressed a tender kiss against my knuckles. The mere act sent a flurry of butterflies scattering throughout my stomach. Despite the rush of emotions, I couldn't shake the sinking feeling that lingered at the back of my mind, casting a shadow over the moment.

"How many more life-threatening situations will I have to watch from your pocket? How many more witches will we have to run from, Jo?" He shook his head sadly at me. "It is no way to live."

"But we can—" I started.

"I'd like to believe that perhaps…" Aneurin trailed off and nodded, apparently deciding his next words. "Perhaps I could find *her* wherever he plans to send me."

"Twenty-four hours isn't a long time," I cautioned.

"Indeed, it is not," he agreed. "But it could be enough."

I wanted to pinch him. *Hard.* Was he listening to himself? His chances were slim to none. He had to know that.

"I can't just watch you throw your life away. You mean so…" I swallowed the rest of the thought and tried again. "You deserve…"

He smiled, making my cheeks warm.

Even that scared me. Maybe that confirmed my feelings. Ones that I hadn't accepted or fully comprehended until now. I had *feelings* for Aneurin. And I didn't want him to get hurt—to make a deal he'd later regret.

When he didn't say anything, I hoped it meant he understood what I was trying to say.

His next words proved me wrong.

"I want you to send Josephine home."

Did that sound like he was accepting? "You have to give him a fair chance," I cut in, glaring at Rumpelstiltskin before he could take it as a binding agreement. "Wherever you're sending us—him—there has to be a fair chance he can succeed."

"'*Fair*' is all up to interpretation, my dear," Rumpel replied.

"Then your deal is bullshit," I retorted. "If you're giving him twenty-four hours or whatever, it should include the moment his chances are at best. How can he stand a chance if his twenty-four hours begin at a time when there's no hope?"

Rumpel smirked. "Isn't that the thrill of a good bargain?"

"No," I replied. "The rules must be clear and concise." I wasn't going to leave anything unsaid in this disastrous deal. "Isn't that how you like your deals? So it's undeniable who won?"

Rumpel huffed. "'Tis true."

"That's what I thought," I replied. "I want your *word* that Aneurin will have until the midnight during the ball." Maybe it wouldn't let him have the *whole* event to search, but it was better than nothing. If Aneurin really was the brother of Prince Charming, and if we were really about to embark on journeying into the story, there *had* to be a ball.

"A ball?" Rumpel repeated curiously.

"You said you'd take him 'somewhere filled with eligible royals.' Is that not the definition of a ball?" I asked with the most nonchalant shrug I could muster. "It could be the easiest win, or the hardest defeat."

Rumpel studied me. "He could be rejected," he finally said.

"He could," I repeated.

"Or you could."

I stared at him. *What?* I wanted to know what he meant, but I was also afraid of his answer, so I kept silent.

He smiled wide, almost smug at finally rendering me speechless. "Fine, my lady. I shall concede to your requests. The prince will have until midnight of a party, a soirée, or a 'ball,' as you put it. If by the last chime of the night rings out, he still has not been kissed... he will be mine. Does this satisfy you?"

No. Aneurin belonging to this man would never be okay.

But before I could press for more details, Aneurin spoke up.

"I'll accept the deal," he stated solemnly, abruptly releasing my hand. "With the condition that you will help Josephine, my friend, go home. Regardless if I am successful."

"Of course, of course. Worry not about her," Rumpelstiltskin said with a pleased smile. "After all, she has already paid the debt of another. She's bad for business in my book."

Seriously? Helping someone was bad for *business?*

"I—" Aneurin started, but I cut him off.

"*Wait,*" I urged.

He shook his head at me and pressed on, staring at Rumpelstiltskin once again. "I accept the terms of having to find my true love and receive a true love's kiss by the midnight of a ball. If not, I shall…become yours."

"Delightful!" the magical man replied, a small, sinister smile growing on his lips until the corners nearly reached his ears.

It made him look inhuman. Like a predator.

A chill shot through me. But there was nothing I could do now. Aneurin had accepted the offer, so I watched in horror as Rumpelstiltskin extended his hand.

"Say no more. It's a deal, *Your Highness.*"

TWENTY-THREE

"Happy hunting, Your Highness." With a snap of Rumpelstiltskin's ridiculously long fingers, the room began to spin.

Esmeralda's eyes were wide with fear and amazement as the golden bobbins of thread began to unravel and twist around us.

Aneurin wrapped his arm around my shoulders, pressing me to him.

"Where are we going?" I shouted into his shirt, tucking my face into the crook of his arm, clinging onto him for dear life. If something didn't happen soon, I was going to be sick.

"He's sending me home," Aneurin replied against my ear.

A flash of light enveloped us. It was just like before. A new story. But this time, it was *his*.

I squeezed my eyes shut and dug my fingers into Aneurin's shoulders even harder. In response, his arms held me tighter.

My heart surged with a strange excitement. Throughout our journey, he'd in my pocket or on my shoulder, a constant companion with our endless debates and banter. Now, with his transformation, a shift had occurred. Now *I* depended on *him*.

But despite his altered appearance, he remained fundamentally unchanged. He was still…him. Him with all his must-be-royal stipulations.

Suddenly, the light disappeared, dropping us. I screamed as we plunged into a pile of something soft. Whatever it was, I was grateful that it wasn't water again.

But I would have done anything for a shower right about now. My dress was still damp from the thunderstorm on the cliff, and now slightly smelly from the straw in Rumpelstiltskin's story.

The scent of sweet grass filled my nose. I opened my eyes and saw small pieces of hay drifted in the air above me. The urge to sneeze was almost impossible to resist, but I didn't want to make more noise. With a hand over my nose, I waited anxiously, hoping our presence hadn't drawn unwanted attention.

When it passed, I realized there was something warm next to—and around—me. It took me a moment to register it was his arms.

Aneurin.

He groaned and shifted next to me, his hand moving to the small of my back.

"Where do you think we are?" I asked softly, doing my best to keep my voice soft and low.

He opened his eyes and scanned the wooden roof above us.

"It appears we're in the royal stables," he murmured.

"Seems fitting, huh?" I replied, lifting a small fistful up for him to see. "To go from straw to hay."

"At least it's not water." He pulled his arm from around me and took some of the hay from my hands. "Small miracles, no doubt."

I nodded, silently mourning the loss of his warmth. The absence left me feeling inexplicably empty. "At least we're not hanging off the side of some cliff—"

"I feel as though I am," he confessed. Before I could ask what he meant, he leaned forward, bracing himself with his elbows and climbed out of our landing spot.

While it was a struggle to find my balance, I adjusted myself enough to see my surroundings. Wooden beams held the roof in place, supported by a foundation of stone and brick walls. The space was empty, but the wooden door, thankfully, was wide open. Each stall had a similar barrier that opened into what I imagined was a courtyard of some sort. I turned back to Aneurin.

The corners of his lips were turned up into a small but brilliant smile. Some brunette curls were matted against his forehead. When he wiped the small strands away, I wondered if they were as soft as they appeared. Even in a stables, he looked like he could have stepped right out of a men's cologne commercial. He was a handsome man for having once been a frog. But was it weird that I missed him being an amphibian?

His gaze met mine, catching me gawking like a teenage girl. "Are you feeling ill, Josephine?"

I licked my bottom lip then shook my head. "I'm fine! Totally fine." Sliding a hand through my tangled hair, I successfully pushed myself to my feet. I tried to walk down the heap of hay but stumbled when the skirt of my dress got caught under my foot. I tugged on the green kirtle and heard the fabric rip.

In an instant, strong hands were around my waist and gently pulling me upright.

I turned my gaze to Aneurin, only to find him focused on leading us in the opposite direction. His warm chest was next to my cheek. If I looked up, I was sure he'd see my face red with embarrassment.

When our feet found the wooden floor, I averted my eyes and used the moment to steady my feet before taking a step back from him. I placed my hands on my waist and flashed the best fake smile I could muster.

"Thanks." I nodded and tucked some of my hair behind my ear. "I'd do anything to get out of this thing." I looked down at my dress, feeling a little ungrateful complaining about it. When I thought about all the hard work that I was sure Snow-White had put into her creation, or the time that Stitches had spent with her...I never wanted to part with it. But after everything, it sorely needed a wash. My sneakers were in bad shape, too.

I looked back up at Aneurin, secretly watching as he rolled his sleeves up to his elbows. His arms's toned muscles were now on display. His pants left nothing to the imagination. His thighs were firm but muscular. Just below his knees, he wore black leather boots, with thick laces wrapped around the tops to keep them in place.

Once again, I felt like a start-struck teenage girl. And then I noticed he was watching me, too. I met his gaze.

"I wish you could see your face. You stare at me as though you've never seen a man before." He smirked at me, only embarrassing me further for being caught ogling him.

I knew my cheeks were a brilliant shade of red by now. There was no way I was going to be able to deny that. I tried to shrug as nonchalantly as I could before replying, "I guess I've just never seen one in an outfit like that."

He looked down at his clothes and lifted a brow. "I'm not any different from the others…"

He was right. Snow's men—they'd all worn similar attire.

Having caught me in a lie, he flashed me a knowing smile. "Am *I* now to be scrutinized for my attire?"

"Not at all," I quickly replied, lifting my hand. "I was just…you know. It's different. *You're* different."

Aneurin slid his hands to his hips and nodded slowly in understanding. "Yes, this must be quite different for you."

"I'm used to you being like…four inches tall," I explained.

He exhaled softly. "Well, would you like a reintroduction?"

"I wouldn't want to tarnish my memory of you calling me a 'peasant' during our first encounter."

"Perhaps not my best moment," he admitted, holding his hand out to me. "I apologize for my behavior."

"I think we're past the necessity of apologies, Aneurin," I replied before stopping myself. "I'm…still allowed to call you that, right?"

He chuckled softly and nodded. Then, he gently enveloped my hand with both of his, holding it securely.

My heart pounded in my chest. What the heck was happening to me? I couldn't even remember a time when Nico had had this effect on me. Maybe it was the boots. It *had* to be the boots.

We stared at each other for a long moment before a loud *neigh* interrupted us.

He dropped my hand and looked at the empty courtyard again. "I should seek my parents," Aneurin explained, gesturing out toward the cobblestone courtyard.

"I'm sure they'll be more than relieved to see you," I replied with my best encouraging nod. "Especially if it's really been three years."

"It is strange to think I've been away from home for so long," he agreed with a heavy sigh. "My brother was only seventeen when I last saw him."

That would make Charming only twenty years old. Most twenty-year-old's in my world were busy navigating college life, buying tacos on Tuesdays, watching sports with friends, and snapping weird selfies on social media platforms.

"You never mentioned him before," I murmured. "I didn't even know you *had* a brother."

Aneurin shifted, glancing back over at me. "I didn't feel he needed to be a part of my story. But now that he has been named to be next in line for the throne…"

"Were you close before what happened?"

"There are eight years between us," he replied with a shrug. "And we both received different instruction in our education. I was educated to become the next king. He was able to enjoy the benefits of the title, without the weight of the role."

"Do you think he'll be happy to see you?"

Aneurin leaned his hand against the stall's wooden frame, his attention on the empty courtyard. "There is only but one way to find the answers to your questions, Josephine," he replied, gesturing at the open door.

"What about Henry?" I asked.

Aneurin raised his brow, curiously. "What about him?"

"I just hope he's still not wandering about the forest, looking for a princess for you."

He pressed his lips together thoughtfully before nodding. "Then I shall hope we find him here, too." He extended his hand out to me once again.

I stared at his hand for a moment before meeting his gaze.

"Will you think differently of me if I admit that I fear I may not fulfill my end of the bargain with that man?" Aneurin murmured.

I swallowed before shaking my head. "No. Why would I?"

"I wondered if you thought me foolish for my agreement."

I sighed. "I…understand why you did it."

"Will you still help me? As you originally agreed?"

"I'm still here, aren't I?"

He nodded. "I expected a vastly different response from you."

"Like what?"

"That you lack the choice," he jabbed.

I rolled my eyes and took a step forward, reaching for his hand with my own. Then it hit me. I was holding his actual, *human* hand. Aneurin was still a stranger to me—how much time had we *really* spent with each other? But when I stared up into his eyes, I felt like I could have melted into a puddle.

"Aneurin, I will help you in whatever way I can," I replied as I squeezed his hand gently with mine. I wanted to believe that we had a fighting chance in finding his true love. Ignoring the bittersweet feeling that the result would never be me. If this was really the story of Cinderella, maybe *she* was his destined princess.

I pushed away my dreams of him. Hazy memories of us dancing in the middle of a large candle-lit ballroom. Him, dressed in his royal attire, and me, in one of the most beautiful gowns imaginable. Him whispering into my ear that he'd wait for me.

But those had only been dreams. Aneurin was a fictional book character, and I…was real. I didn't belong here, and I never would. I needed to stay focused on finding him his real true love and getting back home to Mom and Dad. Everything else, I'd have to figure out later. Because all of this was nothing more than a wild fantasy.

"This is still a little strange," I admitted, breaking the silence. "You being so...tall."

Aneurin laughed, and his smile met his eyes again. "It is a little strange," he agreed. "But I do like that I'm not being carted on your shoulder, or in your pocket. I can finally take the lead."

"By all means," I replied. "The clock is ticking. Let's go find your family and figure out how we're going to find your true love."

He nodded and squeezed my hand. "Aye, let's go."

Just as we left the stables, I could hear a clock off in the distant chiming midnight. The sound made my heart sink into my stomach. I couldn't let Aneurin lose his bargain with Rumpelstiltskin. I didn't know exactly what the man wanted from Aneurin, but I couldn't bear the thought of my friend being lost to such a villain.

We raced across the path, leading from the stables to a structure made of large white stone.

Ahead, I saw a guard, dressed in his uniform, standing by a rounded door. In his hand, he held a long spike, with a pointed edge. Maybe this wouldn't be as easy as I had originally thought. Despite the late hour, the castle was far from being asleep completely.

Aneurin must have seen him, too, for he stopped and pulled me toward the closest outset wall. "How could I be so foolish?" he sighed, shaking his head. "Of course, the doors are guarded."

"Is there a different way in?"

"If I were a frog, it would be as simple as me going ahead..." He turned, looking all around him. "Come, this way," Aneurin said, pulling me to a small, narrow staircase that led up to another round door. This one was not guarded by anyone.

"It leads to the upper floors of the kitchens," he explained softly from over his shoulder.

"The kitchens? As in your Missus Alden's kitchens?"

He paused, turning to look at me. "You remembered?"

"You spoke so highly of her sponge cake."

I was almost sure that Aneurin's eyes glistened in the darkness. "Yes, it's my favorite."

"I know," I said with a shrug. "I didn't forget."

Aneurin looked down, contemplating what I'd just said. "Trust me, you'll have to try one," he finally whispered before continuing up the stone stairs.

I stayed as close as I could to him, wanting to keep within the shadows, in case anyone could see us.

We halted in front of the rounded door, which he took care to open it quietly. After he peered inside, he looked at me, tilting his head to the side. "Come, we'll cross through the kitchens. When we get to the end, there will be a door that leads into the Great Hall."

"Do you think there's a chance we'll find your family there?"

"At this hour? I doubt it. I'm sure my father and mother have long since retired to their chambers."

"What happens if we're caught?"

Aneurin raised a brow. "Josephine, while I might have been missing for several years, I am still the first-born son of the king and queen. Nothing bad will come of us if we're seen."

"Then wouldn't it have been easier for us to just go up to a guard and explain?"

"I'm sure that you would think so. However, I'm not sure every-one would believe that I'm the prince. It *has* been three years."

I sighed, but couldn't argue against that logic.

Aneurin continued, "I suppose we should both be grateful that we're not running from a flesh-eating witch."

"I guess," I murmured, rising onto the tips of my toes to peek over his shoulder into the kitchens.

"Come," he replied. "All will be well. You can trust me."

"I do," I admitted with a nod. "I know that you thought I didn't…" My words drifted to silence as I looked up at him. "I'm sorry that

I didn't tell you everything before. I just didn't know what I could say and—"

"Josephine," Aneurin said my name softly, shaking his head. "I understand. You need not explain yourself to me."

"I know, but—"

"I trust that you would tell me the things I needed to know. I know that I wanted to know, to understand more. But I..." He trailed off, then nodded slowly. "I understand. And there's no need to apologize for anything. Without you, I wouldn't be here."

"I'm not entirely sure you want to go thanking me for that, just yet," I remarked. "What if you don't find her?"

"There's always that chance. But at least I'll have tried."

"But what if twenty-four hours isn't enough? Have you thought about what will happen if he comes to collect you?"

Aneurin leaned back against the door of the kitchen. "In truth, Josephine, I could only think of my family. What I'd do to see them again. To put right the wrongs I left behind. And for you to see me... as I am now."

"What?"

"I know it might sound a little strange," he replied, glancing down at his hands. "But I wanted you to see me as I truly am." He flashed a dazzling smile. "That is why I made the bargain. I had nothing to lose, but everything to gain."

"You have *everything* to lose," I countered.

"I refuse to spend a lifetime as an amphibian."

"I understand not wanting to be a frog for the rest of your life, but there's a hefty price to this bargain. To *belong* to someone? Especially *him*?" It couldn't be a good thing.

"Then we'll do our best to ensure I find her, won't we?"

He brushed his hair from his eyes, and a twinge of jealousy filled me, filling my chest. I didn't know why I felt a twinge of anger as I imagined him with someone else—some wildly beautiful woman, who was perfect in every way. And I'd be sent back home. Back to my reality. A world where Nico's betrayal stung sharply—where I was all alone.

I could feel Aneurin's attention, but I ignore it and him as I pushed through the door. "Come on," I urged. "Every minute is precious here. We don't have time to lose."

"And wher' do ye scavengers think ye goin'?" a voice asked, startling us both.

I turned and saw two male servants, one with long hair hanging around his shoulders while the other had his black hair pulled back, standing in the kitchen. Both were moving crates of apples.

"We've been summoned to the Great Hall," Aneurin answered. "We're coming from the stables."

"Aye, I know abou' the gatherin'," the man with the loose hair said, shaking his head. "Ye says yer names be?"

"We didn't," Aneurin replied, taking my hand. "We'll be taking our leave now." He yanked my hand and led us down a narrow hallway. He stopped just short of the long hall, pushing aside a tapestry that lined the wall from floor to ceiling.

"What are you doing?" I hissed, glancing over my shoulder.

But Aneurin didn't respond. Instead, he opened a door in the wall and tugged me through it. As soon as he shut it behind us, we were in the dark. Over our heavy breathing, I faintly heard music, laughter, and conversation.

"What is that?" I asked softly.

"They must be holding a celebration," Aneurin replied. "Come…"

"I can't see enough to go anywhere," I retorted.

"Hold on. You won't get lost with me," he whispered again as he squeezed my hand in his.

It was the longest I'd ever held a man's hand, and surprisingly, I didn't mind it. I wanted to tell Aneurin to never let go, but deep down, I knew he'd have to, eventually.

"This is a servant's stairwell up to their quarters. If there is a ball, no one will be up in their rooms. We can cut across to the main hall…" He paused, deep in thought on how to navigate to his destination. "My mother and father should be in their suite."

"If this is a celebration, shouldn't they be dancing?"

"My father has never been one for dancing," he explained. "But he does enjoy watching others."

I could barely make out his face in the darkness. Was he anxious to see his parents? I was afraid to ask.

His boots tapped on the stone steps as he quickly led me up the winding staircase.

I followed, sliding my free hand against the wall. Only as we approached the next floor did I finally see a small candelabra. The candles were lit, but they were dim, only illuminating a bit of the staircase ahead. We rounded one more flight of steps and stopped in front of a wooden door that looked aged and worn.

When Aneurin pushed open the door, a long hallway of opened doors came into view. As he towed me behind him, I peered into a few of the opened doorways. A servant's room only had a simple bed, neatly made, and a stand with a bowl upon it.

"This is all the servants have?"

"They spend much of their day away from their rooms," Aneurin explained over his shoulder. "I assure you, they have everything they need below."

"So, says you. Everything but freedom."

He stopped walking and looked at me with a raised brow. "Don't let this luxury fool you, Josephine. No one in this palace, including the royal family, has the sort of freedoms you imagine."

"But you *have* lived a privileged life," I countered. "You've had choices many of these individuals who share this space have not."

"Are you truly arguing with me right now?" Aneurin shook his head, probably in disbelief at the turn of conversation, then gestured to the door in front of us. "I'm going to go seek my parents. It is your choice if you wish to come with me." He opened it revealing another set of stairs, and started up them without another word.

I followed behind him even though my legs were tired of climbing. *I* was tired. "Of *course*, I'm coming with you," I replied to his back. How could he think I'd leave him alone after this?

Aneurin opened another door to reveal a long, tiled hallway.

I covered my mouth with my hand as I surveyed my surroundings. Everything glowed with candelabras and glittering chandeliers. This was more beautiful than I ever imagined.

Beautiful, decorative tapestries lined the walls, depicting characters from stories I wasn't familiar with. Between each one stood a looming marble pillar, holding up a gilded arch of the ceiling.

Feeling a tug on my other hand, I let Aneurin gently pull me further down the hall.

As we continued walking, I admired the tall, wide paintings of royal members, all of whom I assumed were Aneurin's ancestors. There was even a knight's full suit of armor on display in a nook.

I bumped into his back when he unexpectedly stopped in front of a lone, long desk, covered in plates of meats and cheeses, bowls of fruits, and sugared candies. Beside those dishes was a porcelain tray with an assortment of masks. Some of them were adorned with golden weaving with pearls, while others were painted with colors that resembled a butterfly's wing.

There was one mask that was plated in gold with a deep, black fabric behind it. I'd certainly never seen anything like the intricate and unique carvings on it.

Aneurin exhaled as he lifted the mask from the tray.

"What is it?" I asked, peering down at it in his hands.

He brought the accessory to his face and lifted his face to mine. "I'll make quite the entrance, won't I?"

TWENTY-FOUR

If there was one thing I'd learned about Aneurin, it was that he enjoyed his dramatics. The only thing I could do was smile and offer to help to tie the mask around his face.

As he looked at me, he smiled gently. "Wait here. I'll be just a moment."

"But—"

He didn't wait to hear what I had to say and stepped through a set of ornate doors stepped into another large room. As soon as the door closed behind him, the panic of the situation settled in my gut. What if his parents weren't thrilled to see him? What if…what if all of this was a disaster in the making?

Would it be simple enough for me to kiss him myself? But what if that didn't work?

Out of the corner of my eye, I saw movement across the hall. Without a second thought, I lifted another mask from the tray and hastily tied it around my eyes. There was nothing I could do about my gown or my hair, but I could at least hide my face.

Music filled the space with a song I didn't recognize, but it was gentle, and whimsical. In my imagination, I could see Cinderella and her prince dancing away for hours. So many aspects of her story suddenly seemed to make so much sense. How easy it was to forget about time and identity. Under these chandeliers, under this mask…I'm sure in a beautiful dress, I could become the Josephine I'd only dreamed of.

And in the arms of Aneurin…

When I saw another servant cross the hall again, I quickly stepped through the door, following Aneurin into the room where he had disappeared. I tucked myself closest to the wall, not wanting to be detected by anyone, but let myself look with wide eyes. I realized it was a balcony hanging over a gigantic theater. At the center sat what I assumed were the thrones of the king and queen.

Aneurin, who had been standing between the two magnificent seats when I first walked in, took a step to the side of his mother's throne and reached for her hand, startling her.

She pulled her hand away and turned her head quickly. And then there was a moment of recognition, and she rose to her feet.

His mother pressed a hand to her lips and shook her head before she reached for his hand. Despite her distress, she was a beautiful woman—thin and still quite youthful looking. Her golden hair, piled in curls and adorned with a simple golden crown, sat atop her head. Her gown was auburn silk and shimmered against the light emitting from the ballroom below. She also wore a sash of white and blue wrapped from one shoulder to the other side of their hips.

Noticing the silent commotion next to him, the king stood as well. He wore a matching sash to his wife over a deep maroon tunic with gold embroidering around the collar and down along the front. His expressions seemed surprised and yet, filled with regret as he slowly approached Aneurin and gestured to the mask.

I wished I could hear what they were saying, but I knew, without a doubt, by how quickly his mother reached for a hug from him, there was nothing but joy to be found in this reunion. I tried to tuck myself farther into the curtained wall, but smacked into one of those tall suits of armor. My face turned hot red as the entire thing tumbled near my feet. I shot my gaze back to Aneurin and his parents, who were now all staring back at me.

What an introduction to royalty.

Aneurin smiled and looked to his parents, before lifting his hand in my direction. "That is Josephine."

The queen peered over her shoulder and looked at me with a warm but concerned smile. It must have been what prompted Aneurin's own.

I timidly walked towards the three of them. Was I supposed to curtsy or bow? How formal did I need to be? How was I going to explain where I was from? Or how I'd met Aneurin? Did I have to start calling him by his title?

When I finally reached Aneurin's side, I quickly did my best to half-bow-half-curtsy and kept my eyes level with the floor before peering up at the queen curiously.

"Good evening, Your Majesties," I murmured softly.

Aneurin touched the small of my back and he untied the mask around my face.

My cheeks warmed when it fell into my hands. I quickly slid it behind my back.

"Mother," Aneurin began, keeping his attention on the conversation at hand. The one that I had so ungracefully interrupted. "I need your help."

"I do not understand," she replied, shaking her head. "You only just arrived."

"I know," he replied, nodding. "And there's so much to say. So much to explain..."

"Then *do* so," the king commanded from behind his wife. "Where have you been all this time?"

Aneurin stood straighter than before, and studied his father before releasing a soft, but heavy sigh. "As you'll recall, I went in search of how to break the spell that was cast upon me."

Just the mention of the situation caused their faces to pale.

"Where is Henry? I thought you left with your manservant," the queen asked as she pressed a hand to her cheek and glanced backwards at the door, where a suit of armor now lay riddled on the floor. Concern colored her expression as she returned her gaze back to Aneurin.

It seemed to be a question without an answer.

Where *was* Henry?

"I did leave with him," Aneurin said. "I hoped to hear of his safe return to the castle by now."

"I care not where your manservant is," his father retorted. "I care about where *you* have been."

"*Pierre*," the queen hissed, peering at him over her shoulder. "Our son has asked for our help. Let him speak."

"Explain yourself then, Aneurin," the king replied, crossing his arms against his chest. "What is it you need?"

I didn't understand what was going on here. While I knew his mother had genuine concern, it was his father who confused me. I thought Aneurin's parents would be more grateful, at least more *relieved*, to see their son.

The king's gaze briefly met mine before I lowered my eyes down to the floor.

"After Henry left to find help, I found myself in a slight dilemma after being found by two lost children," Aneurin began. "And then I met Josephine. We've traveled a great distance together. *She* has traveled a great distance to have me returned to you as I am now."

The queen's soft hazel eyes met mine briefly. A small smile graced her lips before she returned her attention back to her son.

"I met a magical man," he continued, "who agreed to allow me to remain human, if…I found and received a kiss of true love before the midnight of a ball."

The king groaned and shook his head. "Another spell…"

"It's not," Aneurin explained. "It's a bargain. An agreement."

"And if you do not find this true love's kiss?" his father asked. "What does this man want? Jewels? Riches?"

"Me." The single-word answer was said in a whisper.

"Did you put him up to this?" the king accused, jerking his attention in my direction.

I shook my head, lifting my hands in defense.

"She did *nothing* of the sort," Aneurin interjected.

"So, you've returned to us to find your true love's kiss."

The king's derisive tone made everything inside me curl into an uneasy knot. Based on how his wife's posture stiffened, I assumed she felt it, too.

"It appears I've missed this celebration," Aneurin continued, gesturing towards the ballroom floor just below the balcony. "There's a masquerade."

"For your brother" the queen explained with a small nod. "To help him find a suitable bride. He has come of age to settle down—"

"And, from what I understand, is also the new *crown* prince."

"How were we to know you would actually return back to us," his father hissed. "After three years of nothing, Aneurin. *Nothing*. You know not how worried your mother and I were about you. How we thought about what might have occurred over and over again. I thought about the decision I made…"

And there it was. The *real* origin of the king's rage.

"I'm sorry, father," Aneurin replied, shaking his head. "I'm sorry you were forced to make the decision that you did. But you know not how hard these past three years have been for *me*. To be nothing more than a small, helpless amphibian, reliant on…" He lifted his hand, gesturing to me.

I could practically hear the king think *peasant* the same way Aneurin used to hurl the insult at me.

"Wait a second," I said, shaking my head, suddenly not caring how informal I sounded. "There is nothing wrong with having to rely on someone like *me*. And however short the time has been since our first meeting, I think we both have sincerely earned each other's respect," I replied, glancing at Aneurin.

He nodded. "I concur."

"Secondly," I continued. "This conversation should not be about whose woes were bigger. I'm sure things were not easy for your parents. They must have felt helpless, too."

Everyone nodded.

"And Aneurin hasn't had it easy. He nearly became a delicacy to a witch who enjoyed eating children and frog's legs. Then we tried to save a princess from a vain queen set on poisoning her." I could only hope that the seven men had succeeded in reviving her. "We exchanged some valuable treasures for a poor miller's daughter's freedom. And your son…" I stared at his father. "Your *son* wanted to be himself again. I'm sure after three years, being stuck as a creature that you never wished to be…you'd miss being yourself, too."

When no one responded, I sighed. "While I think twenty-four hours is a little quick…"I do think it is possible for him to find his kiss of true love. And if a ball is where Aneurin must find it, then I think he is entitled to his chance."

"But his brother…" his mother tried to interject, only to be cut off by the doors swinging open.

I jumped in place and turned to see a younger version of Aneurin, with the same sharp nose and firm lips, running to where the three of us gathered. He wore a soft auburn tunic, with dark brown pants, with those same leather boots to match his brother's. And on the top of his head, sat a band of gold, his own royal crown. The main difference between them was, in contrast to his older brother's brown curls, this man's hair was a soft blond.

"Father! I must speak to you at once!" the man called out urgently as he burst into the room. His eyes scanned the space until they landed on Aneurin—freezing him in his tracks.

"B-Brother? Is that really you?" Charming's voice quivered with disbelief, his eyes widening as he stepped closer to him. The way Charming stared at his brother was endearing. His eyes were wide, and his lips turned into an almost relieved smile. "It is you, isn't it?"

Aneurin hesitated for a moment, taking in the sight of his long-lost brother. Despite the years that had passed, the resemblance between them was striking. "Aye, Char. It's truly me," he finally replied with a smile of his own.

I almost wished the younger prince would reach for a hug. But they both remained where they stood, eyeing each other before Charming turned his gaze back to his parents.

"He is back!" he said with enthusiasm.

"He is," the queen replied with a nod before crossing the small distance between the two of them. She brushed a stray strand of his hair back into place before raising a curious brow. "You needed to speak to your father, Charming? Is something wrong?"

"Mother," he started, adjusting his hair on his own before shaking his head. "I have come to inform you and His Majesty that I have found the woman I wish to marry."

"What?" the king asked, startled, turning on his heel to look over the balcony railing. "Where is she at, then, my boy? Let us meet her and tell her the good news before we announce it to the kingdom tomorrow night."

"I would. However, it is just that..." Charming explained wistfully. "She's gone."

I could see where this was going.

"*Gone?*" his parents both asked in unison.

"Yes!" he replied, seemingly more distressed than before. "We must hold another ball, not an engagement banquet, tomorrow night. I know if we do...she would return."

"Impossible," the king said firmly, crossing his arms.

"*Please...*" Charming whined. "If we do, I know she will return. And when she does, I can finally propose to her and—"

"Another ball would do just nicely," the queen agreed. "It would serve Charming with his missing princess. And it would help Aneurin. There must be an eligible maiden..."

It was just as I'd hoped. With the promise of a second ball, Aneurin would have a real chance to break his spell.

"We'll have you in the arms of your future bride before midnight, Aneurin," his mother promised as she kept her focus on the ballroom below. "Yes," she said, seemingly more to herself. "All will be well. Tomorrow night, we will host the largest ball you have ever seen. Both you and your brother will find exactly what you are look-ing for, and the entire kingdom will finally be at ease knowing our sons will be settled in marital bliss." She said the last part to the king, as if she were trying to talk him around to the idea.

"Mother, I'm not entirely sure—" Aneurin began, but I stepped on his foot. He grimaced, silently mouthing the word "ouch" at me as he jerked his gaze in my direction.

I shook my head, narrowing my eyes. This was the *only* way he might get out of Rumpelstiltskin's clutches.

"Another ball," the king repeated beside his wife, nodding slow-ly. "I suppose someone will need to notify the chef right away."

"Leave it all to me," she replied, patting his hand.

If the queen had been from my world, I imagined those words would broadcast that event planning wasn't just a hobby for this woman. She was clearly an expert.

I could only hope it would be enough to save Aneurin.

TWENTY-FIVE

I didn't know what to expect after that, but it wasn't to see the queen turn on her heel so quickly, leaving us to ponder what she was about to do. Or rather, me. It appeared that the other royals had already anticipated her behavior.

The king let out a heavy sigh, his expression weary as he ran a hand over his cheek. "You both should prepare yourselves," the king said, flicking his hand in the air. "Your mother will have you in front of the archbishop within a week."

"For a just cause," Charming replied.

Aneurin snorted.

I stared at the two of them, slightly confused.

"For whatever the reason," the king continued, lifting his finger. "Remember that you asked for this."

"I did not," Aneurin mumbled under his breath, and I resisted the urge to step on his foot again.

His father paused in front of him and crossed his arms against his chest. "You have the most to lose from this if you do not succeed, Aneurin," he said. "With every eligible maiden in the kingdom coming to see you and your brother…"

He trailed off, but I could still hear what he hadn't said.

Find a match. Get the kiss. Break the spell.

"Yes, Father," Aneurin nodded, bowing slightly as the king passed him.

The king stopped in front of Charming, pressing his hand on his shoulder, then disappeared from view through the same doors the queen had exited.

Charming was the first to break the silence between the three of us. "I can't believe 'tis really you," he said, shaking his head in disbelief. "There were so many rumors that you were dead."

"You know how the court likes to gossip," Aneurin replied with a soft smile. "I'm far from dead, Char."

"I know but..." When the younger prince looked down at his hands, I was almost sure he was about to cry. "They gave me your title, when they declared you missing."

"Char..." Aneurin crossed the small distance between himself and his brother in a few steps. His hands grasped Charming's shoulders. "I'm so sorry."

"I never wanted your vapid title."

"Of course not," Aneurin said with a small chuckle. "No one wants a vapid title."

"It was always meant to be yours," Char continued. "I was so afraid that you would..." His words drifted to silence as he stared up at his brother.

Aneurin's brow furrowed. "I don't—What were you afraid of?"

"There are stories, you know," Char explained. "Stories of royal brothers killing each other off for their titles."

Aneurin tilted his head, obviously unsure of what to do with such a comment. "They're just stories. Did you truly think I would kill you for such a thing?"

"I hoped not, but it has been three years."

"Three years or thirty—I would never kill you for a title."

"For a title," Char repeated, lifting a brow as he smirked.

Aneurin laughed then and rolled his eyes. "You're impossible." He grasped his brother and embraced him tightly.

I smiled at the show of fraternal love.

As they eased from each other, Charming finally relaxed. "It is yours, though."

"It *was*," Aneurin corrected. "And now, it is yours."

"Until mother and father change their minds."

"Neither of them will make that determination. At least not until I either break this spell or…" He didn't finish his sentence.

Charming pressed his lips together and nodded before turning his gaze to me. "It seems you already have a lady here. Perhaps your worries are for naught."

When Aneurin glanced towards me, I thought I saw something there. A sparkle—a small glimmer of hope. But, in an instant, the gleam was gone.

He turned his attention back to his brother. "This is Josephine."

I felt my heart shrink at the change.

"Josephine," Charming repeated before crossing the room to where I stood.

He took my hand and lifted it, pressing a soft kiss against my knuckles. He definitely did live up to his name. *Charming*.

"'Tis a pleasure to meet you," he greeted me.

"Josephine helped me," Aneurin explained as he came to stand beside him. "We've ventured here together."

"You'll have to tell me about your journey," Charming said. "All of it."

"Where to start," I said with a laugh, tucking my hands behind my back nervously.

But from how Aneurin looked at me, I could already tell he didn't want me to divulge anything further.

"But I'm afraid it's been a long day," I began. "And if we're to prepare for a ball tomorrow, I think we all should think of getting some rest."

Charming lifted a hand, gesturing to the event already occurring below. "I must go make my rounds with the guests in place of my father and mother, but you—"

"I can show you to a room, Josephine," Aneurin cut in. "It's not like we lack space."

"Right," Charming said with a nod. "We can most certainly reconvene our conversations tomorrow morning as we break our fast."

"And before mother finds us," Aneurin teased with a wink.

"Right again," Charming replied with a smirk. "Well then, I shall take my leave of you both. Send word if you need any assistance."

"I think it best if my presence remains unknown," Aneurin said.

Charming nodded thoughtfully. "I will make sure to send the most discreet of servants to tend to you," he replied, pressing a hand to his brother's shoulder.

"I'd prefer you didn't," Aneurin said. "We can tend to ourselves."

I was a little shocked by what he said. For being as snobby as he was as a frog, I couldn't imagine Aneurin "tending" to himself. Could he stoop to completing tasks that a peasant would do?

Charming seemed completely unfazed by Aneurin's response. He shrugged, as if silently saying, "suit yourself," before saying, "I must admit, it is *good* to have you home, brother."

"It is good to be home," Aneurin replied softly. "I want to hear everything about this maiden you met."

Charming's eyes widened with surprise and delight as a smile grew on his face. "She is the most exquisite woman I have ever met. And the most graceful...and so kind," he explained, his smile growing wider. "I must see her again." His expression spoke volumes to how hard he'd fallen for her. For Cinderella.

"Are you sure you didn't imagine her?" Aneurin asked.

When Charming looked up at his brother, I saw the worry in his eyes. "Of course not," he said. "She was *real*."

"Indeed, you did not," Aneurin consoled. "For your sake, let us hope she returns."

"And let us hope you find what you are looking for as well."

When Aneurin didn't respond, Charming turned his attention in my direction before bowing his head in a polite nod.

"I shall see you both in the morning." He turned and disappeared through the same set of doors his parents had.

Down below, music and another set of dancing began. The sounds of laughter and talking floated above the music, and it made me so curious to see for myself. I'd seen the regency and fantasy movies, with ballrooms aglow with tall candelabras, and orchestras. And it was always the costumes that the actresses and actors wore that captivated me the most.

I eased a bit closer to the balcony's edge, peering down at the group of partygoers, their luxurious gowns of fine silks and satins, and the men, who wore tunics of what looked like suede or fur. There were quite a number of couples on the dance floor, keeping an arm's length between them.

"They look beautiful from here," I mused. "Almost like a dream."

"I suppose attending one could feel like a dream for a mere peasant like you."

The jab caused me to turn my gaze in his direction.

"I merely jest," he reassured me with a smirk.

I smiled and slid my arms around myself, trying to suppress the shiver that suddenly enveloped me. I was still slightly damp and cold—utterly exhausted from our long adventure.

"Come," Aneurin said softly, his hand tucking under my elbow. "We both need to rest."

He didn't need to say anything more to convince me.

I let him lead me back out into the hallway. Despite my grumbling stomach, I ignored the table that still had the assortment of foods, and instead followed Aneurin as he strolled down the length of the hallway.

He was quiet as he turned down another corridor, leading us further away from the ball.

"I like your brother," I blurted. "He seems nice."

"Everyone seems to favor my brother," Aneurin responded softly.

"I'm sure that's not entirely true," I replied. Aneurin raised his brow as he turned his gaze to meet mine. "I prefer *your* company."

Aneurin snorted and shook his head. "Let us be frank, Josephine," he began. "You prefer the company of individuals much like Arch—not me."

"We've already had this conversation," I said, crossing my arms against my chest. "I just appreciated that he was open and gave me the space to share my thoughts."

"And, so, you preferred him."

"That's not *true.*" I shook my head. "I meant what I said."

When he didn't reply, I touched his shoulder. "Aneurin…"

"It matters not to me, Josephine, whom you decide to spend your time with."

"I think you worry about it more than you like to admit," I replied. "If you didn't, my preferences wouldn't have ever been a topic of discussion to begin with."

He didn't reply and we walked in a deafening silence down another darkened hallway. Here, only a few candelabras illuminated the path before us.

Aneurin stopped by one of the only doors around. "I'll leave you here," he replied, reaching to turn the knob.

"And where will you stay?" I asked, looking at him.

He lifted his hand, gesturing further down the hallway. "My quarters are just beyond the next corridor."

The thought of sleeping alone filled me with dread—but why?

Maybe my face had given too much away, because Aneurin picked up one of the lit candles from a nearby candelabra and stepped into the room meant for me.

A few moments later, I saw the room become dimly lit with a few more candles that were scattered about. The space reminded me of an old illustration I'd find in a fairytale. The bed was large, and had a dark wooden frame, with thick, red drapes hanging down around it. Almost like the bed I'd seen millions of times in the various adaptations of *A Christmas Carol.*

There was one large tapestry on the wall, depicting a sleeping kingdom—people in a courtyard and farm fields dozed. Up in a tall, looming tower, a young, beautiful woman was sleeping in a bed surrounded by hundreds of roses. I knew this story.

Taking a step closer, I searched the tapestry. Hidden among the bushes just below, there was a young man on a white horse. His eyes were set on the tower.

"W-what is this?" I asked, pressing a hand against the fabric.

Aneurin turned away from the hearth where he had been building a fire, a small flame coming to life in front of him. "It's an old folk tale."

"But I know this story," I replied softly.

Slowly, he met my gaze. "Many of us do, truth be told. A young princess sleeps for one hundred years until a prince from a distant land finds her and breaks the spell of her slumber with a kiss."

Another spell broken by a kiss.

"It's just...odd," I confessed, turning my attention back to the tapestry. "It's a story told within a story..."

"A story *within* a story," Aneurin echoed. "For the briefest of moments, I forgot..."

The sound of the crackling fire behind him filled the space between us.

Aneurin looked down at the floor before turning to give the fire his attention again. He carefully began to add a few of the lingering logs of wood from the neatly stacked pile in the nearby corner of the room. Adding one more, he took a step back with a sigh.

"If you add a few more before you retire, it should last you through the night."

I wished I knew what he was really thinking. I wished I knew what to say in response to what he hadn't.

Instead, I crossed my arms and replied, "Easy enough. I didn't even know you knew how to do things like that."

"I might be a prince, but I do know how to start a fire," he replied with a raised brow.

I gave him a small smile. "I can't say that I do," I admitted. "Thank you. You know, for doing that."

"It's no trouble," he said. "It's the least I could do."

He stared at me for a moment more before turning on his heel, towards the door.

I didn't want him to leave. Throughout all the trials and tribulations we had faced together, he had become my constant companion. Why did I suddenly feel so lost without him by my side?

I reached out and caught his arm, a desperate plea slipping from my lips. "Aneurin…"

He glanced back at me, his expression mirroring my own conflicted feelings.

"I like you," I blurted out.

He furrowed his brow, clearly taken aback. "What do you mean?"

"I mean I *like* you," I reiterated, determined to get it out despite his confusion. "More than Arch, more than Trapper and Stitches, more than your brother—"

"Josephine…"

I shook my head, needing to get it all out. "Please, just hear me out," I pleaded. "I want you to know that after everything…"

"You don't need to say anything," Aneurin interrupted, his smile strained. "Tomorrow, I'll find my true love, and you'll return home."

His words felt like a punch to the gut, final and crushing.

Before I could respond, he added, "I'll only be down the hall."

I knew he was trying to get away as quickly as he could.

I released my grasp on his arm and nodded.

"Right," I whispered.

Home.

I'd be back where I belonged. And he'd be with his princess.

I had to remember I was falling in love with a fictional character—one that I'd never be able to be with.

"Sleep well," he remarked before disappearing through the door.

As I shut it behind him, I wondered if he, too, was beginning to feel the same way that I did.

TWENTY-SIX

I hadn't expected to fall asleep so quickly. It might have been from just how comfortable the bed was, or how warm the room had become. Or it could have simply been the fact that I'd finally been able to remove my dirty dress, in exchange for a long, soft tunic I'd found in the chest at the end of the bed. Either way, just as I heard a clock striking two, I covered myself in the thick blanket covering the feathered-padded mattress and gave into the slumber I so badly needed.

I slipped into the same dream that seemed to always haunt me now. I was surrounded by glimmering chandeliers, and the soft laughter of the crowd. As I descended a grand staircase down into the marble-floored ballroom, Aneurin was waiting for me at the bottom.

His hand was outstretched as he smiled at me.

A strange relief filled me as my hand slipped into his. He twirled me around the room until a new arm snaked around my waist, pulling me away.

I turned to find Rumpelstiltskin's wrinkled face near mine.

His amber eyes glowed with a mischievous delight as his long fingers curled around my wrist.

"Such a brave, yet foolish girl," he hissed in my ear. "A wanderer of pages…"

The weight of those strange words pulling me out from the dream—pulled me from Aneurin and the ball.

A small yelp erupted from my throat as I jolted under the pile of blankets.

I laid still, trying to catch my breath. When I heard something rustling, I opened my eyes and found three women, dressed in dark brown gowns, tending to different tasks.

One woman with silver strands was rebuilding the fire that Aneurin had fixed for me. Another with a tight bun of golden hair was laying out a new, clean dress on a chair while my dirty green gown was draped over her arm. The third had soft brown locks was pouring a kettle of hot water into a bowl near the bed.

Our eyes met.

"Good morning," she said with a soft smile.

"Hello," I replied and slowly began to push myself up to sit. Brushing my untamed hair from my face, I squinted my eyes, adapting to the brightness of the room. "What time is it?" I asked groggily.

The one near the fire turned to look over her shoulder, a wisp of silver shifting in front of her eyes. "Half past two." Her voice was older and deeper than the brunette's.

"Did you just say *two*?" I asked, unable to keep the surprise out of my voice. I had slept for twelve hours?

When she me nodded, I slid my gaze to the door.

"And Aneur-I mean, the prince? Is he awake yet?"

"Which one?" The golden-haired woman asked, coming to stand by the side of the bed. "If you are referencing Prince Charming—"

"No. Prince Aneurin," I corrected.

She smiled. "He sent us to check on you."

He'd sent servants to check up on me, instead of himself? I guess it made sense. We weren't hiding away in a tree house anymore, where social rules didn't apply. Here, in a castle, I knew there were certain things that Aneurin could and couldn't do.

I'd seen enough period movies to know that at least.

When I didn't respond, the woman continued, "He suggested that we bring you something new to wear. However, Her Majesty has requested for one of her gowns to be brought up to you for this evening's festivities."

"The queen?" I asked, leaning forward. She was going to lend me a gown? Me? A stranger? "Are you sure?" I asked, as I looked from one woman to the other.

"Of course. There is to be another ball this evening. In celebration of Prince Aneurin and his brother, Prince Charming."

It was weird and yet oddly familiar to hear someone mention Prince Charming in front of me. He was a real person. Or as real as a fictional character could be.

"I heard the prince danced with one particular woman several times last evening," the silver haired woman said with a knowing smile. "And that he's quite smitten with her."

"I wonder who the lucky bride shall be," the brunette said to the others as she draped a short piece of linen next to the bowl, full of hot water.

The golden-haired woman looked at me, she raised a brow. "Is it true that you're his betrothed?"

"Me?" I laughed and shook my head. "Oh, no, no," I replied. "I simply helped the lost prince get home."

My response seemed to puzzle them a little bit. The brunette woman raised a brow before nodding. "Oh. I see."

"It appears, perhaps, the rumors are wrong," the silver haired woman remarked.

Of *course*, there would already be rumors. I didn't imagine that our presence—or at least his—would go undetected for long. However, I was surprised that *I* was a part of them.

"Can I go see the prince? Prince Aneurin?" I asked, pushing the blankets away as I pulled myself up from the bed.

"He's out riding with his brother," the golden-haired woman said. "And in an hour, we'll need to begin preparing your attire for the celebration. Unless you're not planning to attend?"

There wasn't an option for me to not go. Releasing a sigh, I pushed myself to the edge of the bed.

"Oh no," I said, rising to my feet. "I'm going to that ball."

*T*he rest of the afternoon passed by me in a whirl of eating some of the most delicious foods I'd ever tasted, washing up after God-only-knew how many days of going without a bath, and being pampered by the three curious servants, whose names I finally learned. The eldest woman was Bess, the blonde was Fern, and the brunette was Joan.

Between bites of sweet breads and meats, Bess and Joan continued to inquire who I was, and why I was there.

I felt bad about lying. Or rather, telling a fabrication of the journey we'd experienced together. I was careful to leave out the parts of us traveling to different stories. There was no real way of explaining that. Instead, I told them that I'd stumbled upon Aneurin at a pond and had agreed to help him.

"I wouldn't have ever dared to pick up a toad," Joan said, wrinkling her nose and crossing her arms over her chest. "Prince or not."

"Oh, watch your tongue Joan," Bess retorted. "We all know you would have been the first to pick up that frog and kiss him yourself."

Fern laughed at the two as she lifted the next strand of my hair. I wasn't entirely sure if I trusted her with the hot rod in her hand—a medieval curling iron that would most definitely fry my hair. But the beautiful spiral of curls that fell over my shoulder with each pass kept me sitting still.

"Did you not try to kiss him?" Joan asked me. "Were you not tempted to see for yourself?"

Had I been tempted to see what he looked like? Maybe. But definitely not at first. When I'd first met Aneurin, he'd been rude and offensive. Even if he hadn't been, I'd been too disgusted by his slimy skin to even *think* about kissing a frog—even to release him from a spell.

But in the span of time we'd shared in the tree house, amongst Snow-White and the seven men, something had started to change. He'd been so clear in his wanting of a princess that I knew that no matter how I felt, I'd never be enough.

I'd never be what *he* wanted.

"No," I said softly, shaking my head. "He requires a kiss from his true love. Not a stranger."

"We all begin as strangers," Bess said just as a knock on the door echoed through the room. She answered it, letting in four new women who were carrying a soft ivory gown between them.

They laid it out on the bed.

"Her Majesty has sent her warmest welcome to you," the tallest woman of the group announced, stepping out of place amongst the others. With a small curtsy, she gestured towards the gown before her eyes met mine again. "A gift for you, milady."

Fern took a step back from me, allowing me to take a look closer.

Lace flowers circled the bust and went down the center of the bodice, which, like the sleeves, was embroidered and small pearls. Sheer ivory skirt cascaded from the waistline down to the floor.

"It's beautiful," I admitted softly, sliding a finger along an embroidered flower.

The woman who had spoken to me curtsied and led the others out of the room.

"Come so that I can finish your hair," Fern said, gesturing back to the seat. "And then we can get you dressed."

As she finished and helped me into the dress, with Bess and Joan's help, my thoughts kept focusing on how everything would be over after tonight. One way or another, I would be returning home. But I couldn't help but worry.

What if Rumpelstiltskin had something up his sleeve? What if Aneurin couldn't break his spell? What if none of the women who came to the ball were interested in him? It didn't seem probable...

After all, I liked him—despite all the things about him that annoyed me. He'd been there for me. Listened. And when he didn't agree with me, he told me. Simply put, he had become my friend.

Joan slid a delicate golden band atop my head, startling me.

"There now," Fern said, smiling behind Joan. "You're ready."

I looked down at the exquisite gown adorning my frame, tracing my fingers over its intricate design as I rose to my feet. The fabric felt luxurious against my skin, its soft texture a comforting reminder of the surreal events unfolding. I wished to catch a glimpse of myself, but the lack of mirrors in my room made it impossible.

"Go get her the shoes, Fern," Bess ordered, rolling her eyes with a huff. "She can't go to the party without something on her feet."

Fern turned on her heel quickly, dashing back towards the door.

"It's okay," I replied with a laugh. "I have my own shoes."

"Those clumps of...whatever they were," Bess said, wrinkling her nose. "They were thrown out with your clothes."

"You threw out my shoes?" I asked, my eyes wide with alarm.

She raised a brow and clicked her tongue, as if I was overreacting. "We will have new shoes for you tomorrow."

Fern finally returned to our side, she carried two delicate and clear shoes in her hands.

"You've got to be kidding me," I mumbled under my breath as I realized that the shoes were made of *glass*.

"I can't wear—" I took a step back. "Those don't belong to me."

"Well, of course not. They belong to Her Majesty," Bess said.

"These are supposed to be worn by someone else," I continued, shaking my head. "Not *me*."

"Oh? Then who?" Bess asked, pushing her hands to her waist.

"I'm not sure I'm allowed to say..." I muttered.

"If you can't say, then you're going to wear them," Fern said before placing them down on the floor, setting them in front of me.

"But these aren't meant for me," I replied, shaking my head.

"Well, they're most certainly not meant for *us*," Bess quipped.

This was *wrong*. How would Prince Charming find his Cinderella if *I* was the one wearing her glass slippers? What did my wearing these do to the rest of this story? What would happen to them?

"Come, come," Bess commanded, pushing the shoes closer to me. "We don't have time to spare."

Nothing else spoken in all the time I'd been in the room had been truer. We didn't have time to spare. Aneurin would only have mere hours left. *Hours*. And yet, I hadn't seen him since the night before. And I wanted nothing more than to see him again now.

"Where is Prince Aneurin?" I asked again, looking between the three women.

"I imagine he's getting ready himself." Bess knelt and picked up one of the shoes. "The sooner you put these on, the sooner you'll see him for yourself."

I admired her directness.

"Alright, alright," I replied and slid a foot into the cool glass. It was strange just how perfect they felt against my skin. I didn't know what to expect in wearing real-life glass slippers but putting them on made me feel regal and almost magical. For a moment, I felt like I could have easily been a princess—*his* princess.

I lifted the hem of the gown from the floor. It wasn't the golden dress I'd dreamt of so many times, but it was more beautiful than anything I could have ever hoped for.

Joan held the door open for me.

Before I crossed the threshold, Fern grabbed my hand. The action was far more informal than I expected from her, I wondered if she'd truly meant to do it until I saw her smile.

"Milady," she started, "if I may be so bold, might I remind you that just because the prince is no longer a frog, it doesn't mean it's too late to kiss him."

I furrowed my brow, resisting the urge to nervously laugh. "I'm sorry, what?"

Fern tilted her head, studying me. "There have been stranger things, yes?"

She wasn't wrong. But I couldn't believe she was encouraging me to do the one thing I knew I couldn't.

"I apologize for my boldness," she added, bowing her head. "But I saw the look in your eye whenever you mentioned the prince."

My cheeks warmed. If she had noticed, had the others?

Fern leaned closer, speaking low so that only I could hear her. "It's never too late…Until it is."

TWENTY-SEVEN

Her words echoed in my mind with an almost prophetic power. If only I'd heard those words years ago. Maybe I would have done things—so *many* things—differently. But if I had, I wouldn't be within the pages of a fairytale world.

As I carefully navigated my way down the hallway towards the staircase Bess directed me to, I focused on how it wasn't too late. Not yet, at least. I still had time. *We* still had time.

But what if Aneurin didn't want me? What if I wasn't his true love? Could I even consider him mine? Did I love Aneurin in the way that almost every fairytale painted love? Was it really this all-encompassing, can't-live-without-them, there's-no-air-in-my-lungs-without-them sort of feeling?

Aneurin was my friend.

He'd been a frog that crept into my hand, who was sweet to a scared little girl, who had gone to get help after a harrowing encounter with a narcissistic witch.

He was the man who had once told me he hoped his future bride would be just like *me*.

I stopped and peered down at the gown I wore once again. It was a beautiful gift from the queen, and one that I wasn't sure I entirely deserved. My feet felt a little sweaty against the glass shoes. Lifting the skirt of the dress, I lifted my foot to peer at it again. Against the glow of candelabras lining the hallway, the crystalline material gleamed.

The swell of the music from the ballroom interrupted my thoughts. I was pretty sure I was going to be sick. I didn't know anything about dancing. The last time I'd gone to a party at this scale, I'd been going to my senior prom. But this was a far cry from any high school dance—prom or not.

Inhaling deeply, I slowly began to descend the steps of the staircase, leading down to the ball. When I reached the main landing, I could see the marbled floor with the gliding dancers.

The women were dressed so elegantly in their blue and burgundy gowns, and the men, fashionably attired in dark tunics. I was probably sticking out like a sore thumb in my ivory white.

My gaze roamed the guests for him. Other side of the room, I saw the two brothers standing side-by-side. Charming wore a dark tunic with several silver fleur-de-lis patterns embroidered across it. While he wore a crown, decorated with an assortment of jewels, Aneurin did not. But despite the lack of a crown on his head, he looked like a fairytale prince in his soft ivory tunic with a gold pattern embroidered on his chest and a gold chain hanging from his shoulders, gleaming in the candlelight. His hair, still wild with curls, was combed neatly into place. He was by far one of the most beautiful men I'd ever seen.

Charming lifted a hand in my direction and leaned in toward his brother's ear.

A moment later, Aneurin's gaze lifted, meeting mine. Even from across the room, his emerald gaze was piercing. The corner of his lips turned into a small, discrete smile. I could see his lips move to form the words, "There you are."

I bit my bottom lip nervously, suppressing a smile.

Aneurin looked to his brother and gave a brief nod before stepping away. Carefully, he moved through the crowd toward me.

I continued my descent, keeping my gaze on his. Just as I reached the last step, the crowd parted, creating an easier path for us. It felt like a dream—a story that didn't belong to me.

Now that the dancing had stopped, my glass slippers clicked against the marble floor, filling in the distance between us.

There was admiration in his gaze when we finally stopped in front of each other.

"Aneurin," I said softly, unable to keep a smile from forming on my face.

"I've been waiting for you," he murmured softly. "I was afraid you wouldn't come."

"You thought I wouldn't show?" I asked, tilting my head curiously. "Where would I have gone instead?"

"I didn't know what to think, honestly," he replied, shaking his head. "This whole day has been…" His words drifted off. He released a heavy sigh. "There's been a lot for me to consider."

"Like what?" I asked. "Tell me, what can I do to help?"

Aneurin shook his head as a corner of his lips curled into a small, yet sad smile. "You've already helped me so much," he confessed. "I couldn't ask for more from you."

"I haven't done anything that you couldn't have done yourself," I countered.

When Aneurin shook his head again, he chuckled softly. "You know that's not true."

I bit down on my bottom lip. "We don't have time to argue the small details," I finally replied. "It's already so late."

"I know…" he agreed with a nod.

"I thought I would have seen you today," I offered, hoping Aneurin would share something about his day with me, something to indicate what he'd done.

"I spent some much-needed time with my brother," Aneurin replied after a pause. "I told him the entirety of our journey together."

"I hope you left out the part where the witch threatened to make frog legs out of you," I said, hoping some humor would bring a smile to his face again.

A dimple appears, and his smile grew a little wider. "Of course." He held his hand out to me. "Josephine, I was hoping you'd honor me with the privilege of a dance."

"You want to dance with me?" I asked, a little startled by his request. Didn't he need to focus on finding his true love? "Isn't the whole point of this for you to find—"

"I want to dance with *you*," he remarked, interrupting me.

I furrowed my brow, confused. "But...are you sure?"

Aneurin took a step closer to me, leaning down to speak in my ear. "There's nothing to be afraid of."

That was such a lie. There was *everything* to be afraid of. Especially his bargain with Rumpelstiltskin.

"I'm not afraid," I lied. "I'm just more concerned with your—"

"Don't be," he encouraged, sliding his hand to my waist.

I could feel the warmth of his palm against the fabric of the dress before he drew me closer against him. I released a breath while his gaze held mine.

"I don't know the steps," I added. "And I have two left feet."

"You can trust me," he reassured me before the orchestra in the room began to play another slow, yet beautiful song. He took my hand in his own, while the other moved from my waist to the small of my back.

Carefully, Aneurin began to lead me around the ballroom floor. While other dancers swirled around us, he was careful to keep us from encroaching too close on the others. I could feel the eyes of the guests, watching the two of us glide around the room. I wondered if his parents were watching us from their balcony above—if they were watching to see who would break both his bargain and spell by midnight.

But despite the attention on us, I felt safe. Held securely in his warm embrace.

"I must admit," Aneurin said softly, breaking the silence of our dancing. "I'm grateful that you are at least able to see me as I a human, and not just as a frog."

"Why?" I asked, raising my brow.

"My being a frog, forcing you to face danger—"

"You didn't *force* me to do anything," I replied, shaking my head. "There was nothing I wasn't willing to do."

"I wanted you to see me as I truly am," Aneurin reiterated, his voice gentle as he began to spin me once more.

When I turned to face him again, I felt a blush on my cheeks. "But, Aneurin, I did see the true you," I said. "I have all this time."

"I was a frog." The teasing glint in his narrowed eyes elicited a soft laugh from me.

"Yes, I'm well aware. But you were always yourself. After all that we've been through, I came to know you as you...without the pretense of what you look like, physically. You were always *you*, Aneurin. Tongue-flicking and all."

He studied me for a long moment, his green eyes piercing me. "I was not always kind to you."

My heart raced in my chest when he pulled me close to his chest. "Neither was I," I replied.

"Despite all that, I am grateful that our paths crossed, Josephine. I'm grateful to have met you."

"And I'm grateful to have met you too, Aneurin. I hope…" I released a heavy sigh, trying to formulate what I wanted to say. It was as though he was trying to say goodbye to me. But I wasn't ready to say farewell yet.

"I hope the princess that you choose tonight is everything that you want and more. Truly."

As I spoke the words, the sparkle in his eyes dimmed, as though he suddenly remembered who we were, and why we were there. The curve of his smile disappeared soon after.

"The princess I choose…" he softly echoed.

"Have you considered anyone yet?" I asked. Even though I didn't really want to know. And I didn't want him to tell me.

"My brother, Charming, has arranged a few dances for me."

"Oh," I replied, nodding quickly. "Well, I'm glad."

I wanted to kick myself. I'm *glad*? That was the best I could do?

"You're glad?" he echoed, raising a brow. Great. Even he didn't believe me.

"Of course," I said. "I want you to be happy...to be free."

"I'm not so sure both are possible anymore," he murmured.

After the song came to an end, Aneurin escorted me to the side of the dance floor.

Several ladies, dressed in beautiful gowns, eagerly watched him as we approached.

He politely nodded at the swooning women.

The women quickly flicked their fans and began to whisper behind the fluttering fabric, their gazes drifting from him to me.

The idea of sharing Aneurin tonight with anyone else filled me with dread. I wanted another dance, another song, another moment to be swept up in his arms. But I knew he wasn't mine to keep. He wasn't *my* prince, and I wasn't destined to be his, no matter what I hoped—or wished—for.

Charming appeared at Aneurin's side. "Brother," he said. "The Princess of Foix de Lille has arrived. I recall you agreed to a dance—"

"Yes," Aneurin replied uneasily, giving him a glare before returning his attention back to me. His gaze seemed to challenge me to speak up—to ask him to stay.

I swallowed back words that I wanted to desperately say. I couldn't ask him to turn away a chance at freedom. There was nothing more that I could do to save Aneurin. I wasn't his true love, and I would never be a princess.

Charming's crystal blue gaze met mine before pressing his lips into a tight, polite smile. I knew he was waiting for me to say something, to release Aneurin out to the crowd of possible future brides.

"You should go meet her," I said, breaking the silence between us. "You don't have much time." I looked away from Aneurin's searching gaze, turning my eyes to the crowd behind him. "This woman might just be the one you've been searching for all this time." My chest tightened as I forced the words out.

He released a heavy sigh. "Perhaps..."

"Come," Charming said, patting his brother on the back. "Let's not keep her waiting."

"Aren't you waiting for your *own* guest to arrive?" Aneurin asked.

Charming's cheeks flushed as he chuckled. "Well...yes, I am. In the meantime, I plan to assist you." He tried to pull his brother from me, tried to direct his attention towards the woman who awaited on the wings of the ballroom floor.

Aneurin turned his attention back to me, as though he were inviting me to disagree.

"I'm parched," I announced. "I could use a drink."

"Please," Charming said, gesturing towards the other side of the ballroom. "There are more than enough refreshments."

I flashed the warmest smile I could muster for him. "I hope your visitor arrives soon." I hoped when Cinderella appeared at the ball, she and Prince Charming would find a path that would lead to a new, happy life.

"As do I," he replied with another polite nod.

I tried my best to curtsy, just like I'd done last night, and turned on my heel. I couldn't bear to watch Aneurin flirt and court the women who were waiting fo him.

But Aneurin had given me his *first* dance. He'd made sure to see *me* before anyone else.

"She's so lucky!" I heard one woman say behind her fluttering fan. "To have danced with the prince."

I'd done so much more than just *dance* with the prince. I'd shared my food with him on a number of occasions. I'd shared a bed, a pillow...I'd carried him in my hand, on my shoulder, in my pocket. I'd listened to him tell stories of his past and tried to remember all the things he liked and disliked.

I'd come to love Aneurin. And now, I had to watch him choose another. It was a miserable situation—and I thought all fairytales ended well.

The idea of going home, back to the ordinary, was not appealing anymore. But maybe moving on was simply my own version of happily ever after?

I couldn't help myself and looked over my shoulder.

Charming was crossing the room to the grand staircase, his hand extended out to a woman dressed in a glittering blue dress. That must have been Cinderella.

But what I cared about more was that Aneurin stood in front of a beautiful woman.

She wore a soft golden gown, her red hair curled and piled on top of her head. There was something about her that seemed almost *too* perfect.

He chuckled at whatever she'd said, and she, in turn, responded with her own perfectly white-toothed smile.

I'd known this was coming. The sooner Aneurin found his bride, the sooner I'd return home. Still, I needed something strong to drink. I headed straight to a server with wine. Maybe it would take the edge off.

I smiled in thanks when he handed me a goblet.

But just as I was about to drink, someone spoke from behind me.

"A good sip of wine makes everything easier to swallow," a *familiar* voice said.

I spun in place and set my drink down on the table. A good thing, too, because Rumpelstiltskin was *here*.

"Hello there, wanderer of pages."

TWENTY-EIGHT

"What are you doing here?" I asked, grabbing his wrist, dragging him away from the table. "You *can't* be here."

"Ah, but you know why I'm here…"

"It's not midnight," I countered. "He has time. You still have to give him the time you promised!"

"Calm yourself, dearie. I'm here to enjoy a party!" Rumpel said with a grin as he gestured towards the partygoers. "Everyone loves a good soirée."

"You don't belong here!" I hissed. "This isn't your story."

I pulled him into a secluded corner of the ballroom, hoping for privacy from any interruptions.

"You were certain to spoil my own, weren't you?" Rumpel snarled. As a servant passed us with a tray of wine goblets, he grabbed one and took a long swig. "I came to make sure I collected what was mine."

"I didn't *spoil* anything," I replied. "I just helped someone in need."

"I *knew* there was something off about you," he snarled, lifting a finger to my face as his amber gaze trailed over me from head to toe. "It's not often I meet such unique travelers."

Had Merle Lynn traversed these pages before?

"So, there have been others? Before me?"

"Just one…" Rumpel said with a careless shrug. "But he never toiled with the tales. He seemed to know better."

"So, there was someone," I whispered, understanding what this meant. I hadn't been the first.

Rumpelstiltskin gave a fake yawn, as if this conversation bored him. "I never cared to know, nor ever *needed* to," he said. "But here we are thanks to you. And now, I'm here to either celebrate my success, or...a future wedding."

I shook my head and dug my nails into his wrist. "You have to release him."

"*I* don't have to do a thing," he replied, tugging his arm free. "He struck a bargain with me. And I will see it through to the end."

"What do you want in exchange for his freedom?" I asked.

"There is nothing *you* could give me," he said, his voice dripping with malice. "Unless..." His flashed a wicked grin.

"*Unless?*" I echoed, my heart pounding in my chest.

"You give me your life."

I recoiled. "You want to kill me?"

"Just think of it as relocation from this world to the next," he replied, examining his nails. Like this, too, was a boring topic.

"Why do you want to kill me?"

"That is such a harsh word," he mused. "I could make it painless for you. A simple exchange." He raised a brow, picking up a goblet of his own off the nearby server's tray. There was a hint of a smirk on his lips before he took a sip. "I think it's only a fair trade in the end, wouldn't you agree? A life for a life."

"You can't think I'd actually agree to that sort of deal." I said, shaking my head.

"Wouldn't you? What says true love more than being willing to give up your life for the other?"

"Is that what true love is?" I pressed. "Leaving the other behind?"

Rumpelstiltskin laughed. "I forgot how feisty you are." When I didn't respond, he took another sip with a shrug. "Then there's no deal, and when the clock strikes midnight...the prince will belong to me."

"He's not an object you can possess."

"Actually, per our bargain, he *is*."

I couldn't let Rumpelstiltskin win. Even if Aneurin found a woman tonight, there was no guarantee he'd kiss her. His endeavors of dancing with a seemingly endless line of women didn't seem like such a bright idea any longer. Especially when I felt as I did. And maybe…just maybe, he felt the same.

I stared at the magical man through narrowed eyes. "And what makes you think I'd agree to this deal?"

"You love him," Rumpelstiltskin replied without a second thought. "It's very obvious."

"You don't know—"

"Is that not what true love is, Josephine?" he asked, peering at me with wide, serious eyes. "To do whatever is necessary to ensure the happiness of the other? Even if it means you are no longer a part of the equation?"

"You could just send me home."

He slid a finger along the table, nodding. "I could but, I'm afraid that leaves room for your return."

"What if I can't return? Isn't that enough?"

"I'm a selfish man, Josephine," he hissed between his teeth. "And I require what I'm due. A life for a life, or nothing at all."

Lively music filled the room once again, spurring more dancers back to the floor.

Aneurin and the red-headed woman were amongst them.

"Perhaps you're not his true love after all," Rumpel mused with a shrug. "And maybe he will be successful all on his own. Maybe he never needed you to begin with."

"Maybe," I countered. "But I don't want to leave it to chance."

"Nothing about true love is *chance*," he said with a smile. "It certainly isn't just luck that you're here, is it?"

"Are you trying to imply that *I'm* Aneurin's true love?" I asked, raising a brow.

"Are you going to finally admit that you are?" He asked with a clever smile.

Maybe it really could be that simple. Maybe we had been the answer to each other's problems all along. He'd been looking for his perfect match, and I'd been looking for ways to heal—to learn to trust and love again, without even knowing it.

Just as I started to leave the table, I felt Rumpelstiltskin's hand wrap around my wrist.

He yanked hard. "Oh no you don't," he hissed, shaking his head. "You're not going to just ruin this for me, too."

"Let go of me," I commanded, tugging on my hand.

But his grip was hard as he pulled me away from the table of wine, and away from the eyes of the guests.

I saw the glimmer of a crystal dagger in Rumpel's hand as he turned the pointed edge towards me.

"You're going to stay as you are," he snarled, pressing the weapon closer to my chest. "It is either you or the prince. But I will have *one* of you before the night is through."

"If you're so desperate to have one of us," I started. "Then just take me. Spare him."

Rumpelstiltskin laughed, shaking his head. "And to think he had the solution to his own bargain right under his nose this entire time. What a fool…"

"There is only one fool here tonight," came a commanding voice from the middle of the dance floor.

The music filling the room came to a halt, and everyone's attention moved to gaze upon the figure, shrouded in a billowing, oversized cloak. When the new arrival pulled back the hood, I was surprised to find a familiar face.

The woman from the estate sale—the one who had given me the book of fairytales. As I scanned her features, I noticed where I'd once found creased wrinkles in the corner of her eyes, she now had smooth skin. Her white-blonde hair was darker than when I'd first met her—more golden. She easily looked decades younger. But I still recognized her.

"I know you…" I whispered, shaking my head. "I *know* you."

The woman crossed the distance of the room, moving closer to both Rumpel and me. With each step she took, a burst of light erupted from beneath her shoe. Her cloak dissolved, transforming into a glimmering gown of emerald and silver, and her hair curled and grew longer until it flowed over her shoulders. She was glowing now, too, and looked as regal as a queen.

"Oh, look who has arrived to help the damsel in distress! It is her fairy godmother!" Rumpelstiltskin mocked, raising a brow. "You always think it's acceptable to be fashionably late to a party."

"I'm warning you, you little *imp*," she said, pointing a finger at him. "Choose your next words wisely."

The light around her began to shine even brighter, filling the ballroom. While she didn't appear to be the kind of person I'd want to upset, Rumpelstiltskin was unafraid.

I could feel his body ripple with laughter. From above, I could see the King and Queen peering down from their balcony, watching the scene unfold.

Aneurin emerged from the parted crowd, his eyes moving from the enchanted woman to me.

"I'm only here to take what belongs to me," Rumpel taunted, pulling me tighter against him as the crystal dagger moved from my chest to the curve of my jaw, pressing the cool blade against my skin. "It's either the dashing froggy prince, or the little wanderer…"

"Release her," Aneurin ordered, pushing his way closer to us. "Your bargain is with me, not her."

"Things can change, Prince Aneurin," he said with a laugh. "But you knew that already, didn't you? T'was me who turned you into a frog, and me who turned you back!"

My eyes widened at his confession, and I stared at Aneurin in astonishment. How could he agree to this deal, knowing this was the magical, dangerous man who was responsible for his frog form?

He gazed back at me sheepishly.

"Why?" I asked, my voice thick with emotion.

"You deserved to go home…" he murmured.

"Your dealings will be with *me*," the enchantress interjected. She took a careful step, crossing the distance between the two of us.

Rumpel laughed gleefully. "What shall you give me instead?"

"What belongs to you," the enchantress answered.

Before he could reply, she flicked a finger at him.

Rumpelstiltskin skidded across the room, pushed by a powerful force, and fell into a wall with a grunt.

It took me a moment to realize I was free. I was only left with a soft sting from the blade that had been against my jaw. A second later, Aneurin's arms were wrapped at me, pulling me out of the way of the fight brewing between the two magical beings.

"You cannot have what is mine!" Rumpelstiltskin roared, pointing the crystal blade at the powerful woman.

"There is nothing here that belongs to *you*," the enchantress retorted. "This time, your bargains have gone too far. You have no right to harm this wanderer of pages." She curled her fingers again as she continued to hold up her hand. "*Rumpelstiltskin.*"

Aneurin's grip on me tightened, and I leaned closer into him.

It was the first time I'd heard anyone say his name aloud. Even I hadn't dared to speak his name.

"What did you say?" Rumpel asked, his eyes growing wide. "How *dare* you speak my name!"

"There is a power in welding a name, is there not, Rumpelstiltskin?" she said, this time the corners of her lips curled into a smile. "Dare I say your name again?" she taunted, "Or will you go?"

"That is not fair!" he exclaimed, lifting the blade again. "The prince is *mine*! The prince promised!"

A searing bolt of light emerged from the tip of the blade, shooting toward her.

The enchantress didn't move other than to flick her finger again.

The blade snapped in half.

"You have caused enough trouble. There is no deal to be had here. Go back where you belong, Rumpelstiltskin."

This time, he didn't argue. But he raised his hand to snap his fingers, a sudden and blinding burst of light enveloped him, and then the entire ballroom.

I squeezed my eyes shut, turning my face into Aneurin's chest. His hand cradled my head gently.

Then there was only an uncanny silence.

When I opened my eyes, Rumpelstiltskin was gone. The only trace of him was the broken blade on the floor.

"Josephine," I heard the enchantress say, drawing my gaze away from where the villain had been.

Slowly, I eased myself from Aneurin's arms and watched as she crossed the rest of the distance between us.

"Josephine," she began again. "You've reached the final story. It's time to close this chapter and return."

"Return?" I asked. "But—"

"There is nothing more for you here."

"But Aneurin," I shook my head. "Aneurin still needs—"

"You were never meant to remain here for as long as you have," she explained as her gaze met mine. "No matter which page you turn to, You will always face a new set of dangers. Don't you see? This is for the best."

"But, Aneurin—" I tried again.

"Isn't this what you wanted all along? To return home?" She asked, a small, kind smile appeared on her lips. "I came here to help you return."

"But why now?" I could feel tears begin to stir behind my eyes. I had wanted to go home. I'd wanted that in the beginning. But now... "Why does it have to be *now?*"

She took another step closer and stretched her hand out to me. Her expression was soft as held my gaze. "You are not of this world, sweet Josephine."

"I don't want her to go," Aneurin interjected as he reached for my hand. I felt the strength of his fingers as they locked with mine.

But, looking down at our hands, I knew no matter how I felt—no matter what I wanted—I knew she was right.

"Please," he begged. His voice broke as he continued, "I…I don't want her to go. I…" he paused, looking at me. "I love her."

The words he'd said seemed so easy, and yet, carried such a complexity. I could see the love in his emerald gaze as he continued to stare at me. A love that I had wished for. It had started off so small—so soft and quiet—but it had grown into something more.

"You can't take her from me," he whispered as he pulled me closer into his arms. "Not when I've just found her."

Aneurin tucked a strand of my loose hair behind my ear.

Tears stung my eyes as I looked at him. "She's right," I whispered. "I was never meant to stay here forever. I was always supposed to go home."

"I know, but I…I'd hoped…" he started before lifting my hand to his lips. He kissed my palm before closing his eyes. "I've been such a fool, Josephine. I've wasted so much time denying how I felt about you…about us. And all because of a stupid title. You must forgive me…"

"You don't need to be sorry, Aneurin," I murmured. "I understood why."

Why did this have to be the way our story ended? Maybe it would have been easier if he'd just fallen for another. And yet, I couldn't bear the thought of sharing a single moment of him with someone else. I couldn't imagine another offering the warmth of her bed the way I had…

"I never needed any of this," he lifted his hand to the wide-eyed party around us. "I always knew my true love was with me all along."

"Aneurin," I tried, shaking my head. "It's alright."

"Josephine," the enchantress interrupted, causing the both of us to look at her. "It's time to go home."

Off in the distance, a clock chimed.

"It's midnight," Aneurin whispered.

How had the time moved so fast?

I laid my hand on his shoulder and inched closer, bridging the small gap between us. I didn't even care that there were others watching us.

Aneurin lifted his hand, brushing his thumb over the curve of my cheek. "I love you, Josephine. I will do whatever it takes to find you again."

My eyes began to fill with tears as I shook my head. Why did he have to be so perfect?

As another chime rang out, I could only do the first thing that popped into my mind. I was wearing glass slippers. And there was only one thing to do with them. I stepped out of one and lifted the lone shoe from the floor. I tried to smile and pressed it to his chest, I tried to smile.

"Find me then," I murmured, despite knowing he'd never be able to.

I wasn't of his world, and he was only a fictional character in mine. Still, I leaned forward and pressed my lips against his. His arms suddenly wrapped around me tightly. Everything about the kiss felt magical...*perfect*. I'd waited my entire life for this kiss. For *him*. And now, I had to leave him behind.

As he moved his lips against mine, I felt the familiar burst of warmth surge around me. I knew what it meant. I hold onto him tighter and tried to ignore the blinding light I knew was starting to envelope me.

"I love you, Josephine," he whispered in my ear.

I parted my lips to reply, but could only muster out, "I lov—" before everything around me erupted into a searing, bright light.

Squeezing my eyes closed, I tried to picture his face in my mind—tried to carry the look in his eyes in my memory. I felt my heart shatter when the feeling of his arms disappeared. There was nothing and no one left for me to hold on to. All the stories we'd traveled through, all those who we'd met, were gone.

And so was the warmth.

I opened my eyes.

I was back in my room.

Alone.

TWENTY-NINE

Tears rolled down my cheeks as I stared up at my bedroom's ceiling. I was *home*. Back where I started. The rest of the house was quiet. I didn't know what time it was, or how long I'd been gone. A sob threatened to break through, but I suppressed it and focused on my breathing. I just needed to *breathe*.

But it still erupted from deep within me, sending a new wave of tears to flood my eyes. I pressed my palms to my closed eyelids, wanting to push the sadness back within me. The only thing I did know was that Aneurin was gone.

I will find you. That's what he'd said to me.

How would he ever find me, when he was inside the book, in his world, and I was out here?

"Find me," I said out loud. But my only answer was silence.

Maybe I just needed to say the spell again. Would that be the way back? I needed to find the book.

With tears still trickling down my cheeks, I pushed myself up, scanning my bed. My phone still sat beside my thigh, turned off from when Nico had texted me. It was then I also noticed I was back in my shirt and shorts.

But the book…Hadn't it been right beside me?

Desperate, I pulled myself to my feet and began to look behind my pillows and blankets. It would be even crueler if the book had disappeared with my return.

Just as another bout of tears flooded my eyes, I felt something hard against my toes as I tripped against the corner of my bed. Looking down, I saw the bound book of fairytales under the bed.

The gleaming vines on the cover taunted me as I pulled it from its hiding place.

"Those who wander through these pages," I gasped trying to remember the words. "...those who wander..." If only I'd remembered it verbatim.

I sat on the edge of my bed and opened the book with desperate fingers. I just needed to find the spell.

Right on the first page of the book, I found the scribbling of the handwritten spell, just like before. "For those who wander through these pages," I started. "Listen well to the tale of ages." There wasn't any flickering of lights like before, but I kept going. "For deep within one's heart will find their past and present intertwined."

Holding my breath, I waited. I waited for anything to happen. But there was still nothing. Nothing but all-encompassing silence.

"For those who wander through these pages!" I shouted at the page, "listen well to the tale of ages! For deep within one's heart will find their past and present intertwined!" I didn't care how loud I was. I needed whatever magic resided in the book to hear me—to let me back inside. "Aneurin!" I yelled, peeling back the rest of the pages. But the yellow-stained pages were empty. All the stories, all the words that had once been there, were gone. All. Gone.

"No, no, no, no..." I whispered, sweeping each page back, one by one. And then a gathering. I slammed the book closed and tried again. I didn't know why I thought that would work. Whatever trick this was, it was cruel. There was no evidence of anything between the covers.

Forcing my attention away from the book, I stumbled onto my feet and bolted towards my door. As I opened it, I saw the house was exactly as I'd left it. The margarita glasses Mom and I had bought at the estate sale were still sitting on the table.

Had no time passed since I'd disappeared into the book? Did that mean that Mom and Dad were still on their way to pick up the desk she'd bought at the estate sale?

The same estate sale that I'd received the book from.

The woman. The one person who could answer my questions. The *enchantress*.

The kitchen light over the sink was still on, evidence that my parents were still out. If they hadn't gotten to the estate sale yet, maybe I had a chance to go back.

I turned back to my room, reaching for my phone. Grabbing the device from the blankets, I pressed the button on the side and waited for the touchscreen to light up.

"Come on," I mumbled to myself, trying not to lose my patience as I waited for the spinning icon to disappear. Finally, when my home screen appeared, a dozen unread texts from Nico appeared.

Not now, I thought to myself, brushing them away with my thumb before pressing the phone icon. Mom's name was the first to appear and I clicked on it.

She answered after the first two rings. "Jo?" she asked, her voice sounding slightly alarmed.

"Mom!" I replied. "Are you at that house yet?"

"We just got here, why?"

"Whatever you do, don't leave. Wait until I get there."

"What? Why?" she asked. "Josephine? What is this all about?"

"Mom. Can you just…can you tell that woman that I want to bring her back the book?"

"I doubt she wants that back."

"Please!" I exclaimed, shaking the phone in frustration. "I need to talk to her!"

I could hear Dad's voice in the background, and Mom replied with, "She wants to bring back the book."

"Mom," I said again. "I'm on my way." There was no alternative. I was coming, like it or not.

I grabbed the book off of the floor and my purse from my bedroom doorknob. In the kitchen, I nabbed my car keys from where they hung on the wall.

"Josephine. It's already late. This is going to take us like two minutes and then we'll be home. We'll bring you dinner."

But it wasn't just a book. It was *my* book. But I couldn't tell Mom the truth. She'd never believe me, let alone understand. I pressed End Call without another word and shoved my phone into my back pocket. If I'd been a teenager, I'd be grounded for the next month and a half for hanging up on her. And another month for leaving the house without permission.

I guess there were a *few* perks of being an adult.

Even if there weren't, all that mattered now was getting the answers I needed.

As I turned into the familiar neighborhood, I saw the estate sale house. There was no evidence of any occupants inside, except for a soft light shining through the living room windows. *Someone* was inside.

It easily felt like a week had passed given how much I'd gone through while in the book, but I now knew only mere hours had passed. My dashboard clock read 8:56 P.M., and while I knew that was late, this couldn't wait until morning. Just as I unbuckled my seat belt, my phone flashed with a text from Mom.

Where are you? We just got home and you're not here.

I'll be home soon. Just ran to the gas station.

Hopefully she'd buy my lie. I didn't bother to wait to see her reply. Instead, I shoved my phone back into my pocket and grabbed the book from the passenger seat. Pressing it against my chest, I closed my eyes for a moment before climbing out of the car.

There was a soft drizzle coming down from the sky, a far cry from the downpour I'd experienced as I'd climbed a set of cliffs in the middle of a thunderstorm on the cliffs, chasing after the disguised queen. Trapper's determined face flashed in my mind; had he freed Snow-White from the spell of the poison apple?

After dashing up the driveway, I leaned into the front door, trying to keep as dry as I pressed my finger against the doorbell.

I could hear the ringing through the door and waited with bated breath. As soon as the door opened, I locked eyes with the woman through the screen door.

Her eyes shifted from my face to the book in my arms. After a pause, she opened the door. "I suppose I should say that I was expecting you. Your mother mentioned something about you wanting to talk to me about the book."

"You know exactly why I need to talk to you about the book."

Her eyes narrowed as she studied me, crossing her arms over her chest. "I'm not entirely sure I do. I saw you today at the sale. But is there something more I'm supposed to know?"

"Yes," I replied sternly. "I'm here because of what happened. Because what you caused to happen."

"What I caused?" she asked as she tilted her head curiously. "I'm not quite sure I follow."

She was going to make this harder than necessary, wasn't she?

"I know you know what I'm talking about. And I get it if you don't want anyone to know who you actually are. I promise I won't tell anyone."

"And who do you think I am?"

I bit my bottom lip, trying to keep my frustration in check. "I need you to help me get back into the book," I eventually answered. "There has to be a way, and I'm pretty sure you know what it is."

She furrowed her brow. "Getting back *into* the book?"

"I know it sounds crazy—"

"I don't know if this is some sort of prank or joke, but—"

"This isn't a joke at all," I replied quickly, peeling back the cover to show her the scribbling on the front page. "See this passage?"

She leaned forward. "My uncle used to write in his books all the time," she answered with a shrug. "They're all over his books. Just his scribbled thoughts."

"It isn't just that," I said, shaking my head. "This is a spell."

"He loved to perform magic tricks for children in the hospitals."

"But this is *real*. And I think you know just how real it is."

She exhaled before taking a step back. "I'm not sure why you think I know—"

"Yes, you do!" I insisted. "You're the reason why I'm here now. And I need your help getting back to Aneurin."

"I wish I knew how to help you, sweetie," she said, retreating further. "But I think the best thing for you to do right now is to go home and maybe get some sleep."

I tucked my hair behind my ears and released a heavy sigh. "But this is real…"

"All stories can feel that way when we love them as much as we do," she agreed with a stagnant smile. "I'm sure my uncle would have been delighted to know his book of fairytales has brought so much joy to you."

"But these aren't *just* stories. You were there."

"I think you must have had some wild, vivid dream," she started. "And I'm so sorry that it felt as real as it did for you. But I've been here at this house all day. I have no idea who this Aneurin person you speak of is, and I know for certain I know nothing about spells or secret identities."

"But the stories," I tried to explain as I started to flip through the pages. I had to show her that they were missing. But the stories were completely restored. There wasn't a single empty page.

Maybe I *was* going crazy.

There was no way any of this had been real, right?

I lifted my gaze back to hers through stinging tears. I blinked them away. Maybe I'd just wanted an escape, and I'd created one in a book of something familiar. My cheeks burned with embarrassment. I'd been so rude, and I'd acted insane.

"I'm so sorry," I whispered, shutting the book before pressing it against my chest.

The woman narrowed her eyes at me, probably searching for dishonesty, then flashed a sympathetic smile. "There's no need to apologize," she replied.

"Right," I said, lowering the large book now that there was nothing special to show her. "I'm sorry for disturbing your evening."

Why had I thought this was the answer? I should have taken a moment to really think about everything. It was more logical to see that all of this had been a dream. There was no such thing as magic.

"Be safe, Josephine," the woman added.

It only took me a second to realize I'd never told the woman my name. But if she wasn't the enchantress...how else could she have possibly known?

The door clattered closed before I could stop her. The lights from the front room flicked off, and I understood no matter how many times I asked, no matter how much I begged, she'd refuse to help me.

The entire neighborhood remained still and quiet, despite the drizzling rain.

Tears flowed down my cheeks as I accepted that, if any of it *had* been real, it no longer mattered. I'd never find a way back into the book—never see Aneurin again.

"Even if he's only written on the page," I whispered into the darkness. "It doesn't make him any less real to me." I held onto the book more tightly in my arms, pressing it against my chest like the prized possession it was. "This doesn't make my love for him any less real either..."

I walked back to my car, each step felt heavier than the next.

My phone buzzed right as I settled in the driver's seat. I tugged it free to see a notification from Mom.

It's time for you to come home, Josephine.

THIRTY

"Mom! Dad!" I shouted as I opened my bedroom door, glancing down at my phone with a smile. When they didn't respond, I tried again. "Mom! Dad! I got the job! I *actually* got the job!"

I didn't know why the email offer felt as surprising as it did, but a wave of relief filled me as I'd read over the message repeatedly. Whatever I'd done during the interview two weeks ago had worked in my favor.

"Did you just say you got the job?" Mom asked from the kitchen, as she lowered a department store pamphlet onto the counter.

"I did!" I said, flashing a smile. "*Finally.*"

"Finally!" she agreed with a laugh before walking towards me. In an instant, she wrapped me in a tight hug. Her hands gently rubbed against my back. "Oh honey, I'm so happy for you."

"Me, too," I sighed. I'd never imagined getting a job at a local community college library, but when I'd seen the position posted online…after everything with the book…it spoke to me.

I'd lost count of how many days had passed since my magical journey. Some days were harder than others. The first night had been the hardest. After coming back home, thoroughly soaked by rain, I had shut myself away in my room, only to find the pages of the fairytale book empty again. I'd had to accept there was no way of returning back to Aneurin. Days later, when I'd finally gained enough courage to go back to the house where I'd gotten the book, I'd found it boarded up, awaiting its next new owners.

At first, I'd spent my evenings saying the spell again and again as I flipped through the pages of the book, hoping that I'd see a flicker of light—a promise of something about to occur. But there was only silence. Always *nothing*.

Eventually, I tucked the book of fairytales under my bed and tried not to think about it. But no matter how hard I tried to push the memory of Aneurin out of my mind, I couldn't.

What would he have said about my having a job in a library?

As Mom took a step back and smiled at me. "Wait until you tell your dad. He'll be thrilled."

I glanced toward the silent living room. If he wasn't watching the television, where was he? "And he is...?"

"He had to go run some errands. His honey-do-list was getting a bit long." She laughed. "Speaking of which..." She lifted the set of keys on the counter. "I was planning on running some of my own. Have any interest in coming with me?"

"I should actually respond to the email," I said, lifting my phone. "You know, to tell them I accept before they change their mind."

"I don't think they're going to, Josephine," Mom remarked while she picked up her purse from the kitchen table. "But if you're sure..."

"Yeah, I am," I replied, flashing her a small smile.

"When we get back, we can all go celebrate."

"Tacos?" I asked with a laugh.

She wrinkled her nose. "I was thinking of something nicer."

"It's just a job, Mom," I replied.

"Not to me," she countered, grabbing an umbrella by the side door. "It's a new chapter."

I heard the words of the enchantress echo in my ears.

It's time to close this chapter and return...

By the time I came back to the present, Mom had already left. I was alone. Releasing a sigh, I lifted my phone again and started a response back to the college. Hopefully, they'd allow me to start soon—anything to keeps me busy and distracted.

Maybe once I had a steady paycheck, I'd start piecing my life back together. I just needed to focus on one thing at a time. I walked into my room and sat on the edge of my bed while I drafted the most professional response I could muster without too many exclamation points.

After pushing send, I released a sigh and laid back on my bed. It was a big step in trying to get myself back on track. But I was glad to finally be taking the steps. I owed it to myself to be happy again—or try to be. And this was a great excuse to buy myself a new outfit or two for my first week. The last thing I needed was for someone to judge me based on my clothes. Like a certain frog had...

Such attire must come from the southern lands...

Placing my phone beside my bed, I lay down and closed my eyes, pushing away the sad ache filling me at the memory of him. I didn't want to cry over him. Again. Not when there was nothing I could do. Nothing I tried worked.

I kept tell myself he'd been nothing but a beautiful dream. One I would cherish forever.

Thumping on the door jerked me from my thoughts.

I bolted upright and quickly brushed away a lone tear rolling down my cheek.

Who on earth was that? Mom hadn't been expecting anyone at the house, had she?

The knocking kept going.

"I'm coming!" I shouted, standing up and making my way through the floor plan. "Give me a second!"

Whoever it was, they were being overly eager.

I yanked open the front door. "Can I help you?" I asked, not doing anything to hide the annoyance in my voice.

But I *knew* those emerald eyes that met and held mine.

My hand trembled on the doorknob and tears flooded my eyes. Was I dreaming? I refused to blink, too afraid I'd open my eyes again, only to find him gone.

But he stood right before me, as though he were truly real. The rain outside was coming down much harder than I'd expected. Droplets fell on his head and shoulders, soaking through the fabric of a blue tunic he was wearing. His appearance was the same, but his attire wasn't nearly as regal as I'd seen at the ball. Wrapped over his shoulder, hung a worn, leather satchel.

"Aneurin?"

His eyes warmed, as though my recognition of him was all he needed. He flashed a smile then whispered my name. *"Josephine…"*

"It *is* you," I murmured, taking a step closer. I reached for him, touching any part of him I could reach. I'd thought about this moment for weeks.

He was really *here*.

"I need your help," he started. "I don't even know where to begin to explain everything to you."

"My help? But I don't understand…" I kept my voice down, trailing off. I tugged him inside, out of the rain. "How did you get here?"

He sighed as he shook his head. "I'm not even sure myself," he murmured. "There's so much…"

That didn't sound good. "You didn't go making more impossible bargains, did you?" I asked, peering at him with concern. "Do you have to be kissed by midnight again?"

He smiled softly and shook his head again. "If only the situation were so simple…"

"I don't recall any part of that being *simple*," I replied.

"It would be simple enough now," he whispered, gaze dropping to my lips.

My cheeks burned. I wished he'd kiss me now.

"I thought I'd never see you again," I blurted.

He slid his hand to my elbow, drawing me closer to him. "I thought the same," Aneurin agreed. "And while these circumstances are less than ideal, I'm certainly relieved to see you again."

"What are these 'less than ideal' circumstances you speak of?"

He released a heavy sigh. "My brother is about to make a grave error, Josephine. I was sent here to retrieve help—*your* help."

"How am *I* supposed to help your brother?"

Was this about the mysterious woman at the ball? The one who I knew was Cinderella? Had something gone wrong because of me? But what could I do? I couldn't even get back into the book...

Aneurin took my hand in his. "My brother has agreed to wed the woman from the ball. But the woman is not who she claims."

"Wait. Is this about her being a...servant?" I started. "She didn't have a choice in that." I was ready to defend he. After being forced to endure her stepfamily's cruelty, it would hardly be fair for Charming's family to turn on her now.

Aneurin shook his head, lifting our linked hands. "It has nothing to do with her social standing."

"Well, that's a first," I retorted before raising my brow curiously. "But if that isn't the issue, what is?"

"He is going to marry a witch."

My mind raced through the story of Cinderella. I wrinkled my nose in thought. "There is no witch in her story,"

Aneurin shook his head and laid his other hand on top of mine, fully encasing it between his own. "I do not know all the answers to your questions. But I need your help in saving my brother from this stranger and her powerful spell."

I studied him. There was so much fear in his green eyes.

His brother was really in danger.

"*Aneurin*," I whispered.

"I was a fool before, Josephine. Even occasionally cruel. But despite everything...despite my flaws, and my stubbornness, you remained by my side. I was nearly too late to realize what had been before me all this time."

"Aneurin—"

"I love you, Josephine. I knew that for a while, but was too cowardly to confess it to you when I had the chance. I regret that."

He was avoiding the question, and I didn't understand why.

"You were searching for a princess," I stated simply.

"I was searching for *true love*, but let my arrogance blind me." He lifted a hand to cup my cheek. "I'm sorry that it took me so long to see you…*You* were the person I'd been looking for this whole time."

I shook my head, swallowing back the tears forming. "And it seems you were the same for me," I confessed.

My heartbeat echoed in my ears. There was nothing else—no one else—but him and me. Nothing else in the world seemed to matter. New job be damned.

He leaned forward slowly, his gaze on mine before he softly pressed his lips against mine. We remained in each other's arms for a moment before he released me and eased away.

"So, will you come back with me, Josephine?"

"Do you even know *how* to get back?" I asked, raising a brow.

"I was hoping you did."

"Don't you think I would have been back already if I did?"

Aneurin paused, before gently nodding thoughtfully. "I suppose you're right."

"You're always leaving me to figure everything out," I teased as I leading him further into the house.

He flashed me the smile I had grown to love. "I did say before that I was willing to learn from you, did I not?"

"Was that after we pushed that creepy witch into the oven? Or after I saved you from a life of servitude with Rumpelstiltskin?"

"Hmmm…I can't quite seem to recall," he chuckled as I pulled him inside my bedroom. "But I'm sure it occurred somewhere close in the middle of all that."

Shutting the door behind me, I rolled my eyes. "You better hope my plan works."

"And what exactly *is* your plan, Josephine?"

"Whatever it is, will you promise to stay with me this time?"

His lips lifted into a soft smile. "Until the last page."

A Hairy Situation

EXCLUSIVE HARDCOVER SCENE

There was a sudden burst of light amidst my scream, the same blinding brilliance that had enveloped me when I was first sucked into the book. But this time, everything around me felt weightless—the speed at which we were falling was abnormal. My immediate thought was that I was about to die. No one survived falls like this.

I'd never guessed this would be the way I'd go—plunging into the unknown depths of a fairytale world, accompanied by a talking frog. It was absurd and yet, somehow fitting. I guess it could be worse. Only, it was—my parents would never know what happened to me.

Squeezing my eyes closed, I willed the moment to end. *I just want to wake up in my bed. Please…*

The air shifted against me again, and the inevitable plummet was instant. It was as though I were coming down the steep decline of a roller coaster. My stomach twisted as I released another scream. The roar of a splash echoed around my ears—I'd landed in a body of water, instantly soaking my clothes. I pushed myself to the surface before they could drag me down.

"It's freezing!" I screeched, using a pruned finger to push my bangs out of my eyes.

Aneurin's coughing made me turn around.

He was clinging to the side of a lily pad, sputtering from his own landing. "*What* in God's teeth was that?" he exclaimed in disbelief, struggling to maintain his grip.

"I-I don't t-think we're in the w-witch's woods a-anymore," I managed, my words shaky as I cupped him in my palms and began swimming toward the shore. My teeth chattering teeth reinforced that we needed to get out of the water before hypothermia set in.

"I would say there is relief in knowing such things," he began, "but do you have any idea of our whereabouts now?"

I shook my head. Peering around me, there were only lines of trees, outlining what appeared to be a forest. *Another* one.

Taking a step out of the murky pond, I sank onto the grass with Aneurin in my hands. I didn't know what I was going to do...or *where* to go. How was I going to help him find his kiss, or find my way home, when we were stuck in another set of woods?

"Perhaps we are not so far away from civilization after all," he said, his voice tinged with hope.

"I'm sure we have very different definitions of 'civilization,'" I murmured under my breath before glancing toward where he'd lifted his small, webbed hand in front of us.

"Look!" he said sharply. "It's a tower. It *must* be a part of a castle."

A castle. A castle could mean help was closer than ever—it could be the promise of home.

"Maybe you'll find your princess there," I blurted. "And then you'll be free of your spell. And I can go home."

"One can certainly hope," Aneurin replied, soft but determined.

"I guess there's only one way to find out," I said, pushing myself back to my feet and steeling myself for whatever lay ahead.

As I stared ahead at a tall, lone tower rising from the midst of the woods, my heart plummeted to my stomach. I had an uncanny feeling that I knew exactly where we were. There was nothing about this that felt at all...*hopeful*.

The imposing building stood above us, constructed of large, white stones. Thick green vines scattered with small blossoms of pink and yellow flowers snaked their way up the structure. The blooms reminded me of a famous painting I couldn't quite place.

Despite its picturesque appearance, there was an undeniable sense of foreboding surrounding the tower. The large window at the top was closed, offering no glimpse of the inhabitant within.

And as I scanned its exterior, searching for any sign of an entrance, my heart sank further.

"Who would live in such a place?" Aneurin asked, breaking the heavy silence between us. His small form shifted on my shoulder as he peered up at the tower.

"Someone who isn't afraid of heights," I remarked wryly.

"And how does one reach the top?"

I bit my bottom lip, debating whether I should tell him the story. It felt like doing so would break an unspoken rule. But maybe the rules didn't apply the same way in this strange world?

"Rapunzel," I finally said.

"*What?*" Aneurin asked, his tiny brow furrowing in confusion.

Before I could delve into further explanation, sticks crackled behind us.

I tensed and grabbed him from my shoulder, then dove into the nearest brush. With my heart pounding in my chest, I cradled him close in trembling hands, trying to suppress the panic rapidly rising within me.

"Don't squeeze me so tightly," he hissed, his voice barely audible over the rustling leaves.

"Quiet!" I whispered urgently, pressing a finger against my lips in a silent plea.

My breath caught in my throat when he called out, "Rapunzel, Rapunzel! Let down your hair!"

"Who or what is this...*Rapunzel?*" Aneurin whispered, his gaze flickering between the tower and me.

"Just watch."

Moments later, a golden cascade of hair tumbled from the window above, unfurling like a waterfall until it reached the waiting man below. Then he tugged gently for a moment, before starting his ascension up.

"Is that *hair*?" Aneurin asked in awe.

"Yeah," I replied.

I nodded. The sheer volume she possessed was mind-boggling. I couldn't fathom how long it took her to wash and brush it.

"If there is no way to the top without the maiden, how did she find *herself* there?" Aneurin pondered aloud, his webbed fingers tapping thoughtfully on my palm.

"I'll give you three guesses. And the first two don't count."

"The first—?"

"A witch," I sighed, cutting him off before he could finish.

"Gods," he muttered in response. "*Another*?"

"If there's a plot of unoccupied forest," I mused, "there's bound to be a witch lurking nearby."

"He has nearly reached the top," Aneurin interjected, redirecting our conversation back to the scene unfolding before us.

The prince's cape billowed in the breeze as he neared the large window at the tower's apex.

As if on cue, a young woman emerged from the shadows. Her expression radiated joy when her prince reached for her.

His hand caressed her face with gentle tenderness before he leaned forward and pressed a kiss against her cheek.

She laughed then pressing her lips against his. Her hands sought his, pulling him into the safety of the tower's interior.

Their laughter echoed faintly through the air as they vanished from sight.

My heart twisted with a strange mix of envy and longing.

"Well," I murmured, glancing at Aneurin. "I don't think you'll have any luck *wooing* her."

"I suppose not," he sighed, his shoulders slumping while his chin dipped down.

Guilt gnawed at me as I realized how my response to the situation had affected him. I'd dejected a frog, struggling to break what felt like an impossible spell.

"We'll find her," I offered, tapping his head in reassurance.

"All of this seems pointless," he muttered.

I couldn't deny that his words held some truth. I wasn't entirely sure where we were going to find his princess. But I couldn't afford to give up.

I knew that Rapunzel wouldn't be of any help to us, given her lifelong confinement in the tower. But maybe, just *maybe*, the prince was the key to a solution.

With a sudden burst of determination, I rose to my feet, settling Aneurin back on my shoulder.

He shot me a bewildered expression and tugged on the shoulder of my shirt. "Where are you going, Josephine?"

"To climb the tower!" I said.

"We're *what*? Why?"

"Maybe the prince will know where we can go," I explained. "Maybe he'll have a sister or a cousin or—"

"It is hardly proper for us to march up to a royal prince and ask such a thing."

"We wouldn't be *marching* up to him," I countered. "It would be climbing. And besides, *you're* a prince, too! Doesn't that make you equals or something?"

"I am currently short and green, Josephine," he replied with a sigh. "Look at me."

It was unusual to hear him openly express his insecurity about his appearance.

"My predicament isn't a joke," he continued, his tone somber.

I shifted uncomfortably, feeling a pang of sympathy for him. "I agree, it's not." Nothing about this situation was *funny*.

Casting my gaze up to the lone window of the tower, I released a heavy sigh. I never imagined in a million years that anything in my life would lead up to this moment.

Here goes nothing.

I lifted my hand to cup against my mouth. "Rapunzel! Rapunzel!" I called out. "Let down your hair!"

And so, we waited, the tension thick as I fervently hoped for the famous golden cascade of hair to descend.

ACKNOWLEDGMENTS

In the interest of full disclosure, this book has been a lifetime in the making.

But it was really sparked by Dustin and Suzie's duet of *The NeverEnding Story* song in the Netflix series *Stranger Things*. Much like the majority of the world that watched the show, I, too, couldn't get the song out of my head. I also spent countless mornings driving to work, thinking about another tv series that I had just recently finished watching *W: Two Worlds* (a K-drama in which a young woman is dragged into a comic series that her father created, and falls in love with the male lead character).

I knew I really wanted to write a similar story—but involving the use of fairy tales instead. I kept thinking about how crazy it would be if a person from our modern world was transported into a book (like what happens to Macaulay Culkin in *The Pagemaster*)—and through their adventures found that their character sidekick is actually their love interest all along.

I hope this book felt like all of those things to you—with the perfect added amount of humor from *The Princess Bride*, sprinkled on top just for fun.

Writing *Until the Last Page* has been a challenging, yet fun adventure. I really enjoyed diving back into my favorite classic Disney films like *Cinderella* and *Sleeping Beauty* and shows like *Shelley Duvall's Faerie Tale Theatre* and *Once Upon a Time* to capture the essence of what a fairy tale feels like to me. There's a sense of familiarity that I wanted the readers of this book to feel as though you know this world, and yet it's still new, but magical!

It was interesting to investigate what a frog felt like when I caught them in our yard (and safely relocated them to ponds). Each time I found one, I began to really imagine myself as Josephine, carrying a snarky frog through the woods. What was even more meaningful in this writing process, was the healing I found within its pages. Writing *Until the Last Page* was a period of healing—of ending a chapter in my life and beginning a new one. While Josephine was experiencing self-growth in this book, I was experiencing the same. To say there is so much of me weaved into this story, is an understatement.

And there is so much more of this story that belongs to others. To start—my family. In almost every one of my stories, I have tried to incorporate both of my parents.

For Dad, to keep him alive. Every page read, to me, is the opportunity for him to be alive somewhere in the world, beyond just my memories of him.

For Mom, it's my way to show my gratitude for her and the love of reading and writing she instilled in me.

Mom, you are my best friend, and I love that you always encourage me to do the things I love. I'm grateful for your editing of this book—and even though I know your eyes were rolling every time we got to a passage of "darting a glance"—I appreciate you took the time to read this book, and to enjoy it as much as you did. I may not be able to give you that island you always wanted, but I can give you a place in my heart, and my books.

Of course, to my sister (who, by the time this comes out, will be a mother of her own), you spent hours helping me to figure out this story one afternoon as I was sick in bed. I appreciate you taking the time to talk about frog princes and evil witches. I love you.

A huge thank you to Inimitable Books—to Zara—who took the chance to bring this story to all of you. And thank you so much to everyone who helped create the finished book—especially Keylin, for the gorgeous cover.

This book wouldn't be what it is without the help of my friends—A.M. Davis, Brianna Sugalski—you both took the time to read and help me with the development of the characters. You talked me through the stories and situations, and encouraged me to keep going. The amount of support I received from you will make me forever grateful.

To Janelle, who was gracious enough to do a round of editing for me in the early stages, and made sure that everyone was age appropriate. Thank you for being such a cheerleader!

To Finn Honeycutt, for your friendship, for all of your amazing art, for your support—for everything. Having you be a part of this process with me is an honor. There are no words for how much I sincerely love you.

To Dustin—who strolled into my life almost like magic. You completely swept me up, almost the way I imagined any Prince Charming would. I wasn't expecting to meet someone like you, but I'm glad and grateful that I did. You were worth the wait, and I love you.

To all my students who I spend (or spent) my every-day with: the students who encouraged me to write, to not give up, who taught me how to be the best version of myself. I hope you know that working with you all has been one of the best things ever in my life.

To my work-bestie, who is so much more than just my work-bestie, Nickala—thank you for being such an incredible friend. I'm so grateful to have the chance to not only work alongside you in our day-to-day responsibilities, but to share a pretty incredible friendship too.

To Erin Craig—the author of *A House of Salt and Sorrow* and *Small Favors*. Your warmth of welcoming me into your Camp NaNoWriMo the summer of 2022 is honestly what fueled the fire to complete *Until the Last Page*. I have always admired your storytelling ability, and I'm so grateful you gave me the chance to work alongside you—even if it was just sharing a space on a website. I wouldn't have finished this book without that act of kindness!

There is a quote from the 1999 film, *Never Been Kissed*, that has stuck with me since I first saw the film as a twelve-year-old. Josie Geller (played by Drew Barrymore) said: "To write well, you have to write what you know..."

Here are the things that I know, that I hope I encompassed in *Until the Last Page*:

I definitely know a lot of fairytales and the differences between the original stories and the Disney movies. I know that frogs typically sink in water, rather than float. I know that my Google Search history after this book made me look like an absolute weirdo to whoever is monitoring me—"Sweeney Todd Walk-In Oven" made me feel a little like a murderer. And I know *Sleeping Beauty* could not have actually pricked her finger on a spinning wheel, as there isn't really a sharp needle.

I also know that I believe in the power of love, and how it can change others, and at times—save others. I know that writing will always be a way that I express myself, whether it be a way of working through painful experiences and trying to heal from them, trying to share a memory of a loved one, or to simply share pieces of myself, in hopes that it will make getting to know me—as a person—easier to do.

I know to never take this opportunity for granted. I know I would not be here without the individuals who took the time to make *Until the Last Page* what it is.

Lastly, to you, reader: thank you.

ABOUT THE AUTHOR

Chantal Gadoury is a best-selling fairytale-retelling and romance author, living in the beautiful countryside of Muncy, Pennsylvania with her mom.

When Chantal isn't pursuing her next writing endeavor, she enjoys spending time with her loved ones, and taking long walks to the sounds of BTS. She is a TikTok enthusiast, loves all things Disney and loves a good, romantic K-Drama.

Chantal first started writing stories at the age of seven and continues that love of writing today. After graduating from Susquehanna University with a degree in Creative Writing, writing novels has become a dream come true.